- Alexander Moran (1962-)
  - m
  - Eamonn Alexand[er]
- Aisling Montgomery (1969-)

- Aisling (1969-)

  - Catharine Cavanagh (1949-)
  - m 1st
  - Justin Waller (1947-2000)
  - m 2nd
  - Eamonn Gallagher (1941-)

  - Grace McDermott (1925-)
  - m
    - Robert (1947-)
    - Catharine (1949-)
  - Gordon Cavanagh (1922-1999)

- Alexander Joseph McDermott (1886-1960)
  - m
    - Hugh (1922-1990)
    - Grace (1925-)
    - Lucille (1927-)
- Mary Grace Johnson (1889-1970)

Aisling of Eire

by

Dorothy Keddington

Copyright © 2002 by Dorothy McDonald Keddington
All Rights Reserved

This is a work of fiction. All characters are fictional and any resemblance to persons living or dead is purely coincidental.

No part of this book may be reproduced in any form whatsoever, whether by graphic, visual, electronic, filming, microfilming, tape recording, or any other means, without the prior written permission of the authors, except in the case of brief passages embodied in critical reviews and articles where the title, authors and ISBN accompany such review or article.

Published and Distributed by:

GRANITE
PUBLISHING & DISTRIBUTION L.L.C.

Granite Publishing and Distribution, LLC
868 North 1430 West
Orem, Utah 84057
(801) 229-9023 • Toll Free (800) 574-5779
Fax (801) 229-1924

Page Layout and Design by Myrna M. Varga, The Office Connection, Inc.
Cover Art and Design by Steve Gray and Daina Jones

Library of Congress Control Number: 2002107719
ISBN: 1-930980-83-3
Printed in the United States of America

First Printing June 2002
10 9 8 7 6 5 4 3 2 1

For my Family ... Past,
Present & Future

A Gaelic Blessing

Deep peace of the running wave to you,
Deep peace of the flowing air to you,
Deep peace of the quiet earth to you
Deep peace of the shining stars to you
Deep peace of the gentle night to you
Deep peace of the Son of
Peace to you.

Acknowledgments

Throughout the years of writing and researching *Aisling of Eire,* I have received encouragement and assistance from many. To my friends, family members, distant cousins, members of the Clifford Association, the staff of the Family History Library in Salt Lake City, the Heritage Center in County Leitrim, and the wonderful people of Ireland ... my heartfelt thanks and gratitude to each and every one of you.

Special thanks go to ...

Margie Butler and Paul Espinoza of "Golden Bough," along with their manager, Nina Black, ... Your music has been a source of true "Celtic" inspiration for the book, and your friendship, a gift beyond price.

James Keigher, of County Mayo, Ireland ... for the gift of your beautiful song, "The Dreamer." I know Esther Clifford would love to thank you if she could. The lyrics and the music are truly inspired.

Carol Warburton, Ka Hancock and Charlene Raddon, friends and fellow writers, my heartfelt thanks for your friendship, steadfast encouragement and insightful critiquing.

Doris Sailor Platt, Special Advisor to the President of the Republic of Georgia. Your belief in me and in this story has been a solid anchor through stormy writing seas.

Heartfelt thanks go to Nancy Hopkins who has given much time and effort in the research and development of this novel. Thanks, Nancy, for your faith and belief in me.

Lou Ann Anderson, for providing not only valuable critiquing and enthusiastic support, but a cabin in the mountains, where frustrated writers could create without interruption.

Katherine Johnson, thanks for your patience and expert instruction in helping me "search for clues," and for being a wonderful traveling companion on research trips to Grass Valley, California, and Ireland.

Mrs. Ann McCutcheon, of Berkshire, England, member of the Clifford Association, for her kind assistance and generosity in sharing our Clifford ancestry in County Leitrim, Ireland.

Mary Boland of the Heritage Center in Ballinamore, County Leitrim; Teresa & Brian Kennedy of Glenmore House in Ballinamore, County Leitrim; Rob and Lorely Forrester of the Old Rectory, Easky, County Sligo; and Ronald and Colette Downey of *Pairc na Bhfuiseog* in County Dublin. Your kindness and hospitality will be remembered always.

Loving tribute is given to my father, Jack Alex McDonald, who passed away in January 1998. He was instrumental in instilling a deep love of family history in me and members of our family. Dad taught by example, and always with great love. His stories, combined with his brilliant mind and memory, have greatly blessed my efforts.

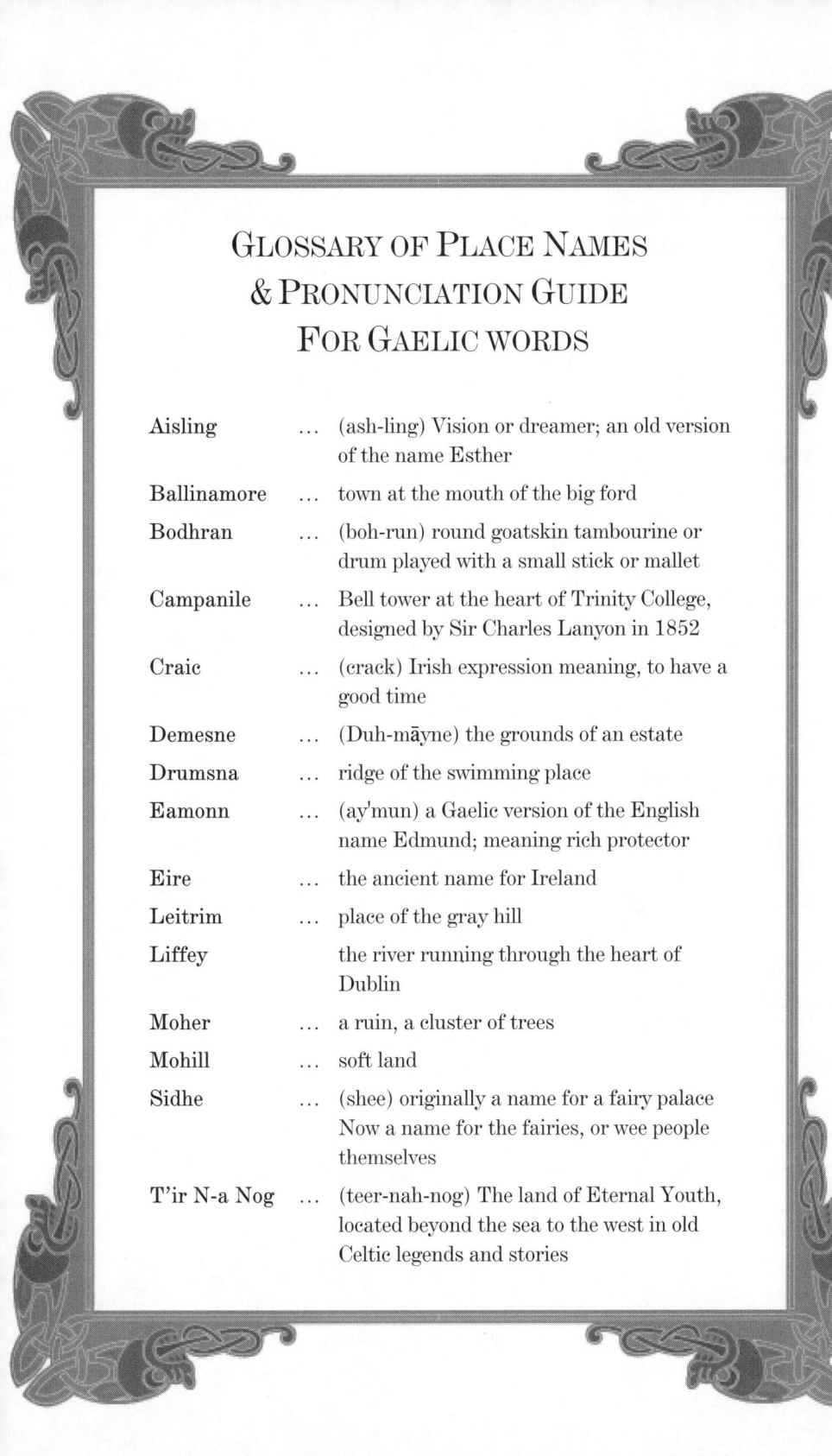

Glossary of Place Names & Pronunciation Guide for Gaelic Words

Aisling	...	(ash-ling) Vision or dreamer; an old version of the name Esther
Ballinamore	...	town at the mouth of the big ford
Bodhran	...	(boh-run) round goatskin tambourine or drum played with a small stick or mallet
Campanile	...	Bell tower at the heart of Trinity College, designed by Sir Charles Lanyon in 1852
Craic	...	(crack) Irish expression meaning, to have a good time
Demesne	...	(Duh-māyne) the grounds of an estate
Drumsna	...	ridge of the swimming place
Eamonn	...	(ay'mun) a Gaelic version of the English name Edmund; meaning rich protector
Eire	...	the ancient name for Ireland
Leitrim	...	place of the gray hill
Liffey		the river running through the heart of Dublin
Moher	...	a ruin, a cluster of trees
Mohill	...	soft land
Sidhe	...	(shee) originally a name for a fairy palace Now a name for the fairies, or wee people themselves
T'ir N-a Nog	...	(teer-nah-nog) The land of Eternal Youth, located beyond the sea to the west in old Celtic legends and stories

Aisling of Eire - the CD

This CD is a unique musical journey, an enchanting blend of story and song, to accompany the novel, *Aisling of Eire*. Two acclaimed musical groups, *Golden Bough* and *Men of Worth* have captured the essence of traditional Celtic music as well as composing original songs especially for the book. It has been said that music is the 'language of emotion.' If so, then the hauntingly beautiful language of Irish music combined with Dorothy Keddington's evocative storytelling is truly a marriage made in heaven.

Songs

"... fresh from the land of 'Saints and Scholars.'" John and Esther Clark sail to America with thousands of their Irish countrymen. *(Chapter 1)*

1. **Planxty Burke/farewell to Ireland**
Turlough O'Carolan/Traditional; arranged and produced by Margie Butler and Paul Espinoza. Published by Forest Moon Music.
     Guitar, octave-mandolin: Paul Espinoza
     Whistle, bodhran: Margie Butler
     Violin: Allison Bailey

"... the hard fabric of decision." Esther Clifford elopes with her coachman and is disinherited by her family. A century and a half later, Esther's gt. gt. granddaughter finds herself in a similar situation when she falls in love with a poor young Irishman. *(Chapter 2)*

2. **The Dreamer**
Words and music by James Keigher. Produced by James Keigher. Published by Mahog Music.
> Vocal, mando-cello: James Keigher
> Pedal steel guitar: Frank Sullivan
> Fiddle, pipes: Kevin Carr
> Bass fiddle: Sam Cuenca
> Concertina: Donnie Macdonald

"... and as they danced, the separateness disappeared." Catharine imagines John and Esther dancing in a moonlit conservatory. *(Chapter 6)*

3. **Mary, Young & Fair**
Traditional, arranged and produced by Margie Butler. Published by ARC Music; Forest Moon Music (USA).
> Celtic Harp: Margie Butler
> Guitar: Paul Espinoza
> Violin: Florie Brown

"... days passed in a happy blend of sharing and caring." Catharine and Eamonn spend an evening with friends at the *Singing Kettle*. *(Chapter 7)*

4. **Sporting Pat Medley**
Traditional, arranged and produced by Margie Butler & Paul Espinoza. Published by Forest Moon Music.
> Celtic harp, bodhran: Margie Butler
> Accordion: Paul Espinoza
> Violin: Sue Draheim

"... all too soon her world would be full of weeping and good-byes."
Catharine and Eamonn visit lovely Glencar in County Leitrim. *(Chapter 7)*

5. **The Stolen Child**
Words by William Butler Yeates; music by Loreena McKennitt. Arranged and produced by Paul Espinoza. Published by Loreena McKennitt.
> Vocal: Margie Butler
> Violin, vocal: Florie Brown
> Guitar: Paul Espinoza

"... song after song echoed in the old hall." Catharine, Grace and Aisling attend a Golden Bough concert in Grass Valley, California. *(Chapter 13)*

6. **Ballyconnell Fair**
Traditional; arranged and produced by Margie Butler and Paul Espinoza. Published by Forest Moon Music.
> Guitar, accordion, vocal: Paul Espinoza
> Harp, bodhran: Margie Butler
> Violin: Alison Bailey

"... an aching river of lost love swirling around her in the confusing eddies of the present." The music brings back haunting memories of Eamonn. *(Chapter 13)*

7. **Song of the Swan Maiden**
Words: Margie Butler. Music: Margie Butler & Paul Espinoza. Arranged and produced by Paul Espinoza and Margie Butler. Published by ARC Music; Forest Moon Music (USA).
> Vocals, harp: Margie Butler
> Guitar, vocal: Paul Espinoza
> Flute: Lief Sorbye

" ... the pulse of past times, a heartbeat from the long ago ..." The music beckons Aisling, Grace and Catharine to come to Ireland. *(Chapter 13)*

8. **Pilib an Cheoil/a Wet December/tarbolton Reel.**
Traditional, arranged and produced by Margie Butler. Published by Forest Moon Music.
>Wire & nylon strung harp, whistle, bodhran: Margie Butler
>Violin: Alison Bailey
>Accordion: Paul Espinoza

" ...a longing for her own people – to find them and know them." *(Chapter 13)*

9. **Song of the Celts** (Aisling's Song)
Words & music by Paul Espinoza. Arranged and produced by Margie Butler and Paul Espinoza. Published by Forest Moon Music.
>Vocals, whistle: Margie Butler
>Guitar: Paul Espinoza
>Violin, Viola: Kathy Sierra

"... who's to say Heaven is all that far away?" A lullabye to Esther and Aisling from their mothers. *(Chapter 17)*

10. **Deep in My Heart**
Words and music by Paul Espinoza. Arranged and produced by Paul Espinoza. Published by Golden Bough and ARC Music/Forest Moon Music (USA).
>Vocal, harp: Margie Butler
>Guitar: Flavio Cucchi
>Accordion: Enrique Ugarte

"... her memory was pressed upon his heart like a flower kept within the pages of a book." *(Chapter 27)*

11. **Nancy Spain**
(Eamonn's Song) Words & Music by Barney Rush. Men of Worth. Arranged by James Keigher. Published by Mahog Music.
>Vocal, guitar: James Keigher
>Octave-Mandolin: Donnie Macdonald

"... The winter inside her was over at last." *(Chapter 27, 28)*

12. **I Remember Erin**
(Catharine's Song) Words & music by Jim Hinton. Arranged and produced by Paul Espinoza & Margie Butler. Published by Forest Moon Music.
>Vocal, harp: Margie Butler
>Guitar: Paul Espinoza
>Violin, vocal: Kathy Sierra

Golden Bough Music, P.O. Box 818 Pacifica, CA, 94044 USA. Website: www.goldenboughmusic.com

Men of Worth c/o MAHOG Music, P.O. Box 1256, Talent, OR, 97540 USA. Website: www.menofworth.com

Aisling of Eire - Song Lyrics

The Dreamer

The lonely sad call of the seagull
Was the last song she heard on the quay,
The sorrowful wave of the immigrants,
The boat sails out for Amerikay …

Leave behind the heart and soul,
A longing nothing can replace
Shattered dreams of what might have been
A suitcase full of memories; tears rolling down her face.

One day she'll come home, to all the paths the future brings
One day she'll return to the heart and the hands of the golden ring.

A starving land; a broken place
No room for truth to cross the line
The joy of love in a youthful kiss
A moment forever held in time.

A father's shame and foolish pride
A nation blinded by the Cross
Banishment is the price to pay
He is firm in all his ignorance,
But inside he feels the loss.

One day she'll come home to all the paths the future brings
One day she'll return to the heart and the hands of the golden ring.

There's a flower she carries in this parting,
To the land where dreamers can be free
And the vision of their sweet embrace is married
By the gentle weave of lover's poetry.

The sails are full as they round Bantry.
The distant shore is fading into sea
And the pain inside, it's advancing
All that's left behind in the place where the heart remains.

One day she'll come home to all the paths the future brings,
One day she'll return, to the heart and the hands of the golden ring…

The Stolen Child

Where dips the rocky highland of Sleuthwood in the lake,
    there lies a leafy island, where flapping herons wake
    the drowsy water rats, there we've hid our faery vats,
    full of berries and the reddest stolen cherries.

Come away, oh human child, to the water and the wild,
    with a faery hand in hand,
For the world's more full of weeping than you can understand.

Where the wave of moonlight glosses the dim grey sands with light.
Far off by furthest Rosses, we foot it through the night,
    weaving olden dances, mingling hands and mingling glances,
    'til the moon has taken flight, to and fro we leap,
    and chase the frothy bubbles,
    while the world is full of troubles and anxious in its sleep.

Where the wandering water gushes from the hills above Glen-Car,
    in pools among the rushes that scarce could bathe a star,
    we seek the slumbering trout and whispering in their ears,
    give them unquiet dreams, while leaning further out
    from ferns that drop their tears over the young streams.

Come away, oh human child, from the water and the wild,
    with a faery hand in hand,
For the world's more full of weeping than you can understand.

Away with us he's going, the solemn eyed,
  no more he'll hear the lowing of the calf on the warm hillside,
  or the kettle on the hob, breathe peace into his breast,
  or see the brown mice bob round and round the oatmeal chest,

For he comes the human child, from the water and the wild,
  with a faery hand in hand,
 for the world's more full of weeping than you can understand.

Ballyconnell Fair

Two brothers bold called Pat and Mick, they lived near Derrylynn,
They had a darlin' springin' cow, her name was Mary Jane.
But hay was scarce and cash was scarce and both their suits threadbare,
So Mary Jane she had to go to Ballyconnell Fair.

The morning of the fair arrived, a shocking fog and mist,
Come rollin' down the hills of Doon, you couldn't see your fist.
Says Pat to Mick, "You walk in front and I'll bring up the rear.
With Mary Jane between us both to the Ballyconnell Fair."

At Gortary now, Mary Jane, she played an awful trick,
She stepped into a byroad there, unknown to Pat and Mick.
She ate a feed from Drum's haystack, there she made her lair,
While Pat and Mick they welted on to the Ballyconnell Fair.

They reached the green at half past eight, approaching the daylight,
The fog had lifted all at once, the drovers hove in sight.
Says Pat to Mick, "Where's Mary Jane, I can't see her nowhere.
By the Holy Lord, it was me you drove to Ballyconnell Fair!"

Now both are dead, God rest their souls, but still the story's told,
Around the fires of Derrylynn, enjoyed by young and old.
And children cry when going to bed and dashing up the stairs,
"Was it Pat drove Mick or Mick drove Pat to the Ballyconnell Fair?"

Song of the Swan Maiden

(Chorus) The people of the town say she's crazy, the people of the town say
  she's mad.
As she wanders by the shore long hours, Dreaming of the love she once had.

Many nights I've seen her weeping, underneath the darkened sky.
Many days I've heard her singing, the same sad lullabye.
I have wandered by the ocean, just to hear her mournful song,
Her heart so filled with longing, to the night she does belong. (Chorus)

In the cold light of the dawning, just as the morning sun did break,
I thought I saw her swimming, with the swans upon the lake.
On that silent day she vanished. Of her song there was no trace,
I walked the cliffs and meadows, I searched in every place.

They say some strange enchanted magic has taken her away.
Bewitched so by her sorrow, they say she'll always say.
Some say that she's become a swallow, and out to the sea has flown.
Some say into a willow, weeping she has grown. (Chorus)

Through the seasons I will wander, through the heather, through the snow.
I'll sing it to the willow, surely she will know.
I'll sing it to the morning, the song that she has given me,
Likewise into the evening, someday I know she'll see. (Chorus)

Song of the Celts (Aisling's Song)

I wasn't born in Ireland, I didn't grow up in the land of the Gaels,
I was raised on some distant sand, far from the stories and the tales.
Long time ago from Ireland, my mother's mother's family came,
To find a new life on new soil, a new home, new dignity to claim.

And yet I hear the song of the Celts, in my heart and in my soul,
Still I hear the song of the Celts, evoking mem'ries of long ago.

I long to know my ancestral home; a yearning calls me to return,
To a land I have never known, other than the dreams that in me burn.
Now I am far from Ireland, haunted by ancient memories
Of a land that's known suffering, of a people gave my life to me.
And still I hear a song of the Celts, in my heart and in my soul,
Still I hear the song of the Celts, calling me to memories of long ago.

A fire burns inside of me, a restless flame that consumes my soul,
To realize my destiny, my hidden past that I have come to know.
Deep in my heart I feel the thread that joins the past with what yet will be,
To understand the poet's words that sing of that green land across the sea.

And now I sing a song of the Celts, in my heart and in my soul,
When I sing the song of the Celts, I am no longer alone.

Deep in My Heart

Deep in my heart, I will be holding you,
Safe in the warm trust a mother's love makes,
Deep in the night, I will be close to you,
Hold you in my heart, until the dawn breaks.

Deep in my heart, all I would do for you,
Has not to do with your beauty and grace.
Deep in my soul, there is a place for you
Shielded from suffering by love's warm embrace.

You called to me and I reached out my heart to you,
Embracing your dreams and offering mine,
Many's the month you were a part of me,
Now I will ever be with you in time.

Still in my arms, dreaming in soft repose,
Tomorrow comes while you quietly rest,
Let not a tear or a worrisome thought prevail,
Yours is the moment, your future be blessed.
Yours is the moment, your future be blessed.

Nancy Spain (Eamonn's Song)

Of all the stars that ever shone not one does twinkle like your pale blue eyes,
Like golden corn at harvest-time, your hair.
Sailing in my boat the wind gently blows and fills out my sail.
Your sweet scented breath is everywhere.

Daylight peeping through the curtain of the passing night-time is your smile
The sun in the sky is like your laugh
Come back to me my Nancy, and linger for jus a little while.
Since you've left these shores I've known no peace nor joy.

No matter where I wander I'm still haunted by your name,
The portrait of your beauty stays the same.

Standing by the ocean, wondering where you've gone, if you'll return again.
Where is the ring I gave to Nancy Spain?

And on a day in spring when snow starts to melt and streams to flow,
With the birds I'll sing a song.
And in a while I'll wander down by bluebell grove where wild flowers grow,
And I'll hope that lovely Nancy will return.

No matter where I wander I'm still haunted by your name,
The portrait of your beauty stays the same.
Standing by the ocean, wondering where you've gone, if you'll return again.
Where is the ring I gave to Nancy Spain.

I Remember Erin (Catharine's Song)

The hollow hills and winding ways, the wild wood and the dale,
Are drifting on to dream lit days, along the twisted trail.
The sunlight and the shadows play, upon the rock and stone
The whispering voices seem to say, "You wander not alone."

I remember Erin, cries the wild wind
And I'll return to Erin, to see my journey's end.

Somewhere in the fading light an image can be seen,
Of romance, wilderness and night, among the hills of green.
The moonlight falling on the sea and gentle in the glen,
The magic mists upon the lea, her song is on the wind.

I remember Erin, cries the wild wind
And I'll return to Erin, to see my journey's end.

So take your sweet child by the hand and give your hand to me,
And we will walk the hollow land where poets wander free.
The good earth lies beneath our feet the sun upon our brow,
Our journey soon will be complete, our long lost time is now.

I remember Erin, cries the wild wind
And I'll return to Erin, to see my journey's end.

Author's Foreword

I remember well the first time I stood by her grave. There was no marker. No stone. No man-made memorial to indicate this forsaken spot in Utah's Tintic Mountains was the final resting place of my great-great grandmother. My father had consulted the sexton and carefully mapped out the location of her burial site, but even with this knowledge, it had taken several minutes of searching through sagebrush and cheat grass to find the place.

Now, staring down at the dry rocky soil where rabbit brush and twisted branches of sage had managed to survive, my mind was filled with unanswered questions. What was she like—this woman of family legend and stories that seemed more like a romantic fairy tale than real life. Running away ... shipwreck ... the search for gold....

I was no more than five or six the first time I heard her name. Sitting on my grandfather's lap, I can still remember his craggy face, the gray stubble on his chin and those incredible Irish blue eyes.

"My grandmother was 'Lady Day' Clifford of Ireland," he'd told me in a gravelly, rumbling growl that was filled with pride.

Just the sound of that name was enough to spark my childish imagination and set it wandering. Knowing what she had done, all she had given up, tugged at my heart and endeared her to me even more.

As years passed, I was too busy living the pages of my own life to become overly preoccupied with the blurred book of someone else's—even an Irish great-great grandmother. Yet somehow, she was always there, waiting patiently in the background—a faded, fascinating persona from the past—someone whose life and loves and decisions had shaped who I would become.

And this is where that life ended.

The strings of silence were plucked by shrill cicadas and the occasional buzz of a horsefly. Now and then, the distant whine of a passing car on the highway served as a reminder that I was indeed part of the twentieth century, however far my thoughts might stray.

My gaze lifted from the plot of rocky soil and I glanced around the little cemetery. Names like O'Leary and O'Toole gave solemn greeting from headstones carved in granite and marble. Great Grandmother Esther had lots of good Irish company at least. Beyond the boundary of the cemetery, rose the scarred slopes of the Tintic Mountains, with their unsightly tailings of rock and rubble from the glory days of mining a century before. Everywhere I looked, the landscape was bleak and barren—dusty, gray-green sage, ochre rocks and sandy soil—a far cry from the 'Emerald Isle' she had left so far across the sea.

Was it worth it? I wondered. Did she have any regrets?

Turning to the west, across the expanse of sage and sandy desert, my eyes found a small patch of green. The richness of the color seemed strangely out of place, like an emerald brooch pinned to a dress of rough homespun cloth. Yet, there it was—a small verdant island shimmering in the desert sun.

Gazing at that distant patch of green, I silently wished I could discover more about her. Esther Clifford Clark had died nearly half a century before I was born, but somewhere beyond the legend and the stories, was a flesh and blood woman who had laughed and loved and dreamed her dreams.

How did I know she had been a dreamer? I had nothing to confirm this. No journals. No diaries. Not even a photograph to offer any clues.

If you could speak to me, Esther, what stories would you tell? If I listen closely enough, could I hear your voice whispering across the years? Is that you I hear, or the lonely sigh of the desert wind....

1

Catharine

He was waiting at the gate, dark eyes moving over the deplaning passengers with expectation and more than a hint of anxiety. His stance was deceptively casual, both hands in his pockets, an overcoat draped across one arm. But his eyes betrayed him.

Catharine Cavanagh Waller sat barely two feet away, watching discreetly as the man's gaze moved past two businessmen with their leather attaches and black, wheeled carry-ons ... past a gray-haired couple and a weary young mother with a fussy infant in one arm and a tired toddler clinging to her other hand.

Then the man's body tensed ever so slightly and the hint of a smile lifted one corner of his mouth. The hands left his pockets and his entire body seemed to breathe relief.

Following his gaze, Catharine saw a young woman with short brown hair weaving her way through the maze of passengers. There was nothing extraordinary about her features or dress, but her eyes were luminous and filled with shining, unspeakable joy as they found the man. She flew into his waiting embrace, dropping her suitcase at their feet as his arms pulled her close.

Catharine drew a quick, involuntary breath and felt her chest tighten with inexplicable longing as the two held each other, not speaking or moving. They drew briefly apart to look into one another's eyes with an amazed sort of gratitude. Then he pulled her close once more.

It could have been the scene out of a book—*one of my books,* Catharine thought with a wistful smile. She glanced at the eager press of humanity hurrying by on either side, most with indifferent, uncaring eyes. So many comings and goings, so many journeys. Yet here were two people who had arrived because they had found each other. It was a miracle, really, to find someone.

Tears suddenly stung her eyelids and she glanced down, trying to blink them away. When she looked up again, the man was bending over to pick up the discarded carry-on. He smiled at the young woman, took her hand, and they walked off together down the crowded concourse.

Watching them go, Catharine felt more tears blur her vision. What was wrong with her? If she chose to allow it, there were several things in her life right now that might merit a good cry. Why should the meeting of two strangers elicit such an emotional response? Was it tiny threads of memory tugging at her from the past, or the weary fabric of the present unraveling before her eyes?

Catharine refused to think about either possibility and fumbled in her handbag for a tissue. She was tired, that was all. Anything could be blown out of proportion when one was tired. After the pressure of the past two days, she felt like running away somewhere safe and warm and sleeping for a week. New York in January was not her favorite place to be. The bitter cold and gray skies heightened the remoteness of concrete and steel. Christmas holidays were past, so was the excitement of a New Year and new millennium. New York, along with the rest of the country had survived Y2K, and it was back to business as usual. That's what she saw on the faces of people rushing by in the concourse of JFK Airport. Business as usual. No joy. No excitement.

And that's probably what someone would see on my face, Catharine thought. She didn't like herself this way. Running away would solve nothing. Neither would sleeping for a week, or a year or a hundred years, unless, like Sleeping Beauty, her problems could be magically solved when she awoke. And that wasn't going to happen.

Catharine had known when she flew to New York for meetings with her publisher that there might be some unpleasantness. More than two years had elapsed since her last novel. The powers that be at Random House were very sympathetic about her personal circumstances, the long illness and recent death of her father, but readers were waiting for the next book by Catharine Cavanagh, and readers would only be patient for so long.

Catharine had assured them she was back on track and had some solid ideas for a new story, when in reality she sometimes wondered if she would ever write again. How could she write when there was this terrible deadness inside, and the very thought of putting words on paper made her so unutterably weary? *I have no dreams left to write about,* she thought in a moment of stark, terrifying honesty. But she hadn't told them that. How could she look into Hal Kellerman's face, her editor and friend for over ten years, and tell him that she didn't really care about writing any more. Just seeing the mute sympathy in his eyes made her more determined than ever not to disappoint him.

"Catharine!"

She glanced up at the sound of her name, then stared in surprise as the middle-aged object of her thoughts hurried toward her through the crowd.

"Hal?"

"I'm glad I caught you before your flight left," he panted, dropping into the empty seat next to hers. "That damned traffic."

"My flight's been delayed or you wouldn't have," she said, wondering what on earth could be worth the rush. Her meetings with Random House had concluded the previous afternoon and she and Hal had said their good-byes last evening over dinner.

Hal Kellerman ran a hand through thinning gray hair and blew out a relieved sigh. "That's the best news I've had all morning. How long before you leave?"

"At least forty minutes."

"Great. Let's go somewhere we can talk. Here, let me take that." He reached for the handle of her carry-on and stood up. "Is the Medallion Room all right with you? I'd rather have someplace more private."

"Yes, of course." Catharine gave him a curious look, then shouldered the case containing her laptop and fell in step beside him.

Her curiosity shifted into a sense of unease as they were seated on comfortable leather couches in the airline's private Medallion Room and offered a choice of beverages. She'd never seen Hal so edgy. What could have happened since last evening to prompt this sudden trip to the airport?

"Will your husband be meeting you at the airport in San Francisco?" Hal asked, after the attendant left with their orders.

"No. I talked with Justin last night. He's got some sort of real estate deal pending near Tahoe, so he'll probably be gone for a couple of days."

"Hmm. Right."

Chapter 1

Catharine watched as her editor nervously clicked his ballpoint pen and frowned at nothing in particular. Hesitancy. That was it. Hal never hesitated. He knew what he wanted to say and do, then said and did it. His bluntness had been disconcerting to her at first, but she had come to not only admire this trait over the years, but depend upon it.

"What's wrong, Hal?" she asked, deciding that a little of that same bluntness might be needed just now. "You know I'm always glad to see you, but I thought we said our good-byes last night."

"We did, but I—" Hal stopped clicking the pen and met her blue gaze with a disgruntled sigh. "Oh, hell! I couldn't let you leave without apologizing."

Catharine's expression was blank. "Apologizing? What on earth for?"

There were only half a dozen occupants in the spacious room, and none within hearing, but Hal's voice lowered to a discreet tone. "Because I wasn't able to get you the advance."

"What advance?"

"The advance on your royalties."

"Advance on my—" Catharine stared at him in total bewilderment.

A flight attendant arrived then, handing Catharine a chilled glass of orange juice and Hal a V-8.

"Is there anything else I can get for you?" the young man asked. "Bagels, sweet rolls, or something from the bar?"

"Tempting, but no—nothing for me," Hal answered. "Catharine?"

"No, thank you."

The attendant lingered a moment longer than necessary, giving her a smile that held awkward admiration. He was slender, no more than medium height, with short dark hair that had been peroxided a bright blond on top. Catharine thought the current fad in young men's hairstyles was ridiculous and made them look like badgers with a bad hair-day. The attendant had an engaging smile though, and nice eyes. They were honest eyes, she thought, returning his smile.

In a sudden gesture of bravado, he thrust a paper napkin toward her and gulped, "My wife really loves your books. Would you mind signing this for her?"

"I'd be happy to." Catharine set her glass on an adjacent table and took the napkin. "What's your wife's name?"

"Lisa."

Hal handed Catharine his pen, watching as she wrote a quick note and talked a moment with the young man. In all the years they'd worked together, he'd never once seen her treat anyone with the condescending politeness he detested in some authors.

"Thanks." The attendant pocketed the napkin with a pleased grin. "My wife will be really jealous when I tell her I met her favorite author. Do you have a new book coming out?"

Catharine hesitated only slightly. "Not right now—but there will be." *There had to be.*

After the young man had gone, she picked up her glass of juice and sipped it thoughtfully before leaning back against the soft leather. "Hal, do you mind if we start this conversation again? You were saying something about an advance?"

He nodded, tight-lipped. "A few weeks ago, Justin called and said you were strapped for money. He wanted to know if I could arrange to get you an advance on your royalties." Hal saw the humiliation flood her face and hurried on. "Believe me, I understand the circumstances. I think it's great you want to help your mother with the medical bills—but without a book proposal in hand, there's no way I can get that much cash."

"How much did Justin ask for?" she asked quietly.

Hal's usual confidence deserted him and he replied in a dry croak, "Seventy-five thousand. I know that's not an unusual amount for one of your books, but—"

"Mother doesn't need money for doctor bills," Catharine told him. "There was more than enough from my father's savings to pay what the insurance didn't cover." She paused, noting the perplexed frown that creased Hal's forehead. "Will you believe me if I say I never asked for an advance?"

Hal blew out a relieved sigh and reached for her hand, giving it a reassuring squeeze. "You know I will. But why would Justin ask for such a large sum of money without your knowledge?"

Catharine looked down, her voice as small as she felt. "Because he—he has a gambling problem."

"Oh, Lord," Hal muttered under his breath. "How long has this been going on?"

She gave a helpless little shrug. "I became aware of it about ten years ago." There was no point going into all the pain and disillusionment of that time. Few people knew the full extent of how much she and Justin had lost financially, let alone their deeper loss of trust. "I really thought he was doing better," she said finally.

Hal drained his glass and set it on the table with an angry thump. "Can I speak frankly?"

Catharine regarded her editor with a wry smile. "With you, I didn't know there was a choice."

"Point taken," he chuckled. His hazel eyes regarded her with an expression she didn't often see. The cool, crusty New Yorker was gone and an underlying tenderness that she'd long suspected was there, suddenly surfaced. "We've known each other a long time, Katie, and you know I don't like sticking my nose into my authors' personal affairs—but I've been worried about you."

She said nothing, just waited for him to go on, her blue eyes suspiciously bright.

Hal had to stop himself from putting his arms around her right then and there. What was it about this woman that always brought out the raw male protectiveness in him? Something more than just her beauty. When they'd first met some ten years before, Catharine had been forty, almost forty-one, and she'd immediately gotten under his thick New York skin. Slender, with dark brown hair, a fair English complexion and the most expressive blue eyes he'd ever had the pleasure of looking into, she had baffled and delighted him right from the start. The woman was intelligent and strong-willed, yet there was an undeniable softness about her, almost a fragile vulnerability. She never played games, never flirted or whined to get her way, and sometime, in her past, she'd been deeply hurt. Hal knew this as surely as he knew that, if he weren't happily married, Catharine Cavanagh could do some serious damage to his heart with just one of those spectacular smiles of hers.

Hal cleared his throat. "Anyone looking at you and Justin would see what appears to be the perfect couple—Catharine Cavanagh, the best-selling author who hasn't aged a day in ten years and could put any one of her heroines to shame—"

"Hal, don't—"

"I'm just stating the facts the way I see them." He grinned, enjoying the heightened color in her cheeks. "Then we have Justin Waller, a successful realtor and investor who adores his beautiful wife and—to make matters worse for guys like me—looks like a walking advertisement for Gold's Gym. On the surface it makes quite the pretty picture, but there's something about your husband that's bothered me for a long time. The guy's too smooth, too image-conscious. Every time I see that big smile of his, I can't help thinking it's just a performance for my benefit."

Catharine's rueful expression acknowledged the truth of his words. "It's in the genes," she said. "If you combine the Waller background of 'old money' with his mother's dedication to appearance, you can understand Justin a little better."

"I don't know that I really want to understand your husband," Hal said bluntly. "And since when does appearance or old money excuse someone's gambling addiction?"

"It doesn't, of course," she agreed with a weary sigh. "It's just—I think money's become something unhealthy for Justin. It's too much a part of his identity. He was the only son and thought he should have whatever he wanted without having to work for it or even put forth much effort. After his father died, Justin inherited an enormous sum, but he went through it in no time, most of it due to gambling losses."

Hal gave her a close look. "Do you think he's jealous of your success?"

She was silent for a moment, considering his words. "I don't think so. Justin's too full of him—" She stopped herself mid-word, but Hal was grinning.

"My feelings exactly," he said, then shook his head. "You and your husband are such opposites. Makes me wonder how the hell you ever got together."

"Timing had a lot to do with it. I met Justin at a family party, about a year after his first wife died."

"That's right. Wasn't she killed in a car accident?"

Catharine nodded, her blue eyes pensive. "In the beginning, I was touched by what I thought was Justin's vulnerability. He seemed so lost, and I really believed he needed me. Then there was David. He was only two when his mother died." Catharine paused before admitting, "I'd just turned thirty-one and was feeling very old and very much alone. Marrying Justin and being David's mother sounded quite appealing."

Hal rubbed his bottom lip the way he always did when he was puzzled. "Excuse me—am I missing something here? During this whole scenario, you haven't said one word about love."

Color flooded her cheeks and Hal Kellerman couldn't keep back a smile. "Don't look so surprised. I haven't edited your last nine books without knowing how you feel about that particular subject. In fact, my wife has commented more than once that your husband must be quite the—er, really something, to inspire such incredible love scenes. Makes me feel damned uncomfortable."

Catharine's lips parted in a wistful smile, but she said nothing. A strong face suddenly surfaced from the past, ever clear and fresh in memory's keeping.

Now what have I said? Hal wondered, watching the sudden play of emotion that lit her eyes. Aloud, he joked, "Okay, so Justin's not the grand passion in your life. Does that mean there's hope for me?" He grinned then gave an exaggerated sigh. "Forget it. Other than my wife, there aren't many women who'd get excited about a balding, middle-aged man with an expanding waist-line."

Catharine came back to the present and gave Hal's arm an affectionate squeeze. "Oh, I wouldn't say that. Sean Connery's beyond middle-age and you have a lot more hair than he does."

"I may have more hair, but I don't have the accent. The Bronx is a far cry from a Scottish brogue." Hal's smile faded as he searched her face. "Are you going to tell Justin that you know about the $75,000?"

"I'll have to. It's one thing to have him throwing away his own money. I'm not going to let him do it with mine."

"Good for you." Hal glanced at his watch then swore. "I'd better be going. I'm supposed to meet Frank Haddon in twenty minutes and he's not going to like what I have to say about his latest manuscript. The man's so in love with the sound of his own words, he takes 1200 pages to write a story that could be told in half that." He leaned over to give Catharine one of his bone-crushing hugs. "I'm sorry to add to your load, Katie. You've had more than your share lately. That business last year with the stalker was bad enough. I meant to ask if you've had any more trouble with the guy."

"The restraining order put a stop to most of it," she answered, unable to repress a small shudder.

Hal stopped straightening his tie to give her a close look. "Most of it?"

"The past month I've found some rather sick notes on the windshield of my car."

"Not good. Have you told the police?"

Catharine shrugged and glanced away from the worried scrutiny of Hal's look. "Justin talked to the detective on the case and he's checking into it."

"Like I said, you've had more than your share." Hal's mouth tightened. "It's been what—only a couple of months since your father died. And now, this ugly business with Justin."

"It's all right," she said. "Who knows? I can always use it for story material."

Looking at her brave, bruised smile, Hal found himself wishing Justin weren't on the opposite end of the country so he could tell him a thing or two. Planting a fist in the middle of his smug, handsome face sounded even better.

"Give me a call when you get back," Hal told her, getting to his feet. His tone made it an order rather than a request.

"I will."

"And Catharine...."

"Yes?"

Hal bit off the sudden impulse to tell her to be careful. She had enough to worry about without him frightening her in the bargain. He leaned over and kissed her on the cheek. "Nothing. Do me a favor though and don't beat yourself up about not having another book in the works. I know you. It'll come."

Catharine was touched when Hal insisted on walking her back to the gate and made sure she was checked in and settled. Somehow, she managed to keep control over her emotions until his stocky figure disappeared into the crowd. Only then did she allow the shock and anger of what Justin had done to sink in. That he had the nerve to call her editor and feed him some sob story about needing money for doctor bills shouldn't stun her, but it did. How much was he in for this time, and did he honestly think she wouldn't find out? Or was he so desperate for money he didn't care. Still, he'd been clever enough to call Hal instead of her agent. If Justin had called Max Russell, he would have been given a flat refusal and a colorful lecture in the bargain. Justin must have known that and bypassed Max in hopes of getting money directly from the source.

Catharine took some deep breaths, feeling a familiar tightness close about her chest like a vice. The doctor said it was stress and not her heart that caused these attacks, but they were too painful to be ignored. She quickly fished three *Advil* out of her handbag, then headed for the nearest drinking fountain.

She had to do something to get her mind off Justin and the pain. Returning to her seat, she got out her notebook and pen. Writing always helped. It released things inside her that could find expression no other way. Whenever or wherever she had to wait, it had become a longstanding habit to pass the time people-watching and sketching little characterizations. Very often, those brief sketches found their way onto the pages of her books and assumed lives of their own.

Airports were ideal places to discover new characters. Especially JFK. Only in New York, Catharine thought, as a solemn cluster of Hasidic Jews approached the ticket line. Directly ahead of them, a buxom young blonde was fishing through a massive leather handbag for her I.D. The line might be sluggish, but the blonde's tight chartreuse tee shirt and hip-hugging skirt were definitely on the move. And that hemline had a mind of its own. Every time the blonde shifted position, whether to check her luggage or the time, the skirt crawled dangerously up her thighs.

A smile curled one corner of Catharine's mouth as she watched the little tableau in the ticket line. Those black-garbed men might be duly shocked out of their solemnity if the young woman found the need or occasion to bend over.

Catharine continued writing, waiting for the tight pain in her chest to ease. Over her right shoulder she could hear portions of a rapid, noisy conversation in Italian. Moving past her down the long concourse were two black youths, each pushing an empty wheelchair toward the gate with singular rhythm and grace. Only in New York, Catharine thought again, marveling at the myriad mix of cultures and ethnic diversity that passed daily through the airport.

What had it been like a century ago? she wondered suddenly. Then, as now, New York had been the main gateway for streams of immigrants coming to the land of dreams and golden opportunity. Her own ancestors had been among those coming to America. They were Irish—Cavanaghs on her father's side, Cliffords and McDermotts on her mother's.

The Cavanaghs had immigrated during the latter part of the nineteenth century, when transportation was well established and the perilous Atlantic passage took days instead of weeks. Her mother's people had arrived much earlier, by nearly forty years. They had been part of the tragic *diaspora* that sent millions of Irish immigrants fleeing from death and the hopelessness of Ireland's potato famine.

Catharine had been fascinated with their story since childhood, although only scant details were known. Her great-great grandmother, Esther Clifford, was especially intriguing. According to family legend, Esther had committed the unpardonable sin of eloping with the family coachman, John Clark, a deed which resulted in her being disgraced and disinherited.

Catharine adored the romance of the tale—the lovely young Irishwoman falling in love with her dashing coachman, and the two running away together to make a new life in America. Years ago she had considered writing a story based on her great-great grandmother's life. Her first attempt had been in the seventh grade. Despite an abundance of adjectives and melodramatic metaphors, her efforts had been rewarded with an A+ from her English teacher. She'd tried again when she was nineteen. Several momentous chapters in her own life had been written during that long ago summer spent in Ireland. The traumatic events which followed, took precedence over fiction. Catharine had placed the unfinished manuscript in a box, along with other mementos. Somehow, she couldn't bring herself to throw those pages away, any more than she could rid herself of the memories they evoked. Putting time's soothing salve on the pain, she had gone on with her life, making the idle promise that someday, when the time was right, she would finish the book.

Why not now? a voice deep inside seemed to ask. The strength and suddenness of the idea caused her to sit bolt upright on the seat. Could she do it? Should she? There would be a tremendous amount of research involved. Catharine set her notebook aside with a little sigh.

It wasn't the research that made her hesitate, but the memories and pain of setting a book in Ireland. Her historical sagas and romances had had many settings over the years, but never Ireland. She couldn't put herself through the bittersweet torture of writing a romance in the very place where her own heart had found the answer to its longing some thirty years before.

Yet she couldn't deny the excited tingling inside her. The feeling was like an unerring compass that told her when a story idea or plot direction was right. She didn't understand it. She didn't need to. The time had come to write Esther Clifford's story. That's all she needed to know.

The announcement of her flight's initial boarding brought Catharine to her feet. She took a moment to glance around the crowded concourse. It was fitting somehow, that the idea and its confirmation should come here in New York, the very place where John and Esther had arrived a century and a half before.

Then, shouldering the strap of her laptop and grabbing the handle of her carry-on, she left thoughts of the past behind and headed down the ramp to face what lay ahead.

2

Esther

Catharine's thoughts made their own journey as the '747' winged its way westward across the country. There were miles of hurt and humiliation, and miles of anger, during which she confronted her husband in a masterful mental dialogue. It was amazing how brilliant one could be at 36,000 feet. Rebuttals and recriminations flowed freely. She was fearless. If only she could file away her acerbic brilliance and replay it when the actual moment of confrontation arrived. Inside, she knew what would probably happen. Justin would either explode with self-righteous anger or stalk away, wounded and hurt. She had learned long ago that nothing was ever his fault. No matter what the problem or issue might be, in the end, the blame would be skillfully shifted to something or someone else.

To be fair, she and Justin had had fewer confrontations since her father's stroke some eighteen months ago. Catharine had been more than grateful for his consideration and concern. Now she found herself doubting Justin's sincerity. Had it all been an act to keep her in the dark, outside the tangled strands of his financial web? How could she have been so blind not to realize he was gambling again?

Was she really that unaware or was he becoming more devious at concealing his actions?

Thinking about it all, she felt a wave of weary sadness. Sadness for them both.

Catharine pressed a hand to her forehead and leaned against the seat's headrest. Outside the plane's small oval window was a sea of billowing clouds. Wave after wave of pure, untroubled white sailing along an airy ocean of clean blue sky. It was like a dream world ... fragile and ethereal ... totally untouched by the mundane matters of earthbound mortals. Cloud castles rose in airy magnificence before her eyes, complete with snowy turrets, towers and battlements.

Present worries faded as Catharine's wandering thoughts traveled back to another place and time—Ireland and Esther Clifford. Images and phrases took shape in her mind as effortlessly as the clouds forming outside her window. Ideas. Words. Ghosts and whispers from the past. At first, insubstantial as the vaporous sea, the ideas swelled and grew, calling to her, urging her to give them form and substance.

Catharine didn't take the time to get out her laptop. It would be blasphemous to put these words into a machine, to listen to its mechanical hums and metallic clicks. No. These words must be born with ink and paper, the way Esther herself might write them. Reaching down, she took a notebook and pen from her bag. Then, with a quiet intake of breath that was half-prayer and half-fear, she began to write.

> *In the land of 'saints and scholars,' I was always a dreamer. That would not have been so difficult if I had been born a man—a man who dreams he can be a poet, or a visionary, or even a prophet. A woman who dreams is simply foolish. Yet, a dreamer I am and ever will be. Even my*

name in the soft Irish tongue means dreamer—Aisling. In English, the name becomes the more prosaic—Esther. I doubt my parents were aware of this when they chose to name me after a maternal grandmother, yet even Esther is decidedly distinctive when placed beside the myriad ranks of Marys, Catharines and Bridgets which were born in Ireland during the 1800's.

I entered this world the day before All Saints' Eve, October 30, in the year of our Lord, eighteen hundred and twenty-two, the second child of Henry and Rose Marie Clifford. My elder sister was one of the many Marys, and the epitome of everything that name implies—dutiful, submissive, and obedient. Everything I was not.

I do not mean to imply that I was wicked. My conscience and love of God would never allow for too much carnal wickedness, no matter how I might be tempted. Rather, I was not what others, my father in particular, expected a genteel young lady of the times to be.

Mother understood me much better, may God and the blessed Virgin bless her soul. I suspect she was a bit of a dreamer herself.

As a child, my dreams were fanciful, but to me, not at all unreasonable. I saw no reason why I could not be a fairy queen with the host of other fairy folk who lived in the old rowan tree behind our home. Oh, how I loved the idea of flying on gossamer wings. I was always a curious child and there were so many secret places I longed to explore. Wings would make a handy addition to such quests. As for fairy attire, I must admit my desires and dreams were a bit on the scandalous side. Encumbered with layers of petticoats, itchy woolen stockings and toe-pinching shoes, I hope I will not be censured too sharply for finding the idea of wearing a diaphanous veil loosely entwined about one's naked bosom and limbs, highly pleasurable as well as romantic, except perhaps on a cold Irish morning of drizzle and rain. Then, on such days, any fairy queen worth her weight in bee pollen and moon-dust should be curled up snugly in a bed of soft leaves and flower petals inside the hollow of a tree.

Need I say that one cannot be a dreamer without also being something of a romantic, and my dearest dreams were drenched in its rosy hue. The idea of falling in love was to me, quite enticing, even mysterious. Living in an age when it was common practice for parents to arrange the marriages of their children, love held all the fascination of the forbidden. My dreams on the subject were sheer poetry, while most of the time, life itself was plain prose.

How did other young women do it? I wondered. Calmly submit to marrying the wart-nosed son of some farmer in a neighboring townland, without a word to say about the matter? He might be the owner of half a dozen milk cows and a fine house with a slate roof, but if truth be told, I doubt any young bride would be thinking of milk cows or a slate roof on her wedding night.

'Tis the simple fact that I much preferred the idea of being swept off my feet by a tide of passion for my true love, to that of sweeping the floor for a man I barely knew.

Amazingly, I do have a practical side, fleeting though it may be at times, and an unquenchable thirst for knowledge. I adore books, and in my dream library, I own shelves and shelves of them—many with fine leather covers and wondrous print. Other volumes might be more humble in appearance, but are none the less interesting for all that. Books are much like the people who own them, coming in all shapes and sizes. But their content! Ah, how rich it is to discover the depths and pleasures that both people and words can bring.

To be truthful, my own words tend to run on at times, like a brook in the spring tide. As a child, I received many a scolding from Father for talking so much, but for me 'twas something akin to breathing itself. To please him, I did my best to remain silent, but even that didn't prevent me from having grand conversations in my head.

Dreams have a way of changing with time. Some simply fade with the passage of years, while others grow dearer still. At the age of fifteen or thereabouts, I happily abandoned my secret desire to possess flowing locks of gold, when John Richard Clark told me that my hair reminded him of glossy chestnuts shining in the sun.

John Richard was the son of our family's coachman and, consequently, his opinion shouldn't have mattered to me at all. Yet I cannot deny that his words sounded very fine, and the roguish glint in his dark blue eyes was finer still. Remembering them sent a happy warmth into my thoughts for days afterwards.

But I am forgetting myself. Talking of John Richard often has that effect on me. I was speaking of dreams and how they change over the years. Yet, some are constant like an ever-burning fire, and so *dear that even the greatest sacrifice seems a sweet thing to bring about their birth into reality.*

Sooner or later, for any dream to become real, one must make a decision and take action. Decision is such a hard word, is it not? Even the sound of it is dressed in the drab, difficult fabric of reality and not the gauzy stuff from which dreams are woven.

I had such a decision. It changed my life and my world. And the cost . . for years I could not speak of it, because of the pain. My dream and the decisions that followed created a great gulf of separation and a chasm of change which once, crossed, could never be bridged again.

Catharine set down her pen and stared at the rush of words across the page. Her throat ached and there was a tortuous longing inside. Already, it seemed as if Esther's life and decisions had become entangled with her own. The 'separation' and that 'chasm of change' ... dear God, why had she written those words? She must be insane to even consider writing this story. What possible good could it do to go through it all again? It wouldn't change anything, only add more pain to her life.

Catharine stared unseeing out the window. *We're both dreamers, Esther, but you had more courage than I.* She tried to turn her thoughts into less emotional channels, but the words she had written kept repeating in her mind. More than words. It was almost as if Esther herself were speaking, urging her on.

Catharine looked down at the handwritten pages, then picked up her pen once more. *Maybe I can't change the past,* she thought, *but I can learn from it. Help me, Esther. I'll do the work—only help me to understand your people and your heart.*

To understand the way of things in my time, one needs to have knowledge of my father's time and his father's and his father's before him, peeling away the years of pain and pride, enlightenment and misery.

There are those who say that Irish history is much like the skin of an onion. The more layers you peel away, the more you weep. One can blame Ireland's troubles on this king or that king, but simply put, the history of Ireland is two dogs and a bone—the Irish being one of the dogs and Ireland itself, the bone. The other dog changed breed and size quite handily over the centuries—from Vikings to Normans to the English—but the purpose was always the same: To take the bone away from the Irish.

I'm sure there are many who would say I am oversimplifying the matter, that there are more important issues at stake—religion and race, complex creeds and changing cultures. To this, I answer simply, men have always tried to justify and defend the reasons for their own selfishness and pride. Strip away all those invented titles and self-righteous excuses and you still have selfishness and pride.

What else can you call it, when one man feels he has more right to a morsel of food and a plot of ground than the next? I like to think there will come a time when men will learn to share and give freely to all their neighbors, no matter who his kith or kin may be. But then, as I said before, I am a dreamer.

The early years of my childhood were a lovely, innocent time. I had little idea what the world was like beyond the limited boundaries of our home and its demesne. We lived in.. . .

Catharine paused, then ceased to write altogether. Where was Esther's home? She had no idea. Not so much as a town, or even a county in Ireland in which to place the setting. During her earlier attempts she hadn't bothered with such details. All she had wanted then was to immerse herself in the romance of Esther's meeting and elopement with her dashing young coachman, and those events were readily created and embellished by her fertile imagination. Now, she felt she owed it to John and Esther to be as accurate as possible.

Someone in the family must have information about the Cliffords. Birth and marriage dates. Pictures or letters. I'll call Mother the minute the plane's on the ground, Catharine decided with a burst of determined energy. Better yet, I'll go see her. Justin would be involved in his questionable 'business' dealings for another day or two, so there was no need to hurry home. Amazing, she thought with a wry smile, how Justin and his problems suddenly ceased to be so critical.

Catharine was so intent on making a list of various questions and facts she needed to know about the Clifford family, she scarcely noticed the flight attendant who paused beside her row with a refreshment cart.

"Would you care for something to drink, Mrs. Waller?"

Catharine glanced up and gave the young woman a quick smile. "No, thank you. I'm fine."

And she was. The pain in her chest was completely gone. In fact, she felt as light and airy as the clouds billowing outside the plane window.

Glancing at the drifting currents of white, Catharine discovered a cloud portal had opened, allowing a gauzy glimpse of the earth below. Patchwork fields wore winter's hues of drab gray and raw umber. There was no green to be found, yet in her mind, she could see the verdant fields and hedgerows of a distant isle. Ireland.

She smiled, basking in a renewed sense of purpose that had been missing from her life for a long time. "Thank you, Esther," she whispered. "You and I are going to write a wonderful book!"

3

Barrett

The sky was overcast and a fitful wind blew dust and scraps of paper into dancing spirals as Catharine walked swiftly down a row of vehicles in the San Francisco Airport's long-term parking area. Looking up at the ominous passage of clouds, she knew rain wasn't far behind. Already, she could smell the faint salt tang from the bay and feel its moist chill on her face. Good! she thought, enjoying the wild portent of the wind as it whipped the dark brown waves of her hair into tangles. She loved the coastal storms, whether it was a pounding sou' wester off the Pacific, or a mild mist kissing the land. She'd lived in northern California all her life, growing up in Alameda across the San Francisco Bay, then moving to Marin County after her marriage to Justin.

Catharine gave her watch a quick glance as she reached the space where her Subaru *Outback* was parked. Four-twenty five. After a long flight and emotionally trying day, she was relieved she wouldn't be driving home to San Anselmo at the height of commuter traffic. Nor was she in the mood to tackle the bumper to bumper stream across the Bay Bridge to Oakland. Instead, she'd drive south and take the San Mateo Bridge across the bay to Alameda.

Setting her laptop case on the hood of the *Outback*, she was reaching in her handbag for the car keys when a sick chill suddenly gripped her insides. Tucked snugly against the windshield beneath the wiper blade was a plain white envelope.

For a heart-pounding moment, Catharine could only stare at the envelope, feeling powerless to move or think. Then her nervous gaze darted to the surrounding parking aisles and vehicles. She could see nothing out of the ordinary, only fellow travelers like herself, searching for their cars or loading luggage into trunks.

Catharine hurriedly unlocked the car, jarred by the thought that he might be in one of the nearby vehicles, watching her even now. Her mind tried to insert the possibility that the note might be totally innocent and not from *him* at all, even though her racing heart and tightening nerves insisted that it was.

The envelope was the same size and shape as two others left on her windshield during the past month. How could he have known when she would be returning from New York? Other than flight times, the airline wouldn't give out passenger information. The man had an almost uncanny way of ferreting out her every move.

Reason wrestled with fear as Catharine put her luggage in the back seat. If the man had really wanted to harm her, he could have done more than leave an anonymous note. So why torture her with these insidious messages? Anger gave fear a healthy shove and she snatched the envelope from beneath the wiper blade. Slapping the envelope down on the passenger seat, she grabbed her handbag and searched an inner pocket for a small card. Detective Adams would want to know about this latest addition to her collection.

Catharine paused, card in hand, to glance at the unopened envelope. There was no point in calling Lyle Adams unless she knew the contents of the letter. Drawing a tense breath, she opened the envelope and removed a single sheet of neatly folded white paper.

The typed words were like dirty hands groping over her body. Dropping the note with a shudder, she reached for her cell phone and hurriedly punched in the numbers. *Please be there!* she pleaded silently. Relief rushed through her when the gruff voice of Lyle Adams answered.

"Detective Adams ... I'm so glad you're in. This is Mrs. Waller. I–I thought you should know that—"

"Excuse me, who did you say this is?" The detective's puzzled tone interrupted.

"Catharine Cavanagh Waller," she said more slowly, and took some steadying breaths.

"Oh, yes. Sorry." The gruff voice registered embarrassed recognition. "I haven't heard from you in a while. How's everything going?"

"At the moment, not very well. I just found another note on my car windshield and—"

"Hold on. What do you mean, another note?"

The unexpectedness of his question left Catharine stammering. "I—it's—a note in a white envelope—from Barrett Saunders—like, like the one my husband gave you a few weeks ago."

"Mrs. Waller, this is the first I've heard about any note."

"But Justin said that—"

"And I haven't heard from your husband since we issued the restraining order," Adams put in, a new edge to his voice.

"I don't understand...."

"Obviously, there's been some kind of miscommunication," Adams told her with weary patience. "Now what's this about a note from Saunders."

Catharine bit her lip, then blew out a shaky breath. There had to be a reasonable explanation why Justin hadn't talked with the police detective as he'd promised. He wouldn't just forget....

"Mrs. Waller—"

The detective's gruff voice interrupted her worrisome stream of thoughts.

"I'm sorry. I'm still feeling a little unnerved."

"Where are you calling from?"

"The airport. I just got back from New York and, when I got to my car, there was a white envelope beneath the wiper blade."

"An envelope," he repeated. "And what makes you think it's from Saunders?"

"Well, because—it's exactly like the others, and he—" Catharine broke off, reluctant to describe the contents.

"The others," he prompted. "How many others."

"Two ... not counting the ... uh, the package he sent before Christmas with—" Catharine drew a ragged breath. "I'm sorry. I know this must sound all mixed-up and confused, but I honestly thought you knew—"

There was a moment of silence on the other end of the line. Then Catharine heard a muttered expletive.

"My feelings exactly," she said.

"Why don't we start this conversation from the beginning," Adams suggested. "And take your time."

Going over the incidents of the past month, Catharine felt her taut nerves begin to relax. Detective Adams was thorough in his questions and unequivocal in his support. Only once did she falter, and that had been when he asked her to read the contents of the note.

Glancing down at the sick sexual message, Catharine couldn't make herself repeat the words.

"Would you mind if I just gave it to you next week?" she asked, her voice trembling a little. "I–I just can't—"

"That's okay," he said, the gruff tone softening considerably. "It can wait until Wednesday. If I could get out of these court commitments I'd meet with you sooner, but I'm afraid that's not possible."

"I know and I understand. I'm just glad I was able to reach you today."

"So am I. If I hadn't been stuck in the office getting this paper work ready for court, you wouldn't have. Do you have the number for my cell phone?"

"I don't believe so."

Catharine repeated the number he gave her and wrote it in her planner.

"If you have any concerns or problems before Wednesday, be sure to call me," Adams said. "It doesn't matter how early or how late. You can reach me at that number."

"Thank you."

By the time Catharine left the airport, a measure of calm and confidence had returned. In a way, talking with Lyle Adams was like making a doctor's appointment. It didn't take away the illness or need for the appointment, but just having it gave one the hope that things could be made right again.

Reaching for her phone once more, she dialed a familiar number. "Hi, Mother! I just got back from New York and wondered if you'd like a little company this evening."

"Catharine, how nice. I'd love to see you."

No questions. No polite inquiries about Justin. *Bless you, Mother,* she thought, and told her, "I'm driving south to San Mateo, so don't expect me right away."

"That's fine, dear. It will give me time to cook us some dinner. What are you in the mood for?"

"Whatever you feel like fixing will be wonderful. But don't go to a lot of trouble."

"I won't. We'll keep it simple."

She smiled, knowing that to Grace Cavanagh simple was usually a seven-course meal. "Thanks, Mother. I'll see you sometime within the hour."

Traffic was heavy, but Catharine encountered no more than the usual slowdowns on her way to the bridge. In spite of her determination to do otherwise, she caught herself checking the rearview mirror more often than necessary and casting quick glances at the occupants of passing vehicles, the sight of a long thin face a recurring image in her mind.

Just ten months ago, she had been the keynote speaker at a writers' conference in San Jose. The audience was predominantly middle-aged and female, with sprinklings of hopeful young writers of both sexes to add spice to the creative brew.

A few minutes into her presentation, Catharine had glanced down and encountered the rapt gaze of a man sitting on the second row. Hair the color of moldy straw framed his narrow face, with unruly wisps sticking out on either side. His nose was high-bridged and bony, the jaw angular and dusted with stubbled growth that looked more like blond lint than a beard.

Catharine quickly shifted her attention back to the audience in general, but throughout her talk, she couldn't help being aware of the unwavering interest of the man on the second row. He didn't take notes or ask questions, just watched her with a dazed sort of fascination, his long-fingered hands nervously twirling a pencil.

Although she did her best to avoid the man's heavy-lidded gaze, there had been a disturbing moment when her eyes encountered his. Strangely shaken, Catharine had glanced down at her notes, sensing that something was not quite right about his mental state.

Afterwards, he'd approached her and asked if he could talk with her about a story he was working on. There had been dozens of people around at the time, and although she hadn't felt threatened in any way, his intense gaze was more than a little unsettling. Catharine ignored the man's request and suggested he might want to attend a workshop she was giving later that afternoon.

He did and left a three-inch typed manuscript on the table before she could explain that she wasn't doing any private editing.

Curiosity compelled her to read a portion of the manuscript later that night in her hotel room. The first two or three pages were ample evidence that Barrett Saunders had a strong command of the language, but Catharine was unable to grasp any sense of direction in the plot. Even if fantasy/science fiction had been her *forte*, she would have found it difficult to understand, let alone enjoy the man's writing. Saunders had invented curious names and a bizarre jargon that she was clueless to decipher.

Catharine skimmed the first three chapters, finding a certain brittleness in the characterization, as if protagonist and antagonist were merely cerebral automatons moving through the muddled machinations of their author's will. Occasionally, she stumbled across a striking image or simile, but overall, she felt a confused darkness about his work.

Honesty prevented her from giving the man any encouragement, yet her innate sense of fairness required that she make some kind of response. Finally, Catharine scribbled a brief note thanking Saunders for the opportunity to read a portion of his manuscript, complimented him on his unique command of the language (which was true, even though half the time she didn't understand what on earth he was saying), and wished him all the best.

She left the manuscript with the conference director, inwardly praising the heavens she wouldn't have to worry about dealing with Barrett Saunders again.

Two weeks later, Catharine was addressing a workshop for *Writer's Digest* in Long Beach, when she glanced down and recognized the scarecrow-like hair and rapt gaze of Barrett Saunders in the audience. Despite efforts to avoid him, he'd sought her out afterwards and asked if they couldn't meet somewhere and talk. Her polite but firm refusal had little effect.

During the weeks and months that followed, the man's attentions became more persistent. Roses showed up on her doorstep—fat, dark red and scentless—and additional chapters of his book arrived in padded envelopes through the mail.

Justin had taken one look at the pages and snorted, "The guy's nuts. I hope you're not encouraging him."

"Of course I'm not encouraging him!" Catharine shot back. "I have no idea how he got our address."

"Getting an address isn't all that difficult," Justin replied in the condescending tone that never failed to irritate her. "The guy probably thinks you're his ticket to fame and fortune. Get rid of him!"

Catharine sighed and remained silent. She'd received many letters from readers over the years, including requests from eager would-be writers who were generally more interested in talking about their books than writing them—but she'd never encountered anything like this. Her novels consistently made the *New York Times* best-seller list, and her name garnered instant recognition in the literary world, but it wasn't as if she had the celebrity status of a film or recording star.

Chapter 3

What was it that motivated the man? Catharine prayed Saunders didn't have any ridiculous romantic notions. Although he was clearly a nuisance, somehow he didn't strike her as dangerous. Maybe Justin was right, and Saunders had the mistaken idea that she could further his writing career.

Catharine finally decided that ignoring the man was the least painful course of action. She sent back his packages unopened, refused delivery of his flowers, and began canceling speaking engagements, using her father's illness as a legitimate excuse.

Weeks passed without incident and Catharine began to believe the uncomfortable episode was over and done with. Saunders and his idiosyncrasies ceased to matter altogether when her father suffered another series of devastating strokes.

Judge Gordon Cavanagh had fought his way back from the partial paralysis and debilitating effects of the first stroke, determined to show those "damn doctors" that he would walk and talk again despite their grim prognosis. And for a time, it seemed as if the good judge's verdict for himself would be carried out in the same way his courtroom decisions had been honored for over forty years.

The second stroke totally defeated him, leaving a shrunken shell of the man that Catharine had both loved and feared all her life. She spent more and more time at his bedside, hating the illness that ravaged his body, yet sadly grateful for the chance it offered to serve and grow closer to him.

Then came the November afternoon, just ten days before her father's death. At Catharine's insistence, her mother had left the house to do a little shopping and get her hair done. The home-care nurse had been by to administer the necessary injections which gave her father a few hours' respite from pain. But this afternoon, Gordon Cavanagh was unusually agitated, and nothing Catharine said or did could calm him.

Looking into her father's sunken blue eyes, she was surprised to see tears slipping down his cheeks.

"It's all right, Dad. I'm here," she murmured brokenly, her own eyes smarting.

Gordon Cavanagh's good hand took his daughter's in a fierce grip, and the drooping, half-frozen mouth struggled to move.

Watching his futile efforts, Catharine felt as if her heart would break. She tried to offer reassurance, but tears tightened her throat.

When he released her hand, it was to point to the dry erase board kept next to the bed. For the past month it had been their only means of communicating. Catharine would patiently point to the letters of the alphabet in turn, and her father would either squeeze her hand or blink rapidly to indicate the letter he wanted. Closing his eyes indicated the negative. The method was painstakingly slow, but provided a much-needed way for Judge Cavanagh to communicate with his family.

"All right, Dad," Catharine told him, wiping her eyes with her hand and trying her best to smile. "What do you want to tell me?"

Taking the dry erase marker, father and daughter went through the now-familiar process, with Catharine writing down the letters indicated.

She stared, speechless, at the simple message on the board. *I'm Sorry.* It was a phrase she'd never heard from her father's lips. And never expected to hear.

Catharine looked at her father, seeing pain in his eyes that had nothing to do with his physical condition.

"I don't understand," she said gently, taking his hand. "Why are you sorry?"

Tears filled the man's eyes again, and his grip on her hand tightened.

"Is it the stroke? That's not your fault."

Judge Cavanagh closed his eyes.

"No? Then what's troubling you? Can I do anything?"

He glanced at the board once more, and Catharine let go his hand to take the marker. Slowly, they went through the letters and Catharine covered her mouth to stifle a sob, as the sentence became clear. *Remember I love you.*

"I love you, too," she whispered, tears slipping down her face.

Not long after, her father had fallen into an exhausted sleep and Catharine quietly left the room.

Pensive and emotionally drained, she had driven back to San Anselmo in the misty gold light of late afternoon, her father's painful apology haunting her thoughts. Pulling into the driveway of their hillside home, she pressed the garage door opener, noting that Justin's sleek black *Porsche* was gone. No surprises there, she thought wearily. Entering the house, she moved from the utility room off the garage into the kitchen. There, she found a note taped to the microwave oven.

"FYI. There's a big investor in town. Stan and I will be wining and dining him tonight. Hope you had a great day. Wish me luck. XOXO Justin."

Catharine snatched the paper off the microwave and tossed it angrily in the garbage. She knew he had no way of knowing what her day had been like, or how much she needed a pair of strong arms to hold her close right now, but somehow, seeing that flip FYI was enough to make her blood boil.

Too upset to eat, Catharine changed into a T-shirt and some jogging pants and left the house.

Glowing ribbons of gold streaked across the autumn sky as she jogged along San Anselmo's residential streets at a punishing pace.

Finally, out of breath, with a sharp pain in her side, she was forced to slow to a walk. Just ahead, she could see the hilltop retreat of the old Montgomery Hall.

Catharine had long been fascinated with the place and her evening walks often found her there, strolling the wooded grounds. Massive oaks and evergreens grew alongside stately palms, ivy climbed old stone walls, and flowering shrubs and bushes hugged the walkways. Decades before, the place had been the site of a thriving parochial school with an impressive library, lecture hall and chapel. The business district of San Anselmo was only blocks away, yet somehow the old school seemed centuries apart from its contemporary rush. The buildings were constructed in the massive, gothic style of Richardsonian architecture with arched windows, stone walls and castle-like turrets.

There are stories here, Catharine had thought the first time she discovered the place. Despite the buildings' parochial history, her imagination sometimes saw Bronte's *Jane Eyre* peering from one of the tower windows; other times a forlorn but proud Elizabeth Bennett waiting in the garden near the sundial for her Mr. Darcy. The wooden bench half-hidden in a secluded corner of vines and branches was the perfect place for a lover's tryst or secret assignation.

On this Indian summer evening, there were no stories or hints of romance. Only stillness and the dusky scent of dry oak brush mingled with pine.

What was it her father had been trying to tell her? That it was something important she had no doubt. She could still feel the painful grip of his bony hand holding hers, and see the remorse in those sunken, tear-filled eyes. What could be troubling him so deeply?

Intent on her thoughts, Catharine turned the corner of a wooded path and found herself face to face with Barrett Saunders. Her heart gave a painful lurch as she stared at the tall man blocking her way.

Chapter 3

His blond hair was as unkempt as ever, his tee shirt too small, and his jeans too loose for his angular frame. The man's heavy-lidded eyes regarded her with something more than pleasure. They seemed desperately alight with a rapt purpose known only to him.

Catharine's throat was painfully dry, but she knew she had to say something. Lifting her chin with more confidence than she felt, she demanded, "What are you doing here?"

"You didn't answer my letters, so I had to find you. I have to talk to you."

"Mr. Saunders, I don't want to—"

"Why didn't you answer my letters?" he asked with an almost innocent sort of bewilderment.

"I–because … Look, whatever it is you want I can't help you. I'm sorry, but I have to go—"

"If you'd read my letters, you'd understand! You'd know we've known each other before.…"

"No. No, we haven't."

Catharine turned on her heel and began walking in the opposite direction. Saunders caught up to her in a few easy strides.

"But we have!" he insisted. "I've written about you, and – and dreamed about you!"

Catharine paused, fighting to keep her voice calm, even though her heart was pounding wildly and her palms were clammy.

"Mr. Saunders, I don't want you to follow me or try to see me again. Do you understand?"

"No, I don't."

The expression in his eyes was so confused that, in spite of her fear, Catharine felt a small stab of guilt for having hurt him. Without another word, she had walked away, forcing herself to keep her pace at a deliberate walk.

"I was meant to be in your life," his voice called after her as she took the stone steps down to the street below. "You don't understand now, but you will...."

One week later, at Justin's insistence, a restraining order was issued.

A police investigation into Barrett Saunder's background produced no criminal history, other than the occasional parking ticket or speeding citation. Saunders lived alone in an older Oakland neighborhood, had never been married and was self-employed, developing and selling fantasy games for computer software.

The officer in charge of the case told Catharine that Saunders had been properly shaken up by the order. "You shouldn't have any more trouble with the guy," he'd assured her.

Three days after that, her father passed away, and any concerns about Barrett Saunders faded into the background. Funeral arrangements, visiting relatives, and assisting her mother with the financial mountain of estate matters, took nearly all her waking hours.

By the time life began to settle down once more, Christmas was only weeks away. It was a strange, limbo-like time of adjustment. Justin was gone more than usual on business trips and Catharine found herself making frequent visits to Alameda, trying to ease her mother through the loneliness of the holiday season.

On a December afternoon of drizzling rain and leaden skies, she had picked Grace up to do a little Christmas shopping. Catharine put on a cheerful face, determined to give her mother a pleasant time, and Grace did the same, yet both women were acutely aware of the new emptiness in their lives, and the loss of the obstinate man who had been so difficult to please.

Grace couldn't walk through the men's department without seeing something that would have looked wonderful on her husband. A handsome tweed sportcoat. A navy wool sweater.

Sensing her mother's pain, Catharine soon regretted her plans to go shopping. Finally, Grace had turned to her daughter with a little smile. "I don't think either one of us is in the mood for Christmas shopping, so I have a suggestion."

"What's that?"

"Why don't we buy something totally outrageous for each other!"

Catharine gave her mother a grateful hug. "You're on."

Skies were clearing and the approach of evening promised a glowing sunset of winter roses as they wound their way through the crowded maze of vehicles to Catharine's car.

"I hope you realize you've totally spoiled me," Catharine said, unlocking the car door.

"It's about time *someone* did," Grace answered meaningfully, putting an armful of packages in the back seat.

Walking around to the driver's side, Catharine noticed a white envelope beneath the wiper blade.

"Don't tell me they've started giving parking tickets in the malls," Grace said.

Smiling, Catharine removed the envelope. "Let's hope not. Besides, it's the wrong color." Her smile froze as she read the typed message inside.

> *Going to the police won't do anything except make me angry. Bad things happen when I get angry. Don't tell anyone about this and we'll both feel better. If you let me, I can make you feel a lot better…*

"Is anything wrong, dear?"

"No. No, it's just another way to lose weight in thirty days," Catharine answered, hoping her voice didn't reveal the cold current of shock running through her. It had been so wonderful to see a return of her mother's usual sparkle. She wasn't about to let Barrett Saunders ruin their day. Crumpling the note, she tossed it into a nearby waste receptacle, then climbed into the car.

Three days before Christmas, a small padded envelope arrived in the mail. Catharine had opened it without a moment's thought, then felt her stomach twist into a hard knot as she saw the scanty contents of black lace, accompanied by an obscene invitation.

Shaken and repulsed, she'd thrown the envelope and its contents into the trash without telling anyone, not even Justin. At the time, her mind was too shocked to realize she was throwing away what might be considered important evidence. She only knew she had to get rid of it. Not let it touch her.

Some ten days later, another white envelope appeared on her windshield. Catharine had just come out of the grocery store a few blocks from her home, and her pounding heart immediately told her this was not a handbill or some other harmless solicitation.

With trembling hands, she put the sacks of groceries in the car, then snatched the envelope. Catharine felt herself begin to shake from the inside out as she read the sick message.

Driving home, confusion and fear clouded her thoughts. As unnerving as they had been, there was nothing of a sexual nature in Saunder's previous contacts. Why this sudden change? Perhaps anger over the restraining order had propelled him over the edge of harmless fantasy to some darker purpose.

Justin had known something was wrong the moment Catharine entered the house. Without a word, she handed him the note. His dark brows narrowed as he read the graphic words. Then he swore under his breath.

"Where the hell did this filth come from?" he demanded, anger flashing in his eyes.

Her voice shaking, Catharine told him, and Justin wrapped her in his arms, pressing her head against his shoulder. The unexpected tenderness was her undoing, and tears spilled down her cheeks.

"I'm sorry, honey," he said. "I thought the business with that creep was over and done with."

"I'm so frightened ... I don't know what to do."

"You don't need to do anything," he assured her. "I'll go see Detective Adams first thing in the morning."

PELLETS OF RAIN spattered against the windshield of the *Outback* as Catharine drove across the metal expanse of the San Mateo Bridge. Far below, the gray-green swells of the bay were as troubled and unsettled as her thoughts.

Over two weeks had passed since Justin had promised he'd take Saunder's note to Lyle Adams. There had to be a reasonable explanation why the detective knew nothing about it. Perhaps he was out of the office when Justin came by, and someone neglected to give him the message. But that still didn't explain why Justin hadn't called back or made another attempt to reach him.

Catharine drew a shaky breath and tried to relax her white-knuckled grip on the steering wheel. Another half-hour, forty minutes at most and she'd be safe at her parents' home. And she'd better find a way to wipe the fear from her face and voice before then or her mother would be certain to know something was wrong.

Grace Cavanagh was aware of the situation with Barrett Saunders, but Catharine had purposely downplayed its seriousness, wanting to spare her mother additional stress during the difficult months of her father's illness. As far as Grace was concerned, the problem with Saunders had been nothing more than a harmless, albeit irritating episode that was long since past. And Catharine was determined to keep it that way.

For now, at least, she was safe. Catharine tried to let the feeling wash over her, but the envelope on the seat beside her was an uneasy reminder that safety was a transient condition, at best.

4

Grace

Porch lights gleamed softly through the darkness and a fine rain was falling as Catharine turned onto a quiet, tree-lined street in one of Alameda's older neighborhoods. From early childhood until her marriage, Catharine had never known any home other than the stately Queen Anne Victorian. The two-story gray house with its white gingerbread trim was well over a hundred years old, but proud upkeep and loving care by three generations of Cavanaghs had kept it looking gracefully young.

Dignity combined with ageless charm and a warm welcome were distinctive facets of the Cavanagh home's personality. Catharine had always been sensitive to the spirit of a house, particularly older homes that had felt the sorrows and joys of the families who lived within their walls.

Justin thought she was being fanciful and overly romantic, and said so, but Catharine was convinced that houses had personalities. In her travels and writing tours over the years, she had visited many homes. Some were weighed down with an oppressive atmosphere of gloom and sadness. Others wore the artificial glitter of wealth and expensive furnishings, but had no soul. One could admire their surface beauty, but there was no depth of character. Character had nothing to do with a home's size, cost, or even its architectural design. Often, Catharine had felt more nobleness of spirit in a simple cottage than the costliest mansion. Character came from within.

The Cavanagh home had known its share of sorrow as well as gladness over the years. Her grandparents had died there, as had her father. Yet grief had added a refining element, rather than an atmosphere of despair. The home was softer, warmer now than her childhood memories recalled. But the welcome was always the same. Even though it had been nearly twenty years since her marriage, Catharine still felt the warmth of that welcome whenever she returned, as if the house itself were reaching out to her, offering the safety and security of its walls.

As she turned onto the drive, a pizza delivery van was just pulling away from the curb. Catharine switched off the motor and smiled at the sight of her mother standing on the vine-trellised porch with a large cardboard box in her hands.

Getting out of the car, she called in mock disappointment, "What – no nine-course meal?"

"I told you we'd keep things simple," Grace answered with a laugh.

Catharine met her mother on the porch and gave her a kiss on the cheek. "You look good, Mother."

"Thank you, dear."

Dressed in navy slacks of brushed wool and an ivory sweater, with pearl studs in her ears, Grace Cavanagh radiated an air of casual elegance. She was a small woman, with a fine-boned face and a youthful spirit that made her seventy-five years seem impossible. The beauty which had been hers as a young woman was still evident in her smile, but softer now, and more finely polished, like the satin luster of old silver.

She's too thin, Catharine thought, observing her mother in the porch's mellow lamplight, but she was relieved to see an absence of the strain and hollow-eyed pallor that Grace had worn since the death of her husband.

"It smells wonderful," Catharine said, giving the pizza an appreciative sniff. "What kind did you get?"

"I couldn't decide between the 'hefty Hawaiian' and the 'cowboy special'—although what on earth Hawaiians and cowboys have to do with Italian pizza is beyond me. At any rate, I ordered an extra large and had them make one-half of each."

Catharine laughed and followed her mother inside. "From the size of that box, you'll be eating pizza for a week. But I hope you ordered breadsticks."

"Of course I did, but I draw the line at 'buffalo wings.' They're nothing more than a fancy name for heartburn and indigestion."

In spite of their light banter, Catharine was immediately aware of the strange new silence that had taken up residence in the house since her father's death. Gordon Cavanagh had been a work-driven man, not often home, and intensely occupied with his own world. Yet strangely, now that he was gone, there was this silence she'd never felt before.

She and Grace sat in the kitchen where her father's presence, or the lack of it, was less keenly felt.

Grace Cavanagh's kitchen was merely an inside version of her garden. Light and airy with a large bay window and creamy walls, bouquets of flowers bloomed on china plates, as well as in clay pots on the windowsills. Function was fine in its place, but Grace needed the beauty of living things around her.

Talking about snippets and trifles, they ate hot pizza and buttery breadsticks, while outside, the soft patter of rain added its calming voice to their conversation.

Catharine felt a welcome distance from the day's disturbing revelations—Justin's underhanded attempt to get $75,000 of her royalties, the obscene fantasies of Barrett Saunders—none of that could touch her here.

Grace silently observed her daughter as they ate, grateful to feel the air of unspoken tension about her gradually relax. Something was bothering Catharine, she knew, but not until the food was put away and dishes cleared did she venture to ask more pertinent questions.

"How did the meetings with your publisher go? I know you were feeling a bit tense about it before you left."

"It was awful," Catharine said bluntly. "If they'd been angry and raked me over the coals, it would have been a lot easier than so much kindness. Even Hal was less blustery than usual. By the end of the first day, I was wallowing in guilt. I knew what everyone wanted to hear—that I had a new book in the works, or at least an outline for one—and at the time, I seriously doubted whether I could ever give that to them again." Catharine saw the painful expression in her mother's eyes and went on with a happy rush of excitement. "Not to worry," she said, smiling. "I have something for you to read, but my notebook's in the car. Be back in a second."

Moments later, Catharine placed the notebook on the table in front of her mother. "It's still a bit rough, but I—"

Grace let go a delighted laugh as she put on her reading glasses. "After all these years and all your books, you're still caveating. I'm your mother, not your editor."

"I know," Catharine answered with a grin. "That's the problem. Hal can tear a scene apart and it doesn't even phase me, but you—well, just read a few pages and tell me what you think."

Chapter 4

Catharine sat on the edge of her chair, as rigid as a schoolgirl waiting for test results. After a moment, she heard her mother's quick intake of breath and a murmured, "Oh my..." followed by a barely audible, "Oh, Catharine...."

Grace finished reading the first three pages, then glanced up from the notebook to stare at her daughter. "When—how did this happen?"

"I wrote it on the flight back, but I think the story's been inside me for a long time."

Grace nodded, then glanced down and smoothed the notebook page with a reverence that made Catharine want to cry. "It's wonderful," she said, adding crisply, "And I'm not saying that because I'm your mother!"

Catharine laughed. "I know. I could hardly wait to get back and start pumping you with questions about Esther and the Cliffords. I don't know why I've been so dense. The story's been here all along and I didn't see it."

"You're not dense," Grace corrected. "You just weren't ready, that's all." Picking up the notebook, she read the first sentence aloud. "'In the land of saints and scholars, I was always a dreamer'...." Grace sighed and shook her head in amazement. "I never knew my great-grandmother, but reading this makes me feel as if she were alive again and speaking through you. By the way, how did you know her father's name was Henry? I don't think we have that in any of the family information."

Catharine shrugged. "I don't know. I just wrote it. But I do remember you telling me once that her mother's name was Rose Marie. What else do we know about the family?"

"Not very much, I'm afraid. There's a box of pictures and a few things up in the attic. I haven't looked at them in years."

"Would it be too much trouble to find them?"

Grace smiled at her daughter's barely restrained eagerness. "Of course it's no trouble. Are you going to drive back to San Anselmo tonight?"

"I'd rather not. Justin's in Tahoe on business and won't be home for a day or two. If you don't mind, I'd love to stay the night." Catharine was amazed how normal her voice sounded. So normal she almost believed it herself.

Something's terribly wrong, Grace was thinking, but she doesn't want to talk about it. Aloud, she told Catharine, "You know you don't ever need to ask me that. Since you're staying over, would you mind helping me go through your father's clothes? I haven't felt up to tackling that job yet, but I think it's time."

"I'll be glad to. First thing in the morning."

Mother and daughter left the kitchen to climb the curving oak staircase to the second floor, where spring-blue carpet and wallpaper sprigged with blue and white posies, always made Catharine feel as if she were walking up to a flower-filled sky. Beyond the landing, a narrower column continued, curving upward in fan-like steps.

Grace accomplished the ascent with a spry agility that made Catharine smile, while her own legs felt the tired pull of muscles that had been sitting too long.

A breath of cool darkness met them as her mother opened the attic door, then flipped the light switch on the wall.

As a child, Grandmother Cavanagh's attic was a shadowy realm of the past that both frightened and fascinated Catharine. Her active imagination was quick to create sounds and sinister possibilities from the most innocent noise or object. Mystery lurked in the dusty corners and stories spoke to her from the shelves, where books, boxes and musty memorabilia lived a forgotten half-life.

Chapter 4 — Grace

The camelback trunk was a veritable Pandora's box which, in the daytime, might contain nothing more than old quilts and clothing smelling of moth balls—but at night, who knew what sort of creatures might creep out to furtively roam about the house. And the tall, footed dresser with its carved drawers and oval mirror must surely have belonged to a wily wizard who used the mirror's magical powers to watch young Catharine and her brother at their play.

The transition from childhood to teens brought a disappointing discovery. Somehow, the attic had shrunk in size and its mysterious image was forever altered. The mystique of the past still lingered, however, as did Catharine's fascination with the long ago. She'd written some of her first stories there, curled up on quilts beneath the dormer window that looked out over treetops and offered a tantalizing glimpse of the bay.

In those years, the history of her own ancestors had seemed less thrilling and romantic than someone else's past. Now she acknowledged with amazement and new poignancy, that the lives of her own had a far greater pull and fascination than any characters history or fiction could offer.

The glow of a single bulb chased the darkness into the corners as Catharine followed her mother across creaking floorboards to the wizard's bureau. Grace removed a cardboard box from one of the drawers, then sat down in a nearby rocker with the box in her lap.

Catharine found a folding chair and pulled it close beside her mother's, as Grace fingered through the loose pictures, letters and cards.

"This is Esther's daughter, Annie," she said, handing Catharine a small photo of a stern-faced woman well past her youth.

"Annie was your father's mother, right?"

Grace nodded. "She had gorgeous red hair. I'm told her looks caused quite a stir when the family first arrived in Grass Valley."

"Life must have been very hard for Annie," Catharine said, noting the woman's firm, unsmiling mouth and strong chin.

"It certainly was," Grace agreed with a sigh. "Annie lost three of her eleven children, and her husband died of emphysema before she was fifty."

That's younger than I am now, Catharine thought, looking at Annie's photo with new understanding. No wonder she looks a bit grim.

Grace picked up two sepia-colored photographs. "And these are Annie's brothers—James Edward and Henry Clifford Clark."

Catharine studied the photos of John and Esther's sons with interest. Both men appeared to be in their early twenties, but there was little resemblance between them. Certainly not enough that would easily identify the two as brothers.

One had dark wavy hair, a dapper handlebar mustache, and a roguish gleam in his dark eyes.

"That's James, the eldest of the two," Grace said. "The other is poor Henry."

'Poor Henry' was a good-looking fellow, clean-shaven, with a prominent chin and smooth hair parted neatly on the side. What was there about his face that suggested weakness? Catharine wondered, studying the young man's features. Something about the mouth.

"Henry was only twenty-five when he was shot and killed in Cassidy's Saloon," Grace filled in.

"I'd forgotten about that," Catharine said, seeing the young man's weakness in a new light.

"Oh, yes, Henry was quite the gambler. He and a man named 'Saxey' got into an argument one night over cards and—" Grace broke off, seeing the look that tightened Catharine's mouth. "I'm sorry, dear. I didn't mean to bring up a painful subject."

"That's all right." Catharine smiled and shrugged, wishing her mother weren't so blasted sensitive to her every thought.

Grace remained silent, but the look on her face plainly said she knew things were far from all right.

"Justin's been gambling again," Catharine said after a lengthy silence.

Her mother's expression showed little reaction to the news. Catharine gave her a close look. "You knew?"

"Let's just say, I'm not surprised. I've had the feeling for some time now that he was hiding something."

Catharine shook her head. "Why didn't I see it?"

"For one thing, you're too close to the problem. How much has he lost this time?"

"I have no idea. But a few weeks ago he called Hal and asked for a $75,000 cash advance to help you with the doctor bills."

This time it was Grace's mouth that tightened in a firm line. "How generous of him," she said with a healthy bite of sarcasm. "And how totally out of character."

"Mother!"

"Well, isn't it?" Grace tossed the question back to her daughter.

Catharine sighed and nodded.

"How much longer are you going to put up with this sort of nonsense?" Grace asked.

When Catharine recovered from the bluntness of her mother's question, she could only murmur, "Well, I–I haven't thought much about it."

"Yes, you have. You've been thinking about it for years. You just don't want to face it, that's all."

Catharine stared at her mother in a long moment of stunned silence.

"Are you angry with me?" Grace asked.

"No ... not angry. I–I guess I find it difficult to believe we're having this conversation, that's all."

"We should have had it years ago," Grace said, "but I was afraid you might think I was trying to interfere in your life. It's not always easy to know when to say something and when to remain silent."

Catharine nodded. "Yes, I know."

"I've been doing a lot of thinking since your father died," Grace went on. "About Gordon and me ... about you and Justin ... about a lot of things. Your father was far from perfect, but I loved him dearly, faults and all." Grace paused, then gave Catharine's hand a little pat. "I guess what I'm trying to say is, I've known for a long time that there's more wrong with your marriage than Justin's gambling addiction. I want you to be happy, dear, and I know you're not."

"Mother, are you suggesting...."

Grace shrugged her slender shoulders. "It's not my place to suggest anything. Only, I'd hate to see you let a misplaced sense of guilt keep you from being happy."

"Guilt?" Catharine tried to mock the word and failed miserably in the process.

"Yes, guilt," Grace said. "Because you don't love Justin. You've been beating yourself up over that fact for years. It's not your fault, Catharine. The success or failure of any marriage is never the sole responsibility of one person."

Catharine tried to swallow an uncomfortable lump in her throat, but it refused to budge. Leaning forward, she put her arms around her mother and whispered, "Thanks, Mother. I love you...."

"I love you, too, dear."

Grace held her daughter close, savoring the sweet understanding of the moment. When Catharine drew back, Grace saw tears sparkling in her daughter's eyes—tears and something else—a strong inner resolve that released worry's burdensome hold. She's going to be all right, Grace thought. Things will probably get worse before all this is over, but she's going to be all right.

Catharine handed the photos of James and Henry Clark to her mother. "Don't we have a picture of Esther?"

"If we do, I've never seen it," Grace answered, taking her cue to change the subject. "But we do have this one of her brother."

Taking the photograph, Catharine felt a strange stirring inside. A face, fascinating in its planes and hints of character, gazed back at her. Prominent cheekbones, a noble nose and chin. The forehead, high and smooth. Studying the man's features and serious expression, Catharine could see the poise and dignity of English aristocracy—something entirely different from the roguish charm and weak good looks of Esther's sons. And the eyes ... even without knowing their color, she saw clear blue creeping out from the sepia tones of the old photograph. Intelligence was there as well. The kind that was on comfortable terms with Shakespeare and the classics. And something else—something that struck a sensitive chord deep inside her. This man had suffered great pain and loss.

"What was his name?" she asked softly.

"I'm not certain, but I think it was Henry. Maybe that's why you gave Esther's father that name."

"Perhaps ... I wish I knew more about him. About all of them. Don't we have any letters or documents from Esther's family? Anything at all that belonged to her?"

Grace shook her head with regret. "There isn't much. My sister has an old silver spoon that Esther supposedly brought with her from Ireland." She glanced down, rifling through the remaining cards and photos. "And there's this...."

She handed Catharine a small funeral program with the heading: *In Loving Memory: Mrs. Esther Clark Died: April 17, 1904 Aged 82 years.*

A familiar poem from the time followed. *Peaceful be thy silent slumber, peaceful in thy grave so low. Thou no more wilt join our number, Thou no more our sorrows know...*

How sad to begin the study of someone's life with her death, Catharine thought, as she read the quaint, old-fashioned lines. *I don't want to begin with the ending. I want to know about the living woman—her hopes, her dreams, even her disappointments.*

"Tell me about Esther," she said. "Anything ... everything you can remember."

Catharine had heard the story many times before, but this time, as she listened to her mother relate various events in her ancestors' lives, Catharine felt herself responding to the people and their experiences in a way that was much more immediate and personal.

Esther ... defying her family and her father's wishes to marry a man beneath her social station ... the young couple fleeing from famine and the hopelessness that ravaged Ireland in those years ... the voyage to America aboard one of the many famine ships, where human ballast was crammed into living conditions not fit for cattle.

Arrival in America had not given the young couple any relief from adversity. For Esther, there was the pain and hardship of giving birth to three children somewhere in the crowded squalor of New York's tenements. And for John, instead of wealth and golden opportunity, there had been sharp-faced censure and prejudice, simply because they were Irish.

Chapter 4

Catharine couldn't blame him for succumbing to the lure of 'gold fever' and its fickle promise of easy fortune. She could almost hear his excited voice assuring Esther and the children that it wouldn't be long—a few months at most and he would send for them. Then her father would have no cause for complaint. John could look any man in the eye with pride, knowing his Esther would be well provided for and have a home far grander than any she'd ever known.

But instead of wealth—seven long years of separation had followed. Seven years of backbreaking labor in the Grass Valley mines, struggling and scrimping to save enough money to send for his wife and children.

What had Esther's life been like during that time of separation? How had she managed to provide for herself and her children? Cast ashore in a rough new land, in a fast-growing city with thousands of other immigrants like herself, how had she coped with the loneliness and homesickness that must have engulfed her at times?

When word from John and the passage money finally arrived, there was yet another journey for Esther to face. This time she endured the perilous voyage from New York down to Panama, across the Isthmus by mule train, then sailed up to San Francisco, where the family would travel by stagecoach to Grass Valley.

Catharine tried to picture their reunion after so many years apart. Did Esther still love him? Did the touch of his hand and the feel of his arms about her reawaken the love that had once been theirs, or had she felt as if she were looking into the eyes of a stranger?

There must have been some shock as well as pleasure for John in seeing the changes time had wrought in his wife and children. His sons were more than half-grown, and his daughter no longer a child, but a young woman of sixteen.

How had John and Esther felt, when, after the initial meeting, they had once more lain side by side as man and wife? Was it awkward and unfamiliar, or was the deep channel of their love strong enough to withstand the time-altering current of separation....

Late that night, lying awake in her old room, with its dear familiarity and the comforting balm of clean sheets and soft pillows, Catharine listened to the rain outside. Her thoughts were not of John and Esther's separation, but her own—thirty long years—from a man living somewhere in Ireland.

"Eamonn...." The name moved from a safe room in her memory to become a soft moan on her lips. "Eamonn...."

5

Eamonn

"Tell me something. Did Dad ever throw anything away?" Catharine asked her mother. "I thought women were supposed to be the ones who kept everything."

Grace laughed, then sighed as she looked around the room. Surrounding her on the bed, suits and slacks had been piled high. The large closet where Catharine sat cross-legged on the floor was half-empty. Black plastic garbage bags had been filled with shoes, shirts and other items for Goodwill. The sacred contents of dresser drawers which Grace knew better than to touch or go through while her husband was alive, were now emptied and sorted. She was more grateful than she could say that Catharine was here to help share the emotional aspects of the task, as well as the work itself. It wasn't an easy thing seeing the remnants of someone's life either discarded or sorted into nostalgic piles of memory.

"I think your father's possessions were a lot like medals for him," she mused." Each one represented a certain milestone or achievement in his life. Take this for example…." She picked up a faded football jersey, and the corners of her mouth twitched in a little smile. "Gordon was never a very good football player, but he looked wonderful in the uniform."

Grace hesitated, not knowing where to place the jersey. Sentiment won out and she put it in the 'keep' stack with a fond little pat.

"What about this?" Catharine asked, holding up a navy blazer worn by members of the Veterans of Foreign Wars.

"Oh, heavens, I certainly won't mind getting rid of that thing," Grace said with feeling. "I think your father only wore it twice in his life, and the last time was a dreadful experience."

"Why? What happened?"

Grace hesitated a moment, not sure she wanted to introduce the painful memories of that time, for Catharine's sake as well as her own. "It was when he was running for Congress. I–uh, I think you must have been living with your Aunt Lucille by then."

Catharine felt a familiar tightness take hold inside, but met her mother's eyes with what she hoped was a normal expression. "What happened?" she asked again.

"It was a few days before the election. Your father was scheduled to speak at a VFW convention in San Francisco, and he was more than a little tense about the prospect."

Catharine could understand why. In 1968, the war in Viet Nam was still raging, despite President Johnson's decision in March of that year to end U.S. bombing in the North. The decision came a month too late to save the life of her brother Robert, who was killed during the bloody battle at Khe Sanh. The wrenching loss had torn Catharine apart and made a ghost of her usually vibrant mother. Her father shouldered the loss of his only son with stoic grimness, promptly made the decision to run for Congress, and threw all his energies into the upcoming campaign.

Chapter 5

The election of '68 was unlike any other in the nation's history. All across the country, angry protests and youthful demonstrators kept the emotional climate in a highly combustible state. Anti-war sentiment grew along with the rising death toll. But the killing that year was not confined to the battlefield alone. In April, Martin Luther King had been gunned down during what was supposed to have been a peaceful protest. Then in June, Bobby Kennedy had been shot and killed in the kitchen of a Los Angeles hotel.

While the nation mourned the loss of its 'Bobby,' Catharine and her mother privately grieved over the loss of theirs.

Death in the jungles of Viet Nam. Death in the streets. Death on campuses and L.A. hotels. When would it all end? Catharine wondered. There was so much she didn't understand. Patriotism had always seemed to her to be a simple thing, something good and right. Yet in the face of her brother's death and thousands like him, she was left with painful questions that had no easy answers.

And there was something else. Something more disturbing than the political rightness or wrongness of the war.

Often, during the fevered months of her father's campaign, Catharine found herself observing his behavior with a sadness that bordered on shame. Public opinion and the press were fond of praising Gordon Cavanagh for his strength and "selfless patriotism in the face of such deep personal loss," but Catharine would have given anything to see him show some emotion, or any evidence of grief. Whatever caring was there, and Catharine had to believe it existed somewhere inside her father, was tightly controlled. There were times she even had the feeling that, for him, Robert's death had somehow moved beyond tragedy to become a political asset, helping to sway public opinion and win votes.

"When your father arrived at the building, there was a large crowd of anti-war demonstrators waiting outside," Grace was saying.

"They were young, mostly students from Stanford and Berkeley. If Gordon had just ignored them and gone into the building, things might have been different, but he didn't. You know your father's temper...."

Catharine nodded, feeling the tension growing inside her.

"One of the hecklers shouted something rather explicit to Gordon and he shouted back, calling the young man a—well, let's just say things got very ugly. Right or wrong, your father loved his country, and he couldn't understand the young man's anger. Only his own. I think having some student his son's age yelling in his face must have brought a lot of pain to the surface. Anyway, your father reached out and shoved the young man so hard he fell backwards into the crowd—" Grace shuddered with the memory, as if she were trying to shake away its unpleasantness. "The media had a heyday with it," she went on. "I doubt if anyone will remember that pathetic young man, but the incident probably cost your father the election."

Catharine sat motionless, the navy blazer in her lap. "I never knew...."

"How could you, living with George and Lucille in Seattle? It was a big item in local news, but thankfully, after the election the incident died away. Your father never talked about it, and he certainly didn't wear that jacket again."

"I always thought it was me," Catharine said quietly. "That I cost him the election."

"Oh, Catharine, of course it wasn't you...." Silence filled the space between them, until Grace gathered enough courage to broach a subject even more sensitive than the incident in San Francisco. "Please believe me, dear. Your father losing the election had nothing to do with you—and the baby."

Catharine blinked furiously, trying to stop the tears that were threatening, and busied herself with checking the pockets. Her fingers found a tube of lip balm and some loose change in one. The crumpled program from the convention in another.

"More *Chapstick*," she said, her voice sounding brittle in her ears. Shoving her hand into an inside pocket, she felt something smooth and rectangular against the lining. A letter.

"Catharine...?"

Grace stared at her daughter's pale face and felt her heart constrict with worry. Getting to her feet, she took a step in Catharine's direction, then caught her breath.

She saw little more than a foreign stamp and her daughter's name written in a bold, masculine hand. She didn't need more than that to know who the sender was. That the letter had been opened was immediately obvious from the envelope's torn flap.

Catharine sat unmoving, the letter clutched in her hands, tears trickling down her cheeks in a quiet stream.

"I'll be downstairs if you need me," Grace said faintly, and left the room.

CATHARINE HAD NO idea how long she sat there, staring at Eamonn's letter through a misty veil of tears, her heart pumping with shock and anger that her father had kept this from her. Part of her was terrified to know what Eamonn had written. Whatever he might have said, it was thirty years too late for any of it to matter now. Another part of her desperately wanted to know. Needed to know. Dear God, who was she trying to fool? It did matter.

With trembling fingers, Catharine removed the pages from the envelope. Seeing the familiar handwriting, feeling the smooth touch of the paper in her hands, the past and present blurred into insignificance. She heard his voice, saw his face as if it were only yesterday and not thirty years of yesterdays, and the aching gap between them disappeared.

October 18, 1968

Darling Girl,

There was a chill wind out of the north blowing all day. The kind which sends an unmistakable message that autumn days are past and winter is not far behind. Feeling its sting on my face, I thought of the unnamed poet who once felt as I do now.

> *'O Western wind, when wilt thou blow,*
> *That the small rain down can rain.*
> *Christ, that my love were in my arms,*
> *And I in my bed again!'*

Did you know it has been eighty-two days since I last held you in my arms? And nearly a month since your last letter. Your silence tells me something is wrong, yet how am I to know what it is? I phoned ten days ago, and your father said you didn't want to see or hear from me—that I was not to call or contact you again. The tone of his voice left no room for discussion, but until I hear those words from your own sweet voice, I cannot make myself believe them.

Silence is a cruel companion, Katie darling. Far worse than separation, I think. Won't you write and tell me what's wrong? Whatever it is, surely it can't be so terrible that the two of us couldn't work things out.

Do you remember the day we stood by that stream in Derrycarne Wood, with the water running so high and fast that we neither of us could get over, no matter how the other side called? And then how we searched up and down the bank, looking for a place to cross? I'm still searching for that place. Trying to cross over to you. But now I need to know that you're waiting on the other side—that you still love me, in spite of the silence and separation.

As I love you, and always will.

Eamonn

GRACE MADE TEA and forced herself to drink a steaming cup. She scrubbed the already spotless kitchen, reheated the tea, and finally threw it out. Several times, she walked to the foot of the stairs, wanting to go up, aching to do something, yet feeling totally helpless. Finally, she put on a sweater and went outside to the garden. The ground was still too wet to do any weeding and the air held a damp chill from the previous night's rain. Pulling off her gloves, she tossed them aside and returned to the house.

It was silence that finally drove her back upstairs. A terrible stillness that she would remember for years after. Tears, sobbing, anger or rage she could have dealt with more easily. Especially anger. Her husband's outbursts and grumbling over the years had become no more feared or dreaded than summer thunder. It was loud and startling at the time, but like a summer storm, soon over, with the sun seeming warmer than ever after its passing.

But this stillness. How does one comfort a sorrow deeper than tears? What consolation can one give when confronted with the face of hopeless grief? And that face belonging to her only daughter.

When Grace entered the bedroom, it seemed as if the only sound in all the world was the painful thudding of her own heart.

Catharine sat on the floor near the closet, pale and dry-eyed, still clutching Eamonn's letter in her hands. More than anything, Grace wanted to gather her into her arms and kiss away the hurt, as she had done when Catharine was a child. Instead, she could only stand there, mute and helpless.

Catharine glanced up then, and, as if it were some great weight to be lifted, offered her mother the letter.

Reaching for her glasses on the bedside table, Grace found that her hands were trembling. Silently, she read the words of longing and love, then sank down on the edge of the bed.

When she looked up at last, there was pain and pleading in her eyes. "Catharine, dear...."

"Eamonn never got my letter—the one I wrote telling him about the baby," she said in a tight voice.

"I don't understand," Grace murmured, but inside she felt the stirrings of a terrible fear.

"It's not so hard to understand," Catharine answered in the same tightly-controlled tone. "My letter was never mailed because Dad must have destroyed it. I wanted to call Eamonn and tell him about my pregnancy, but Dad convinced me that a phone call wouldn't be fair to either one of us. He said a letter would soften the blow—give Eamonn a chance to recover from the news, so to speak." Catharine slowly shook her head. "And I believed him."

"But ... how would your father get hold of your letter?"

"I gave it to him," Catharine answered simply. "I spent hours writing and rewriting that letter—stayed up half the night, trying to make sure everything was said just right. I guess the worry and stress took its toll, because I was coming down the stairs the next morning to mail it, and fainted dead away. Dad found me in a heap at the bottom of the stairs. I remember, he helped me into bed and promised he'd mail the letter for me." Her mouth trembled slightly as she glanced at the letter in her mother's hand. "Eamonn wrote this more than a month later, so it's fairly obvious what must have happened."

Grace set the letter aside and drew a ragged breath. "Catharine, I don't know what to say. I knew your father was against you marrying Eamonn, but this—I had no idea...." Her voice broke, and she shook her head. "Where was I? Why don't I remember any of this?"

Catharine got slowly to her feet and moved beside her mother. Understanding gentled her tone as she took one of Grace's cold hands in hers. "If I remember right, you had a doctor's appointment that morning."

Shock and grief had taken its toll on Grace Cavanagh that year. Trying to cope with the loss of her only son and deal with the demands and pressure of her husband's political campaign had brought about a near nervous breakdown, followed by months of depression.

"I'm not blaming you, Mom, so please don't blame yourself," Catharine said. "I can't help wondering though, how many other letters and phone calls Dad intercepted. It would have been quite easy for him after I moved to Aunt Lucille's."

Grace agreed to this with a sad nod. "I'm so sorry. When I think what you went through...."

"I wasn't the only one hurting," Catharine said, bitterness sharpening her tone. "God only knows how Eamonn must have felt when I didn't answer his letter. All this time ... I thought he didn't want me or our baby ... and he never knew...." Catharine paced about the room, trying to control her emotions. "And now, thirty years later, he still doesn't know. I keep trying to understand, trying to forgive Dad for what he did—but if you think about it, the whole thing is so ludicrous! All he lost was a stupid election! Eamonn and I lost each other—and—and our daughter!"

Grace couldn't speak. She stood and held out her arms, but Catharine had turned away to grab some tissues from a box on the dresser.

"I'd better go," she said, wiping her eyes. "I think I need to be alone for awhile."

Grace nodded, her heart twisting within her. "Of course, dear." Please God, help me not to cry, she pleaded silently. Help me not to add to her pain.

Catharine looked at her mother's face, and knew she couldn't leave. Not this way. Without a word, she put her arms about her.

"I'm so sorry...." was all Grace could say.

"I know."

"What are you going to do?"

Catharine gave a hopeless, helpless little shrug. "I don't know."

Shock muffled some of the pain and Catharine was only half-conscious of her surroundings as she drove. It was as if her mind were on autopilot and functioning on a previously programmed level. Somehow, she managed to stop when traffic signals dictated, and take the right freeway entrance or exit. She even dealt with the busy weekend traffic, but as yet, she had no idea where she was going. She only knew she couldn't go home. Not yet. Even if Justin weren't there, her heart couldn't face the shallow surroundings of her life with him.

Eventually, Catharine found herself driving north along the winding stretches of the Coast Highway, where rugged headlands and rocky bluffs met the pounding sea. The road's twistings and turnings were a perfect match for her tortured thoughts.

The reason behind her father's apology was now fully clear. Yet in spite of her anger and the utter unfairness of what he had done, Catharine couldn't hate him. Hate would accomplish nothing. It wouldn't bring back Eamonn or the baby daughter she had given up at birth. Besides, there wasn't enough left inside her to hate or cry or feel much of anything. There was only this aching hole ... this colorless void of thirty years lost, with no hope of recovery.

The afternoon sun breaks that had kept weekenders hoping for some respite and relaxation disappeared in a shroud of gray. Rain fell, intensifying from a teasing drizzle to a steady downpour. Before long, Highway One was transformed from a pleasant scenic route to a lonely road by the edge of the sea, buffeted by gusts of wind and rain.

Catharine drove on, mindless of the miles, needing the rain and the solitude. Somehow, if she could only drive far enough, she might be able to escape the pain and betrayal.

Daylight was fading and the rain showed no signs of abating when the road itself brought an end to her flight. Passing through a small seaside town, she noticed flashing red lights up ahead. She slowed and saw a highway patrol car straddling the narrow road. Not far beyond the patrol car, an angry brown torrent had completely engulfed the road in its rain-swollen rush to the sea.

As Catharine approached, an officer was directing people to turn back. Catharine slowed and pulled off to the side of the road. Rolling down her window, she stared at the rushing stream that blocked her escape. Only six to eight yards farther on, the road continued over a small rise, but crossing the flooded river at this point would have been risky, if not impossible.

" ... *remember the afternoon in Derrycarne Wood when the water was running so high and fast that we neither of us could get over no matter how the other side called ... and how we searched up and down the bank, looking for a place to cross? I'm still searching for that place. Trying to cross over to you...*"

The tight ache inside her chest burst like the river's swollen banks, releasing a flood of pent-up anguish. Tears streaming down her face, she turned the car around and headed back the way she had come.

Nightfall and her own weariness finally necessitated some kind of decision. She couldn't face going home to San Anselmo, and she was too emotionally and physically spent to drive back to Alameda. Then, not far distant, she caught the welcoming gleam of lights and Jenner's Inn near the Russian River.

A gust of wind slammed the door behind her, announcing her approach, but the night-manager in the motel office was too engrossed in the vicarious thrills offered by a steamy paperback romance to notice.

Catharine took in the hard-faced woman sitting behind the desk, with her streaked hair and sallow skin, and couldn't help comparing her with the voluptuous maiden portrayed on the book's cover. Painted in full fleshy detail, a raven-haired beauty was perilously close to losing the bodice of her dress, among other things, as she struggled in the brawny arms of a bare-chested Viking.

I guess we each find our own ways to escape, Catharine thought, and cleared her throat.

"Sorry, I don't have a single." The woman answered Catharine's inquiry in a smoke-roughened voice. "All I have left is the bridal suite, but you can have that for $75."

"Thank you. That will be fine," Catharine said and discovered much to her amazement, there was still enough life in her to find irony in the situation. "Is there a phone in the room?" she asked. "The battery's dead on my cell phone and I need to make a call."

"Nope." The sallow-faced woman put the novel down with a reluctant sigh to take a key from a rack on the nearby wall. She glanced at Catharine, seeing her for the first time, and the smoky voice softened noticeably. "If you need to make a call, you can use the phone here."

"Thank you."

It was easier than she thought to give her mother the proper reassurance that she was safe and well. Somehow the phone created enough distance to mask some of the pain and hurt.

"Try not to worry about me, Mother. I'll be in touch."

"You're sure there's nothing I can do?"

"Not a thing, but thanks for the worry ... and the love."

I really am doing rather well, Catharine told herself after the steamy therapy of a long hot shower. She toweled her dark hair, undressed, then climbed into the softness of the king-size bed.

Outside, the wind howled and rain pelted the room's steep-pitched roof. Catharine lay, listening to the storm's wet fury, her surroundings a weary blur. Turning on her side, her gaze focused on Eamonn's letter, lying on the table beside the bed.

She reached for it in much the same way she had once reached for him, needing his words and his love, even if they were only on paper. She read the letter again and yet again, gladly suffering the pain of its contents for the bittersweet pleasure of seeing his words and hearing his voice in her mind.

The punishing reality of the present, the aching uncertainty of the future, all that would be waiting for her in the morning. Tonight, with the storm raging outside and the bed a warm cocoon enveloping her in its softness, Catharine allowed herself to visit the long ago loveliness of the past.

6

Ireland - 1968

Long before they ever touched, and long before she said the words, Catharine fell in love with Eamonn Gallagher's words. Whether they found expression on the written page or in casual conversation mattered little. Both forms possessed the power to move her.

She heard his voice for the first time in a classroom at Dublin's Trinity College, and while her mind was not yet ready to acknowledge the fact, her heart knew that Eamonn was the reason she had come to Ireland. The summer course, "Literary Ireland," was merely the vehicle which brought them together.

Catharine's father had done his judicial best to convince her that she should stay home and help him with his campaign, using guilt, sense of duty, and every other emotional weapon available. Even when he attacked her dream of becoming a writer, labeling it sheer foolishness and a waste of good intelligence, she had remained firm and quietly unyielding in her resolve. Gordon Cavanagh never realized how determined his daughter could be. And Catharine was determined to go to Ireland.

He couldn't argue the fact that the class would further her education, and being selected was something of an honor, since only twelve students out of all those applying had been chosen to participate. Judge Cavanagh had examined the course description the way he would critical evidence in the courtroom, and could find no fault with it. Three weeks of class work studying the lives and works of Ireland's literary giants would be followed by a ten-day tour around the island. The course would conclude with a two-week writing retreat where students would work on their final papers and have time for individual projects.

Somewhat reluctantly, the good judge pronounced his verdict of approval, not realizing, that in Catharine's mind, there was no other answer.

Grace Cavanagh had been supportive from the beginning. Since her son's death the previous February, she had watched the colors fade from Catharine's usually brilliant world into the grayness of grief and despair. The girl's grades had dropped, along with her weight, and her interest in friends and activities. When the summer course in Ireland became a possibility, Grace had seen a glimmer of hope return to her daughter's eyes, along with a shining thread of purpose. Pushing aside the clouds of her own depression, she did her best to help Catharine prepare for the trip. If spending the summer in Ireland could bring her daughter some happiness, then by all means, she should and would go.

Catharine entered the classroom that first morning, fairly bursting with nervous excitement. From the moment she'd walked across the worn cobblestones on the main entry grounds and stared up at the magnificent Campanile, she'd been in a state of dazed wonder. Above her, the soft blue of an Irish sky wore a hazy scarf of clouds. The lawn had to be at least three times greener than any grass at home, and the ancient brick and stone buildings fairly breathed history. That she was actually here in Ireland was nothing less than a miracle—and miracles needed to be savored.

Catharine took a few minutes to wander the grounds, bidding a respectful good morning to statues of Swift, Goldsmith and bygone provosts of the college. By the time she found the building and room where her class was to be held, several of her fellow students from Berkeley had arrived and the room echoed with the eager buzz of their conversation.

Catharine's roommate, Penny Sims, was sitting near the back and looking more than a little lost. Poor Penny. Short, square, and bland as a bowl of oatmeal, one would never suspect she relished writing bloodthirsty who-done-its. For a brief moment, Catharine considered sitting beside her, but couldn't tolerate the thought of being a back row participant in this, the first day of her Irish adventure. Giving Penny a wave and a smile, she walked straight down the aisle and took a seat on the front row.

According to the schedule, a Dr. Anthony Hilliard would be teaching the history of Irish literature during the nine o'clock hour. Catharine's mind immediately conjured up the image of a distinguished, if somewhat portly man in his mid-fifties, with a bulbous nose and bushy gray eyebrows. She would have been amused to know that her mental image wasn't far from the mark, although Dr. Hilliard was in fact, only forty-six, and the size of his nose had always been a sensitive point with him.

It was not Anthony Hilliard, however, who stood in front of them to welcome the class. Catharine was pleasantly surprised when a tall young man with curly brown hair and a rakish grin, introduced himself as Eamonn Gallagher and announced he would be substituting for the ailing professor.

Her front row vantage point afforded ample opportunity to observe Mr. Gallagher throughout the hour. Catharine assured herself it was merely habit and not personal interest that prompted her to take in all the details of his appearance, from the brown tweed sportcoat and brawny width of his shoulders, to the way his blue broadcloth shirt brought out the deeper blue of his eyes. When he turned to write on the board, she immediately noticed how the dark brown tangles of his hair brushed against his shirt collar. That firm, straight mouth might look very forbidding when he was angry, she suspected, but when he smiled—as he often did—it curved in the most delightful way.

Several times during the morning, their glances met and each time, Catharine tried to convince herself that it meant nothing. A good teacher often made eye contact with his students. Still, she couldn't dismiss the effect his slate blue gaze had upon her or the warm connection that seemed to vibrate and sing between them until she was forced to focus her attention elsewhere.

Watching his hands was much safer. Broad across the backs, with strong, blunt fingers, Catharine found them fascinating. Eamonn Gallagher had the hands of a laborer, not those one might expect of a scholar. And, although she cursed herself for checking, there was no wedding band.

From his brief introduction, Catharine learned that Eamonn was a graduate student finishing his Masters Degree, and had worked closely with Professor Hilliard. Before the first week of class work was over, Catharine knew she would be forever grateful to Anthony Hilliard's gallbladder for necessitating the change in instructors.

Eamonn had a way of making Irish prose and poetry sing with meaning. Ancient history seemed as close as yesterday with his telling. Folk tales, myths and legends held more magic. Catharine found herself listening with her heart as well as her mind, loving the compassion and passion that Eamonn had for his country. Ireland, with her abundant wealth of beauty and abject poverty of her people; Ireland, with her brilliant scholars, poets and playwrights; Ireland, with all her wisdom and foolishness, where cold prejudice and warm hospitality often shared the same hearth. All this and more was painted daily for her in a brilliant canvas of words. Eamonn Gallagher's words.

The hours spent in Eamonn's classes were easily the most anticipated and shortest hours of her day. With his easy-going charm and quick wit, Eamonn enjoyed a warm rapport with all his students, Irish and American alike. The female portion of the class might not be able to recount the main points of a particular day's lecture, but if called upon, any one of them could give a detailed description of what Mr. Gallagher was wearing, the deep blue color of his eyes, and the sensual appeal of his lilting voice.

Many an evening after the dinner hour, Catharine had to endure the sweet torture of listening to her American classmates as they launched into provocative discussions of Eamonn's various attributes.

"He's not *really* handsome, I mean, not *really*," Shanna Melville commented with a dreamy look and healthy dose of italics. "But there's *something* about him ... I mean, he practically oozes masculinity."

"It's the mouth," sighed Carolyn Bickmore. "Have you noticed his mouth?"

"Is the Pope Catholic?" Penny Sims inserted dryly.

"His hair drives me crazy," Shanna went on. "It's so thick and so – so untamable. Whenever I think what it would be like to get my fingers tangled up in those curls, my brain fogs over and I totally forget to take notes."

"You're all animals," Ann Ridd pronounced, glancing up from her book. "A bunch of prowling, predatory jungle cats."

Catharine smiled at this. Ann's father was a psychiatrist and her mother a social worker. With Ann, everything had clinical or Freudian overtones.

"Mmm, you're right," Carolyn agreed with a feral look in her green eyes. "And Eamonn Gallagher's the king of beasts."

"Catharine, don't *you* have anything to say about Mr. Gallagher?" Shanna asked with a significant lift in her voice. "I saw the two of you sitting on a bench at Stephen's Green the other day, and you couldn't have been discussing Irish history."

It required supreme effort for Catharine to answer with a shrug and a laugh. "You're right, it wasn't history. Mr. Gallagher and I were going over a chapter from *The Dubliners*. I don't think I'll ever understand it." Then, before any more questions could be asked, she had left with the excuse she had letters to write.

If the others knew how often she and Eamonn simply chanced to meet after class, at lunch, or in the evening, Catharine would never have escaped the resulting onslaught of questions. And questions would lead to talk. Catharine wasn't at all sure that her faculty advisor for the trip would approve of her friendship with the handsome young Irishman. Constance Duffy Chavez DeBry, thrice married and thrice divorced, had an ongoing love-hate relationship with the male gender, and Catharine was not unaware of the buttery smiles and glances the woman sent Eamonn's way. All Catharine's instincts warned her that Dr. DeBry was capable of implementing some serious interference if she suspected that one of her students had a "relationship" with a teacher, no matter how harmless or innocent it might be.

Catharine couldn't bear the thought that anything or anyone might prevent her from spending time with Eamonn. Her feelings for him were so new and so tender, idle talk would cheapen them somehow. Yes, she adored his mouth, although they had never kissed. And yes, she longed to touch that unruly head of hair. But intimacy meant much more than just the physical.

There were times, when she and Eamonn were talking, that their closeness amazed and frightened her. To know his feelings, to share in his thoughts, and to feel safe and confident sharing hers with him was to know a happiness unlike anything she had experienced. She wondered if it was the same for him. Sometimes she felt as if he could read her very thoughts. Other times she was miserably unsure.

Days passed and their meetings became more frequent. Soon they were taking long walks in the cool summer evenings, sharing the sweetness of soft rain, ribbony sunsets and quiet stars. Their conversations became more personal, shifting effortlessly from the thoughts of writers and poets to their own. As they shared their lives, their families, and their dreams with one another, Catharine was forced to see the disparity in their backgrounds. He, the fifth of seven children born to a poor Catholic family in County Leitrim. She, the wealthy daughter of a notable judge. She had never known want or had a moment's worry whether there would be food on the table. Yet in Eamonn's presence, experiencing the richness of his soul and his passionate love of life, Catharine often felt as if she were the one who had grown up poor and deprived.

Although some of her Irish ancestors had been Catholic, her own family was not overly religious and rarely attended church. In spite of this, Catharine had come to privately cherish the knowledge that there was indeed a loving God who cared and watched over His children. The death of her brother in Viet Nam had not altered that belief, only reinforced it. Inside, she knew that it was man's inhumanity to man, and not God's lack of love that had caused her brother's death and the deaths of thousands like him.

All this and more she shared with Eamonn—thoughts and feelings she had never spoken aloud to anyone, even her dream of someday becoming a published author. And Eamonn shared his—the longing he had for knowledge, how he wished he could help his parents more financially, and how he hoped that someday the wealth of Ireland's history would become more accessible and appreciated by the world.

The following day, the topic of class discussion centered on the life and poetry of William Butler Yeats. Catharine had been familiar with some of Yeats' poems, but suddenly found herself blinking back the tears when Eamonn looked directly at her as he recited the lines:

> *"Had I the heaven's embroidered cloths,*
> *Enwrought with golden and silver light,*
> *The blue and the dim and the dark cloths*
> *Of night and light and the half-light,*
> *I would spread the cloths under your feet:*
> *But I, being poor, have only my dreams;*
> *I have spread my dreams under your feet;*
> *Tread softly because you tread on my dreams."*

Touched to her heart's core, she was unaware that several class members, including Dr. DeBry, were observing this interchange with considerable interest. Nor did she suspect anything out of the ordinary when Constance DeBry cornered Eamonn after class. Instead, Catharine floated out of the room, still savoring the sound of his voice and the personal significance of the poem. She was in love for the first time in her life.

Eamonn Gallagher never intended to fall in love. After teaching the summer course at Trinity, he had one quarter remaining before earning his Master of Arts degree. His thesis was well underway, and needed just a few months' work before it was completed.

Chapter 6

Ireland – 1968

What with working part time and helping his father on the farm in Ballinamore, it had taken three years longer than usual to reach his goal. Eamonn was the first in his family to graduate from college, let alone earn an advanced degree, and every time he saw the pride in his father's eyes, the long struggle was more than worth it.

Eamonn had originally planned to spend the summer in Leitrim with his family, but when Professor Hilliard had asked him to take his place, there was no way he could refuse. Anthony Hilliard was a good friend as well as mentor, and Eamonn considered it a privilege to be asked. Then, too, teaching the "Literary Ireland" course would look good on his résumé, and he could always use the time at the writing retreat to work on his thesis.

Yes, it promised to be a very pleasant summer, with just the right amount of relaxation, and a little travel to ease the pressures before the final push come fall. Looking down the smooth road of his immediate future, Eamonn could see no curves or complications.

Then he met Catharine Cavanagh. He'd been drawn to her from that first day in class. It was all he could do to keep his eyes off her, in fact. With her crisp white blouse and her sweater and skirt in the same deep blue as her eyes, it was as if a bright piece of morning sky had fallen to light up the room. With current fashion dictating pale lips and raccoon eyes, it was refreshing to see a girl who looked so alive and blooming. Her dark brown hair fell in thick waves against her shoulders, and seeing the soft shine of it, that hair looked all too touchable, especially when compared with the strange assortment of styles worn by other girls in the class. Everything from shaggy jungle manes to stiff bouffant bubbles and towering beehives greeted him each day, and were instantly forgettable, even laughable, while the image of Catharine Cavanagh sitting on the front row, curled up very nicely in his thoughts. The girl refused to fit his preconceived image of the female American college student—a loud, gum chewing, materialistic young thing who cared more about nail polish and makeup than books or current affairs.

Eamonn smiled when he thought of Catharine's small hands, with their short, unvarnished nails. As a matter of course, at least one was broken or newly chewed on. Along with her warm smile and friendliness, he had been surprised, even touched by her shyness at times. It seemed as if American girls could still blush, after all.

Catharine's comments in class were insightful and intelligent, with never an attempt to impress or merely go along with what others said. She had ideas and opinions of her own, she did, and didn't hesitate to voice them.

How this girl could be so intelligent and so beautiful, constantly amazed and unsettled him, besides making it damn difficult to concentrate in class. Many's the time he told himself he was doing just fine, then he'd look down and see those blue eyes of hers shining up at him with a warmth that shot straight to his insides and made him act the fool. Why else had he launched into all that story telling and poetry, but to elicit a smile, or a laugh, or that special look that brightened her lovely face whenever she listened to him.

Eamonn had earned something of a reputation for clever banter and entertaining lectures, but with Catharine in the audience, he outdid himself.

If he'd just left it at that, his heart might have escaped unscathed, but he didn't. The afternoon when he'd seen her sitting alone on a bench, frowning over a copy of *Ulysses*, for example. If he'd had any sense at all, he should have offered a simple hello and walked on by. Better yet, he should have turned around right then and high-tailed it the other way. But no. Without thinking twice, he'd stopped to talk, and teased her unmercifully about Joyce and his writing. Catharine had rewarded his efforts with a blush and silvery laugh that spurred him on to greater foolishness.

Chapter 6 — Ireland – 1968

Without knowing quite how it came about, he found himself asking if she had seen the Long Room of Trinity's ancient library. She hadn't. Eamonn knew in that moment, he wanted to be with her when she gazed up at those towering shelves with thousands of volumes dating back to the seventeenth century and beyond.

Eamonn had loved the library from the moment he'd seen it, Loved the history and knowledge that breathed in the solemn air of the room. To him it embodied the very heart and soul of Ireland—the love for learning and reverence for books that had survived in spite of bitter centuries of conquest and chaos.

He and Catharine entered the Long Room in late afternoon when the light was a soft, burnished gold, much like the rich bindings and embossed letters on the books themselves.

Lifting her head, Catharine gazed in speechless wonder at row after row of dark-timbered shelves that climbed a full two stories to the great barrel-vaulted ceiling. Her eyes shone and her voice, when she finally spoke, was no more than a whisper.

"Oh, Eamonn, it's magnificent. I never dreamed there was such a place...."

He had difficulty responding after that. Hearing his name on her lips did all kinds of things to his equilibrium, not one of which would be described as scholarly. Thus far, she had always addressed him as Mr. Gallagher, in polite deference to his position, and she was strictly, "Miss Cavanagh."

In that unguarded moment, they became Catharine and Eamonn and an unspoken intimacy was born.

There were times when reason asserted itself and he tried to convince himself that she was too young for him, only nineteen to his twenty-seven years. Their backgrounds and social stations were just as conflicting as in the old days when wealthy Anglo-Irish Protestant and poor Irish Catholic had inhabited the same country, but lived worlds apart. Old days, hell. The stigmas and cultural clashes were all too alive in the Ireland of today, with frequent disturbing headlines of "troubles" in the North.

If he were smart, he'd find a way to distance himself from Catharine Cavanagh before he had "troubles" of his own and things got too complicated. But he didn't. He couldn't. Her smile and voice warmed his days like the fickle Irish sun breaking through the clouds. And when she looked at him that certain way, with her blue eyes shining, he knew there wasn't anything in the world he couldn't do.

Even though Catharine was far from helpless, Eamonn found himself wanting to protect and defend her from any hurt or criticism. Like the day in creative writing class, when she read a scene from the story she was writing about her Irish ancestors. Granted, the darling girl was a hopeless romantic and her sense of idealism might even be described as 'rose-colored,' but that was no reason to attack her writing the way a few students had.

Catharine had taken their criticism in stride, but seeing the bruised look in her eyes suddenly made him fighting mad. Eamonn could partially excuse Randall Atwood, whose pseudo-intellectual attitude labeled most the world as sadly lacking, but that cocky little runt, Wally Benson would never know how close he'd come to having his face smashed in good and proper. One more snide comment and Eamonn would have asked him to stay after class to exchange more than a few verbal punches.

Determined to take away or at least soften the hurt, Eamonn invited Catharine to dinner that evening, and offered to help with the research for her story. She'd been reluctant to talk about it at first, and that bruised look had returned to her face. Eamonn mentally damned Wally Benson to hell, then threw caution to the winds.

"You know, I had the very devil of a time in class today," he said as they sat at a corner table for two. "—trying to make up my mind whether to permanently rearrange Benson's face, or just toss the fellow in the Liffey."

Catharine's lips twitched into the semblance of a smile. "And what did you decide to do?"

"Well, after givin' the matter some serious consideration, I decided the Liffey had enough garbage in it already, and although smashing Benson's face would have been highly satisfyin', it might have prevented me from seeing your lovely face across the table tonight."

The glowing smile this inspired warmed Eamonn's thoughts long after they said an awkward goodnight, and he left her to walk back to his flat alone.

It wasn't long before Eamonn found himself fighting a far different battle—one between his heart and his head. As much as he enjoyed his conversations with Catharine and their time together, it was no longer enough. He ached to hold her in his arms, touch her smooth dark hair, and kiss her mouth. Yet, while his heart was fair to bursting, his mind was telling him it would never work. There were too many obstacles in their way.

Poetry became a way of expressing what he dared not say or do. Eamonn derived a reckless sort of pleasure in quoting the passionate words of Synge and Yeats before the entire class, knowing all the while, they were intended for her ears and her heart alone. Synge's sensual lines... *My arms are around you, and I lean Against you, while the lark Sings over us* ... may have been referring to "The Oaks at Glencree," but Eamonn had something else on his mind altogether. Feeling the warmth of Catharine's blue gaze on his, caressing her with his voice when he couldn't hold her in his arms, at least got him through the days.

THE WEEKS OF class work ended all too quickly, and so did Catharine's and Eamonn's opportunities to spend time together. The ten-day tour around the island was like an endless, frustrating ride on a merry-go-round, with Catharine strapped to one horse and Eamonn astride another, while they circled round and round in the midst of a noisy, hovering crowd. And like the whirling scenes outside the merry-go-round, so the beauties and historic sites of Ireland passed by them in an aching blur: ring forts and round towers, ruined abbeys and Norman castles, lovely Killarney and the Ring of Kerry.

To Catharine it seemed as if every minute of every day was rigorously outlined and accounted for. When Eamonn wasn't surrounded by a bevy of adoring students, it was Constance DeBry who preened and pranced and vied for his attention. Even during mealtimes, when Catharine thought they might have a few moments of conversation, Dr. DeBry would magically appear with some issue or excuse that needed his attention.

As the tour wore on, Catharine discovered more than Ireland's 'forty shades o' green.' Her own shades of jealousy easily topped that amount in bilious variety. Even more disturbing was the unexplainable distance she felt between Eamonn and herself. He was friendly enough, but no more so than with anyone else. He didn't avoid her, but neither did he seek her out. Their conversations were light and painfully brief, with none of the warmth and subtle intimacy she had come to love.

The next to the last day found them in County Clare, driving mile after mile through the bleak, rocky area known as the Burren. In midafternoon they made a stop to see the Cliffs of Moher, where sheer sides of basalt plunged nearly 700 feet to the surging Atlantic below.

The hike from the parking area to the cliffs was a fair distance, but Catharine was grateful for the chance to leave the bus and walk off some frustration. With Penny huffing and puffing at her side, they made their way to the edge of the precipice. Catharine had seen pictures of the cliffs in travel books, but nothing could have prepared her for the rugged splendor of the place itself. Although she had never been overly afraid of heights, standing near the edge was a dizzying experience. Nothing but wind and sky above her. And far, far below, the endless expanse of the sea. Never had she felt so insignificant.

Satisfied with a brief, nervous glimpse, Penny decided to explore the safer surroundings of the gift shop, leaving Catharine alone.

From where she stood, the cliffs curved inward, forming several u-shaped headlands as they continued down the coast. Shading her eyes with her hand, she glanced across the chasm to the opposite side. Silhouetted against the sunlit sky and green cliff top, were several of her classmates, looking like Lilliputian figures out of *Gulliver's Travels*. Catharine tensed, suddenly recognizing Eamonn's tall form standing slightly apart from the rest.

Longing tightened around her heart as she stood on the lonely edge of her world, and he on his, with an empty chasm of sea and sky between. With only the wind to hear, she whispered, "I love you, Eamonn," then turned and walked away.

The tour concluded with a visit to Yeats' Country and Drumcliffe Churchyard where the poet's tombstone uttered an epitaph cold as the granite on which it was carved: "Cast a cold eye on life, death, Horseman pass by."

Catharine's mood was no less grim.

In late afternoon, when slanted sunlight cast a mellow glow across patch-work fields and hedgerows, the bus with its weary travelers turned down a long, tree-lined lane. At its end, a large gray-stone country house surveyed the surrounding demesne in all its faded glory. Built in the late eighteenth century during the twilight of the Protestant Ascendancy, and sadly neglected in the nineteenth, the stately Georgian mansion was in the process of being reborn in the twentieth as a luxury hotel/bed and breakfast. The current owners, a wealthy Irish/American couple with an eye to the future and respect for the past, had graciously agreed to host the group of students in the finished portion.

In atmosphere and appearance, the accommodations couldn't have been more ideal, combining all the ambiance of the past with creature comforts of the present. Ordinarily, Catharine would have been in the throws of rapture. Instead, she sat quietly with the others in the nineteenth-century splendor of the *salon*, only half listening as Dr. DeBry went over their daily schedule.

"Breakfast will be served between eight and nine, after which you will have three hours to work on individual projects and final papers...." Catharine sighed and stared up at the elaborately scrolled plasterwork on the ceiling, while Constance DeBry's imperious voice droned on. "... afternoons will accommodate individual pursuits as well as more writing time...."

Individual pursuits. At this, Catharine risked a sidelong glance across the room where Eamonn's dark curly head was bent in frowning concentration over a thick stack of assignments. *What's wrong?* she asked him silently. *What have I done?*

"Following the dinner hour, we will all meet here in the *salon* where Mr. Gallagher and I will oversee an evening of reading and critiquing." This, with a purring, feline smile in Eamonn's direction.

But Eamonn was nowhere to be seen after that first day, and made only a brief appearance at breakfast the next. Like the burning sting of iodine in an open wound, Catharine applied ruthless realty on her raw emotions. She was a fool for daring to believe that he might care. How could she have been so blind to mistake friendship for something more? Probably, Eamonn suspected she was in love with him, and avoiding her was his way of letting her down without a painful confrontation. Heartsick and humiliated, there was nothing to do but plunge into the task of writing her final paper. Concentration was far from easy, especially when she felt certain that everyone was watching her with eyes of pity, or worse still, secret amusement.

By mid-afternoon of the third day, Catharine was too restless to study or stay inside a moment longer. Grabbing a sweater, along with her notebook and pen, she left the house to wander the grounds alone.

Even the day offered her no sympathy. The morning's gentle rain had long since blown away, leaving a few lazy skiffs of cloud brushing against the sky's blue. The air was warm with color, scent and drowsy sound. Bees hummed in the blossoms of honeysuckle and wild rose ... doves cooed their sleepy songs from dense green branches overhead ... and from the hillsides came the bleat of black-faced lambs, grazing beside their mothers.

Refusing to be thus distracted from her misery, Catharine wandered away from the house toward the shade of oak and beech woods, and the crumbling ruin of a gray stone wall. Here, the grass grew long and wild and the earth felt spongy beneath her feet. She touched a hand to the worn stone, idly wondering how many centuries it had occupied this place and whose hands had built it. Looking toward the adjacent woods, she was tempted to explore its tangled green paths, but knew that kind of excursion needed slacks and sneakers, not a slim summer sheath with a hemline several inches above her knees. Already, the wet grass had seeped through her thin black flats, and she knew her tights would never survive the brambles.

Then, some yards to her left, she noticed a domed glass conservatory standing in shabby splendor, its white paint peeling and faded to gray, the glass panes dirty and weather-stained. Intrigued, Catharine approached the arched doorway and found it unlocked.

Entering the conservatory was like stepping through a time portal into another century. No matter that the marble floor was dusty and strewn with dead leaves, or that the graceful urns and plaster pots sat empty, some cracked and broken. In her mind, she could easily envision how it must have looked long ago.

Observing her with sightless eyes from their stone pedestals were half a dozen classical figures of life-size proportion. Her breathing quickened with sensual awareness as she stared at two lovers locked in a marble embrace. Time had added layers of dust and grime, but could not diminish their ardor. Shapely limbs entwined in passion's symmetry. One of the maid's slender hands caressed her lover's sinewy shoulder, while his muscled arms held her white stone nakedness close to his. Only a breath apart, his mouth reached for hers, yearning, but never quite touching.

Catharine sank down on a stone bench with a sigh, thinking the conservatory would have been an ideal place for a lover's tryst. She could almost see them ... two lovers from the long ago, slipping furtively away from the house to laugh and kiss amidst the greenery perhaps even to dance in the moonlight....

The next moment, a scene took shape in her mind and the lovers yielded their anonymity to become Esther Clifford and her dashing coachman, John Clark. Catharine opened her notebook and forgetting all else, began to write.

Some time later, how long she had no idea, the creak of hinges and scrape of shoes on the dusty floor sent her plummeting out of her ancestors' world, back to the present. Glancing up, she discovered Eamonn standing in the doorway, a tentative smile curving his mouth. Dressed in a dark pullover sweater and casual jeans, he looked at once younger and more rugged than the classroom Mr. Gallagher in his correct tie and tweeds.

"So this is where you've disappeared to," he said, sounding a bit breathless, as if he'd been on the run. "D'you mind if I trespass in your world for a bit? From the expression on your face, it looks to be a pleasant place."

Chapter 6   Ireland – 1968   91

Catharine tried to find her voice, her happiness at the sight of him suddenly blotting out all else. "I'm afraid I'm the one who's trespassing," she said at last. "I don't know if it's all right for me to be here, but I—well, sometimes it's hard to concentrate around the others."

"More interested in playing with the words from their mouths than in putting any on paper," he commented with a chuckle. Then, sitting down beside her, he asked in a far different tone, "And what sort of magic might you be weaving today?"

Catharine felt self-conscious warmth spread in her cheeks, and one hand moved automatically to cover the page in her notebook. "Oh nothing, really. It's just a–a scene from the story I'm writing."

"The one about your great-great grandmother?" he pursued.

"Yes."

"I'd like to hear it."

"Well —I don't know. It's still pretty—"

Eamonn's smile widened. "Don't tell me. I think we're about to hear a variation of the famous 'Cavanagh-Caveat,' are we not? Something along the lines of how rough it is?"

Catharine couldn't help laughing. "Yes, but—it is rough. This is only the first draft."

"Rough paths are often more rewarding than smooth roads," he said, and something in his eyes sent her pulse racing.

She glanced down, still trying to come up with some excuse. "I–I'm not sure the scene will read well—taken out of context."

"I think I have a pretty good handle on the story," he persisted. "Besides, anything reads well coming from you. I'm sure if you were to read the Dublin phone directory, I'd find it highly entertaining."

Catharine met his smiling glance. "Well, all right, but—"

"No buts, girl. Just read."

She glanced down at the notebook and took a shaky breath. "*Esther made her escape from the stifling heat of the crowded ballroom, out into the—*"

"Hold on, girl, hold on." Eamonn broke into her breathless narrative with a laugh. "Could you slow the pace a bit? Unless Esther's trying to escape from an ax murderer, there's no need to rush things. Let's back her up to the starting gate."

Catharine's nervousness dissolved into laughter. "All right. One more time...."

'Esther made her escape from the stifling heat of the crowded ballroom, out into the softness of the summer night. She was bored. Bored with the advances of young dandies whose smiles were as stiff and starched as their collars. Bored with the idle gossip of silly young girls.

A stone path, shining pale across the moon-washed lawn beckoned, and she lifted her silk skirts to follow. Standing apart from the formal gardens was a large conservatory with a domed room and glassed-in sides. Seeing it there in the moonlight, it seemed a magical place indeed, one full of mystery and romance.

She glanced about, but could see no one to either grant or deny her permission. Then, with a little tug on the door and a swish of her skirts, she was inside.

Tropical plants and flowers grew in lush profusion on every side, filling the night air with their fragrance—palms, citrus trees and glossy white magnolias. Roses, too, Esther thought, detecting their heady scent even before she saw them. The floor beneath her feet was a checkerboard of polished black and white marble, with curved benches beside potted plants, inviting one to sit and dream a while.

It was not the sight of lush greenery alone that caused her to gasp and place a hand on her breast. Standing amid the ferns and flowers were life-sized statues, gods and goddesses all, she supposed.

Moonlight glanced off smooth white stone, revealing rounded curves and graceful limbs. Staring in guilty fascination at the statuary, she wondered briefly why gods and goddesses rarely seemed to wear clothes; indeed, if their lofty expressions were any indication, they scorned them.

Esther cast a critical glance at one young maiden whose only item of apparel was a wreath of flowers in her hair. Her own figure was every bit as good, she decided. Perhaps even better. Her waist was smaller by several inches. So were her hips. Esther glanced down at the modest curve of her bodice which revealed little more than a few inches of smooth white throat and a hint of shoulder. With an impish smile, she wriggled and pushed the silky fabric off her shoulders, then shivered with pleasure as the night breeze caressed her bare skin.

Drifting in from outside, the muted strains of a waltz came to her ears, the melody piercing sweet and faery-like on the evening air. Esther closed her eyes, succumbing to its spell. Then, lifting her skirts in one hand, she began to dance. Soft silk rustled across the marble floor as she whirled in graceful response to the tune's lilting strains.

So caught up was she in dancing with her imaginary partner that the very real footsteps entering the moonlit conservatory went entirely unnoticed, as did the coachman's sharp intake of breath.

John Richard felt sure he must be dreaming. The radiant vision before him with her pale white shoulders and smiling lips, couldn't possibly be the passionate child he had teased and tormented for years.

In mid-whirl, Esther saw the young man who stood motionless in the doorway. Her imaginary partner disappeared into the netherworld of the night.

Giving a stilted bow, John stepped closer. She answered with a breathless curtsy, aware in one tumultuous rush of her disheveled appearance—the revealing state of her dress, and her hair, flown loose from its pins, tumbling about her bare shoulders. What must he think of her?

His eyes, even partially shadowed as they were, gave her the answer.

Without a word, John extended his hand, and without a word, she placed hers in his. As they danced, the separateness disappeared. Titles, class, all the man-made stigmas that had divided them melted in the softness of the moonlight. They were John and Esther. A man and a woman. Nothing more.

The music rose and fell in silken cadence, and John found confidence in the supple response of her body. Her eyes offered an invitation and his smile accepted. His arm tightened around her slim waist, pulling her closer. Then his face bent nearer until his lips touched the softness of her cheek ..."

CATHARINE DREW A shaky breath and closed the notebook. "I–I'm sorry. The rest is—well, it's just too—" She bit her lip before the word 'rough' came out, but there was no teasing glint in Eamonn's eyes.

"Is this the first time John has kissed her?" he asked, his voice a shade huskier than usual.

"Yes."

"But he's wanted to kiss her for a long while."

"Yes."

"Well then, if I might make a suggestion or two...."

She nodded, moistening her lips.

"The way I see it, John wouldn't be offering your Esther any polite pecks on the cheek. Not when the blood's fair boilin' in his veins! The poor lad's had a hard time of it for a long while now—lovin' the girl and wantin' more than anything in life for her to be his—yet knowing this is pretty nigh impossible."

"But it's not impossible—"

"I think you're forgetting something. There are powerful walls keeping the two of them apart—walls they had no part in building, made from stones that existed long before they were born—their religion, their social station—" Eamonn paused and a fatalistic bleakness drained his voice of its usual life and color. "No matter how much he loves her, there are those walls to be torn down."

Catharine stared at him, feeling the hard pounding of her heart in her chest and in her head. "I know that—I mean, Esther knows that. But she loves John and—"

"And you think love is strong enough to break down those walls."

The words, spoken in an offhand manner, wore a protective covering of sarcasm that stung her.

"Yes, I do," she answered hotly, daring to meet his eyes. "And there's something you're forgetting. This isn't just a fictional story about my ancestors. Their lives were real! Their love was real! John and Esther didn't let walls or—or anything else stop them from being together. If they had, I wouldn't be here right now!" Taking a shaky breath, she plunged recklessly on. "I know what you're saying, and I know those walls exist—but if two people really love each other— why can't they just help each other climb over the stupid bloody walls, instead of wasting all that time and effort trying to tear them down!"

Eamonn stared at her flushed face and burning eyes for a stunned moment, then drew a deep breath, like a drowning man breaking the surface of the water. "Darling Katie … why can't they indeed," he said, taking her face in his hands. Then he was kissing her, again and again, as if each time was the first and the last they would ever know.

The notebook fell unheeded to the dusty floor as their restraint crumbled into ashes. Held close against his chest, Catharine could feel the wild pounding of his heart. His breath was her breath. His passion, a thundering echo of her own. There was thrilling newness and frightening familiarity in his touch. How it could be both things at once, she had no idea. She was too happy to care. All the poetry and romantic musings in her young life couldn't have prepared her for love's sweet reality and she gave to him the only way she knew how. With her whole heart.

"I love you, Eamonn."

"You're sure, darlin'?"

"Oh, yes...." Laughing now, she kissed his face, his eyes and his mouth. "I was afraid you didn't care."

"Not care? Sweet mother of God," he groaned. His arms pulled her closer and his mouth took hers in a hard kiss that left them both shaken and breathless. When he released her, it was to look quietly, almost gravely into her eyes. "I love you, Catharine Cavanagh. By all that's dear and holy, I do."

Tears sparkled in the blue of her eyes. "And I love you."

"Then give me your hand, darling girl, for it looks as if we've some walls to climb."

7

County Leitrim, Ireland - 1968

The days following held beautiful blindness and exquisite clarity, such as only lovers know. Misunderstandings were smoothed away and doubts discarded. Lost in the wonder of discovery, each moment together was more precious than the last. Eamonn and Catharine met often in the old conservatory, priding themselves on slipping away unnoticed from the others, and never realizing there is nothing quite so obvious in the world as two people who are desperately in love.

Catharine's female classmates watched with a combination of envy and wistful admiration as the drama unfolded. Catharine Cavanagh and Mr. Gallagher? The prospect was amazing and deliciously wicked, and more than worthy of intense discussion.

"I told you they were talking about more than Irish history!" Shanna pronounced triumphantly.

Carolyn blew on her elegant red nails and decided the couple's future with a careless flip of her blonde jungle mane. "It'll never work," she said. "Never in a million years."

"Well, I think it's wonderful," Penny put in, who adored Catharine and thought Mr. Gallagher was approaching sainthood.

"It may be wonderful now, but what about ten years down the road?" Ann Ridd asked with a skeptical frown. "And where will they live—his world or hers?" She sighed and broached a more immediate danger. "I hate to think what Dr. DeBry is going to do about this."

In fact, Dr. DeBry wasn't at all sure what to do about Catharine and Eamonn. She had sensed trouble weeks ago, felt it coming from the moment she'd first discovered the two laughing and talking after class. A few days before the tour, Constance decided that something had to be done. As unpleasant as the task might be, she'd taken it upon herself to have a frank discussion with the beguiling Mr. Gallagher before this ridiculous infatuation got out of hand.

Constance had chosen her words carefully, as she always did. Never accusing. Only suggesting. Never telling. Simply pointing out the facts, in case others failed to see things as clearly as she did.

Eamonn hadn't been at all pleased, but he was too polite not to listen. People were beginning to talk, she'd told him. No matter how innocent a relationship might be there were bound to be others who didn't see it that way. A teacher and his student? And not just any student. The daughter of a circuit judge who was running for Congress. Surely Eamonn could see the damage a scandal involving Judge Cavanagh's daughter might do. He wouldn't want to be the cause of Catharine being sent home in disgrace. Nor would it be wise to risk ruining his own reputation and career at such a critical time. The administration at Trinity might be understanding. Then again, they might not. But of course, he knew all this. She was only pointing out the obvious because she sincerely cared about them both. Catharine

Chapter 7 — County Leitrim, Ireland – 1968

might be hurt for a little while, but wouldn't it be wise to end things now and spare them both a lot of embarrassment?

For a time, it seemed as if Eamonn had taken her advice to heart. He'd definitely pulled back from Catharine during the tour. All for the best, Constance thought. And highly gratifying. Even more gratifying was the opportunity this afforded her of sitting beside Eamonn on the bus, and finding subtle occasions to lean against those broad shoulders as she gazed out the window.

Constance did her scintillating, cerebral best to engage him in conversation, but his response was less than satisfying. Oh, he was always polite and very witty, but no more personal than he was with the bus driver, a round-faced, red-cheeked man from County Tipperary. As annoying as it might be, Constance finally had to admit that Eamonn Gallagher was completely oblivious to the benefits that she, an older, more experienced woman could offer him. Not that much older, she amended. She was only forty-one, and not unattractive. Ah, well. Perhaps if she were patient, gave him a little time to get over the girl….

A few days into the writing retreat, Constance DeBry was confronted with undeniable evidence that her efforts had failed. She didn't know how it had happened or when, but Catharine and Eamonn were suddenly inseparable. Moreover, as much as it pained her to do so, she was forced to admit something else. Their relationship was not infatuation, nor anything remotely like it.

Watching them, the woman found herself drawn to the couple with an almost unholy fascination. Constance tried to pin it down, to mentally define what it was about the two that intrigued her so. Certainly there was nothing overt or blatantly objectionable in their behavior. Just the opposite.

At mealtimes, whenever Catharine entered the room, Eamonn would glance her way and say with a smile, "There she is." Simple words, yet there was something in his voice, as if he were announcing the sun's rising after a dark lonely night.

And on rainy afternoons, Constance had observed them sitting in the library, heads bent studiously over their books, each seemingly intent on his or her own work. Yet, magically, as minutes passed, their bodies would gravitate closer and closer, as if some powerful magnet were drawing each inexorably toward the other. Before long, their shoulders would be brushing and Catharine would reach out to touch his arm. The simplest smile or glance could turn into an intimate conversation understood only by the other.

One morning, Constance had been passing by the large dining room where the group met for meals and noticed Eamonn slipping something inside the cloth napkin at the place where Catharine always sat. Tight-lipped, with chin held high, Constance continued on her way. Then, despite all her intentions to the contrary, she'd returned to the dining room after Eamonn had gone. Hating herself for displaying such weakness, yet driven by a force she didn't fully understand, Constance approached Catharine's place at the table and carefully lifted the fold of the napkin. Inside she found a small note addressed to: "The love of my heart."

A bittersweet ache tightened her mid-section and a sigh escaped her lips. Carefully smoothing the napkin back over the note, Constance left the room.

Much as she might wish to avoid it, observing Catharine and Eamonn often prompted an uncomfortable examination of her own relationships and past marriages. No man could accuse her of being cold or unfeeling, but somehow, so much seemed lacking in the face of what she was witnessing now. There was a new radiance about Catharine that made her youthful beauty even more enchanting. And Eamonn. Seeing his rough male protectiveness and the light in those slate blue eyes that only Catharine could inspire, held Constance in a state of resentful awe. A smile. A glance. The touch of a hand. Their simplest gesture had a way of making Constance painfully aware how shallow her own dabblings into love had been.

The end of the first week of the writing retreat brought some painful realizations for Catharine and Eamonn as well. The summer, which had stretched so endlessly before them, was suddenly drawing to a close and the cold reality of separation loomed ever nearer.

Eamonn spent one all but sleepless night, mulling over the few short days that were left to him and Catharine, knowing he couldn't bear the thought of wasting a single minute of that time. Early the next morning, he sought out Dr. DeBry and found her in the sitting room drinking a solitary cup of coffee.

"Could I have a word with you?" he asked.

"Certainly." Constance straightened up and set her cup on the side table. *What in heaven's name was ailing the man?* she wondered, as Eamonn sank into the wing-backed chair opposite hers. His eyes were shadowed and weary, the rugged jaw unshaven. But there was something in his face—a kind of raw determination.

"I've been going over the schedule for the next few days and I thought I should let you know about a few changes," he said.

"What sort of changes?" she asked, frowning slightly.

"Nothing you need worry about, and nothing that will affect the others. I just thought you should know that Catharine and I will be leaving today after lunch."

"Leaving?" Constance croaked. "What do you mean leaving?"

"Just that. I'm taking Catharine to Ballinamore in Leitrim to meet my family. We'll be spending the next week with them."

Constance could only stare, stunned speechless at the brazen effrontery of the man. "Mr. Gallagher, have you forgotten your responsibilities—"

"I certainly have not," he said, meeting her gaze with a look that made Constance drop her eyes and reach for the coffee cup. "Everything Dr. Hilliard asked me to do has been done," he went on. "There's no need for me to be here for the critiquing sessions. Not with a capable person such as yourself to keep things running smooth and proper."

"But I – but what about Catharine? She has—"

"You don't need to worry your head about Catharine. Her final paper is finished and I'll be leavin' that with you." His voice deepened then, taking on a note of pride and ownership that made Constance ache inside. "No harm will come to her. I'll see that she gets safely back to Dublin when the time comes."

"And just how do you propose to accomplish that without a car?" Constance asked tartly.

"Jimmy Shanley will give us a lift."

"Jimmy Shanley?" she repeated stupidly.

"He's one of the fellas working on the place here. Jimmy has to drive over to Mohill this afternoon to pick up some supplies and Ballinamore's just a few miles farther up the road."

"Well...." Constance released a long sigh, then cleared her throat. "I hope you know what you're doing."

At this, Eamonn's firm mouth curved into a grin. "Aye. That I do," he said and walked away.

FOUR HOURS LATER, Catharine and Eamonn were bouncing along a narrow road in the back seat of Jimmy Shanley's dilapidated *Fiat*. Jimmy was sixty-five if he was a day, with close-cropped white hair and a young face. His small eyes were bright as a leprechaun's and topped with grizzled brows that jerked up and down whenever he laughed, like furry puppets on a string.

Chapter 7 — County Leitrim, Ireland – 1968

With the *Fiat's* small trunk already loaded with tools and supplies, one of Catharine's suitcases had been propped upright in the passenger seat next to Jimmy, and the other two were crammed on the seat and floor in the back. This not only encouraged, but necessitated that she and Eamonn find a way to occupy the small sliver of space remaining. A lovely dilemma, Catharine thought, and one happily solved by sitting on Eamonn's lap. The fact that her head often bumped against the vehicle's low roof was a minor concern. Nor did it matter that the car's upholstery was blistered and torn in places, or that its suspension and springs were long gone, emphasizing every bump and chuckhole along the way. As far as Catharine was concerned, they were traveling in the lap of luxury. Occasionally, the transmission emitted a grinding groan when Jimmy shifted from first gear into second, but he was quick to reassure them that even this was nothing to be worried about.

"Old Nell likes to complain a bit now and then," he told them. "But she never fails to git me where I'm goin'. Hope you don't mind the close quarters."

Mind? Catharine laughed and assured Jimmy that she didn't. Her state of happiness had risen steadily that morning, until now she was sure there were no words left in the English language to properly describe it. At the moment, her left arm was around Eamonn's neck, leaving the other free to caress his face, stroke a muscled forearm, or rest against his chest where she could feel the sure, solid rhythm of his heart.

Outside, skies were gray with low-lying clouds. Before long, rain was spattering against the windshield and drumming a tinny rhythm on the car roof.

"'Tis a soft day," Jimmy observed, turning on the wipers which sang a squeaking cricket-song as they scraped against the glass.

A lovely day. A perfect day, Catharine thought, smiling into Eamonn's eyes. I love you, she told him silently, and he answered not in words, but by pressing a lingering kiss into her palm.

Her breathing quickened and she whispered close to his ear, "Do you think Jimmy can see us in the rearview mirror?"

Eamonn grinned at this and his eyes held a mischievous gleam. "I have a question for you, Jimmy," he called to the man in the front seat.

"Ask away then, and I'll be doin' me best to answer."

Catharine cringed and shook her head, but Eamonn went right on. "Would you be havin' any objections if I felt the need to kiss someone I dearly adore?"

"I would not," Jimmy chuckled, "unless the someone you have in mind is meself, and thin I'd have to tell you to shove off and find another way home."

"'Tis not yourself I have in mind," Eamonn answered.

The older man chuckled again. "I thought not. Mind you don't steam up the windows. The defrost isn't workin' like she should."

There was no answer from the back seat.

Some time later, Jimmy rolled his window down a crack and rubbed the steamy windshield with the side of his sleeve. His eyes were tender as they glanced up at the rearview mirror, and he said not a word.

By the time they reached the market town of Mohill, the rain had stopped and a late afternoon sun was tossing mottled light like golden coins on the narrow cluster of houses.

Eamonn was pointing out the statue of Ireland's legendary blind harpist, Turlough O'Carolan, when Jimmy piped in: "D'ye see that church over there?"

Chapter 7   *County Leitrim, Ireland – 1968*

Catharine glanced in the direction he was pointing. "Yes."

"That's where me good wife put this on me finger, thirty-seven years ago," he informed them, holding up his left hand where a simple gold band adorned the fourth finger.

Catharine smiled, touched by the fond note of reminiscence in the man's voice.

"That's a long time, Jimmy," Eamonn said.

"It is, that it is. And they've been good years, every one. Would y'mind if I shared a wee bit of advice with you?"

Eamonn smiled at this and gave Catharine's hand a little squeeze. "And what sort of advice might that be?"

"Well now, I've come up with a few simple rules, y'see, for havin' a happy marriage. Nothin' fancy, mind you, just good common sense. But it works. Meself and me wife are proof o'that."

"And what are your rules?" Catharine asked, unconsciously picking up a little flavor of the man's speech.

"There's only three," Jimmy answered, holding up a gnarled hand. "Share, care, and be fair. That's all there is to it."

Catharine found herself making mental note of the words as Eamonn said, "You're a wise man, Jimmy Shanley."

"Aye, and a happy one."

THE GALLAGHER FAMILY lived a few miles outside the small town of Ballinamore in an old farmhouse with lime-washed walls and a kitchen door that was painted a bright, peacock blue. Inside, the furnishings were spare and simple. A long wooden table covered with oilcloth ran nearly half the length of the room, with benches on either side. An old-fashioned cupboard painted the same brilliant blue as the door sat against one wall, with china plates, kettles and crockery filling its open shelves. The kitchen's whitewashed walls and flagstone floor were stark in their simplicity, yet Catharine's first impression was one of warmth and welcome rather than austerity. Part of the warmth came from a sweet-smelling peat fire burning in the stone fireplace, and part from the hearty aroma of soup heating on the stove. The welcome came from the Gallaghers themselves.

Eamonn's mother was putting a pan of scones in the oven to bake when they walked in. "You're finished early today, John," she said without turning around. "The cows must have been right eager to be milked. Supper won't be on for a few minutes yet."

"I can't answer for the cows," Eamonn answered, "but I'm right eager for some of that soup. Would you mind settin' two extra places?"

"Eamonn!"

The woman turned around with a start, her eyes widening along with her smile. Floured hands didn't hinder her from throwing glad arms around her son's neck.

"What are you doing here?" she demanded, wiping her hands on her apron. "We didn't expect you home for another week yet. Is everything all right?"

"Better than all right," Eamonn said with a smile, and turning from his mother's embrace, reached out a hand to Catharine. Drawing her close to his side, he said with quiet pride, "Mum, I'd like you to meet Catharine."

Catharine offered the woman her hand and a nervous smile. "Mrs. Gallagher ... Eamonn's told me so much about you and your family."

Mary Gallagher smiled and her light blue eyes met Catharine's in a moment of unspoken understanding. Behind a somewhat faded appearance of graying brown hair and a pleasant face that scorned makeup, Catharine sensed the calm inner strength of a woman who had loved and given much.

"The name's Mary or 'Mum,'" she said, taking Catharine's hand in both of hers. "Welcome to our home."

John Gallagher entered the kitchen some ten minutes later to find his youngest son smiling like a love struck pup at a dark-haired young woman who was setting the table for supper. *For the love o' Mike, will ye look at that,* he thought, scraping his boots on the mat beside the door. *The lad's smitten sure.*

"Well now, this is a welcome sight," he said aloud.

"Eamonn's surprised us and come home a week early," his wife informed him.

"That's not the sight I'm referrin' to," John said, giving his son a wink and turning his slow smile on Catharine. "Tisn't often a man walks into his house and finds the fairy queen herself settin' the table."

Mary Gallagher tossed him a wry glance over her shoulder. "This is Catharine, Eamonn's friend from America. Mind you, clean all the mud off those boots. I didn't spend half the afternoon moppin' the floor to have you trackin' a path all the way across it."

Catharine smiled as Eamonn's father raised his eyes heavenward and dutifully gave his boots another scrape on the mat.

"Katie, is it?" he said, coming over to the table.

She nodded.

Craggy faced, with a thick shock of iron gray hair and Eamonn's firm straight mouth, John Gallagher would have presented quite the intimidating figure, were it not for the twinkle of mischief Catharine glimpsed in his dark blue eyes.

"And what is it that's brought yourself all the way from America to Ballinamore?" he asked. "Mary's scones have a reputation for bein' the best in the county, but I didn't think word had spread quite that far."

Eamonn smiled and told him, "Catharine's been taking the 'Literary Ireland' course this summer."

"Ah, well now, that explains everything," his father said, the straight mouth curving up in the corners. "No class on Irish literature would be complete without supper at the Gallaghers."

"John, stop your teasing and go wash up," his wife ordered, coming to the table with a basket of hot scones.

"Sure, an' I'm not teasin' a'tall," the man replied, taking one of the scones. "Everyone knows your scones are pure poetry."

Mary Gallagher snatched the scone away from her husband, then gave him a hearty kiss on the mouth. "Flattery will get you nowhere, John Gallagher. Now go wash up."

"It got me a kiss now, didn't it?" the man chuckled, but moved obligingly to the sink. "Eamonn," he said over his shoulder, "why don't you go find your sisters and tell them supper's ready, while Katie and I get acquainted."

Getting acquainted, Catharine discovered much to her relief and delight, was a seamless experience, free from the awkward strings of formality and protocol. Sitting around the table with the Gallagher family, sharing the simple meal and the day's happenings, she felt as if she had known them for months instead of minutes. Steaming ham and bean soup and hot, buttery scones made a perfect blend with their laughter and conversation.

Eamonn's younger sisters, Maggie and Eileen sat across the table from them and plied Catharine with questions about everything American, from the latest movies, to music and fashion. The two sisters were totally unlike in appearance and personality. Maggie, with her dark curly hair and vivid coloring, was engaged to be married in two month's time. Catharine noticed that most of her conversation had a subtle way of circling round to the object of her affection, one Tommy Doonan, the son of the local butcher.

Eileen was two years older than Catharine, yet her shyness and reserve made her seem much younger. Her hair was a light brown, fine textured and straight. Like her mother, Eileen wore little, if any makeup. Observing her, Catharine decided the young woman's pale, freckled face would be quite attractive with some subtle touches of lipstick and blush.

Eamonn's older brothers and sisters, she learned, were all married with families of their own.

"Caitlin and Nora live fairly close by in Mohill," Mary informed her. "You'll be meetin' them and their little ones while you're here, I'm sure. Tom and his family live just outside Dublin, for want of employment here at home," she added with a grieved sigh. "And John Jr. moved to the States three years ago. He works for his wife's father in some place called Detroit."

John Gallagher said nothing, but Catharine sensed from his frowning silence that having his sons leave their home county to find work was a source of sorrow and frustration to him.

Eamonn made a tactful change of subject by telling his family about Catharine's writing and her Irish ancestors.

"Ah, the grand lady and her coachman," John Gallagher said with a twinkle in his eyes. "Now that'll be a tale. When did you say they ran away?"

"Sometime in 1848," Catharine told him. "My great-grandmother was born in New York, later that year."

"They left during the famine years then," John went on with a shake of his grizzled head. "Those were terrible hard times, what with all the sickness and the dyin' and the leavin'...." He paused and looked at Catharine with her youthful beauty and her eyes so full of hope and dreams. She had no idea of the suffering that haunted Ireland during that time. How could she? He could tell her stories of those years. Stories of the 'great hunger' and his own people who stayed behind when thousands were fleeing the country. But he didn't. Let her have her dreams, he thought. Life will teach her about suffering soon enough.

At the evening's end, Catharine followed Eileen upstairs to a small dormer room with a low ceiling and faded wallpaper that was curled and peeling around the edges. Catharine took one look at the old iron bedstead and gave Eamonn's sister an awkward little smile. Sharing a bed was a totally new experience for her, but one she knew must be commonplace in large Irish families.

"It's awfully nice of you to share your room," she said.

"Oh, it's no bother," Eileen told her with a shy smile, and turned back the covers.

In spite of the fact that the old bed complained with her every move, Catharine found it amazingly comfortable. Her pillow was cool and downy soft and the sheets were the whitest, most sweet-smelling she had ever known. She stretched out with a contented sigh, then jumped as something with the frigid temperature of an ice cube brushed against her bare foot.

"Sorry," Eileen apologized quickly. "My feet are always cold as the devil's breath. I usually put a hot water bottle in the bed, but it's been such an excitin' evening, I clean forgot. Would you like me to go downstairs and get one?"

"No, no ... that's all right," Catharine said with a laugh.

Silence settled round the two, and Catharine felt herself relaxing into dreamy contentment.

"Do you love my brother, then?" Eileen whispered into the darkness.

Catharine smiled. "Yes ... very much."

"That's nice," Eileen answered and turned over with a little sigh.

DAYS PASSED IN a happy blend of 'sharing and caring.' While the small town of Ballinamore might not offer some of the more sophisticated city pleasures, Catharine soon discovered there was no lack of things to do. In Ireland, two people meeting on a street corner gave each something to do.

An evening spent at the "Singing Kettle" with several of Eamonn's friends turned into a high-spirited *ceili*, with fast fiddles playing, and the rhythmic heartbeat of a *bodhran* keeping time for dancing feet. In spite of her protests that she didn't know the steps, Eamonn drew her out to the small, crowded space where a few couples were dancing. With his smile as encouragement and hands clapping all around, it wasn't long before Catharine's heart answered the call of the music's infectious rhythm, and her feet soon followed.

As they danced, the separateness disappeared ... Strange that the words she had penned for John and Esther should be just as true for Eamonn and herself. Strange and wonderful. And she didn't need a moonlit conservatory or a silk ball gown to know that all her heart ever needed was here.

During the morning hours, while Eamonn helped his father with the chores, Catharine spent time with Mary Gallagher and Eamonn's sisters. Never having had a sister, she was touched that Maggie wanted her advice and opinion on the choice of flowers and colors for her upcoming wedding. The fact that she and her mother were sewing the wedding dress themselves, Catharine found totally amazing.

"It's lovely," Catharine told her, fingering the soft white satin. "You'll look like a princess, Maggie." Then, noticing Eileen's wistful glance, she asked, "Do you have the material picked out for your dress? I'd love to see it."

Eileen grimaced and shook her head. "Not yet. Maggie thinks I should wear forest green, but I'll look dead as a banshee in that color."

Catharine laughed. "You're too pretty to look like a banshee in any color. And with the right makeup, I think you'd look wonderful in green. I have a few things with me, if you'd like to try them out."

Eileen's pale face brightened, but there was hesitation in her voice. "Thanks, but I wouldn't know what to do with it," she confessed.

"I could help a little, if you wouldn't mind," Catharine offered. "And if you don't like it, you can wash it right off."

"Go on, Eilly," Maggie urged. "It'll be fun."

A short while later, Catharine surveyed her work with a pleased smile. Thinking a light touch would be best, she'd done little more than apply some of the basics. Eileen's fresh, natural beauty did the rest. Catharine handed her a mirror and said, "Take a look."

"Jeepers, is that really me?" she exclaimed. "I look gorgeous!"

Catharine laughed. "You are gorgeous! I just helped bring out what was already there."

"Wait 'til Tim Flaherty sees you," Maggie put in slyly.

"Tim Flaherty doesn't know that I exist," Eileen answered with lofty diffidence, but the color on her cheekbones turned a shade rosier.

"If he didn't before, he will now," Maggie predicted, giving Catharine a little wink.

Eileen stared at her reflection with a dazed smile, then threw her arms around Catharine in an impulsive hug. "Thank you, Katie," she said.

One rainy afternoon, Eamonn's two older sisters came by to meet her, with so many nieces and nephews Catharine knew she'd never be able to remember all their names. That evening after dinner, they all played cards, laughing and teasing one another, with Eamonn and his father engaging in a verbal battle of wits, until Catharine was weak with laughter.

Other times, the family gathered around the hearth to listen as Eamonn's father told stories of the old days that had been passed down by his father and his grandfather before him. Memories and happenings from the reverent to the ridiculous—everything from Great Aunt Minnie's premonitions of death to the time Paddy O'Brien dropped his reading glasses down the outdoor privy—were glibly shared and lived again in the telling.

"You see this chair I'm sittin' in," John told her, running a fond hand along the wooden arm. "It's called a hedgerow chair, for the very reason that the wood came from shrubs growin' along the hedgerows. Wood was scarce in olden times. And if you're wonderin' why such a thing should be in a place as richly favored and green as Ireland, I'll tell you. Hundreds of years ago, the country was everywhere covered with grand oak forests. But after the prolonged visit of the English, the trees began to disappear—cut down they were, to build fine English houses and supply fuel for smelting iron. With the forests gone, the poor folk fashioned what little furniture they had from hawthorn or blackthorn shrubs. Some of it was made by diggin' up the bog oak from the turf itself. My great granddad made this chair nearly one hundred years ago, and there've been Gallaghers tellin' tales in it and warmin' their bones by the fire ever since."

Eamonn's father gave Catharine one of his slow smiles that began deep in his eyes and only reached his mouth as something of an afterthought. The sight of him sitting in the old chair by the stone hearth, with firelight adding gold to the silver of his hair and softening the lines on his work-weary face, became a living portrait in Catharine's mind; one she would cherish and remember for years after.

As the days passed, Catharine found herself quietly marveling at the family's closeness and tough endurance through hard times; at their ability to laugh at life and themselves. Their simple faith touched her deeply. Tacked to a wall in the kitchen was a framed placard which seemed to embody everything the Gallagher family stood for. *Dear Lord, help me to remember that nothing is going to happen to me today, that you and I can't handle together.*

But the sweetest times of all were the hours she and Eamonn had to themselves. There were kisses in the hayloft, talks beside a rushing stream, and walks in the hushed, faery-like spell of twilight, when the only thing that convinced Catharine she was not dreaming, was the firm grasp of Eamonn's hand holding hers.

One morning Eamonn surprised her by announcing he'd been able to borrow a car from one of his brothers-in-law. He and Catharine spent a full day roaming through the county ... past blue *lochs* where white swans glided near the rushes ... past Sheemore, the Faery Hill, the legendary dwelling place of the *Sidhe*. Then they went on to the towns of Drumshanbo and Dromahair, which were once part of the old Gaelic kingdom of Breffni ruled by the powerful O'Rourkes. It was there that Dermot MacMurrogh, the headstrong King of Leinster, carried off the wife of Teirnan O'Rourke—a singular event which led to the invasion of the Normans and Ireland's traumatic relationship with England.

Yet, as they drove by historic sites and villages, events of the distant past were no more tangible to Catharine than the shadow of a dream. Far more real was the knowledge that, however sweet the day might be, this time would soon become a memory in their own past.

At length, they reached lovely Glencar with its wooded paths and cascading waterfalls. Decades before, William Butler Yeats had wandered those same paths and found inspiration for his poem, "The Stolen Child."

Passing by the main picnic area, they found a secluded spot in the deep green heart of the glade, where dappled sunlight danced on emerald bracken and other ferns. There, with the rush of the falls pouring liquid music in the background, Catharine leaned against Eamonn's shoulder, listening to the spell of his voice as he read Yeats' poem aloud.

> *"... Where the wandering water gushes*
> *from the hills above Glencar,*
> *In pools among the rushes*
> *that scarce could bath a star...*
>
> *Come away, oh human child,*
> *to the waters and the wild,*
> *With a faery hand in hand,*
> *For the world's more full of weeping than you can*
> *understand...."*

As she listened, the specter of their imminent parting crept into the day's beauty. Yeats' haunting words suddenly made her heart ache and she wished that somehow, she and Eamonn could run away "to the waters and the wild," for all too soon, her world would be full of weeping and good-byes.

Eamonn closed the book of poetry and set it aside. "Katie darlin', I've made you sad."

"No. No, it's just the poem and this beautiful place...." Tears stung her eyes and tightened her throat, but she made an attempt to smile.

"It isn't the poem, or the place a 'tall. It's the sadness of our parting that I see in your eyes, along with the tears. You can't hide either one, you know." Touching her tear-wet cheek, he said gently, "It's all right, darlin.' The same sadness touches me as well. Why else do you think I wanted to show you the whole bloomin' county, if not to have a memory of you in all the places that I love."

With a little cry, Catharine went into his arms. There was desperation in the kiss she gave him, desperation to hold on to every moment they had together and push away the painful reality of time's passing.

Eamonn responded with a fierceness that left her breathless and trembling, and for awhile, there was no time, only the urgency of their kisses and their whispers of love mingling with the voice of the falls.

"Your going is something that neither of us have wanted to talk about," he said at length.

"Not yet," she begged, stopping his words with another kiss. "Please ... not yet. Oh, Eamonn, I can't stand the thought of leaving you."

Holding her close, he kissed the dark waves of her hair and murmured, "The time will come, darlin', whether we speak of it or not."

"I know," she cried and clung to him all the harder.

THE DAY BEFORE they were scheduled to drive back to Dublin, Eamonn was quiet and frowning at breakfast and Catharine could scarcely force herself to eat.

"There's a place I wanted you to see," he said finally, "but I haven't been able to get a car."

Chapter 7 — County Leitrim, Ireland – 1968

"How far away is this place?" she asked.

"A few miles more than I'd care to walk."

"What about Jigs?" his mother suggested, coming to the table with a fresh pot of tea.

Catharine gave the woman a quizzical glance. "Who's Jigs?"

"The sweetest horse God ever gave four legs to," came the reply.

"Most horses are constructed on that principle," Eamonn said dryly, and Mary Gallagher gave him an affectionate shove. "Thanks, Mum, but I don't think Catharine would enjoy seein' the countryside on the likes of him."

"Yes, I would," Catharine countered.

"Now, darlin', you don't have to be agreein' with me just because—well, because—"

"I'll go change into some slacks while you discuss it with Jigs," Catharine told him. "If he's agreeable, then so am I."

Mary Gallagher gave the two a beaming smile. "You'll be wantin' some sandwiches and a thermos, I wager. I'll pack some straight away."

A short time later, Eamonn and Catharine were heading off through the fields on the back of the big gray gelding. The day was warm, with only the barest hint of a breeze, and Catharine was glad for the chance to exchange her usual attire of skirts and sweaters for a short-sleeved blouse and cotton Capri's.

Past hilly farms and out into the green Irish countryside they rode. For once they said little, content to cover the miles in shared silence, with Catharine's arms wrapped tightly around Eamonn's chest, and her cheek occasionally resting on his back.

She drank in every sight and sound with the painful appreciation of someone facing a long drought—the grassy fields sweetened by clover and spiced with golden drifts of mustard, the liquid laughter of sun bright streams and the raucous chatter of rooks conversing in ancient elms. And Eamonn, most of all. Her mind and senses embraced everything about him from the ease of his hands holding the reins and solid feel of his back against her cheek, to the dark tangles of his hair, framing a face that was ruggedly Irish and infinitely dear.

At length, they reached the somber gray ruins of an ancient abbey. Built many centuries before, the building was little more than a broken shell, with only a few walls remaining of what had once been a thriving seat of study and learning.

Eamonn slid off Jigs' back, then helped Catharine off the horse. Leaving the animal to graze in the long grass, they walked hand in hand toward the ruins. The abbey's roof had long since been demolished and blue sky was now its only ceiling. Dark green ivy climbed the gray walls and crept among the fallen stones. Birds and small creatures of the field made their homes amidst the rubble where centuries before, scholars had read and pondered.

Catharine glanced about with a sense of awe, seeing silent sermons in the nearby gravestones with their distinctive Celtic crosses. Time's fingers had long since erased the words, leaving only blurred symbols of man's presence. Still, there remained about the place a feeling of peace and quiet reflection which kings and armies and centuries of conflict had been unable to destroy.

Her eyes shifted from the ruins to Eamonn's dark blue gaze, and she was filled with a rush of intense gratitude that she was young and alive, and sharing this moment with the only man she would ever love.

He spread the blanket they had brought on the mossy rubble of a low wall, then said almost awkwardly, "Would you sit please, Katie, for I've somethin' to say to you that needs sayin'."

Catharine sank down in a heap of sudden nerves, her heart beating like a small bird startled from the brush.

Rubbing his palms against the sides of his jeans, Eamonn drew a deep breath before sitting beside her. "I brought you here for several reasons," he began. "You'll be leaving me soon. We both know that. Going back to the life you had before. But for me, well—life can never be the way it was. So there's something I want to give to you—a reminder that all the miles and—" He glanced at the crumbling gray stones around them. "—and all the walls in the world can never keep us apart." Taking a small square box from his shirt pocket, he placed it in her hand. "Now don't be cryin' already, darlin', or you'll soon have us both blubberin' like babies."

Catharine swiped at the tears spilling down her cheeks, and opened the box to find a distinctive gold ring with two hands clasping a crowned heart between them. Her lips parted in surprise and delight. "Eamonn … is this the Claddagh?"

"It is. Are you familiar with its meaning?"

"I think so. Something about faith and friendship?" she ventured.

He smiled. "Partly so, but there's a good deal more. As you said, the hands signify faith, or plighted troth, the heart love, and the crown honor and loyalty." He took the ring from its case of dark green velvet and told her, "Among the people of the Claddagh, it was used as a marriage ring, and certain rules apply to how it should be worn. Do you know them?"

She shook her head.

"If you wear the ring on your right hand with the heart turned outwards, the world will know your heart has not yet been won. Wear it on your right hand with the heart turned inwards, and it shows you have friendship and love is being considered." Eamonn's voice took on a husky note. "But worn on the left hand with the heart turned inwards, it means two loves have joined forever. Which is it to be, darlin' girl?"

Catharine held out her left hand to him and said softly, "Two loves joined forever...."

"Forever," he echoed and slipped the ring on her finger.

THERE WAS PEACE. Warm, drowsy peace. And rest at last from the grim march of minutes ticking toward their parting. Catharine lay in Eamonn's arms, feeling only the gentle warmth of the sun and the lilting sigh of the breeze. Overhead, a feathered choir was conversing in the trees.

"'My arms are around you, and I lean against you ... while the lark sings over us,'" she quoted sleepily. "Lovely words. Lovely poem...."

Eamonn stirred slightly to kiss her hair, then her forehead. "They're not larks. They're rooks."

"I know, but rooks aren't as romantic as larks." She sighed and stretched luxuriously. "I love you," she said, as if the words were a sudden discovery or a happy surprise she had come upon. "And I love my ring." Catharine held out her hand, smiling at the sight of the golden ring on her finger. "Do you mind if I ask you something?"

"Ask away, love, and I'll tell you if I mind."

She laughed and kissed the corners of his mouth, while her fingers curled themselves in the dark tangles of his hair. "Well, I was just curious about one thing...."

"And what is it ... that's got you so curious ... at such a moment as this?" he asked between kisses.

"Mmm. I was wondering when you got the ring and when you decided to give it to me."

"If I've still enough brain left for countin', I'd say that's two things," he teased, and Catharine gave him a little shove. He laughed

Chapter 7   *County Leitrim, Ireland – 1968*

and turned on his side to look at her. "I bought it in Longford, the second day of the retreat."

She stared. "That's where you were? When I think how I was suffering and agonizing all that day."

"You weren't the only one suffering," he chuckled. "I had the very devil of a time hitchin' a ride to Longford, and then I had to walk more than halfway back with the ring heavy as a stone in me pocket, and a cold fear inside, thinkin' you might say no."

Catharine put a hand on his chest. "How could I say anything but yes," she murmured with a kiss to seal the words. "And yes … and yes…."

When they could breathe and speak again, she settled herself in the crook of his arm with a happy sigh. "Catharine Gallagher," she said. "What a wonderful name. Don't you love the sound of it?"

"I do."

"It just sort of rolls off the tongue, don't you think?"

"I think you've become very talkative of a sudden. That's what I think."

She laughed. "Only because I'm so happy. You make me happy, Eamonn."

One of his hands stroked her cheek and the soft curve of her jaw. "I hope I always can."

"I'm not afraid—not now," she said. "Two loves joined together…." Taking his hand, she held it close against her heart. "Whenever I'm lonely—until we can be together again—all I have to do is look at my ring."

Eamonn kissed her gently, then kissed the hand that wore the ring. "You've such small hands," he said wonderingly. "I was worried I might not be able to find one to fit proper."

"It fits perfectly," Catharine said, lovingly twisting the gold band. "I never want to take it off."

"One day you might have to," he told her.

Her gaze flew to his face. "Why?" she asked, a thread of worry tightening her voice.

Eamonn met her worried glance with a slow smile. "Seein' as how my mind was otherwise occupied at the time, there's part of the Claddagh tradition I forgot to tell you."

He raised himself on one elbow to look at her, breathing in the sight with wonder and a sense of disbelief—her lovely face, smiling up at him with the love shining in those blue eyes, and her dark hair fanning out beside her like a dusky sky. Dear God Almighty, what had he ever done in his miserable life to deserve her?

"What part is that?" she was asking.

"I told you how the Claddagh was used as a marriage ring."

"Yes."

"In olden times, the ring used to be passed from grandmother to eldest granddaughter on her wedding day. Now it's more common for the ring to go from mother to daughter." Looking into her eyes, he said with husky tenderness, "Someday, God willin', you'll be giving this ring to our daughter on her wedding day. Our daughter Aisling."

The thought of bearing his children filled Catharine with sweet, aching warmth. "Aisling," she repeated. "What a beautiful name. I don't think I've heard it before."

"The name's Gaelic," he told her. "And it means dreamer, or vision. It's also an old version of the name Esther. Seein' how she had a part in bringing us together, I thought your great-great grandmother would be pleased."

"Yes," she whispered, smiling into his eyes. "Someday, I'll give the ring to our little dreamer ... Aisling."

Claddagh

8

Alameda, California – 2000

In spite of Catharine's assurance that she was safe and well, Grace Cavanagh couldn't rid herself of the oppressive hands of worry. Between the storm raging outside and the emotional storm within, there was little time for sleep. Painful memories, throbbing like old wounds, returned to haunt her as she lay with eyes wide to the darkness in the bed she had shared with her husband for over fifty years. But tonight, she wasn't missing him. Tonight she was angry.

Conversations from the long ago returned with brutal clarity, making Grace cringe as if the words were newly spoken. She recalled the misty October day of Catharine's painful admission to them that she was expecting a baby ... followed by Gordon's cold fury and biting words.

From that moment on, he had given his daughter a heavy coat of guilt and shame to wear, adding layers of blame as the weeks wore on.

Of course, he was hurt and disappointed. They both were. But that didn't give him the right to withdraw his love the way he had.

If only she had been stronger, she might have been able to spare Catharine some of the anguish. But could she have altered what happened? The possibility tortured her thoughts as her mind moved through the events of that traumatic time.

Catharine had been so radiant and happy when she returned from Ireland late that summer, exuding a womanly glow and sparkling enthusiasm that had taken both Grace and her husband by surprise. Listening to the girl's rhapsodic account of the class, anyone would have to be blind, deaf and dumb not to notice the frequent mention of one of the instructors, Eamonn Gallagher. Catharine had never been skilled at masking or even containing her emotions, and it soon became evident to Grace that this Mr. Gallagher was the source, the inner spring that fed her daughter's flowing fountain of joy.

One evening as they were looking through some of the photos she had taken, Grace had laughingly remarked, "My goodness, Catharine. Is it Ireland or Eamonn Gallagher you're in love with?"

Catharine had grown very still and her eyes had taken on a quiet, rapt shine. "In a way, Eamonn is Ireland—it's hard to separate the two."

Grace waited for her to go on, knowing what was coming next and desperately trying to contain all the sensible, motherly things she wanted to say. Things like: "You're only nineteen. You have your whole life ahead of you. How do you know you're really in love? Wait. Please, wait. Give it some time."

But she said none of these things. How could she when Catharine's blue eyes were soft and pleading for understanding, her voice so intense, and her young heart so open.

"I love him, Mother. And he loves me. We want to be married in January, as soon as he finishes the semester. I know it seems a little sudden, but wait until you meet Eamonn. You'll love him, too. I know you will."

For the next month and a half, there had been a weekly exchange of letters and one or two telephone calls. It couldn't be more than that, with Eamonn's heavy class load and lack of money. Even the cost of one phone call was an expense he could barely afford.

Gordon had been so preoccupied with his work and the election that he'd taken little interest in his daughter's doings, although it was impossible not to notice her radiant smile, and the way she floated around the house in a happy cloud whenever a letter from Ireland would arrive. Because he wished it to be so, Gordon Cavanagh was convinced that Catharine's involvement with "that Irishman" was nothing more than a frivolous summer romance. He and Grace both knew their daughter's tendency to get a little carried away at times. Give her a few weeks, he'd told Grace, and some handsome new face at Berkeley was bound to make Catharine forget all about this Eamonn who-ever-he-was.

But Catharine did not forget, and soon there were unmistakable signs that her involvement with Eamonn Gallagher was more serious than either of them had suspected. The bouts of sickness and nausea, and then, the painful truth. His daughter was pregnant. Some no-good Irish bastard had taken advantage of an innocent young girl. And Catharine was foolish enough to believe that he loved her.

Grace never doubted for a moment that Gordon loved his daughter and truly cared about her happiness, but those deeper emotions were totally smothered by his anger and hurt pride. There was no love or tenderness offered, only stinging comments of blame and recrimination. To hear Gordon talk, one would think Catharine had intentionally set out to sabotage his campaign and ruin all their lives.

But the largest part of his anger was directed at Eamonn. In Gordon's mind, the young Irishman lost all identity, to become 'the enemy'—someone who represented a tangible threat to the comfortable world he had created. Eamonn became the source of his secret shame; a faceless someone who had humiliated him and discredited all he stood for. Gordon Cavanagh was a man who took pride in dispensing benevolent *largesse* or stinging justice to the rest of the world, but one whose own life was seemingly beyond reproach and the frailties of other men.

The months of Catharine's pregnancy were a painful blur—a throbbing headache of memory that Grace had never wanted to recall in great detail—just take two aspirins of forgetfulness and try to go on with life, ignoring the pain and the throbbing until with time, the pain faded away. Now it all returned, with greater force and clarity than ever.

Gordon insisted that Catharine should move away from home until after the baby was born—someplace where no one knew her, but where she could still get the proper rest and care. Reluctantly, Grace agreed, hating to let her daughter go, but afraid that the stress and tension of being around her father would only aggravate Catharine's fragile state of health. After some discussion, it was decided that she would live with Grace's sister and her husband in Washington State. Aunt Lucille had always adored Catharine. So had George, and both were more than willing to help.

If anyone should ask about Catharine's absence, the excuse was given that she and Gordon were worried about their daughter's health. Catharine had been working too hard in school, and they felt it best that she not take any classes fall and winter semester and visit with some family members out of state.

Grace was forever grateful that Catharine hadn't been home at election time. After a stunning win in the primaries, Gordon had lost the election to his younger, more liberal opponent. The defeat had been a devastating one for the Judge's ego and pride, although publicly, he was never anything but gracious.

Grace struggled through the winter months that followed with depression's hold coloring her world an unrelenting gray. Miles away, Catharine endured the lonely days and nights, believing she had been rejected not only by her father, but by the man she loved.

Then came that dreadful night in early May. Grace could see it still in all its frightening detail. Her husband, sitting on one of those impossible plastic chairs in the hospital waiting room, nervously flipping through the pages of a *Time* magazine he had already read from cover to cover. And she, trying to fill the anxious hours of waiting by crocheting the hem on a flannel baby blanket. Not knowing the sex of the baby, Grace had chosen green material over the traditional pink or blue, a soft lime green with ridiculous yellow chicks and ducklings.

There was a hard thump on the door and Grace glanced up to see the doctor burst into the room and rush toward them with urgency in his eyes and blood on his clothes. There was blood everywhere—bright red on the front of his green scrubs, his pants, and his gloved hands. Then he was shoving a piece of paper at her husband. Even the paper was spattered with blood. Catharine's blood.

"Your daughter's hemorrhaging ... the placenta's burst and we can't stop the bleeding. I've got to do an emergency hysterectomy or we'll lose her."

Staring at the doctor's taut face, hearing the rough urgency in his voice, Grace felt a cold, paralyzing fear grip her heart.

"Sign this. We can't wait."

Gordon grabbed the paper and scribbled his signature with hands that shook like an old man with palsy. Grace hadn't seen her husband's hands shake that way before or since. Without another word, the doctor grabbed the permission slip and ran from the room.

She and Gordon had waited through those endless hours of the night, punctuating the minutes with pleading prayers and fearful agony that Catharine would be taken from them, as their son had the year before.

But Catharine had lived, lived to see and hold her healthy six-pound daughter for a few heavenly minutes. Grace would never forget the rapt shine of maternal love in her daughter's eyes when the baby had first been placed in her arms.

"She's beautiful," Grace had murmured, looking into the small round face of her granddaughter. "Beautiful, and absolutely perfect."

"Aisling," Catharine had crooned, kissing the infant's cheek. "My little Aisling...."

Grace had wondered about the name, but all Catharine would say was that it was Gaelic, and whoever adopted the baby had to agree that this would be her given name. Catharine's only other request was that Aisling be given the unusual gold ring she had worn ever since her return from Ireland.

The adoption arrangements had been taken care of by Lucille's husband, George. As an attorney, he had offered his services and handled the matter with discretion and privacy.

And so it had been done. Catharine left the hospital ten days later with her arms as aching and empty as her heart. And although Grace never failed to thank God for sparing her daughter's life, that didn't eliminate the nights during the months which followed, when she had held Catharine close, listening to the girl's racking sobs. Grace had wept, too, for the loss and the emptiness.

She wept now, in her empty bed and her empty house, with the rain falling and the wind moaning outside.

Oh, Gordon ... Gordon, you were wrong. I know you thought you were doing the right thing—doing what you thought was best for her—but you had no right to take away her choices. Not even God himself does that. As foolish as we might be, He still allows us the right to choose. You took that away from her ... robbed her of her life and her child. You robbed us all...

MORNING CAME. SUN bright, glistening and new. The rain had passed with the night, leaving the air stunningly fresh and clear.

Everything should be clear on such a morning, Grace thought, as she sat at the kitchen table, drinking a steaming cup of tea. Not muddled and confused. Her eyes stung from the previous night's weeping, and although her initial anger and grief had been spent, the remnants of those emotions left her feeling restless and edgy.

Staring at the sunlight dancing through lace curtains, its beauty hurt her. It was as if the light were mocking her pain. She got up, thinking she would pull the blinds and shut out the day, when a flash of movement and color blinked across the window from outside. A pair of chickadees darted and danced from bush to branch, chattering noisily as they flew. Watching them, a phrase from one of Catharine's favorite poems made its way through the tired muddle in Grace's mind.

Hope is like the feathered thing that perches in the soul,

And sings the tune without the words, and never stops at all...

Grace couldn't remember the rest, but she stood for a long while, watching the cheerful flight and antics of the small birds outside her window. *Hope. The feathered thing.* That was what she needed. What Catharine needed. But how and where to find it....

Grace went through her morning routine with punishing precision, and all the while her mind was searching for the answer. She wanted to fix things, but she didn't know how or even if anything could be fixed. What Gordon had done was done. Thirty years had passed. She knew that. But it didn't stop her restless thoughts.

Eamonn Gallagher was probably married with a family of his own by now. For all she knew, he might even be a grandfather. Grace didn't have the slightest notion how to begin finding him. Or even if she should. It was none of her business, really. Catharine herself was married, and although Justin Waller might be a miserable excuse for a husband, he was still her daughter's husband and she had no right to interfere with their marriage.

Grace reached this conclusion while she was cleaning the bathroom. Cleaning a toilet could be very therapeutic at times, and although the toilet didn't really need it, Grace gave it a merciless scrubbing, wishing she could somehow flush Justin Waller out of Catharine's life as easily.

Next, she made herself go through the mail, sorting out various bills, insurance claims and other pertinent letters from the junk mail. Throwing away junk mail could also be therapeutic, she decided, ripping in half all those ridiculous solicitations for credit cards and magazine subscriptions, and tossing them in the trash.

Morning moved into afternoon, with her mind and body never resting. Grace dusted, straightened and paced, wondering where Catharine was and wishing she would call. She was folding and putting away some clean clothes when she snagged the sleeve of her sweater on the corner of a drawer. Fingering the torn threads, she frowned at the small hole. I need to mend *something*, she thought, feeling a desperate ache inside. But how can I mend the holes in Catharine's life?

Going to the hall cupboard where she kept her sewing things, Grace searched for a spool of thread in the soft lavender shade that would match the sweater's weave.

The cupboard shelves were filled to overflowing with notions, sacks of material, and boxes stuffed with sewing projects in various stages of completion—everything from needlepoint to cross-stitch and

Chapter 8   *Alameda, California – 2000*

quilting material. Projects that for one reason or another had been set aside and mentally marked for completion at a later date.

Grace surveyed the bulging shelves with a weary sigh, thinking she really ought to go through the cupboard and organize its jumbled contents; not today, of course, but sometime soon. In spite of this, her restlessness soon had her taking out a few sacks and boxes and placing them in neat piles on the floor.

Reaching up to the top shelf, she pulled down a large plastic bag filled with fabric remnants intended for another 'someday' quilt project. Amidst the kaleidoscope of color and texture, her eyes caught a glimpse of green flannel. Grace stared, feeling her heart pound with painful recognition. Tears blurred the sight of those ridiculous chicks and ducklings, and for a moment she almost gave in to her grief and an overwhelming sense of despair.

Then, something touched her deep inside, calming the grief and replacing the despair with a feeling of quiet peace. It was nothing so obvious as a voice, yet every bit as real, and it told her—here was something she could mend.

Clutching the soft flannel in her thin fingers, her heart uttered a silent prayer. Then, leaving the sacks and boxes on the floor, Grace walked with purposeful calm to her bedroom and picked up the telephone.

When her sister answered she said, "Lucille, I need to talk to George. I don't know if he can help me or not, but it's very important. No–no, I'm all right. Really, I'm fine. It's about Catharine...."

CATHARINE AWOKE TO a feeling of quiet, of utter stillness. She lay for a moment, staring at the unfamiliar motel room. Then awareness and sharp reality returned in an all-engulfing tide, drowning the remnants of memory in its wake and leaving her floundering in the present's painful sea. She turned over with a weary sigh. She couldn't cry anymore. There was nothing left inside, to cry or to feel or to do much of anything. She dressed, packed and paid her bill, because her mind knew this was what needed doing, and it seemed a great thing somehow, just to keep moving and breathing.

Outside, rain-washed air filled her lungs and the winter sun shone tender and clear as a day in spring. Growing alongside the motel was a border of shrubs and flowers. There were calla lilies with long white throats, and pink camellias, deeply whorled and as many-petaled as a rose. Bright prisms of sunlight sparkled in the raindrops still glistening on soft petals and waxy green leaves. It seemed wrong somehow, that the morning should feel so new, when she felt so old.

She put her suitcase in the car and drove away, knowing that she must now drive back to the hillside house in San Anselmo and somehow find a way to go on living.

Since yesterday's discovery, everything had changed and nothing had changed. Finding Eamonn's letter, understanding her father's deceit... all this was old information. There was nothing she could do, nothing to decide, and no clear course to follow. Not now, thirty years after the fact.

There was bittersweet comfort at least, in knowing Eamonn had loved her, that he hadn't abandoned her as her father had insisted. And she loved him. Thirty years hadn't changed that. Nothing would.

"I love you, Eamonn," she said, needing to hear and say the words once more. That much was clear, no matter how jumbled and confused the rest of her life might be. She was driving home, home to Justin. Even the words were jarring, like dissonant notes interrupting a lovely melody. Perhaps it was because, being with Justin, had never felt like home.

The miles passed with her thoughts playing a vicious tug of war with her battered emotions, twisting back and forth even as the road itself curved and twisted through the rugged foothills and steep canyons. At last, she reached the oak-covered foothills surrounding San Anselmo and the landscape of the long familiar.

Driving down her street, she was grateful Justin wouldn't be home until that night, or perhaps the following day, if she were lucky. She needed time, time to rest and hopefully, to think clearly again. She ought to call her mother. Probably, the refrigerator was empty and the sink full of dirty dishes.

Catharine gave the garage door opener a click as she pulled up the drive. The door shuddered up to reveal the gleam of a black Porsche parked inside. She caught her breath and stared at the Porsche. He was home. A stifling, smothering feeling flooded her senses. Yet, strangely, in that same moment, everything became perfectly clear.

9

Justin

Justin Waller sat in the silent living room, frowning at the amber liquid in his glass, his handsome features darkened and contorted by the darkness of his thoughts.

The silence of the house seemed to mock him, ringing in his ears like a jarring echo. Whenever the echoes got too loud, he'd refill his glass and drown them in alcohol.

She was gone. Just like that. With no tears and no tantrums. She'd been gone before during the years of their marriage, with book signings, speaking engagements and promotional travel, and it had never bothered him. If he were inclined to be truthful, he'd have to admit that he was away from home far more often than she. So why was this silence so different? It made him feel edgy and uncomfortable in his skin.

Maybe, because she's never coming back, the echoes answered, and Justin tossed the last of his drink down his throat, needing its raw burn. His thoughts throbbed like a burn whenever he remembered her face, so pale and composed. Her voice, so quiet, yet unyielding.

"I'm tired, Justin," she'd said. "Tired of pretending we're happy, when we both know we're not. And I'm tired of the lies. I don't have room in my life for any more lies."

What the hell was she talking about? he'd demanded, but she hadn't answered. Instead, she just looked at him with sad eyes that spoke more plainly than words. *You know.*

Justin poured himself another drink, trying to douse the prickly edges of fear with indignant anger. So she was upset about the $75,000. He couldn't get the money, so what was all the fuss about? She was a fool to leave him, but his gut told him she was serious this time. He knew that, just as he knew that a divorce would place him in a very uncomfortable position. No matter that California's community property laws would entitle him to half their assets. A divorce would staunch the steady flow of Catharine's book royalties that he had been siphoning for the past year. Half the house would do him no good at all; not when he'd skimmed off the equity and refinanced so many times to get ready cash. Catharine wasn't aware of that, of course, nor did she know about the second mortgage that was two months in arrears. He'd managed to hock some of her jewelry in recent months, but that had made only a small dent in the avalanche of mounting debt.

If she divorced him, he'd be totally cut off from receiving any benefits from the huge trust left to Catharine by her father.

Justin took another swig of whiskey and cursed the old man soundly. The terms of Gordon Cavanagh's will and estate settlement still rankled him. Why, even his son David ended up with more than he had. It was worse than an insult. It had been an obvious slap in the face. And Catharine's portion of her father's money had been neatly tied up and executed in such a way that he couldn't touch a dime.

Justin remembered with stinging clarity, the humiliation he'd felt, listening to the lawyer's obnoxious voice as he spelled out the various debts grew like a many—tentacled monster, threatening to strangle him and everything in sight. Killing Catharine was the only way to free himself from the stranglehold of those tentacles. But how to accomplish this without casting suspicion on himself remained unclear. Then the answer came, one so obvious Justin couldn't believe he hadn't seen it before. All he had to do was produce another suspect, and that suspect had been right under his nose the entire time.

Barrett Saunders. The man's obsession with Catharine was already well established. Saunders had set himself up as the perfect fall guy. The irony in the situation pleased Justin immensely. All he had to do was help things along a little. The notes on her windshield had been a nice touch. Saunders could deny it all he liked, and no one would believe him. The guy was a nut.

There were still several details to work out, but for the past few weeks, Justin had felt no real urgency to act. He derived a sick sort of pleasure in seeing his wife's fear after one of those notes appeared, and congratulated himself for offering such tender support and/or righteous indignation, whatever the situation might call for.

Now, all that had changed. And it was Catharine's fault. She was the one who had rewritten the script, and instigated the changes. So what to do next? Surely there must be someone who owed him a favor. He'd have to make some phone calls. Justin tried to think through the haze of alcohol clouding his thoughts, and decided it could wait until morning.

Reaching for his bottle of liquid courage, he poured himself another shot. Catharine's leaving him didn't change a thing, he decided. The outcome was still the same. Only the timetable had changed.

Raising his glass, Justin saluted the mocking silence of the room and downed the whiskey in a single gulp.

THE TIME FOLLOWING the Sunday afternoon that Catharine left Justin was unlike any she had ever known. Days passed, filled with a confusing mixture of cruel realization, great kindness, and a strange sense of the surreal. Often, she felt as if she were observing the bizarre events in someone else's life rather than in her own.

Her meetings with the attorney and filing divorce papers had been almost painless and amazingly free of complications. She wanted nothing—not the house nor any of its furnishings—only her personal belongings. Let Justin have the rest. He was welcome to it. Then came the shock of learning how little there actually was. Their home was heavily mortgaged. Investments were wiped out. Loans she hadn't known existed were in arrears. One of the biggest shocks had come when she'd gone to the bank to close out her checking account and transfer her savings. Staring at the figures, first with disbelief, then sick realization, she discovered that Justin had somehow managed to drain her finances from thousands down to a few measly dollars—forty-seven dollars and sixty-seven cents to be exact. The fact the money was gone hadn't angered her nearly as much as the ugly stain this might cast on her name and reputation.

Then there had been the meeting with Detective Adams. The man insisted that Justin had never called or come by with a note or any other kind of information. Adams had met with Barrett Saunders who adamantly denied making an attempt to contact Catharine through notes or any other means. More lies, Catharine thought in weary confusion. And more unanswered questions.

She hated the fact that her eyes immediately flew to the windshield whenever she approached her car, hated the feeling of wanting to look over her shoulder whenever she went out, never knowing if he might be watching or waiting for her somewhere nearby. Once or twice, she'd noticed a tan Ford *Escort* following at a discreet distance behind her *Outback*, and wondered if it were the same vehicle she'd seen cruising slowly up her mother's street. She hadn't got a clear enough look at the driver to know whether it was Saunders or not, but she couldn't live this way, with fear in control of her life. One good thing. There hadn't been any more notes.

Through the gauntlet of each day's challenges, Catharine felt the loving support and quiet strength of her mother. It was waiting for her every time she returned home and evidenced in small, but tangible ways: a favorite dish or dessert for dinner, a quiet talk before bed, sympathetic silence and warm hugs. And sometimes, she found herself needing her mother's indignant peppery anger at Justin when she herself felt too tired to care.

Catharine had begun referring to her mother as, "my saving Grace," and knew this was literally true.

Grace insisted on coming along when Catharine returned to the house in San Anselmo to pick up the rest of her clothes and other personal items. Catharine had tried to dissuade her, insisting she'd be just fine, but Grace wouldn't hear of it. "You're not going anywhere near that place, alone," she'd stated in a tone that brooked no argument.

Catharine had smiled and relented, thinking a seventy-five year old woman would pose little threat to Justin or any man. Yet, afterwards, she was infinitely grateful that her mother had insisted on coming.

Justin had not been home, but there was an eerie, almost alien feeling in the house, as if it no longer knew her and resented her presence. Going into the bedroom, taking her things out of drawers and the closet, she'd felt strangely out of place, almost as if she were breaking into someone else's home.

Grace's matter of fact voice and brisk approach to the task at hand had helped more than she would ever know. In less than an hour, they'd gathered Catharine's clothes, her computer, books and a few personal belongings and loaded them in the *Outback*. This done, Catharine locked the door and left without a backward glance.

The old gray Victorian in Alameda became her safe haven, welcoming her back with warmth and comfortable familiarity. But how and where could she find a safe haven for her thoughts, and the limbo-like position in which she found herself? She might be physically and emotionally separated from Justin, but until that nebulous, unknown time when the divorce was final, there was still a tangled, uncomfortable thread that bound their lives together.

Justin had not made any attempt to contact her and Catharine found that both puzzling and strangely unnerving. In spite of everything he had done, she often felt a wistful sadness inside, wondering if she were somehow to blame.

One bright spot had been the visit of Justin's son David and his young wife to give Catharine the happy news that they were expecting a baby. I did something right during all those years, Catharine thought, looking at the glowing couple and David's smiling pride. At twenty-three, the young man was totally unlike Justin. Conservative, hard working and dependable. Even in appearance, David's pleasant but unremarkable looks were very unlike his charismatic father.

Catharine was thankful that a divorce would not alter the close relationship she enjoyed with the young man. The fact that she would be a grandmother in six month's time was more than a little unsettling. A grandmother? It sounded so ancient, and the type of role she had always applied to her mother, never to herself.

As days passed, Catharine's initial weariness and shock began to ease, leaving her with restless energy and the need to put her thoughts and efforts into something positive. With the legal "have-to-do's" largely out of the way, research for her Irish novel took its place at the top of her list of priorities. She haunted bookstores and libraries, bringing home volumes covering every aspect of life in nineteenth-

Chapter 9

century Ireland. Afternoons and evenings were spent reading, studying, and totally immersing herself in the Ireland of her great-great grandmother's day.

In spite of her eagerness and the impressive store of knowledge available, Catharine had to acknowledge there were frustrating gaps as well, blank spaces where she knew next to nothing. The biggest void lay within the lost lives of her ancestors. Only small fragments of information were known, and those dealt largely with the years following the time John and Esther had immigrated to the United States. She had dates to establish when their three children had been born, but nothing to tell her what their lives had been like. Those blank spaces loomed like black holes when it came to the early period of their lives in Ireland.

Curiosity grew into deep longing, a yearning to know more. Did Esther have other brothers and sisters? If so, what had happened to them? What of her husband, John Richard Clark? How had the potato famine that ravaged Ireland during the late eighteen forties affected his life and members of his family?

Equally frustrating was the questionable accuracy of certain 'facts' that family legend had carried through the years. In light of what she was learning, several of those facts now seemed contradictory. The question of religion, for example. Family stories purported that both John Clark and Esther Clifford had been Roman Catholic. That being the case, Catharine wondered how the Clifford family had managed to hold on to their land during the period of Cromwell's confiscation of Irish property, or the bitter years of the Penal Laws when the Crown had denied even the most basic rights to all Irish Catholics. Everything from practicing their religion, to buying land and holding public office was forbidden by English law. Even their language was denied to them, in an attempt to crush and eliminate all that was Irish.

If Esther's ancestors were Catholic, how had they survived those punishing times? Had the Cliffords been among those who conveniently converted to the Established Church in an effort to keep what little they had?

Another puzzle was the name itself. As a surname, Clifford was far more common in England than Ireland, although there were many by that name who lived in the southwest counties of Ireland. In Munster, the surname Clifford had been Anglicized from the Gaelic *Cluvane*. How and where did her people fit into this picture? She had no idea.

Grace made the suggestion once that Catharine simply fictionalize the story, the way she had with some of her other historical novels, and create her own setting for the characters.

"I can't do that!" Catharine had insisted. "It wouldn't be fair to John and Esther. There's got to be a way of finding out more about them."

January slipped quietly into February, with days of fog and drizzling rain. On one such evening, Catharine sat in the living room, curled up in a wingback chair, with a book in her lap, her thoughts pleasantly idle. She had had enough Irish history for one evening, experiencing both anger and anguish as she read about Charles Trevelyan's harsh policies and callous attitude toward Ireland's starving masses during the famine years. How could the man do it? she wondered. How could he dehumanize an entire population and publicly state that the blight which destroyed Ireland's mainstay of food was God's will, divine punishment on the Irish for their perceived idleness? How could Trevelyan permit the export of grain and foodstuffs which flowed unceasingly from Ireland to England, when masses were dying of hunger? How could he justify his actions by stating it would be unwise to interfere with England's economic policies of "free trade."

Thinking about it all put a poignant new perspective on her own situation. In spite of everything that had happened in recent weeks, when she compared her circumstances with those of her great-great grandparents, Catharine had to acknowledge that her emotions were mainly those of immense gratitude, gratitude for her home, her life, and her mother.

In some ways, it felt as if she had been back home forever. She wouldn't consider staying permanently, of course, but it was lovely not to have to worry about finding another place to live just yet. She and Grace had always enjoyed a special closeness. They were friends as well as mother and daughter. Along with a keen awareness of what this time at home meant to her, Catharine thought perhaps it was a good thing for Grace as well, helping to fill the lonely hours and emptiness since her father's passing.

Catharine glanced across the living room where her mother sat at a cherry wood writing desk, surrounded by neat stacks of cards and notes. During the weeks following Judge Cavanagh's death, there had been dozens of cards, letters and other tokens of sympathy from family and friends, as well as from the legal community where he had been a prominent figure for decades.

At the moment, Grace was not working on thank you notes, however. Instead, Catharine found her mother staring off into space with a pleased little smile curving her mouth and a far-off look in her eyes. Observing her for a moment or two, Catharine realized she'd seen that same expression on her mother's face more than once in recent days.

"You're looking awfully pleased with yourself," Catharine commented with a smile. "Did you have a nice day?"

Grace jumped visibly, then laughed at her reaction. "Yes, I did, actually. I was just thinking about something...." The words trailed off and she made a point of straightening an already neat stack of letters.

"And—?" Catharine prompted.

"I have an idea to help you with the research for your book."

"Really?" Catharine sat up a little straighter. "I'm all ears."

"Well, I wouldn't want you to think that I was interfering, or trying to tell you what to do—but I couldn't help noticing how frustrated you've been lately, and—"

"Now who's caveating," Catharine said dryly. "What's your idea? I promise, I won't think you're interfering."

Grace drew a quick little breath and her eyes, when she looked at Catharine, were as sparkling and excited as a girl's.

"I've hired a genealogist to help us find the Cliffords," she said.

"You what?"

"I hired a genealogist." Grace laughed at her daughter's blank expression. "You said yourself that you can't move forward with the story until you find out what part of Ireland the Clarks and Cliffords came from. And I've been curious to know more about my family for a long time now."

"But how—?"

"Oh, I was talking to your Aunt Lucille the other day and she mentioned some friends in Sacramento who are really into that sort of thing. They told her about a firm—some company that specializes in doing family histories and searching out people's roots. They're supposed to be very good. They even have someone who specializes in Irish research, so I called them."

Catharine broke in to her mother's excited rambling. "Called who—the friends or the company?"

"The company, of course. They're called 'Connections.' I had a very nice talk with their Irish specialist and made an appointment. Do you mind?"

"Why would I mind?"

Grace beamed. "Then you think it's a good idea?"

"Mother, you amaze me. You're absolutely brilliant."

"Of course I am. But it's nice to know my daughter has finally reached the same conclusion."

Catharine laughed and felt something hard and hurting that had been living inside her suddenly ease its hold. How wonderful to laugh again. To know that she still could. "So when do I get to meet this genealogist of yours?"

Grace glanced down at her notes and smiled that pleased smile. "The day after tomorrow at one o'clock—if that's all right with you."

"It's fine. I had an appointment with the attorney at eleven, but if we're going to drive to Sacramento, I'd better call and reschedule."

"No need for that," Grace answered airily. "Ms. Montgomery already had an appointment in the Bay area, so she's agreed to come to the house. Just make sure you tell Charles about the appointment, or he'll keep you there all afternoon. You know how long-winded he can be."

"I'll tell him."

"Not that he's long winded," Grace put in quickly. "Only about the appointment."

Catharine shook her head and sent her mother an affectionate smile. "Don't ever change, Mother."

"I'm too old to change, dear."

"No," Catharine said. "You'll never be old."

10

Aisling

Catharine arrived five minutes early for her appointment with Charles Wentworth, only to learn that the attorney was still tied up in court. Several times during the forty-five minute wait which followed, she was tempted to tell the secretary that she couldn't wait any longer, and to please reschedule her another day. But every time she started fidgeting, or stood to get a magazine, the dutiful Miss Humphries offered a hasty apology and assured Catharine that, even though Mr. Wentworth was running "a little behind," he should be back very soon—another five minutes at most.

Charles Wentworth had been running "a little behind" for years, Catharine thought, but he was an excellent attorney and had handled her father's financial affairs with flawless expertise. Now, with the divorce and her own finances in such a chaotic state, Catharine was more than grateful for the man's help and personal concern.

And so she waited, watching the clock and determining to be out of the office and on her way home no later than twelve-thirty. At twelve forty-six, Catharine was dashing to her car and mentally willing traffic between Wentworth's office in Oakland and home to cooperate. All went smoothly until a minor fender-bender in the Webster 'tube,' which connected island Alameda with the mainland, created still another delay.

Catharine's nerves and temper were seriously frayed by the time she pulled into the driveway at eighteen minutes past one. Getting out of her car, she frowned at the sight of a blue-green Honda parked on the street in front of her mother's home. She hated being late and despised keeping others waiting. Giving the car door a frustrated slam, she hurried up the walk.

Where had she put her blasted notebook with the list of questions for the genealogist? What if she'd left it in Charles' office? Catharine swore under her breath, then stood for a moment in the entryway, trying to gather her scattered thoughts into some semblance of order. There was the notebook, sitting on the hall table exactly where she'd left it. Catharine blew out a ragged breath and, picking up the notebook, heard the sound of voices coming from the dining room.

Her mother and a young woman with magnificent auburn hair were sitting side by side at the cherry wood table, with books and papers spread out in front of them.

Catharine hurried in with an apology on her lips. "I'm sorry to be late. Mr. Wentworth was held up in court and—"

"That's all right, dear," her mother said. "Ms. Montgomery hasn't been here long."

The young woman stood up then and faced Catharine with a smile. She had a beautiful smile, Catharine thought, and that hair was incredible. Thick auburn waves fell in a cascade of shining red-gold to the woman's shoulders, and framed her heart-shaped face. She wore a wool blazer of hunter green over a simple white top and charcoal slacks. Catharine found she had to lift her gaze slightly to meet the young woman's dark blue eyes, as she stood taller by a good two inches.

"My last appointment ran late, too," she told Catharine. "I was afraid I'd be the one keeping you waiting."

"Ms. Montgomery is a fan of yours," Grace put in.

Faint color spread along the young woman's cheekbones. "It's true. I must have read all your novels at least a dozen times," she said with a self-conscious smile. "You'll have to forgive me if I start acting a bit dumbstruck. I never dreamed I'd be doing genealogy for my favorite author."

Catharine clasped the hand offered to her. "Then you'll have to forgive me as well. I'm afraid I was picturing some wizened old maid with bifocals three inches thick and a pencil behind each ear. I never thought a genealogist could be so young!"

Ms. Montgomery laughed at this, then wrinkled her nose, which had a light dusting of freckles. "Not that young. I'll be thirty-one in May."

Catharine laughed, too, thinking what a delightful young woman this was. Then she glanced at her mother who seemed to have something in her eye.

"As long as we're making confessions," Ms. Montgomery went on, "I have to tell you, I'm not sure how one should address a famous author. Do you prefer Ms. Cavanagh or Mrs. Waller?"

"Catharine is even better," she answered warmly. "But I don't believe I caught your first name."

"Aisling. Aisling Montgomery."

Catharine felt a curious weakness in her legs, as if the bones had suddenly turned to water. She gripped the back of a dining room chair for support and repeated faintly, "Aisling?"

"It's Gaelic," the young woman explained.

"Yes ... I know. I'm—uh, you don't hear that name very often."

Aisling nodded agreement, giving Catharine's pale face a concerned glance.

Catharine shook herself mentally and gestured to a chair. "Please, won't you sit down? I–I've been so eager to hear about—about everything," she said, trying to tell herself this was only a cruel coincidence and nothing to get worked up about. There must be hundreds of women with that name. Dozens, anyway.

The young woman sat back down and reached for a leather portfolio. As she removed a few printed forms, Catharine caught the gleam of gold on her right hand and recognition seared through her. The Claddagh. Dear heaven ... it couldn't be.

"Catharine?"

Her mother's voice came to her, sounding a long way off, but she couldn't answer. How could she speak or move or do anything at all when her heart was pounding so, and painful doubts pummeled the impossible hope growing inside her. Could it be possible? Was there any way under heaven that this beautiful young woman was *her* Aisling?

"Catharine...." Grace's voice came again, sounding warm and full of love.

With effort, Catharine's questioning gaze lifted from the gold ring to her mother's face. One look at Grace's shining eyes gave her the answer.

She must have said something after that, but she had no idea what. Somehow, she managed to get from the dining room to the kitchen before the tears completely blinded her and her legs refused to function.

Chapter 10

Grace found her there, hunched over a chair, trembling from head to foot.

"Catharine…." She put a hand on her daughter's shoulder, not knowing what to say or do.

"You found her," Catharine choked, looking up at her mother with stunned joy and tears coursing down her face. "You found my little Aisling…." Then, wrapping her arms about Grace's waist, she buried her face in the woman's bosom and sobbed.

Grace held Catharine close, stroking her hair and struggling to keep hold of her own composure. "Oh, my dear … forgive me. I should have prepared you, but I didn't know how. Are you all right?"

Catharine drew some ragged breaths and wiped a hand across her tear-stained face. "All right? I've never been so all right. Mother … how did this miracle happen?"

"I'll tell you all about it, dear," Grace promised, "but I think explanations should wait until later. Right now, your daughter is in the next room wondering what's happened to her favorite author." She frowned and said, "I hate to tell you this, but you look absolutely dreadful."

"Thanks." Catharine gave her mother a wry smile. "That's just what I needed to hear."

Grace's sigh was relieved. "Will you be all right if I go back and talk to her?"

Catharine nodded. "Yes. I just need a minute or two. Could you make my excuses?"

"What excuses? What do you want me to tell her?"

"I–I don't know, but she mustn't know about me. Not yet. It wouldn't be fair."

"I know, dear, and I agree. But I've got to tell her something."

Catharine moved to the sink and began splashing handfuls of cold water on her face. "Then tell her I've been sick or something."

"Catharine, I can't lie. You may look dreadful, but you don't look ill."

"Then tell her I had a terrible time at the attorney's office."

"Doing what?"

"Good heavens, Mother, I don't know. Can't you just make up something?"

"I'm not good at making things up," Grace stated flatly, handing Catharine a dishtowel to dry her face. "Besides, you're the author."

Catharine groaned and glanced up from the towel. "Mother, please. Just say something. Anything! Blame it on Justin, I don't care."

Grace brightened and turned to go. "That I can do," she said. "Don't be too long, dear."

Catharine did her best to listen attentively and take notes on the information Aisling gave them, but the largest part of her was too lost in wonder to do much more than drink in the miracle sitting at their dining room table. Studying Aisling's features, listening to her voice and observing her mannerisms, Catharine could see much of Eamonn. Little things—like the way she tilted her head and held her pen. Even the intent way she had of checking her notes. And her eyes. It was amazing, unsettling, and totally wonderful to look at this lovely young woman and see Eamonn's dark blue eyes. *She has my mouth, though,* Catharine decided with motherly satisfaction. Where that magnificent auburn hair came from, she had no idea, although its thickness and curls were very much like her father's.

Catharine was in total awe. Occasionally, she managed to ask a semi-intelligent question, but for the most part, she considered it a major feat just to keep from staring. *This is my daughter,* she told herself again and again. Hers and Eamonn's.

Grace managed the situation much better, but then, Catharine reminded herself, her mother had the advantage of being somewhat prepared. How in the name of heaven had she found her? she wondered for the hundredth time.

All too soon, Aisling was gathering up her notebooks and the family group records they had filled out during the course of the afternoon.

"I know you're anxious to find the Cliffords in Ireland," she said, "but it's important to start with what we know and work backwards from there. Before I start searching any Irish records, I'll need to make a thorough check of the sources available in this country. A trip to Grass Valley might be very helpful for that. I'll do what I can here, of course, but at some point, I'd like to go to Salt Lake City and spend some time at the Family History Library there. They have microfilms of all the federal census records, and quite a few state census films. And their Irish collection is wonderful. I doubt you could find more information anywhere outside of Dublin."

"Whatever you need to do, do it!" Grace told her with unreserved enthusiasm.

"Would I be in the way, if I came along when you go to Salt Lake?" Catharine suddenly found herself asking. "I–I can see where going to the library there would be very helpful for my research—but I wouldn't want to get in your way."

"In my way?" Aisling burst out. "I'd love to have you come!"

The aftershocks Catharine was experiencing from her moment of bold effrontery, disappeared in the enthusiasm of her daughter's response.

"I'll look forward to it then," Catharine said warmly, and the sparkle in Aisling's blue eyes said she felt the same.

"Do you have time for some gingerbread with hot lemon sauce before you go?" Grace asked.

Aisling glanced at the watch on her wrist, then smiled. "Actually, I probably don't—but it sounds much too tempting to miss."

"Oh, it is," Grace assured her, and getting up, led the way to the kitchen.

They talked easily, as if they'd known one another for years instead of hours, and when Grace slyly offered her granddaughter another "tiny slice" of gingerbread so it wouldn't go to waste, Aisling did not refuse.

"Mmm. How did you know this was my favorite dessert?" she said. "Are you a mind reader as well as a wonderful cook?"

"No to the first question, and yes to the second," Grace quipped, adding, "Actually, gingerbread with lemon sauce is one of yo—is one of Catharine's favorite desserts."

Catharine coughed on a mouthful of cake and sent her mother a warning look. "Ever since I moved back home a few weeks ago, Mother's been baking up a storm," she filled in.

"Grace told me that you're—well, going through a divorce," Aisling said, offering a tentative, "I'm sorry."

"No need to be sorry," Catharine said. "It's all for the best."

A few awkward seconds followed, as Aisling mentally kicked herself for bringing up something so personal, and Catharine administered similar self-punishment for answering in such flip, careless tones.

Observing the two, Grace considered it her duty to salvage the moment. "You know, for the life of me, I can't understand why you're not married," she said to Aisling. "Some dark-eyed Romeo should have snatched you up years ago."

"Mother!" Catharine's tone was only mildly reproving, but her expression was horrified.

Aisling burst out laughing. "It's all Catharine's fault," she said.

"My fault?"

The young woman's blue eyes danced with mischief as they met Catharine's. "It's true. Your novels have totally spoiled me. Sometimes, I think the only fascinating men left in the world exist solely between the pages of a book. Honestly, Catharine, your heroes are to die for. Take Sebastian in *Michelangelo's Mirror*. The man was deadly. And then there was that Anglo-Indian doctor from *In the Hall of Peacocks*—what was his name again?"

"Rashad," Catharine said with an embarrassed smile.

"That's right. Rashad. The man's dialogue alone was enough to melt any woman's bones. It's no wonder Cecilia what's-her-name couldn't resist him." Uttering a blissful sigh she went on, "It's so refreshing to find a man and a woman who can actually talk to each other. I'd just about given up hope that there was a man left on the planet who could make intelligent conversation—something more than bathroom humor and four-letter words. Why can't I meet someone like that?"

Grace was shaking too hard with laughter to answer.

Catharine looked at her daughter with delight. "I suppose that's why they call it fiction," she said.

They said their good-byes on the front porch and Catharine tried to ignore the sharp pang of reluctance to let Aisling go, by consoling herself that in just a few days' time, they would have their next meeting. And there would be another after that. And another.

Yet knowing this didn't help when it came to saying good-bye. Catharine was at a loss, suddenly, to know what to do. A hug might be misunderstood after such brief acquaintance, yet a handshake seemed stilted and sterile.

Grace stepped forward without hesitation and put her arms around her granddaughter. "You drive safely going home," she cautioned.

Aisling smiled at this, but answered dutifully, "I will." Then her eyes met Catharine's.

"Thank you so much for coming," Catharine said, feeling the inadequacy of the words, and fighting the impulse to hold the girl close.

"I should be thanking you," Aisling answered, and gave Catharine a spontaneous hug. "I'll see you soon."

Catharine smiled and nodded, knowing her emotions were too close to the surface to speak.

She and Grace stood on the porch, watching until the blue-green Honda turned the corner and disappeared from sight. Catharine put an arm about her mother's shoulders as they turned to go inside.

"Thank you," she whispered.

IN SPITE OF her best intentions to help Grace tidy up the kitchen, Catharine found she was suddenly too weak to do anything but sit and stare into space.

"How?" she asked after a long moment. "How did this miracle happen?"

Grace got out a package of plastic wrap to cover the pan of leftover gingerbread, smiling with pure satisfaction. "It was far less difficult than I first thought. The day you left Justin, I decided to call your Uncle George. I had no idea if he would be willing or even legally able to help me. I just knew I had to try."

"But wouldn't adoption information be sealed by the courts?" Catharine said. "How would Uncle George have any access to it?"

"Your uncle didn't need to go through the courts. The people who adopted Aisling were good friends of his—Joseph and Helen Montgomery. George told me they were an older couple who'd tried for years to have children of their own. Apparently, Helen had several miscarriages, and the one time she was able to carry a baby to term, the poor little thing died two days later. They were overjoyed when George told them about Aisling." She gave an amazed sigh. "To think, all these years, your uncle's known exactly where Aisling was and never said a word to another soul. Although, it's probably a good thing Lucille didn't know, or she never would have given him a moment's peace."

Catharine took this in with a thoughtful look. "Why was he suddenly willing to tell you?"

"A combination of things, I suppose. Circumstance and serendipity."

"I don't understand."

Grace leaned against the counter and there was some hesitation in her eyes, as if she weren't sure of Catharine's response. "I told George about Eamonn's letter," she said finally, "and what your father had done. Then I asked him flat out if there was any way to find out where your daughter was. And if he could, would he be willing to let us know if she was all right. George said he'd think about it, do a little checking, then get back to me." Grace shook her head, thinking over the amazing events. "A week or so later, George called back and told me about the Montgomerys. You could have knocked me over with a feather. It's a good thing you were away at the library that afternoon. All I could do was wander around the house in a daze."

"Mother, please. What did he tell you?"

"That the Montgomerys had moved away about a year after Aisling was born, but still kept in touch with him now and then—with Christmas cards and an occasional letter. After that, Joe Montgomery's work kept them moving on a regular basis, so—"

"Mother, I'm dying by inches. Do you think you could give me the condensed version of the story?"

"I'm sorry, dear." Grace gave Catharine a contrite look and took a chair beside her. "The Montgomerys have lived in Sacramento for the past nine years. Helen died five years ago and Joe remarried two years after that. He and his new wife live in Santa Clara, or Santa Cruz, I can't remember which. At any rate, George called him last week and asked if he'd have any objection to Aisling's birth mother knowing where she was and how she was doing." Grace uttered a thankful sigh. "Mr. Montgomery said it was fine with him, and to give you his blessing. That was a very generous thing to do, I think," she added softly.

"I was wondering how on earth to arrange for you two to get together when your uncle told me that Aisling was a certified genealogist working for a firm in Sacramento. That's what I meant by serendipity. It's quite amazing, isn't it?"

Catharine closed her eyes and rested her forehead on her hands.

A quiet moment passed with neither one speaking. Then Catharine lifted her head. "She's very lovely, isn't she, Mother?"

"Yes, dear. Very lovely."

"And so bright. I can see a lot of Eamonn in her."

"I can see a lot of her mother as well," Grace added with a tender smile.

Catharine reached out to give her mother's hand an affectionate squeeze. "There's one thing that puzzles me, though. Where did she get that gorgeous red hair? Neither of Eamonn's parents were red-headed, and you and Dad aren't, so—"

Grace let go a delighted laugh. "That's no puzzle at all. Have you forgotten about Annie?"

"Esther's daughter," Catharine breathed.

Grace beamed and nodded. "That's right. Our Aisling got her red hair from her Irish great-great grandmother!"

11

Plans & Presentiments

Ten days later, Catharine returned home from an afternoon at the Berkeley Library to hear her mother's cheerful announcement from the kitchen. "Aisling called a little while ago. She left a number where you can reach her."

Catharine's heart gave a happy leap and she paused in the act of hanging her coat in the hall closet. *Aisling called* ... What amazing words. Would the wonder of hearing her daughter's name and knowing she would actually see her again ever cease? She hoped not.

Going into the kitchen, Catharine found her mother beside the stove, stirring a pot of broccoli-cheese soup.

"How did your afternoon go?" Grace said, turning down the heat and setting the spoon aside.

Catharine didn't answer. Instead she asked, "Where's the number? Did Aisling want me to call back right away?"

"Any time this evening will be fine," Grace answered, trying to keep back a smile. "The number's on the note pad next to the phone."

Grace went about her dinner preparations, getting out soup bowls and flatware to set the table, and observing out the corner of her eye as Catharine nervously punched in a few numbers, hung up, and tried again. It tugged at her heart to hear the breathless anticipation in her daughter's voice as she asked, "May I speak with Ms. Montgomery, please?" And then the warmth, "Aisling? Hello, it's Catharine."

Grace went back to the stove to check the soup, paying little attention to the content of their conversation; hearing instead the welcome lightness in Catharine's voice. That terrible strain and weariness was completely gone. If a bouquet of spring flowers, all bright and blooming, could talk, they'd sound exactly like Catharine's voice, she thought.

Casting a sideways glance in her daughter's direction, Grace found herself smiling at the sight. I never looked that good at fifty, she thought. A snug, wine-colored sweater and tailored gray slacks emphasized Catharine's slender curves and complimented the dark waves of her hair. Her blue eyes were shining and her skin glowed, as if lit from within. Grace indulged herself in a moment of motherly pride at her daughter's mature beauty. *You and I did good work, Gordon*, she told him.

Catharine laughed then at something Aisling said, and the next moment Grace's heart was on its knees, as it had been so often since that first afternoon she and Aisling had met. This happiness was such a gift. Grace closed her eyes, offering a quiet, "Thank you, Lord," as she stirred the soup.

"Aisling's tied up until nearly the end of the week, finishing a big project," Catharine told her moments later. "She wanted to know if we could meet Thursday evening and I suggested we all go to dinner. Do you think that was wrong?"

"Why would it be wrong?" Grace said.

"I don't know. Maybe it's not very professional or something."

Grace shot Catharine an amused glance. "What did Aisling say?"

"She said she'd love to."

"Well then, there's your answer."

Catharine stood in the center of the kitchen, frowning at nothing. "I guess, sometimes I can't help feeling afraid; that all this is too wonderful to be true, and if I make a mistake or do something wrong—she'll disappear."

"Your daughter is not going to disappear," Grace said adamantly.

"What about—after she learns the truth? She might not forgive me."

"Catharine, there's no sense torturing yourself with what might or might not happen. You'll know what to do when the time comes. I don't doubt that for a minute."

Catharine sighed and her voice held more than a little doubt. "I hope so."

"What do you say we leave all the maybe's and what if's until later, and concentrate on the problem at hand."

"Such as?"

"What restaurant did you have in mind for dinner?"

Catharine smiled. "I thought Kinkades might be nice. Aisling will be driving back from San Francisco, so it won't be too far out of her way. I told her I'd make reservations for six-thirty."

"That sounds fine," Grace said, taking a pen out of a kitchen drawer. "I'd better mark it on the calendar. Was that Friday at six-thirty?"

"No, Thursday."

"Oh, that's right. Well, you two will just have to meet without me. I have book club with the girls on Thursday afternoon and we always have dinner together afterwards."

Catharine couldn't help smiling at the mention of 'the girls.' Grace Cavanagh and ten other women, all in their early to late seventies, had been meeting for as long as Catharine could remember, to discuss and review a selected 'book of the month.' The titles ranged from the classics to current bestsellers and nothing short of a major earthquake could prevent 'the girls' from meeting for their appointed rounds.

"You're nervous, aren't you," Grace said, bringing the steaming pot of soup to the table.

Catharine looked at her mother. "Not nervous. Terrified."

THERE HAD BEEN a few awkward moments when Catharine and Aisling met at Kinkades in Jack London Square, with each woman slightly in awe of the other. Aisling had been trying to convince herself for the past week that she ought to be able to treat Catharine Cavanagh like any other client, and not the author whose work she had adored and admired for years. Catharine was doing much the same, desperate for a way to approach Aisling on a friendly, but professional level, instead of the daughter she had once thought would be lost to her forever.

They took their seats at a comfortable booth with a stunning view of the marina and estuary, trying to cover the awkwardness with smiles and politeness. When this didn't help, they hid behind their menus.

Moments later, a server approached and asked if they would care for an appetizer or beverage before their meal. Catharine and Aisling glanced up and said at the same time, "Crab-stuffed mushrooms and a diet Coke."

Momentary tension dissolved into laughter, and suddenly everything was all right. By the time the main course arrived, their enthusiasm for the project at hand had replaced all else. Conversation was effortless and animated.

"I really appreciate your patience with my schedule the past week or so," Aisling told Catharine. "As much as I've wanted to get started on your project, I've had several others that I had to finish first. As of today, I'll be able to concentrate all my efforts on finding your great-great grandmother and her family."

Catharine smiled and thought, *They're your family, too.* Aloud she said, "That's wonderful. I know I'm going to learn a lot from you in the coming weeks."

Aisling reached into her leather portfolio and handed Catharine a copy of an 1870 census page for Grass Valley, California. "I know this doesn't seem like much, but I thought I'd wait to do most of the New York and Irish research until we go to Salt Lake."

Catharine stared at the page of names written by some long ago census taker. There they were. *John Clark, age 50, occupation: car man. Wife: Esther, age 48, keeping house.* Their two sons, James and Henry, were also working in the mines.

"Not much?" she said. "This is wonderful! Just seeing the names makes them more real somehow. But where's Annie?"

"Right here." Aisling pointed a few lines farther down the page. "She's married to Hugh McDermott by now and they have a son, James Henry, age 1. I'm assuming he was named after Annie's two brothers, which is a little unusual, because many Irish at that time followed the custom of naming the oldest son after the paternal grandfather. The second son was named after the mother's father, and the daughters in the family followed the same pattern."

"I think the reason might have something to do with the fact that Annie and Hugh eloped," Catharine said. "From what I've been told, John wasn't too pleased with their marriage in the beginning."

Aisling's lips parted in a little smile. "Like mother, like daughter," she said, and the words had Catharine suddenly catching her breath.

"Yes ... yes, I guess so."

"I'm anxious to find out more about Esther's immediate family," Aisling went on. "Grace told me there was a brother Henry, but without knowing the names and ages of other siblings, it's difficult to make a guess where Esther fits into the birth order. If we knew that, it might give us some clues about her parents' names and ancestry."

"How did you ever learn all this?" Catharine asked.

"The same way you do research for one of your books," Aisling answered with a smile. "You read and you study."

Catharine glanced down and took a bite of her shrimp scampi before saying, "Do you mind if I ask you something personal?"

"Not at all."

"What made you decide to become a genealogist? I've been curious about that since we met."

Aisling twirled a forkful of *fettuccini* and cocked her head to one side. "Several things, really. I graduated from college with a major in history and a minor in humanities, and didn't have the vaguest idea what to do with it, except teach. And that didn't appeal to me at the time. Then I decided it would be fun to actually see all the places I'd been reading about for so many years. I lived abroad for a little over a year, then went back to school, thinking I might enjoy being a travel agent, but—" She stopped mid-sentence and gave Catharine a self-conscious smile. "Sorry. You shouldn't be so easy to talk to. Sometimes I don't know how to answer a simple question without turning it into a major epic."

"No, no. Please go on," Catharine told her, thinking, *If only you knew how hungry I've been to know something about your life.*

Aisling's smile faded as she stared at her dinner plate. "Towards the end of the travel agent phase, my Mom died of cancer, and suddenly, I didn't know what to do with my life." She paused and a pensive expression clouded her face. "I suppose, when you lose someone close to you, you come face to face with your own mortality. Anyway, I wasn't sure what to pursue, but I did know that I wanted to spend my time doing something that mattered—something that would make a difference in someone else's life."

Catharine swallowed and said carefully, "You and your mother were close, then?"

"Yes and no. My mother was a wonderful person, but you can love someone without being really close to them. Does that make sense? I loved Mom and I know she loved me—but we were so different, sometimes it was hard to feel really close...."

Catharine took another bite of her dinner and suddenly found it quite tasteless. "Different in what way?"

After giving the matter a moment's thought, Aisling said, "I think it was because Mom was always content to live in a box, and I wanted to be out looking for clues."

Catharine's smile was faintly puzzled. "Looking for clues?"

"You know—like 'Nancy Drew' or Agatha Christie's 'Miss Marple.' I was always hoping to stumble onto some mystery or grand adventure."

"And did you?" Catharine asked gently.

The young woman's dark blue eyes took on a sudden sparkle. "Yes. Doing family history is all that for me and more—it's like a treasure hunt into the past. I love the research, and I love finding clues. Connecting people with their past and their ancestors is more than just exciting—it's satisfying, too. I'm sure part of that has to do with me being adopted. Not knowing anything about my own roots, it means a lot to know I can help others find theirs."

Catharine could only nod, her throat too tight to attempt an answer. Her heart hurt as she watched Aisling unconsciously finger the Claddagh ring on her right hand.

"I think one of my birth parents may have been Irish," Aisling went on with a sigh. "I don't know, of course, but Ireland has always fascinated me. I love everything about it—the music, the literature and the history...."

Catharine's heart was pounding in her ears, her thoughts ringing with unspoken questions. *Have you ever thought about finding your birth parents? Would you like to know who they are?* Then something else was ringing.

"Is that your phone?" Aisling asked, and Catharine gave a little start.

"Oh, yes. It is. Excuse me a moment." Reaching down, she took the cell phone from her handbag.

Aisling watched as a concerned frown suddenly marred Catharine's features. Then she glanced down at her meal, not wanting to eavesdrop on the conversation.

The shrimp *fettuccini* that had arrived steamy hot and tantalizing several minutes before, was now on the lukewarm side. *When will I ever learn not to talk so much?* she thought. But how could she not respond when Catharine's eyes and voice were so bright and eager. Not just polite, but genuinely interested in everything she said. Still, that didn't explain or excuse why she'd launched into such a lengthy account of her life history. Talking about her background was something she rarely did, even with friends, and never with clients. The trouble was, Catharine didn't seem like a client. Neither did Grace.

Catharine set her phone on the table with a frustrated sigh and searched through her handbag.

Observing the tension in her hurried movements, Aisling asked with some concern, "Is everything all right?"

"Yes and no. That was some man calling to tell me that Mother's had car trouble. He was nice enough to call a towing company, but apparently Mother's waiting for me to give her a ride home. I'm so sorry, Aisling. I don't want to go, but—" Catharine shrugged, then took some bills from her wallet and set them on the table. "Would you like to come over to the house later?"

"Thanks, but I think I'll just drive back to Sacramento."

"I really am sorry. I don't know how many times I've tried to convince my mother to get a cell phone, but she won't hear of it."

Aisling smiled, touched by the disappointment in Catharine's eyes and voice. "Please don't worry about it. I hope Grace is all right."

"I'm sure she is, but I'd better not keep her waiting too long. Stay and finish your dinner. I'll call you tomorrow, if that's okay?"

"Yes, of course...."

Catharine grabbed her handbag and gave Aisling one of her warmest smiles. "Mark your place, will you? I want to hear the rest of the story." Then she was threading her way between tables, hurrying toward the front of the restaurant.

Aisling glanced down at the congealed mass of noodles on her plate and decided there was really no reason to stay longer. Especially when home was a good two-hour drive away. She picked up her portfolio, then glanced around for their server. The next second, she caught sight of Catharine's cell phone lying on the table beside her plate.

Grabbing the phone and her own things, Aisling hurried out of the restaurant, hoping she could catch Catharine before she left the parking lot.

A moist breeze carrying the briny smells of the harbor fanned her cheeks as she glanced about. Kinkades had two parking areas for its patrons, one underground and the other street side. Directly across the street from the restaurant was a multi-level parking terrace which added still another choice to her dilemma.

Then, less than thirty yards off to her right, Aisling caught sight of Catharine heading toward a dark green Subaru at a brisk walk. With Catharine practically within shouting distance, she should have been feeling nothing more than relief. Instead, the sudden presentiment of danger had her breaking into a dead run.

The next few seconds emerged in Aisling's mind like a series of shadowy stills projected on a screen. Only yards away now, she could see Catharine clearly. Standing beside the car with keys in hand, she was reaching for something white on the windshield.

"Catharine!"

At the shrill sound of her name, Catharine jerked around and dropped the keys, then bent down to retrieve them. That same moment, Aisling heard a muffled pop and the tinny splintering of breaking glass. Catharine straightened and glanced Aisling's way as somewhere nearby, an engine roared to life and tires squealed. Aisling had a moment's glimpse of a tan vehicle gunning out of a nearby parking aisle. Before she could get a closer look at the driver or license plate, the car was out the exit and speeding up the street.

Time and movement returned to their normal pace as she reached Catharine's side.

"Are you all right?"

"Yes, I just dropped my keys...."

"Thank God, you did." Aisling put a hand to her chest, trying to calm her ragged breathing.

Catharine turned to look in the direction of Aisling's frightened gaze, and saw a small round hole with a spider-like network of veins in the window of the driver's side. A second hole pierced the windshield, marking the bullet's exit. Catharine stared, her eyes widening with stunned realization, and one hand moved to cover her mouth.

"Someone was shooting at you. If you hadn't bent down when you did...." Aisling bit her lip, unable to finish.

Catharine couldn't speak.

"We need to call the police," Aisling said.

Catharine gave a shaky nod and reached into her handbag. "I'll get my phone."

"It's right here." Aisling held out the cell phone. "You left it in the restaurant. That's why I came out to find you."

Catharine leaned weakly against the car, the night breeze adding its chill to the coldness she felt inside. "Aisling, would you mind … could you call them for me?" Shudders of reaction were beginning to quake through her. She listened, grateful for Aisling's presence of mind and the calmness of her voice as she gave the 911 operator the necessary information.

"It won't be long now," Aisling told her. "The police are on their way." Then, seeing Catharine's trembling, she put a hand on her arm. "You're cold. Why don't you go inside where it's warm. I'll stay here and wait for the police."

The thought of Aisling waiting outside alone brought Catharine sharply back from the blurry edges of shock. "No. I'm not leaving you out here alone." Mustering a smile, she wrapped her arms about her sides. "I'm all right. Honestly. It's just reaction."

Aisling's answering smile was on the shaky side. "Don't feel too bad. My knees are so weak, I'm lucky to be standing at all. I just hope we don't have to wait too long."

Catharine gasped as the word 'wait' triggered her reason for leaving the restaurant in the first place. "Oh, no! I forgot all about Mother. She's still stranded somewhere over on Park Street waiting for me to pick her up."

"Well, you can't leave now," Aisling said. "Isn't there someone you could call—a neighbor or—wait a minute. Didn't you mention something about a tow truck coming to get Grace's car?"

"Yes. The man who stopped to help said he'd called for one, but—"

"The man. Then you didn't actually talk to Grace?"

Catharine felt a nameless fear prick her spine. "No, I didn't...."

"Maybe I'm just being overly suspicious after what's happened, but I find that a bit odd. Why wouldn't your mother speak to you herself? For that matter, if a tow truck was on its way, why wouldn't the driver give Grace a ride home?"

Catharine had no answer for either question. Their eyes met in a moment of tense silence. Then Aisling handed her the phone.

"I think you ought to call your home," she said, shivering. "Just in case—well, it wouldn't hurt to check."

Catharine was already punching in the numbers.

12

"share, care, and be fair"

Grace's voice answered after the second ring, her hello sounding untroubled and welcoming as ever. Catherine found herself responding in kind, concern for her mother overriding her own fears.

"Hi, Mother. I just thought I'd check and see if you made it home okay."

"Of course I did. How was dinner? How's Aisling?"

"Aisling's fine. And we're still at the restaurant. In fact—well, that's partly why I'm calling. There's a lot we need to go over."

"Take your time, dear." Grace's voice was pleased. "No need to hurry home on my account."

"If we're too late, I hate to have her drive all the way back to Sacramento tonight—" Catharine glanced at her watch and sent Aisling a silent message, who gave her a quick, assenting nod. "Could you get the guestroom ready for her? Thanks, Mother. No ... no need to wait up for us. Bye now."

The distant whine of sirens grew steadily louder as Aisling faced Catharine with tight-lipped concern. "Grace will have to know what happened tonight."

"Yes, I know." Catharine looked at the bullet-shattered glass, and the white envelope still tucked beneath the wiper blade. "There's a lot that I'd hoped she would never have to know." Turning to Aisling, she said, "And it's important that I tell you as well."

Aisling's eyes held a puzzled, questioning look, but before Catharine could say more, two patrol cars swung into the restaurant parking lot and the darkness was colored with the dizzying glare of flashing red and blue lights.

A tall, dark-haired officer approached them with swift, purposeful steps, introduced himself as Sergeant Platt, and Catharine readied herself for the barrage of questions that would follow.

Talking helped. Somehow, it brought a sense of reality to a situation which seemed anything but real. Sergeant Platt had a calm, efficient manner that was not lacking in compassion. His questions were direct and pertinent, but his voice held a polite concern that smoothed shock's rough edges and offered a much needed sense of security.

"I'm sorry to have you stand out here," he said, "but after taking two DUI's to jail, the backseat of my car isn't exactly pleasant."

While Catharine and Aisling each gave an account of the evening's bizarre events, a few feet away, other officers examined the Subaru and cordoned off the area around the vehicle. Moments later, one of them approached Sergeant Platt. "You better read this," he said, handing him the envelope with gloved hands. "We just dusted it for prints."

The police sergeant slipped on a glove and carefully removed a single sheet of paper. His expression was a taut, unreadable mask as his eyes moved over the page. Then he glanced at Catharine. "I'm assuming you haven't read this yet?"

"No. I was just reaching for it when Aisling called out...."

Sergeant Platt held the note closer to the car's flashing dome lights, saying briefly, "It's better if you don't touch this."

Catharine nodded and braced herself for more sick sexual propositions. Reading the short message, she tried to swallow and found her throat was too dry. Close by her side, she heard Aisling's sudden intake of breath.

> *It's too bad this has to happen, baby, but it's really your fault.*
> *Thanks to you, my life is a living hell. We could have had it all, but you never gave me a chance.*

Glancing away with a little shudder, Catharine met Sergeant Platt's dark-eyed scrutiny.

"Do you have any idea who wrote this?" he asked, folding the paper and slipping it inside his jacket.

She nodded. "His name is Barrett Saunders. I've had problems with him stalking me for several months now—but never anything like this. Detective Adams has been handling the case."

"Lyle Adams?"

"Yes."

"I'd better give him a call. Excuse me."

As he left them to radio dispatch, Aisling put a tentative hand on Catharine's arm. Seeing the concern in her daughter's eyes, Catharine felt a sudden flood of love and gratitude. The next moment, Aisling's arms were wrapped around her in a warm hug. Catharine held her daughter close, needing the small moment of comfort in the night's chaotic events. The moment ended all too soon as she felt

Aisling's body tense with alertness and heard her muttered, "Oh, no. Here comes the media."

Glancing toward the street, Catharine saw a cameraman and smartly dressed newsman from one of the local TV stations heading their way. Thankfully, one of the investigating officers was nearer the line of fire and took a direct hit from the reporter's volley of questions.

"We understand there's been a shooting ... how many shots were fired? Was anyone injured? Have you made any arrests? Do you have any suspects? What was the motive for the shooting?"

In the midst of this, Catharine noticed another news team enter the parking area and found herself automatically averting her head. The reporter was a brash young woman in a beige trench coat who fancied herself the news room's answer to Katie Couric and Meg Ryan. Sandra Jewett had the same gamine-like features and short blonde hair styled by an eggbeater gone wild, but there wasn't an ounce of softness or vulnerability in her manner.

Catharine had had the brief, but uncomfortable experience of being interviewed by the woman a few years back when her last novel was released. Prior to the interview, Sandra Jewett had asked for an exhaustive list of questions and discussion topics, then ignored all of them to ask in baiting tones why the book didn't contain any graphic love scenes. Catharine's simple answer, "Because I respect my character's privacy," had left the reporter slightly floundering and none too pleased.

"Isn't that Sandra Jewett from Channel 9?" Aisling asked in low tones. "I think she recognizes you."

Catharine acknowledged this with a sigh and met the reporter's glance head-on.

"Ms. Cavanagh? Ms. Cavanagh, could I ask you a few questions?"

"I'm sorry, but any questions will have to wait until we've finished the investigation." Sergeant Platt's tone was as polite as ever, but the expression on his face was unyielding as a brick wall.

"Is she under arrest?" the woman persisted.

"No one is under arrest, and would you step back, please," he directed. Then he turned to Catharine, "Mrs. Waller, Miss Montgomery, if you'll come with me...."

The police sergeant ushered Catharine and Aisling inside the taped-off area and toward another patrol car where they would be out of sight and earshot from cameras and microphones.

"Until we can check into this thing with Saunders, it would be better if you didn't say anything to the media," he cautioned.

"My thoughts exactly," Catharine agreed.

"Good. I just talked with Adams. He's handling another call and won't be able to get here for awhile, but he'll be in touch with you as soon as he can. Later tonight, probably." The sergeant's professional demeanor softened into concern. "With that bullet hole through the windshield, we're going to have to tow your car. Would you like me to arrange for a ride?"

"I have my car," Aisling put in. "I was planning on driving Catharine home."

"That's fine," he said. "Under the circumstances, I'll have one of my men follow behind."

"Thank you." Catharine gave him a grateful look, then asked hesitantly. "Is there any way one of your officers could keep the media people occupied for a few minutes, just until we've had a chance to leave? I'd rather not be on the late news show."

Sergeant Platt's smile held wry understanding. "I think we can manage that."

IT WAS NEARLY eleven by the time Aisling pulled into the driveway of the Cavanagh home.

Catharine glanced over her shoulder at the patrol car that drove slowly past, and gave a little sigh. "I hope Mother's gone to bed. I'd just as soon leave all the explanations until morning."

But Grace was not in bed. She met them in the front hallway, fully dressed with eyes that flashed worry. "Detective Adams phoned a few minutes ago," she said crisply. "He asked me to tell you that the police picked up Barrett Saunders and they're holding him for questioning." Grace met her daughter's eyes and waited.

"Did Detective Adams tell you what happened tonight?" Catharine asked quietly.

"Enough," came the clipped answer. "But there's no sense discussing it here in the hall. Come out to the kitchen, both of you. I've made some cinnamon toast and there's hot cocoa heating on the stove."

Sitting at the table, Catharine watched through a haze of weariness as Aisling and her mother brought a plate of toast and steaming mugs of hot chocolate to the table. She told herself she ought to do or say something, but her thoughts refused to focus. Instead her mind kept repeating a series of frightening images, and she didn't know how to turn them off—the spider web of broken glass with its small deadly hole ... Aisling's white face and frightened eyes ... the sheet of paper lit by flashing red and blue lights....

Grace set a mug of hot chocolate in front of her and Catharine tried to summon the energy to drink it. The hot liquid sent its soothing warmth inside, and she sipped it gratefully.

The comfort of warm, safe surroundings eased the way to tell her mother and Aisling about Saunder's notes and the disturbing change in his behavior.

Listening to the account, Aisling didn't know which was more frightening—Barrett Saunder's fanatic obsession with Catharine, or Justin Waller's negligent response to his wife's situation. Both of them ought to be strung up, she thought angrily.

Grace's emotions were doing a similar dance between anger and fear. Her anger was really nothing more than another face of fear, she knew, but right now, she needed it to keep other emotions at bay. Yet, how could she remain angry, seeing her daughter's weary face with worry shadowing her eyes?

"Honestly, Catharine, I don't know whether to shake you, or praise the heavens," she said when Catharine had finished. She answered the dilemma by promptly getting up and putting thankful arms about her daughter.

Seeing the affection between the two, Aisling felt a painful little tug inside. She glanced down and stirred her chocolate, feeling suddenly alone and apart from such closeness.

Grace sat back down with a sigh and eyes that were suspiciously bright. "When are you going to learn that it's all right to share the worries and the burdens along with the joys?" she asked Catharine. "You don't have to shoulder everything by yourself, you know."

"I know, and I'm sorry." Catharine gave her mother a contrite smile. I've been forgetting the rules, haven't I?"

"The rules?"

She nodded and murmured half to herself, "Share, care and be fair. I didn't want to tell you about Barrett because I care so much—but I can see where that really wasn't very fair of me, was it?"

"I'm sure you know what you're talking about," Grace said with a puzzled shake of her head.

"Share, care and be fair. I like that. Who told you the rules?" Aisling asked.

"A sweet old Irishman gave me that advice a long time ago," Catharine answered. "And as long as we're talking about fairness, I have to say that I don't think it's right or fair to expect you to continue working on our family history. Not after what happened tonight. I couldn't live with myself if I thought I was putting you in any danger."

"Your family history isn't putting me in any danger."

"No, but your association with me could."

Aisling set her mug on the table. "I don't agree. From what you've told us, Saunders is definitely an emotionally disturbed man—but he's a stalker, not a serial killer." She shuddered slightly and added, "Being a stalker is bad enough, I know, but his obsession is with you—not me. I agree with Grace. There's no reason why you should have to carry all this by yourself. And as for being fair—I think it would be totally unfair to take this incredible family away from me now—to ask me to stop when I've barely begun. And it wouldn't be fair to Esther," she went on, brushing back a strand of red-gold hair. "Maybe this sounds a little crazy, but from everything you've told me, I feel like I know her already. Esther wants her story to be told. And she wants us to find her family—to know them and understand their lives. How will you write your book if we don't?"

Catharine listened to this passionate outpouring in a state of dazed wonder, while Grace got up and gave Aisling a hard hug and kiss on the cheek.

"You darling girl! Esther would be proud of you. She is proud of you! And so am I!"

Aisling returned the older woman's hug and felt the hurtful separateness fade away. Then Catharine was holding her, too, and there was no longer any fear or worry, only this sure sense of purpose and belonging.

"Are you always this dedicated to your work?" Grace asked, sitting back down and dabbing her eyes with a napkin.

"I don't know if it's dedication, determination, or just plain stubbornness," Aisling answered. Smiling, she added, "Dad used to say it was the 'Irish' in me."

Grace's brows lifted only slightly. "It could be at that."

"You're sure you want to go ahead?" Catharine asked, giving Aisling a close look.

"Positive. In fact, I've been revising my research priorities, and I've come up with a new plan of action. I think we should go to Grass Valley right away—in the next day or two, if you can arrange it. And our trip to the Family History Library in Salt Lake couldn't come at a better time. If you think about it, it's perfect. You really do need to get away. Saunders can't be so all-knowing that he'd follow us there. Besides, I'm sure the police will be keeping a very close watch on him." Scarcely taking a breath, she went on, "If you like, I can make e-reservations for our plane tickets and we could fly out as early as Tuesday or Wednesday of next week. What do you think?"

Catharine's eyes were sparkling and the color had come back to her face. "I think you're amazing, that's what I think. And you're right. I do need to get away." Turning to Grace, she added quickly, "But I don't feel right about leaving you here alone."

"You won't be," Grace said. "I'd definitely enjoy going to Grass Valley with you and Aisling. I haven't seen the town in years. But there's no need for me to tag along while you're doing research in Salt Lake. George and Lucille have been asking me to visit them for months. There's no reason why I couldn't fly to Seattle and spend a week or so with them."

Catharine gave her mother and daughter a smile that was both grateful and slightly dazed. "You two take my breath away," she said.

"I'm sure I'll have to meet with Detective Adams sometime tomorrow, but what do you say we go to Grass Valley on Saturday?"

Aisling leaned back with a satisfied smile. "You're on."

IT WAS WELL after midnight by the time they headed upstairs. After giving Catharine and Aisling a hug in turn, Grace bid them a weary good night. "Good morning, I should say," she amended with a yawn and closed the door to her room.

The guestroom was next to Catharine's and had once belonged to her brother. It had long since been redecorated and refurbished, but it suddenly struck her as strangely poignant that her daughter should be spending the night there. The tug of tender emotion left her feeling a little awkward and unsure. After showing Aisling where to find fresh towels and toiletries, she turned to go, then paused in the doorway.

"There's something I have to say before I can get any sleep tonight," she began. "Something I've been wanting to say all evening."

"What's that?"

"Thank you," Catharine said softly. "Just ... thank you."

Aisling smiled her beautiful smile. "I'm glad I was there. Sleep well."

WHEN CATHARINE SLEPT at all, it was fitful and haunted by dreams of danger and pursuit. In her dreams, she and Aisling were in a house that faintly resembled the one she had shared with Justin, and someone—a man—was trying to break in. She never saw his face, but his presence was overwhelming and filled with dark purpose. She could feel it. And the sense of dread was more terrifying than anything tangible could ever be.

Catharine went from room to room, frantically locking doors and shutting windows against the unseen menace. But somehow, there always seemed to be another room and another door she had missed. The man was closer now. And so was the chilling presence of danger. Strangely, Aisling didn't seem to notice this, and Catharine couldn't make her understand. No sooner had she closed one door, than Aisling would come along and open it again, completely unaware of the man lurking outside.

In frightened desperation, Catharine pressed her body against the door, her fingers struggling with the lock. Why couldn't she lock it? Why wouldn't Aisling listen to her?

The man was on the other side now. She could feel the darkness of his presence, then the force of it, pushing against the door.

"Eamonn ... help me! Help me save her! Aisling, don't go ... please, don't go...."

The sound of her own voice brought Catharine out of the dream and into a reality that was only slightly less frightening. Her mind knew it had been a dream, yet the feeling of danger still remained, pressing heavily upon her. She turned over, struggling to stay awake, knowing if she closed her eyes, *he* would be there, waiting just behind the door. She mustn't sleep, but she was so weary. So weary....

The dream retreated with the dawn, yet strangely, danger's dark presence did not. Catharine rose and dressed, knowing she couldn't speak of it to Grace or Aisling, but the feeling of dread made her watchful and pensive.

Soon after breakfast, Aisling left to drive back to Sacramento, promising to be in touch with them later that day.

"Are you sure you feel up to going to Grass Valley tomorrow?" she asked Catharine before leaving. "You look so tired. Maybe we should wait."

"No, I want to go," Catharine assured her. "I need something positive to look forward to." *Something to push away this feeling of danger...*

And so they made their plans. She and Grace would drive to Sacramento in the morning and meet Aisling there. But first, there was today to be faced and the meeting with Detective Adams.

Grace had insisted on coming along, and if Lyle Adams thought it a little unusual that Catharine's seventy-five year old mother should accompany her, he said not a word. Instead, he ushered the two women into his office, removed a stack of reports from one chair and went to borrow another from an adjoining office.

Since the time of their first meeting, Lyle Adams had struck Catharine as a combination between an aging linebacker and used car salesman. His sandy hair was cut short and his bristled mustache was too long. The man's features were as heavy and thick-set as his beefy shoulders and arms, while the shape and angle of his nose strongly suggested it had been broken at least once sometime in the past. His suits were a little on the slick side and his ties, 100% Technicolor-polyester.

Adams returned with the chair, and after grumbling an apology for not being able to meet with Catharine the previous night, picked up a police report on his desk.

"I've been trying to put together some kind of scenario for what happened last night," he said. "As near as I can figure, whoever called to tell you that Mrs. Cavanagh had car trouble, was probably making the call from his car outside the restaurant. Do you happen to have your cell phone with you?"

"Yes." Catharine reached into her handbag and brought out the phone.

"Do you have caller I.D.?"

She nodded and quickly pressed the button back to the calls of the day before. "Wireless caller," she told Adams. "But the number's unavailable."

He frowned. "I didn't think we'd be lucky enough to have the bas—to have the guy leave us his number, but it was worth a try. Whoever it was, I think it's a safe bet to assume he was also the one who left that note on your windshield. After that, all he had to do was wait for you to come outside. You taking the time to pick up the note, or even unlock your car door would give him a clear shot, and he'd be out of there in nothing flat. In other words, the guy knew what he was doing." Adams put the report down and said, "The police picked up Saunders not too far from his apartment and questioned him for a couple of hours. He denied writing the note and insisted he was nowhere near the restaurant."

"What about the tan car Aisling saw leaving the parking lot," Catharine asked.

"Saunders does drive a tan Ford *Escort*," Adams conceded, "but without a plate number, we can't establish that it was the same car. Her description of the driver was too general to make a positive I.D., and other than her statement, we don't have any other witnesses. As you can see, there's still a lot we don't know, and much of what we do have is circumstantial. I can tell you this. The bullet fired at your car came from a nine-millimeter handgun and was equipped with a silencer. Saunders doesn't own a gun. That doesn't mean he couldn't get his hands on one, but there's no record of any weapons registered in his name."

Catharine studied the detective's face, felt the hesitation in his voice and manner. "And so?" she prompted.

"So we had to let Saunders go."

"You let him go?" Grace burst out.

"We're keeping a close watch on him," Adams assured them. "He knows that and I want you to know that."

Catharine felt no shock or surprise at the news. This is why, she thought. This is why the feeling of dread won't leave. The danger's still here....

Lyle Adams fixed his gaze on her with uncompromising frankness. "Is there anyone else—anyone at all, who might want to hurt you?"

The question caught her by surprise and brought with it a sudden feeling of uneasiness. "No. No one I can think of."

Adams leaned back in his chair and casually picked at a callused palm. "How does your husband feel about what happened last night?"

Her lips parted. "Justin and I are separated," she said after a moment. "I doubt he even knows about the shooting."

"He knows," Adams said calmly. "I wasn't aware you were staying at your mother's, so I called your home."

"Oh ... I see." Catharine felt a familiar tightness grip her chest. "Detective Adams, my husband doesn't drive a tan car."

"I know that."

"And—and he doesn't own a handgun with a silencer."

Again, Adams nodded agreement, then frowned at his callused palm and picked off a crust of dried skin. "Mrs. Waller, I'm not suggesting that your husband is responsible for what happened—but I'm not ready to eliminate him as a possible suspect."

Catharine glanced at her mother, then back to the detective, trying to take it all in. "But—if Justin was at home in San Anselmo, there's no way he could have been waiting for me outside the restaurant. And it certainly wasn't Justin who called to tell me about Mother's supposed car trouble."

"That's true," he agreed easily. "Like I said, I'm not suggesting he's involved, but I like to consider all the angles."

"Angles," Catharine repeated.

Adams nodded and leaned forward, resting his beefy forearms on the desk. "Motive, in other words. Would you say that Mr. Waller might stand to profit financially by your death?"

Once again, Catharine found herself unable to reply. Beside her, Grace made a restless movement, then said quietly, "Catharine, have you told Detective Adams about Justin's gambling problem?"

The detective's sandy brows shot up a notch. "How much is he in for?"

Catharine sighed and shook her head. "I have no idea." Seeing the man's frown, she added quickly, "I'm sorry, but I really don't know the extent of his debts. My husband has never been very open when it comes to finances. I did learn recently that our home has a second mortgage that's several months in arrears, and—" She paused, not wanting to go into Justin's attempt to get an advance on her royalties. "—and there was nothing left in our savings," she finished.

Adams was silent a moment, then said, "I'm sorry to be so personal, but I wouldn't ask if it weren't important."

"Yes, I know."

"Then, can you tell me if your separation is temporary—or is there a divorce in the works?"

Catharine glanced down at her hands. "I've filed for divorce."

"I think maybe it's time your husband and I had a little talk." Adams leaned back in his chair once more. "That doesn't mean I'm eliminating Saunders as a suspect. That note makes him a prime suspect, and he knows it. Assuming of course, Saunders actually sent those notes."

"But if he didn't—who did?" Catharine asked, feeling the tightness inside her strengthen its hold.

"That's what we need to find out," Adams answered grimly. "I'll be in touch if we turn up anything new. Or you can check back with me tomorrow."

"I won't be home tomorrow," Catharine told him. "Mother and I were planning on driving to Grass Valley."

Adams made note of this. "No problem. Why don't you give me a call when you get back."

"I will. Oh, and the middle of next week, I have plans to fly to Salt Lake City to do book research. I'll be gone at least a week, perhaps longer."

"Maybe that's not a bad idea," Adams said. "Just make sure I have a number where I can reach you." He paused, then asked, "Does Saunders have any way of knowing about your plans?"

"I don't see how he could."

"What about your husband? Does he know you're leaving town?"

"No."

Adams' expression was as terse as his voice. "Good. Let's keep it that way."

13

Grass Valley, California

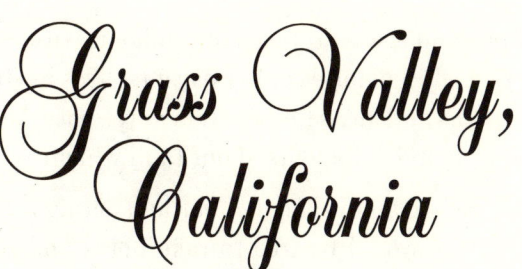

"I love this time of year," Aisling said. "The hills are so green."

She and Catharine and Grace had driven high into California's historic 'gold country.' The lower valleys were behind them and rugged foothills stretched out on either side. The gnarled branches of oaks were fully leafed out in tender new green and roadside fields were adrift with orange poppies and blue lupine.

Grace looked out on the burgeoning spring with contentment and gratitude that the season could still move her. A little over three months had passed since her husband's death and the painful loss had subsided to a bearable ache. Since Aisling's entrance into her life, even the ache was less noticeable. "It's hard to believe it's almost March," she said. "February usually drags so."

"It's been an amazing month," Catharine commented softly, drinking in the luminous beauty of a roadside cluster of lupine. Their deep blue color always reminded her of Eamonn's eyes. She smiled, seeing a similar color reflected in her daughter's eyes.

Aisling's gaze left the road long enough to give Catharine a sideways glance. "After all you've been through, I'm *amazed* you would use that word to describe it."

Catharine glanced down at her notes and said simply, "Oh, it hasn't been all bad."

They had been on the road just over an hour, with conversation drifting from Grace's memories of her parents' lives in Grass Valley, to Catharine's plans and ideas for her Irish novel, with Aisling inserting lively questions and comments about family history.

Aisling had insisted on taking her car and acting as 'designated driver' so Catharine would be free to take notes and photographs along the way. Despite both hers and Catharine's objections, Grace had stubbornly insisted on sitting in the back.

"At my age, I've earned the right to be a back-seat driver," she told them.

"Dad would have said you managed to do that no matter where you sat," Catharine teased, glancing over her shoulder.

Grace laughed good-naturedly at this, her smile acknowledging the truth of her daughter's words. "I only resorted to that when absolutely necessary," she said, eyes twinkling. "Your father may have been Dr. Jekyll in the courtroom, but he could be a regular Mr. Hyde behind the wheel."

Aisling laughed at this and Grace felt a secret thrill as the young woman and Catharine shared a smiling glance. My daughter and granddaughter, she thought, with tender emotion. Despite Catharine's comments to the contrary, she could see a definite resemblance between the two. Their smiles were like twin mirrors, each shining with the same reflection. And they both shared the same eagerness and passionate response to life.

Grace listened with passive contentment as the two engaged in an animated discussion of Esther Clifford Clark's life and loves, puzzling over the gaps in information, and freely throwing out ideas and 'what ifs' for various solutions. Yes, it was a good morning, a good time to be alive. Once or twice the image of Catharine's white face and the threat of shots fired in the darkness came unbidden into Grace's mind, like a cloud passing over the sun, but she shoved it firmly away. She refused to let anything dark or ugly blot out today's sunlight. The darkness and ugliness existed, of course, but for now, it was good to put all that away, and simply revel in the miracle of spring and this time together.

They drove past Auburn with its blend of nineteenth-century 'old town' and twentieth-century sprawl, then headed northeast, with the road climbing higher through forests of Ponderosa pine. Some twenty miles further, the Grass Valley exit brought them around a gentle curve and into the town itself.

In spite of the familiar fabric of chain stores and restaurants, Catharine immediately felt the rich texture of the town's history. Hanging in the closet of present, there were still garments of the past, well cared for and fondly remembered. Boardwalks had been replaced with cement sidewalks, and saloons and mercantiles wore the modern makeup of gift shops and small boutiques, but even this couldn't cover the rustic face of Grass Valley's mining days.

Grace looked at the quaint town through the fond eyes of her childhood, while Catharine saw the narrow streets and buildings as they must have been over a century before in the silver years of the town's prosperity.

Somewhere on one of these narrow, hilly streets was the place where John and Esther had lived, Catharine thought. Here, red-headed Annie had met Hugh McDermott and fallen in love. And here, John and his sons had labored long, ten-hour shifts in the labyrinthine tunnels of the mines, where only a favored few found wealth, and others were glad merely to find work to feed their families.

"Where do you suggest we start?" she asked Aisling.

"I thought the records of the Catholic Church would be a good place. Appropriately enough, the church is located on Church Street, but I'll need some directions from our 'back-seat' driver to get there."

With Grace's guidance, it wasn't long before they were driving down a narrow road with nineteenth-century clapboard cottages on one side, and more modern homes on the other. At its end, Church Street joined Chapel Street near the old Catholic cemetery where towering redwoods shaded the granite headstones. Directly across the street from the cemetery, was an attractive edifice built of creamy white stucco with the fittingly Irish appellation, St. Patrick's Church.

"The building looks too new to have been around when John and Esther lived here," Catharine commented.

"It is," Grace said. "This church was built near the site of the old one though. That's St. Joseph's Hall across the street, and the museum, which used to be St. Mary's convent, is right next door."

"I'm sure the records will be kept here at St. Patrick's," Aisling said, and headed in the direction of a smaller building adjacent to the chapel, where the priest's offices and residence were located.

The receptionist who answered their knock was a gentle-voiced woman with silvery blonde hair and a gracious manner that said she was well accustomed to visitors wanting to search through the parish records. When Aisling introduced Catharine and Grace and briefly mentioned Catharine's plans for a book about her ancestors who had lived in the area, the woman's politeness warmed by degrees to become an interested sparkle.

"Father Patrick isn't here right now," she explained, "but I'm sure he wouldn't mind if you used his office to look at the records."

"That's very kind of you," Catharine told her with a smile, as the woman ushered them from the main reception area into the priest's office. This was an attractive room furnished with a large mahogany desk, a small leather sofa, and white lace curtains at the windows. An ornately carved table sat in front of the window with a few books, religious icons and personal mementos on its polished top.

"Please, sit down and I'll be right back with the ledgers," the woman said and left.

Grace leaned back on the leather sofa, taking in the peaceful simplicity of the room. Aisling and Catharine stood talking in respectful whispers, as if Father Patrick himself were present.

It wasn't long before the receptionist returned with a formidable stack of xeroxed pages in her arms. "Here you are," she said, presenting the stack to Catharine, she left, shutting the door behind her.

"It's not as daunting as it looks," Aisling said, smiling at Catharine's expression. "Since the Clarks and McDermott's only lived here from about 1865 to 1871, we won't need to search through them all."

Catharine stared at the handwritten entries. "They're in Latin."

"That's right. But all you have to do is look for the surnames. I'll help translate the Latin terms. Why don't I divide the records into thirds, and we can each go through some."

Grace waved away her portion with a shake of her head. "I'm here purely as an advisor and to offer moral support. It's up to you two to tackle the Latin."

Catharine took the thick portion of pages Aisling handed her, and sat down beside her mother. Looking at the old records, she felt a sudden pulse of excitement beating inside her. "So this is what it's like ... looking for clues."

Aisling smiled and nodded, then took a chair near the window and bent over the parish entries with intense concentration.

Catharine found it challenging at first, trying to decipher not only the unfamiliar Latin terms, but also the handwriting of various priests. Some wrote in careful, precise script, while others' handwriting was nearly illegible. It wasn't long though, before patterns and similarities in the entries began to emerge, and Catharine found herself searching with more confidence through the various given names and surnames.

The two women worked in companionable silence, with muted sunlight pouring through the lace curtains, and their minds focused on a common goal.

Catharine had examined only a few pages when she heard Aisling's quick intake of breath. Glancing up, she saw her daughter's blue eyes alight with excitement.

"You've found something."

"I think so." Getting up, she moved beside the couch and knelt near Grace. "I want you to see this and give your approval," she said.

The top of the page had been clearly labeled as recorded in the year 1865. Just below the date, in the left margin was the surname McDermott, and beside this, the baptismal record of the infant son of Bridget and Thomas McDermott.

"Look at the names of the godparents," Aisling directed.

Catharine leaned closer to peer over her mother's shoulder and read the names, *Hugo McDermott & Hester Clark*, at the bottom of the entry.

"Hugo and Hester are the Latin names for Hugh and Esther," Aisling explained quickly. "Now we know for certain that the Clarks and McDermott's were here in 1865. Probably, even earlier. In order for Hugh and his mother-in-law to be named godparents, I think it's very likely that he and Annie were married by this time."

"But who's this Thomas McDermott?" Grace asked with a puzzled frown.

"I was hoping you could tell me," Aisling said. "A brother of Hugh's perhaps?"

"Another clue and another mystery," Catharine put in.

Aisling gave her a warm smile. "I'll copy down the entry in my notebook, but you might want to photograph the page."

"I certainly do."

This done, they went back to checking the parish records with new eagerness. In the entries for 1868, Aisling discovered the christening record for Hugh and Annie's eldest son, James Henry, with Esther's son James named as one of the godparents. Grace was totally taken back by this information.

"Are you sure the year is 1868?" she asked. "All our family records list his birth as 1869."

Aisling showed her the page with the year written prominently at the top. "And this would be considered a primary source," she explained, "because the priest made the entry soon after the event took place."

"Well, I'm amazed," Grace said, shaking her head. "Who'd have thought my drunken Uncle Jim was a year older than even he thought he was."

Aisling clapped a hand over her mouth to keep from laughing out loud which seemed, if not irreverent, a disrespectful thing to do in their present surroundings. "Drunken Uncle Jim?" she repeated, lips twitching.

"My mother always referred to him that way," Grace said. "For obvious reasons, I'm afraid. But that's another story."

Catharine advanced the film in her camera and photographed the page with the parish entry. "Well, no matter what he may have become in later years, at this moment in time he must have been a darling bundle of possibilities and hopes fulfilled."

"That's very true," Grace agreed with a sigh. "Poor Jim. I'm sure he never intended to be a disappointment."

Silence settled comfortably around the room as Catharine and Aisling returned to their individual stacks of records. Years and pages went slowly by, with neither one finding anything more of import, and Catharine tried to tell herself there was no reason to feel so disappointed that she had not found anything significant. What they had learned was wonderful, and more than she expected.

Setting aside page 178, she let her glance drift down the following page, carefully checking the surnames. The next moment her heart was thundering in her ears and she felt sudden tears come to her eyes.

"Catharine ... what is it?" Aisling's voice was breathless. "Have you found something?"

Catharine nodded, blinking away the happy tears. "Esther's namesake," she murmured with a radiant smile. "I've found little Esther McDermott."

Grace leaned closer and frowned at the scripted Latin. "Aisling, could you please translate this into plain English?"

Setting her own pages aside, Aisling knelt on the floor in front of them. Sunlight poured through the window, catching the fire of her hair and turning the rich auburn waves into molten gold as she read. *"On the twenty-ninth day of January, Esther, daughter of Hugo and*

Anna McDermott, born on the twenty-fifth day of the same month, entered the sacred font of baptism."

Grace released an amazed sigh. "This must be the baby girl, Ettie, that my mother told me about," she said. "Annie and Hugh had two little girls who died at a young age, but no one in the family had dates or information on either one."

Catharine stared down at the name, feeling a sense of deep, quiet joy. Esther's granddaughter and namesake. Lost in the pages of her family's memories and annals of time—until today.

"You were right," she told Aisling. "Esther does want us to find her family."

They had lunch in a small restaurant specializing in Cornish pastries and meat pies, eagerly talking over the day's finds and planning the afternoon's activities. Aisling suggested that they visit the Searle's Historical Library to see the Great Register, which contained an extensive list of nineteenth-century voters for Nevada County.

"It's possible we might find a marriage record for Hugh and Annie," she said hopefully. "Assuming they eloped some place fairly close by."

Catharine sat, lost in thought, her lunch momentarily forgotten. In her mind she saw Hugh McDermott, the young Irish miner some twelve years older than sixteen-year old Annie Clark, secretly whisking the girl away while her father was working a shift at one of the mines. Had Esther assisted in the couple's plans, or was she kept in the dark until after the deed was done? Catharine could understand John's protective feelings, wanting to shield his young redheaded daughter from the advances of rough, rowdy miners. How had Hugh won Annie's heart, she wondered. And where had they gone to be married?

"Catharine, come back," Aisling said with a laugh. "Either that or take me with you."

Catharine returned to the present with a little jerk, while Grace said, "This is something you'll have to get used to if you're going to work with my daughter."

"It's this place," Catharine said. "I keep drifting off to the past ... seeing scenes in my mind for the book. But I promise, I'll try to keep at least part of my mind in the present."

The present was a little too close when, as they were walking up one of the hilly sidewalks, a car backfired somewhere nearby. Both Catharine and Aisling jumped visibly at the sound, with Catharine reaching out to clutch her daughter's arm.

Throughout the day, none of them had mentioned the shooting incident. The sight of a tan car, whether parked or driving by, was enough to prompt a nervous glance over her shoulder, but for the most part, Catharine had nearly convinced herself that she'd suffered no ill effects from trauma's aftermath.

The backfire changed all that.

"I guess I'm still a little jumpy," she said, waiting for her pounding heart to calm down.

The look in Aisling's eyes held understanding as well as concern. "If it helps any, so am I," she admitted. "Everywhere we go, I find myself staring at tan cars."

"You, too?" Catharine blew out a shaky sigh. "I thought I was the only one."

Thinking of the potential threat to her daughter and granddaughter's safety, Grace felt a helpless surge of anger. "Well, all I have to say is, if I had any inkling who was responsible, I'd make sure he was strung up by his—" She broke off, suddenly finding herself unable to say the word she had in mind.

In spite of her fears, Catharine had to smile. "Strung up by his what?" she prompted.

Grace cleared her throat. "Never you mind, but you can be sure that snake wouldn't be able to walk upright for a good long time!"

"Most snakes don't," Aisling said wickedly. "In fact, I didn't know that snakes had—"

Grace gave her a significant jab with her elbow. "Maybe that's *why*," she said with a knowing look.

AS THE AFTERNOON waned, the past and present moved like cloud shadows over the pine-covered hills. There were moments of sunny illumination, when they found John Clark's and Hugh McDermott's names written in the Great Register, and there were times of confusion, with no clear answers in sight, as they searched in vain for a record of Hugh and Annie's marriage.

With the approach of evening, libraries, offices and businesses closed, and Catharine tried to resign herself to the fact that their day together was nearly over.

"Where would you like to have dinner?" Grace was asking Aisling as they headed back to the car.

"I hadn't really given it much thought," she answered, adding tactfully, "If you're feeling too tired, we can always head back to Sacramento and get some fast food on the way."

"Tired?" Grace shot back. "I'm having a grand time. One of the nicest in a long while. Don't you dare cut things short on my account. In fact, I was going to make a suggestion for the evening—that is, if you and Catharine are *feeling up to it*."

Aisling grinned and took Grace's arm as they crossed the street. "I'm up to anything you are."

"Good! Because I've noticed some posters around town for a concert tonight at the old St. Joseph's Hall."

"Who's playing?"

"A Celtic group called *Golden Bough*," Grace answered. "I can't think of a better way to end the day than to hear some good Irish music."

"It's perfect," Aisling agreed. "How about you, Catharine? Are you up to an evening of good *craic*?"

"That I am," Catharine said in her best Irish brogue.

Grace frowned and asked in stern grandmotherly tones. "Just what sort of 'crack' are we talking about here?"

"It's Gaelic, Grace," Aisling laughed. "And it means to have fun, or a grand time, as you would say."

"Are you sure?" Grace's expression was dubious.

Aisling nodded, still laughing, but Grace was unconvinced. "Well, it might be all right for you to have good *craic* in Ireland, but I don't think you should use that expression here."

By the time they reached the car, Aisling was nearly doubled over with laughter. "Grace, I love you," she said between gasps.

Grace's mouth trembled slightly as she climbed into the back seat. "I love you, too, dear," she said.

THE BUILDING WHERE the Sisters of Mercy had worshipped and taught over a century ago, had been restored in recent decades and converted into a fine meeting hall where community events and concerts could take place. Pews and other sacred emblems of worship had long since been removed, but still watching over the proceedings from high over the front of the hall were solemn Biblical figures in a beautiful stained-glass window entitled, "The Adoration of the Women."

The old wooden floors echoed with the footsteps of arriving concert goers as Catharine, Grace and Aisling found seats on the second row. On the stage in front of them, microphones, sound equipment and an assortment of Irish folk instruments—everything from a mandolin, Irish harp and penny whistle, to a fiddle, accordion and the *bodhran*—lay in readiness.

Catharine got out her notebook, then turned to Aisling with a little smile. "Would you like to know how I search for clues? Clues for characters and stories, that is."

"I'd love to."

"All right." Catharine's voice lowered to a conspiratorial tone. "Carefully observe the two 'men in black' sitting on the front row. One is on our left...." Catharine nodded slightly in that direction where a dark-haired man who was probably thirty-something had just taken his seat across the center aisle. "And one is ..." Her voice dropped below a whisper as she indicated the folding chairs directly in front of theirs. " ... very close by. Notice their physical description. Both men have black hair and mustaches, and might even be fairly close in age. But our first MIB is sitting alone."

Aisling cast a quick sideways glance at the man in question. He was dressed completely in black, from his jacket, shirt and slacks, to his black leather loafers with tassels.

"He's quite nice-looking," Catharine went on, "although a bit on the pudgy side. Now, taking your clues from his clothes and general demeanor, tell me what you think. Is he married, single—a closet member of the Mafia, or a used car salesman from nearby Nevada City?"

Aisling smiled. "Definitely single," she whispered back, entering into the spirit of the game. "As for occupation, I vote for used car salesman. My second choice would be a loan officer at the local bank."

"Very good," Catharine said with an approving nod. "Next we have Man in Black #2. This man is—"

"Drop dead gorgeous," Aisling filled in under her breath.

Catharine choked back a laugh and gave smiling agreement to this assessment.

The man in question was tall, with broad shoulders and a lanky, muscular frame. His black shirt was long-sleeved and collarless, tapering in at the waist, where it was tucked into a pair of tight-fitting black jeans. Black cowboy boots completed the costume, giving him a look straight out of the Old West. So did his raven-black hair, handlebar mustache and tanned, chiseled features.

Catharine's covert glance shifted from the stunning male specimen sitting in front of them to the woman arranging her girth in the folding chair at his side. She was obviously much older than her companion and a good fifty to sixty pounds overweight, with a prominent jaw and straight brown hair pulled back in a tight French bun. Her bulky figure was covered rather than camouflaged by a flowing caftan in swirling shades of purple and black, which resembled a bad bruise rather than anything exotic. Below the caftan, black tights enclosed her sturdy legs, but ended at the ankles, which left her sandaled feet bare. Dangling rhinestone earrings with a matching pendant made up the remainder of the woman's extraordinary wardrobe choices for an evening out.

"And so, we have our MIB #2 and his—rather unique companion," Catharine whispered. Then wrote in her notebook:

Who is the man in black's mysterious companion?

Chapter 13 — Grass Valley, California

Is she: (a) his mother (b) a spinster aunt, recently retired from a lucrative career as a fortuneteller, or (c) his wife.

Grace leaned across Aisling to look at the three choices, then pointed a definitive finger to *(c) his wife.*

Aisling gave Grace an incredulous glance and shook her head, indicating her choice as *(a) his mother.* "Well?" she asked Catharine. "Which one do you think she is?"

"I'm still gathering clues," Catharine answered with an enigmatic smile.

Before they could discuss it further, Man in Black #2 stood up and excused himself, mumbling something to the caftan woman about "coming right back."

"Don't take too long," his companion ordered. "You don't want to miss anything."

Grace pursed her lips and smugly pointed to answer *(c)* once more.

"It can't be," Aisling said under her breath. "I still vote for *(a)*."

Moments later, the woman in the bruised caftan was joined by another couple who took the empty seats beside her.

"Where'd Jim go?" the man asked.

"Said he wanted a drink," came the dubious response, and the woman craned her neck to peer toward the back of the hall. "If he takes too long, I'll have to go fetch him. I don't know what's gotten into my husband lately. Ever since he got his mustache trimmed, the girls have been flockin' all around and he thinks he's really hot stuff."

Grace gave her granddaughter a triumphant, 'I told you so' look, as Aisling sat stunned.

"Unbelievable," she breathed. "What clues did I miss?"

"Appearances can be deceiving," Catharine said. "Don't ever be too quick to accept the obvious."

Fortunately for him, Man in Black #2 returned to his seat moments before the Master of Ceremonies finished a glowing introduction of the husband/wife team, Margie Butler and Paul Espinoza, who, along with fiddle player, Kathy Sierra comprised the Celtic musical group, *Golden Bough*.

Catharine had thought she might write a quick, descriptive sketch of the various band members, but got no farther than a sentence or two when the music began with a medley of lively jigs and reels. Writing anything more was instantly forgotten as the music erased both years and miles. Suddenly she was back in Ireland, with Eamonn's hand holding hers and his blue eyes smiling encouragement as he led her onto the dance floor of the Singing Kettle.... With a sigh, Catharine slipped the notebook under her chair and surrendered herself to the music's timeless spell.

Song after song echoed through the old hall, from the foot-tapping, hand-clapping, "Ballyconnnell Fair" to ancient airs composed by Ireland's beloved blind harpist, Turlough O'Carolan. Margie's haunting voice and flawless ability on the Irish harp, gave sensitive interpretation to traditional melodies passed down for generations, while Kathy's nimble fingers played the fiddle with a vivacious energy and technique that made one wonder if the young woman hadn't made a pact with the wee folk themselves. As one number ended and another began, Paul moved from one instrument to the next with seamless ease and enjoyment.

Watching him, Grace whispered to Aisling, "I don't usually care for a pony-tail and a mustache on the same person—but on him it looks—what was that expression you used?"

"Drop dead gorgeous," Aisling filled in.

"That's the one."

There were songs of hearth and home … songs of myth and legend … of love won and lost. Through it all there was the pulse of past times, a heartbeat from the long ago … calling out for them to remember and come back … come back to Ireland.

Aisling heard the call and felt a longing inside so piercingly sweet it almost resembled pain. A longing for her own people—to find them and know them. A longing to belong to a family—*her* family.

Catharine heard it and felt an aching river of lost love swirling around her in the confusing eddies of the present. Eamonn's daughter sat beside her, with the same dark blue eyes and the same passionate spirit as her father. If only Aisling could know him. She needed to. Deserved to. Was there any way?

Grace, too, heard the call, felt it in the insistent rhythm of the *bodhran* as clearly as she felt the pulse of her own heartbeat, and in a moment of sudden clarity, knew what she must do. Why hadn't she thought of it before now? Catharine and Aisling would go to Ireland … and she would take them.

Glancing at her granddaughter's shining eyes and smiling lips, the rightness of the decision filled Grace with warm, unshakable certainty. Yes, it was time … time for her little dreamer to discover the 'land of saints and scholars.' And perhaps, God willing, the father who had been denied this sweet treasure so long ago.

14

. . . *looking for clues at the FHL*

Plans and possibilities punctuated the days that followed. It was satisfying to have sure, purposeful goals, Catharine thought, as she moved from task to task. She and Aisling had reservations to fly to Salt Lake City early Wednesday morning, with Grace heading for Seattle that same day. Not only was there the pleasurable anticipation of the trip to Salt Lake with her daughter, but the promise of a trip to Ireland in the near future.

When Grace had first broached the subject on the drive home from Grass Valley, Catharine had known immediately that going back to Ireland was necessary and right on many levels. Book research and family history might be the obvious reasons, but there were others even more important.

Eamonn needed to know about Aisling. To deny him that knowledge would be even more cruel than what her father had done. No matter how controlling or selfish his actions had been, part of her father's motives stemmed from his love for her. She understood that much, at least. She must try to summon the strength to contact Eamonn out of a similar motive—not out of duty, or fear—but out of love.

She and Grace had talked until late on Sunday night about Ireland, Aisling, and the future.

"Don't wait too long to tell her," Grace had cautioned. "I know how difficult it will be for you, but it will only get more difficult the longer you wait."

Knowing her mother was right, didn't make the prospect of telling Aisling the truth any easier. Nor did knowing the 'why's' answer the attendant questions of 'when, where and how'.

"There isn't a script for something like this," Grace had said. "Just trust your feelings. You'll know what to do."

Would she? Catharine seriously wondered. All her life she had loved words, delighted in their beauty, power and meaning. For years, the characters in her books had spoken to her and she had written their diverse dialogue; whether realistic or romantic, pithy or poignant, their voices had been clear in her mind. But when it came to choosing the words to tell Aisling that she was her mother, she felt mute and speechless. Words fled and only fear remained.

The evening before their flight to Salt Lake, Aisling arrived at the Cavanagh home, suitcase in hand, and excitement shining in her eyes. She had initially offered to meet Catharine and Grace at the Oakland airport, but Grace insisted there was no need to make such a long drive so early in the morning. "Come over Monday evening for dinner and spend the night," she told Aisling. "Then we can all leave for the airport together."

Now, seeing Aisling's eagerness and enthusiasm, Catharine felt the pressures of a hectic day fade. There had been calls to her editor Hal Kellerman in New York, a necessary check with Detective Adams and her attorney, then picking up her car from the repair shop and a stop at the bank.

Detective Adams' news was less than encouraging. Thus far, the police investigation hadn't produced any leads. No fingerprints had been found on either her car or the envelope. Dealing with an unidentifiable threat, and having no answers forthcoming was like trying to breathe in a plastic bag. It had to have been Barrett Saunders who sent the notes and fired that shot. Her mind couldn't cope with any other possibilities.

Charles Wentworth's latest figures on her finances and settlement dates for the divorce were equally inconclusive. The day's only positive news had come from her editor. Hal was more than enthusiastic with her initial outline for the new book and confident that a healthy advance would be forthcoming. But that didn't help her current circumstances. Catharine had no options other than to draw out a substantial amount from the estate money left to her by her father. At least she had that. Yet, it was frustrating to know there would have been more than enough money for a dozen trips to Salt Lake and Ireland, if Justin hadn't pilfered and gambled away her savings and royalties.

Aisling's presence brought positive energy back to the day. Her smile and laughter warmed the house and brightened the rooms. Listening to her enthusiastic plans for research during dinner, Catharine felt herself more than just relaxing. It was as if life were suddenly whole again instead of fragmented. By seven-thirty that evening, Catharine was humming to herself as she finished a last load of laundry. There was even time enough to permit herself the luxury of sitting down to double check a few research books and writing materials she might want to bring along.

Grace was upstairs finishing some last minute packing and chatting with her sister on the phone, while Aisling was on the computer in the study, doing a little advance preparation on the Internet for their trip to Ireland.

Catharine spread out a stack of books and some maps of Ireland on the coffee table in the living room, and had just begun going over her research list, when she heard the doorbell's chime.

"I'll get it," she called up the stairs, thinking it was probably Charles Wentworth. The attorney had promised to drop by some papers that needed her signature before they left town. Seven-thirty is just about right for Charles, she thought, remembering how he'd assured her he would be by no later than seven.

Catharine opened the front door, then stared. "Justin?"

He stood, hands in his pockets, looking as darkly handsome as ever in a tan shirt and black slacks, with a black and tan windbreaker.

"Surely you haven't forgotten me already?" he said, flashing one of his charming, if slightly mocking smiles. "I'm still your husband, even if it's only for a few more months."

There was a time when a remark like that would have prompted feelings of guilt or a quick apology on her part, even if she had done nothing that required one. Why had it taken so long to see through the smooth smiles and manipulative behavior? Now there wasn't enough emotion left inside to feel much of anything for him, not even anger.

"I was expecting my attorney," she answered shortly.

"I guess I should have called first," he allowed, "but I wasn't sure you'd answer. You look wonderful," he added, and when she didn't respond, went on with a concerned glance. "A lot better than I expected after what Adams told me."

"You've talked with Detective Adams?"

"I just came from his office...." He paused and Catharine knew he was waiting for her to invite him in.

"What do you want, Justin? As I said, I'm expecting my attorney."

"Mainly to make sure you're all right. Ever since Adams called me late Thursday night, I've been worried as hell."

"That was five days ago," she said, not buying the concern in his eyes and voice. "You could have called and saved yourself all that worry."

Her comment caught him off guard, but only for a moment.

"Well, thanks a lot." He gave her a wounded look. "It's not like you to be so sarcastic."

Catharine sighed, knowing there was no point in trying to defend or deny the accusation. Whatever she said, Justin would only twist the words to suit his own purpose. Then, glancing past him, she noticed an older model Toyota parked in the driveway.

"What happened to the Porsche? Have you been in a wreck?"

He gave a mirthless laugh. "In a matter of speaking. A real financial wreck, as you well know. So, I sold it."

"You sold the Porsche?"

Justin answered her incredulous look with a crooked smile. "It might not seem like much, but I had to make a start somewhere. You know, try to salvage a little from the mess I've made of our finances." He paused, then asked, "Can I come in?"

"Now isn't a good time—"

"I promise I won't stay long," he said and edged his way past before she could say another word.

Alarm bells rang out the moment she saw him heading for the living room. The travel pamphlets and her books on Ireland were still on the coffee table. Her mind still balked at the possibility Justin might want to harm her, yet something about Detective Adams' warning had her moving past her husband and quickly gathering up the books.

"You don't trust me, do you?" he said, sitting down on the sofa and casually resting one leg across his knee.

Catharine set the books and pamphlets on a shelf near the fireplace, then turned to face him. "After what you've done, can you give me one good reason why I should?"

Justin acknowledged the truth of this with a shrug. "I know, I know—but I had to see you! Whether you believe me or not, doesn't really matter. I just had to know that you were all right. After what happened, I can't believe the police let Saunders go. The man's unstable—an emotional time-bomb waiting to explode—and they let him go!"

His eyes and voice were full of righteous indignation, yet Catharine found herself listening to his outburst with weary patience, as if she were a disinterested outsider and not his wife of twenty years.

"Have they provided you with some kind of protection?" he was asking.

She sat down in the wingback chair opposite the sofa. "Not yet."

"What the hell are they waiting for? Does it take another attempt on your life before they'll do anything?"

"Justin, please ... I'd really rather not discuss it."

"Sorry, sorry. I didn't mean to upset you, but I feel so damn helpless. I just wish there were something I could do—"

"There's nothing you can do."

"Nothing?" he shot back. "You expect me to just stand by and do nothing?"

"No. All I'm trying to say is—where you're concerned, I have no expectations. None at all." Her voice was calm, without a single thread of anger, but the finality in her tone found its mark.

For a brief moment, the mask of worry and concern fell away and Catharine glimpsed a hardness in Justin's eyes that sent a chill coursing through her.

Then she heard the eager rush of footsteps down the stairs, and Aisling burst into the room. "Catharine! Wait 'til you hear—I've found a fantastic rate on airfare to Dublin! Aer Lingus is running a special and—oh, I'm sorry. I didn't realize you had company…."

"I'm not really company," Justin said, rising to his feet and offering Aisling his hand along with a winning smile. "I'm Catharine's husband, Justin Waller."

"Mr. Waller," Aisling replied, but her own smile was suddenly on the stiff side. Still, she took the hand offered to her.

"Justin, please," he said warmly.

The young woman's smile stiffened even more and she withdrew her hand.

Catharine could have hugged her. "Justin, this is Aisling Montgomery. Aisling's been helping Mother and me with some family history and genealogy."

"Genealogy?" Justin's surprise had to be genuine, but he recovered quickly enough. "That's great! I thought at first, you might be a travel agent." Turning his smile on Catharine, he said with casual interest, "I didn't know you were planning a trip out of the country. Why Ireland? I can think of quite a few places to visit this time of year that are a lot warmer than Ireland."

Aisling saw Catharine's tight-lipped expression, and sensed her hesitancy to discuss their plans. "Will you excuse me, Mr. Waller?" she said. "I have some things to do. It was … nice meeting you." She gave him one of her warmest smiles, thinking, *Not nice at all, actually, but very interesting.*

"Stunning young woman," Justin commented after Aisling had gone. "But she's not really a genealogist, is she."

"Yes, she is—and a very good one. Mother hired her to work on some family lines."

"Ah, hence the trip to Ireland … a visit to the 'old sod'," he said with a poor attempt at an Irish brogue. "The trip should do Grace a lot of good, after all she's been through this past year. How's she doing, by the way?"

"Mother's fine. Was there anything else you needed?"

The handsome mouth tightened. "Very cool, aren't we? I guess I deserve that." He moved obligingly to the front door, then gave her a last, lingering glance. "Take care of yourself, Baby," he said softly.

I'm not your Baby, Catharine silently told his departing figure. Now that he was gone, reaction set in, leaving her legs weak and her hands unsteady as she shut and locked the door.

"Catharine?"

She turned to see Aisling on the stairs behind her. "I just wanted to apologize for bursting in on you like that."

"There's no need to apologize"

"Are you sure? I had the feeling I must have said or done something—you looked so uncomfortable."

"Justin makes me feel very uncomfortable," Catharine admitted frankly. "I wasn't expecting him, that's all."

Aisling's expression remained unconvinced, but she didn't pursue the subject further. "Maybe now's not a good time to look at those airfares…."

Chapter 14   ... *looking for clues at the FHL*   219

"No, I'd love to see them," Catharine said and followed her back upstairs.

The words came easily enough, but Justin's visit left a feeling of disquiet behind, that left her out of sorts and more than a little worried. She tried to console herself with the fact that Justin had no way of knowing when they were going to Ireland, only that they were going sometime in the near future. But it didn't help, not when she remembered the look of surprise in his dark eyes.

MORNING SKIES WERE overcast, with rain threatening and traffic heavier than usual as they drove to the airport. Catharine tried to ignore a nagging headache, the remnants of a restless night, but by the time they arrived, her nerves felt like frayed wires. It didn't help that Grace was certain she'd left the iron on and had visions of the house burning down in their absence. Catharine gave patient reassurance that this was not the case, and even if it were, Mrs. Collins was right next door and would be checking on the house. In spite of her inner tension, she managed to see her mother off on her flight to Seattle with a cheerful face and hugs of assurance that they would call often and report on their progress.

As she and Aisling sat down to wait for their flight to Salt Lake, Catharine felt she could allow herself a brief moment of congratulation.

Then Aisling said, "You're doing it again."

"Doing it?"

"Breaking the rules. 'Share, care and be fair'—remember?"

Before she could protest, Aisling went on, "I'm not trying to pry, but it's obvious there's something bothering you. And if it would help to talk about it, well—I'm here."

Catharine released a tense breath. "Thanks. I think I'm just feeling the backlash from a lot of little things."

"*Little* things?" Aisling repeated. "Like being followed and shot at by some mentally unbalanced stalker, and then having a royal jerk of a husband show up on your doorstep, trying to shmooze his way back into your good graces—" She cut herself off with a grimace. "Sorry. I wasn't going to say that last part out loud. I really don't have the right to ... well, anyway, I shouldn't be so outspoken."

Catharine couldn't help smiling at this. "I'm not offended, but I am curious. How did you know ... about Justin?"

Aisling didn't answer right away. She didn't really understand it herself, but she couldn't ignore the feeling she'd had when she met the man's eyes. On the outside, Justin Waller might be handsome and charming in a carelessly confident sort of way. But on the inside—something about him instantly raised her hackles.

"I don't know all that much," she admitted. "It's more of a feeling. I just don't trust him."

Catharine nodded. "Neither do I. And I wish it hadn't taken me so long to learn that particular lesson." She gave a little shudder, then said with weary determination, "But I promise you, I won't let Justin or anything else interfere with our trip."

"I hope you don't feel like you have to be 'Miss Cheerful' and carry on for my benefit," Aisling said. "Honestly, Catharine, I think the way you're handling everything is, well, pretty amazing. But you're not super human. The stress is bound to take a toll. Anyway, I just wanted you to know that it's perfectly all right with me if you feel like crap now and then."

Catharine didn't know whether to laugh or cry, but laughing felt wonderful and released a hard knot of worry inside.

"As long as I have your permission," she said, and drew a deep breath. "Actually, I'm feeling better already."

Aisling's blue glance was warm. "Good! I'm so glad you're coming on this trip. I know we're going to discover some wonderful things before the week is out."

"I hope so," Catharine said, but her thoughts were not on genealogy.

THE PLANE LANDED in Utah's capital city shortly before noon. Gone were the gray skies and moist, coastal fog, and in its place, air that was dry and biting in its clarity. Riding in the shuttle bus from the airport to the Marriott Hotel, Catharine took in the piercing blue of the sky, and the snow-covered peaks of the Wasatch Mountain Range with a sense of wonder. A gusty breeze from the south lent added freshness, blowing away the last remnants of her 'soul fog' and leaving brisk excitement and anticipation in its place.

A half-hour later they were checked in at the Marriott and had unpacked a few things in their room. It was spacious and attractive, decorated in muted shades of mauve, ivory and green, with thick carpets and thick towels. Two queen-size beds, with a lamp and night table between, were set against one wall, with dressers on the opposite side. In a sunny corner near the windows was a large round table that could easily double as a desk for their work. An added welcome was the bowl of fresh fruit and a vase filled with spring flowers. Daffodils, tulips, lilies and sprigs of heather filled the room with spring's delicate fragrance.

Aisling had gone into raptures the moment she saw the flowers and the accompanying card from the hotel management, welcoming Catharine as their guest.

"Traveling with a famous author has its perks," she teased, glancing around the lovely room. "It'll be rough, but I think I could get used to this."

Catharine gave Aisling a smiling look as she finished putting a few things on hangers. "I'm glad everything meets with your approval." Wanting to respect her daughter's privacy, she had initially offered to reserve separate or adjoining rooms for their stay, but Aisling's response to this was as practical as it was candid. "Why go all that expense? I appreciate the thought, but it seems like such a bother to go back and forth every time we want to talk or discuss something."

Catharine gave casual agreement to the arrangement, while inwardly rejoicing at the opportunity this would afford to spend more time with her daughter.

Now, as they finished a quick lunch of soup and salad in the hotel coffee shop, Aisling gave Catharine a close look. "Tell me honestly— do you feel like taking it easy for awhile, or are you ready to look for clues?"

"More than ready to look for clues!" Catharine said, and knew it was true.

Minutes later, with portfolios in hand, they left the hotel and headed up West Temple Street. The Marriott was within easy walking distance, only a block away, from the Family History Library and Salt Lake's historic Temple Square. Spring was still weeks away from the high mountain valley that had been settled by Mormon pioneers over a century and a half before, but the pansies and primroses blooming in the gardens of Temple Square were colorful harbingers of its approach.

Aisling had suggested they walk through the grounds on their way to the library, and almost the moment they passed through the tall iron gates, Catharine felt a distinct change of atmosphere. The twentieth century trappings of business and traffic and people on the move were only yards away. Yet here, within the old sandstone walls, there was reflective beauty and peace.

"Have you been to Salt Lake before?" Aisling asked, as they walked past the historic Tabernacle and massive granite Temple with its pointed spires.

"Years ago, for a book signing," Catharine said, "but it was a rushed visit; an in and out sort of thing. Do you come here often?"

"At least four or five times a year. Sometimes it's for clients, other times a genealogy conference. But whatever the reason, I always enjoy coming."

Catharine breathed in the contemplative loveliness of the grounds. "I can see why."

The Family History Library was housed in a large granite-faced building directly across from Temple Square. With books, records, and microfilms stored on five floors—three above ground and two below, Catharine was amazed at the library's size and scope. In addition to its massive collection of books, vital records and films, there were computers, microfilm readers, and quiet areas for individual study available to library patrons. Located in a central position on each floor was an information desk and copy center, each with a trained staff as well as with volunteers to assist patrons in every aspect of their research.

Catharine followed in her daughter's redheaded wake as Aisling made a beeline for the second floor where reference books and microfilms pertaining to the U.S. census were located. In minutes, Aisling had made a list of all the John Clarks living in Brooklyn, New York in 1860, then she was off to find the necessary films. Watching her, Catharine was reminded of an Irish step dancer, her movements quick and light, with practiced sureness and grace.

Soon they were sitting side by side in an area of subdued lighting where rows of individual cubicles with microfilm readers were located.

Aisling gave Catharine a few basic instructions on how to load the film and they went to work.

It was slightly disconcerting for Catharine to realize how little she knew about genealogical research. Despite Aisling's instructions, she felt all thumbs trying to thread the film into the machine. Sheer determination finally won out, and she sat down to view the census film.

When the image came up horizontal rather than vertical on the lighted screen, she briefly considered asking Aisling what the problem might be, but hated to bother her. Deciding there must be something wrong with the machine, Catharine craned her neck sideways to adjust to the film's image, and began scanning the names.

Awkwardness was soon forgotten as she discovered the large proportion of Irish immigrants living in the Brooklyn of 1860. Somewhere among them were her great-great grandparents, John and Esther Clark.

Moments later, Aisling glanced over and noticed the awkward angle of Catharine's head and neck. Trying not to smile, she got up and turned the center knob to adjust the screen to its proper vertical image.

"It's a little easier to see this way," she said, not wanting to embarrass her.

Catharine's shoulders began to shake with suppressed laughter at her own ignorance. "It's a good thing you're here, or I might have to go through life with my neck permanently twisted sideways. It's not easy, being mechanically challenged," she said and they both laughed.

Catharine was still searching for the John Clark living in Ward 6 of the city, when Aisling turned to her with a pleased smile and whispered, "I've found them!"

Wonderful words, Catharine thought, and moved her chair closer to Aisling's. Elation turned to puzzlement as she stared at the census page. "Are you sure these are the right Clarks? The name here is Hester, and the woman's age is 50. Esther couldn't have been more than 37 or 38 at the time."

"Hester and Esther were used interchangeably," Aisling explained, "and you might as well get used to the fact that census takers often recorded the wrong age. Look at the names of the children—there's Ann and James and Henry. And from what you've told me, I think you'll be pleased with the added bonus on the next page." Aisling turned the handle and scrolled the film. "It seems Esther had several Irish boarders to help her meet expenses while John was away, and one of them is—"

"Her brother Henry!" Catharine burst out, forgetting to keep her voice down.

"Yes, Henry. And another piece of the puzzle, nicely in place," Aisling said with satisfaction. "I'll take this film to the copy center, then we can move on to the 1850 census."

Catharine's elation at their initial success turned to disappointment when, after checking some two dozen John Clarks living in Brooklyn, they failed to find John and Esther among them.

Aisling was not the least bit deterred. "If they immigrated sometime in 1848, it's possible they were still living in New York City by 1850. Let's check the index."

"Good heavens, there's got to be at least sixty of them," Catharine said as they looked at the long columns of John Clarks marching down the page. "Seeing that list makes me wish Esther ran away with someone named Humperdinck instead of Clark."

"It's going to take some time," Aisling agreed. "Maybe we should try hitting it fresh tomorrow morning."

"Isn't the library open in the evening?"

"Yes, until ten."

"Then let's come back after dinner."

By evening's end, they had checked barely a third of the names on the list, and Esther and her coachman still remained elusively out of reach.

"There's no need to count sheep tonight," Catharine commented with a groan, when they were back in their hotel room and preparing for bed. "If anything, I'll probably dream about census pages and John Clarks marching past in endless succession. I don't know how you do it!"

Aisling just laughed. "You get used to it. It's all part of the hunt. Do you mind if I watch the news?"

"Go right ahead. I'm rarely in bed before eleven. I think I'll read for a while."

Five minutes later, Aisling glanced over to find Catharine sound asleep, with the book lying across her chest. Smiling, she got out of bed, placed the book on the night table, and turned out the light.

CATHARINE SLEPT DEEP and dreamlessly, and discovered much to her amazement that she could hardly wait to get back to the Family History Library the next morning. What had felt like an insurmountable task the night before was only a challenge today, and a stimulating one at that.

Feeling a small sense of personal triumph, she even managed to load the microfilm correctly, and without help.

Aisling gave her a smiling sideways glance. "For someone who's mechanically challenged, you're doing very well."

"I have a great teacher," Catharine answered.

All around them, dozens of other patrons were intent on their own research, yet Catharine was increasingly aware of the common, unifying thread that had brought them all to this amazing place—the family.

Her second film of the day contained a record of residents living in Ward 17 on New York's East Side. It was here at the bottom of the page that she found them, the names smeared and blackened by some census taker's leaky pen. And there was more. Living with John and Esther and their year old daughter, was sixty-year old Kate Clark.

Turning to Aisling, she asked, "Do you think Kate could be John's mother?"

"It's very possible, but we can't be certain without some other verifying source. Unfortunately, those sources are limited. Kate must have passed away sometime between the years the two censuses were taken. My guess is, shortly before John left for California and Esther moved to Brooklyn."

"Aren't there any death records we can check?"

"Yes, but the coroner's reports aren't indexed or alphabetized. If Kate's there at all, it would take quite some time to go through nearly ten years of entries."

"Then what about church records?" Catharine asked, refusing to be daunted. "Wouldn't those help?"

Aisling smiled at Catharine and shook her head. "Oh, dear. I think you've got it."

"Got what?"

"The fever. Doing family history is addictive, you know, but it's never fatal."

"Far from fatal," Catharine said, her eyes sparkling. "It brings people to life!"

15

"Mr. M."

After two productive days and positive finds, Catharine's and Aisling's third day of research was tedious and tiring, with frustrating dead-ends and missing information.

"Maybe we ought to take a break," Aisling suggested as they finished dinner that evening. "We could always take in a movie at the Crossroads Mall."

Catharine toyed with a forkful of cherry cheesecake that had looked so appetizing when she was starving and now, after a full meal, had definitely lost its appeal. "We do need a break, but we haven't been down to the floor where the Irish records are kept. Even if it's too soon to do any research, I'd love to look through the book section. Do you mind?"

Catharine thought she glimpsed a moment's hesitation in Aisling's expression. Then she answered lightly, "Sure, why not? But could we go back to our room first? I'd like to freshen up a bit."

Catharine was amused and faintly puzzled as she observed what Aisling considered "freshening up." This involved a complete change of clothes, with Aisling first trying on a silky top in pale blue, and then a beige blouse, before settling on a snug, ribbed sweater in deep forest green. Next, her *Levi's* were discarded in favor of gray slacks, and she spent another fifteen minutes redoing her makeup and hair.

"Maybe I should change into something a little nicer," Catharine commented, giving her jeans and ivory sweater a critical glance. "Standing next to you, I feel positively dowdy."

Aisling's cheeks took on a rosy tint that had nothing to do with her carefully applied blush. "You—dowdy? You couldn't look dowdy if you tried. Honestly, Catharine, you're so classy. That man sitting across the aisle from us this afternoon couldn't take his eyes off you. Didn't you notice?"

"You mean the one who was close to ninety and wheezed every time he cranked the handle?"

"No, not him," she said, unable to keep from laughing. "The distinguished one with—"

"The cane," Catharine filled in dryly. "I may be a historical romance writer, but occasionally, reality sets in. Even I can't imagine romance blossoming in the Family History Library."

Aisling's mouth twitched slightly as she gave her appearance one last check in the mirror. "You're absolutely right. Neither can I."

As they stepped off the elevator on the B-2 level of the library, Catharine noticed Aisling taking a quick, covert glance around the tables and computer area near the Information Desk. Whatever she was looking for must not have been there, because her manner relaxed noticeably after that.

"Some of the basic reference books are on the wall here to your left," she explained, "and the rest of the Irish books are over on the far wall."

"Lead me to the Irish," Catharine said eagerly, and followed Aisling's lead past the information desk and two rows of computers to the west wall where rows of metal bookshelves stretched from floor to ceiling.

Catharine glanced longingly at the various titles as they moved down the narrow aisles between shelves. "Good heavens, where does one start? I could spend days here."

"It is pretty impressive," Aisling agreed. "There are books covering material on each of the Republic's twenty-six counties, and all of Northern Ireland as well."

They were nearing the end of one aisle when Aisling gasped and did a sudden about face.

Catharine glanced at her in alarm. "What's wrong?"

"He's here," she mumbled, burying her red head in a thick tome listing pedigrees of English and Irish gentry.

Cold, clenching fear gripped Catharine's heart as the image of Barrett Saunders' face shot through her mind. "He can't be...."

Aisling's head jerked up from the book. "Oh, Catharine, I'm so sorry! I'm such an idiot! I didn't think...."

Catharine took in her daughter's apologetic look and flaming cheeks. "I take it, we're not in any danger of being shot at?"

"No." Aisling slowly shook her head.

"Well, that's good to know." Catharine blew out a shaky breath. "But you still haven't answered my question. Who's here?"

Aisling peered between the shelves, then back at Catharine with a sheepish expression. "Mr. Misogynist."

"Mr. Who?" Catharine had to choke down a wild impulse to burst out laughing.

"Misogynist. I–I don't know his real name, but almost every time I come down to the Irish section, he's here."

"Other than the obvious implications of the name, I don't understand why this should be a problem. You visit the library, what—four or five times a year?"

"It shouldn't be a problem, I know," Aisling said with a frustrated sigh. "It isn't a problem. Not really. It's just—whenever I'm here, I always seem to bump into him and—" She raised her eyes, then returned the book to the shelf with a vengeance. "And I just don't function very well when he's around."

Catharine struggled to keep back a smile. "Function in what way?"

"You know—think, concentrate, perform basic motor skills—things like that."

"Oh, I see." Catharine was smiling openly now. "Well, where is he? I don't think I've ever met a real live misogynist. What am I saying? I've been married to one for nearly twenty years."

Aisling let out a shaky laugh, then gestured with a slight movement of her head. "He's sitting at the next to the last table, near the microfilm readers."

Catharine moved a step or two closer to the end of the aisle and peered around the corner. "Mmm. You mean Blackbeard the pirate with the baseball cap?"

"That's the one. Catharine, what are you doing?" Aisling asked in a horrified whisper.

"Nothing drastic, I promise. I was simply going to take this lovely book about Irish landowners and sit down at one of the tables to read. But if you're feeling too uncomfortable—"

"No, no ... that's fine."

Catharine felt a moment's wicked impulse to choose the same table where Mr. Misogynist was seemingly intent on his own research, but seeing Aisling's frozen expression, took a seat two tables away instead.

Nearly ten minutes passed with Aisling dutifully staring at her notebook without turning a single page.

Observing her, Catharine found it difficult not to smile. Her own book on Irish landowners would have made fascinating reading, had it not been for the fascinating little drama going on much closer at hand.

Mr. M.'s dark good looks made him an ideal candidate for a character in one of her books, she decided. His hair was black and wavy with a few tantalizing touches of premature gray. He wore a beard and mustache, both neatly trimmed. A bright yellow tee shirt was an effective contrast to his swarthy coloring, as well as emphasizing a physique that was fit and muscular.

Catharine placed the man's age somewhere in his mid to late thirties. And as far as she could determine, he seemed totally absorbed in his work. A black leather portfolio lay open beside him, along with several microfilms, books and papers. Once, he got up to return a film to its metal filing drawer, and Catharine thought she detected a jerking pause in his movements as he glanced in their direction.

Another time, Mr. Misogynist walked directly past their table on his way to get a book from one of the shelves. His stride was brisk and purposeful, and except for a subtle sideways glance from those dark eyes, there was nothing to indicate Aisling's presence meant anything significant to him.

Ah, yes, he's definitely story material, Catharine thought, mentally replacing the reference book in his hand with a shining cutlass, and the yellow tee shirt with one of those white, long-sleeved affairs that were always open from neck to waist. She had no idea why Aisling would label him a woman-hater, but one thing was certain. This gentleman pirate was as unlike the stereotypical image of a genealogist as her stunning, redheaded daughter.

Her own book momentarily forgotten, Catharine watched covertly as one of the library staff, a pleasant-faced man wearing a white shirt and dark slacks, approached Mr. M. to offer a few words of praise for some recent research find.

Aisling didn't noticeably react or glance up, but Catharine saw her white-knuckled grip tighten on the book she was reading.

Mr. M. flashed the staff worker a bearded grin and answered with an easy shrug, "I'm glad I was able to help." Then he returned to his own table the long way around.

Interesting, Catharine thought. Moments later, she stretched and closed her book. "Well, I suppose we ought to call it a night."

Aisling quickly agreed and nearly knocked over the chair in her eagerness to take their books back to the return shelf. Where she had been openly reluctant to leave the library their first two nights, now it was all Catharine could do to keep up as she sped toward the elevator.

For all intents and purposes, Mr. M. never noticed they had gone.

BY THE TIME they returned to their hotel room, Aisling was back to her cheerful, energetic self, chatting about the day's work and making plans for the next as they prepared for bed.

"I've been going over things in my mind—what we've learned so far," she was saying. "We've tracked John and Esther through five decades of the census—from New York to Brooklyn, to Grass Valley and Silver Reef. But other than verifying a few basic facts, we're not any closer to knowing where they came from in Ireland, or even exactly when they left the country."

Catharine finished brushing her teeth and glanced at her daughter with a little smile. Dressed in pink satin pajamas, the young woman was sitting cross-legged on the bed, completely surrounded by notebooks and copies of census pages. "And so?"

"So, we need to approach the problem from a different angle. In other words, if the doors are closed, we need to open a window."

"What window do you have in mind?"

"Henry—Esther's brother," Aisling said with bright-eyed determination. "We know he was living with Esther and her children in 1860. But what happened to Henry after she left New York to join her husband in California?"

"Good question. I'm fairly sure he didn't follow them to Grass Valley. Do you think he could have gone back to Ireland?"

Aisling shook her head. "When the Irish left Ireland during those years, it was because they had no other choice. Even after the famine, the situation in the country was grim, and not only for the poorer classes. The whole economic system was in upheaval. Many of the wealthy landowners were in debt over their heads and lost entire estates. No, when Henry left Ireland, he must have known it would be permanent, and not just for a few months to help his sister." Picking up a copy of his picture, she stared thoughtfully at the man's aristocratic features. "It's just a feeling, but I think Henry is our window to finding the Clifford's in Ireland."

Catharine smiled softly. "By all means, follow your feelings. What do you have in mind?"

"First thing tomorrow, I want to check the 1870 census for Ward 12 in Brooklyn. We know Henry was there in 1860. I'm hoping he might still be there ten years later."

Catharine got into bed and leaned gratefully against the pillows, while Aisling gathered up her papers and put them in her portfolio. "Tell me more about your Mr. Misogynist," she said lightly. "He's very good looking, by the way."

Aisling glanced up with a careless laugh. "There's nothing to tell. I've never even talked to him. Not really."

"Then how do you know he's a woman-hater? That's a pretty strong label to put on any man—especially one you've never talked to."

"I didn't put the label on him—he did," Aisling explained quickly. "He said he came from a long line of misogynists. And then he laughed. Can you believe the arrogance of the man? I think he's just too—well...." Turning back the bedcovers, she climbed into bed with a disgusted sigh.

Catharine took this in with a little smile. "And when exactly did he make this revealing confession to you?"

"Well, he didn't exactly make it to me...." She turned on her side to face Catharine, who waited patiently, blue eyes dancing. "Oh, all right. One evening, I overheard him talking with a couple of the staff workers. I wasn't trying to eavesdrop," she put in hastily. "I really wasn't. It's like I said before. Whenever I have work on the British Isles floor, nine times out of ten he's there, too, and ... no matter how I try to avoid him, it seems like he's always using the machine next to mine, or doing something nearby."

"Maybe he's a professional genealogist," Catharine suggested, curious as to why Aisling would take such pains to avoid him.

"Oh, yes, I know he is."

"What kind of research does he do?"

"Mostly English and Scottish."

"And is he good—at research, I mean?"

"He's incredible. The staff members are always going to him with questions."

"I see. And is he married?"

"I think he's divorced. But I'm not sure."

Catharine gave her daughter an amused smile. "Well, for someone who doesn't know anything about the man—not even his name—you seem to have gathered quite a bit of pertinent information. How exactly does this happen, if you don't speak to each other? Osmosis, maybe?"

Aisling's answering grin was decidedly on the sheepish side. "This is going to sound crazy, but whenever he's nearby, I–I just can't seem to think straight. I can be right in the middle of studying some eighteenth century land deed and then I'll hear his voice across the room, and my concentration's totally blown. The next thing I know, I'm staring at nothing and making mental notes of everything he says. It's terrible!"

Catharine smiled. "I don't know that I'd call it terrible. There's obviously some sort of chemistry going on between you two."

"But I'm thirty years old!" Aisling burst out, giving her pillow a few punches for good measure. "It's ridiculous for me to react this way to someone I don't even know."

"You do have a few years yet before senility sets in," Catharine said, and Aisling laughed in spite of herself.

"I don't know whether it's chemistry, or what it is," she said airily, and lay back down. "It doesn't really matter to me, one way or the other."

Catharine didn't buy this for a moment. "Perhaps you have the same effect on him."

"I doubt it. Not Mr. Misogynist from the long line of misogynists."

Catharine smothered a smile. "Well, for the sake of your concentration, I suppose it's a good thing we'll be working on the second floor tomorrow and not in the Irish section."

"Like I said, it doesn't matter to me one way or the other." Aisling reached over to turn out the light. Her voice, coming out of the darkness a few seconds later, sounded vaguely disappointed. "Besides, he rarely comes to the library on Saturdays. That's when he spends time with his children. At least, I think they're his children."

"Goodnight, Aisling," Catharine said, and quickly turned her face into the pillow to muffle her laughter.

16

> *"Were our fount of knowledge dry,*
> *Who could to men of rank supply*
> *The branches of their pedigree,*
> *And Gaelic genealogy."*
>
> The Dialogue of the Old Men
(Trans. Lord Longford)

The morning was typical of early March in Utah, with a lusty breeze blowing from the south and a sky that was mixed and unsettled in its emotions—one moment revealing tantalizing patches of bright blue, and the next, frowning over with clouds. Even on a leisurely Saturday, the city was up and awake as Catharine and Aisling made the short walk from the Marriott Hotel to the Family History Library.

In the few short days since their arrival, Catharine had come to enjoy and embrace their daily routine. The leisurely breakfasts, the hours of concentrated research, broken up with walks around Temple Square, and lively discussions on family history or story ideas. That she was actually here with the daughter she never expected to find was a miracle that met her like the sunrise each morning.

Aisling, too, felt the uniqueness of the time. During the busy passage of each day, she often found her emotions doing a dual dance of wonder. One moment, feeling as if she had known Catharine all her life. And the next, thinking she needed to pinch herself to believe she was actually working with her favorite author, *the* Catharine Cavanagh.

By now, others in the library were also aware of Catharine's daily visits. It was not unusual to be stopped at least once during the day, by some patron or member of the staff. Some asked for an autograph, others merely wanted to say hello and tell Catharine how much they enjoyed her books.

During such times, Aisling found her admiration for Catharine steadily growing. She responded to every request with warmth and a smile, never diffidence or patronizing patience. And even though Catharine had joked and laughed it off when Aisling referred to the attention she attracted from men, it was true none the less. Catharine was classy and elegant, but somehow, still soft. Her clothes and make-up were never image-conscious or overdone. Like this morning. She was dressed in trim Levis and a wine-colored shirt, with a tweed blazer in soft burgundy and gray. The dark waves of her hair had been pulled back in a gold clip, and scarcely a wrinkle could be detected in her flawless skin.

Aisling gave Catharine's appearance a silent thumb's up of approval as they walked side by side.

It was not yet nine o'clock when they entered the main doors, but the library, which had been open for nearly an hour and a half, was busier than they had yet seen it.

One of two older women stationed at the main floor Information Desk smiled a greeting and called out as they headed for the stairs, "Oh, Mrs. Cavanagh—would you have time to sign a couple of books for my granddaughter?"

Catharine smiled at the little woman whose tightly permed hair framed her face like a curly white cloud. "I'd be happy to."

Chapter 16

The white cloud disappeared behind the desk, to return seconds later with a hefty stack of hardcover novels. Setting them on the counter with a thump she said, "My granddaughter's name is Amy."

Aisling gave the tower of books an amused glance, and said to Catharine, "See you in an hour or two. I'll be upstairs in the usual place."

THE SECOND FLOOR U.S. Census area was especially crowded, and Catharine reached their 'usual place' only to discover the desk cubicles were already occupied and Aisling nowhere in sight. Wandering down the rows in search of her, Catharine found herself having to rethink her initial assessment that genealogy was a hobby pursued largely by senior citizens. This morning she was pleasantly surprised to see a fair amount of young adults and even a few teens busy at the computers and reader machines. Then, in a far corner, she caught a glimpse of red-gold hair.

"There's a Henry Clifford in Ward 12!" Aisling announced by way of greeting, as Catharine sat down beside her. "And wait until you see who else is there!"

Catharine leaned closer and her eyes had traveled barely a third of the way down the page when her heart began pounding like a trip hammer.

"Oh, dear heaven," she whispered.

"Do you realize what this means?" Aisling said, her voice bubbling with excitement.

Catharine nodded, open-mouthed, unable to take her eyes off the names. *Clifford, Henry. Age 76. Clifford, Henry. Age 39. Clifford, George. Age 34. Clifford, John. Age 31. Clifford, Mary. Age 50.*

"The whole family must have come over from Ireland," she said. "You were right about Henry. He is our window." Her eyes left the screen to meet Aisling's in a shared moment of joyful discovery.

Aisling was beaming. "Look at the rest of the people living in the same apartment with Henry Sr. and his sons. There's Ann Haddow and her five children, and a Francis Munkenbeck with his wife Kate. That makes thirteen people altogether. I know conditions were crowded in the tenements, but I seriously doubt Esther's father would have a bunch of strangers and five young children living with him and his grown sons."

"What are you saying?"

"That Anne and Kate could be Esther's married sisters. We'll have to document it, of course, but I'd be willing to bet that they are. I'm not sure about Mary's relationship though. It's possible she's Henry's wife."

"I don't think so," Catharine said. "Not unless he married a second time. Esther's mother's name was Rose Marie. My feeling is, this Mary's an older sister."

Aisling gave her a teasing smile. "It will be interesting to see if we can document those feelings of yours."

Catharine leaned back with a dazed expression. "This is so amazing, I can hardly take it in. Everyone in my family always thought the Clifford's were fairly well off and living somewhere in Ireland. We never imagined they could have emigrated to this country."

"They must have lost everything," Aisling said. "Otherwise...." She didn't need to go on.

MORNING MOVED UNNOTICED into afternoon, with Catharine paying little heed to the passage of minutes or hours. She was in another time, another century ... somewhere in the teeming tenements of Brooklyn, walking with the Clifford family as they struggled to make a life among thousands of other immigrants. She could almost see the laundry hanging outside the windows, and the horse drawn wagons moving along the narrow streets. There would be the strong, briny smells of the wharf and garbage in the streets, and cabbage cooking on the stoves, with all the smells mingling together to make one crowded, living smell of the city.

By 1880, Esther's two brothers were married with families of their own. George was a baker and John worked as longshoreman on the nearby docks.

It was strange to think of the Cliffords in this way, when for so many years, she had imagined them living a life of wealth and privilege somewhere in Ireland. Had Esther reconciled with her father and other members of her family? Catharine wondered. Did they ever exchange letters, with Esther writing from the small mining town of Grass Valley an entire continent away? Catharine dearly hoped that they had.

In spite of the day's revealing finds, there was also a significant gap, for search as they may, neither Aisling nor Catharine could find any further mention of Henry Sr. or Jr.

"Taking the father's age into consideration, I'm beginning to think we might have more success if we checked the Death Records," Aisling said.

Catharine nodded, although she found the thought less than appealing. It was as if she were being asked to let the family go, when she'd barely discovered them. Leaning back, she stretched the tight muscles in her neck and shoulders, where the hours of intense concentration usually took their toll.

"Are you too tired?" Aisling asked. "We have been working hard for several hours now."

"Not really tired, but what do you say we take a break and go for a walk? My mind's a little bogged down by everything right now."

Leaving research and the past behind, they grabbed jackets and handbags and made their way across the crowded room toward the stairs. The next second, Aisling stopped with a jerk and clutched Catharine's arm. "Not the stairs! Let's take the elevator instead."

"I thought you liked taking the stairs."

"I do, but—well, we're both tired. It won't hurt to take the elevator for once."

Puzzled, Catharine glanced past Aisling to see a bearded man with a baseball cap only yards away, also heading toward the stairway. Catharine gave Aisling a knowing look and shook her head, but obligingly changed course and turned toward the elevators.

"I thought you said Mr. Misogynist didn't come to the library on Saturdays," she said, as Aisling pushed the button for the Main Level and the doors closed behind them with a metal whine and whoosh.

"He doesn't—not usually. Oh, no!"

"Now what's wrong?"

"What do you want to bet, he gets on the elevator at the main floor?"

"If he's taking the stairs, why would he do that?"

Aisling gave her a fatalistic look. "You have your feelings about things, and I have mine."

Before Catharine could place her bet either way, the light indicating the Main Floor flashed green and the elevator stopped with a gentle lurch. The doors parted and there he stood, portfolio and pen in hand. Today, a rust-colored tee shirt replaced the one in bright yellow, but was no less effective in setting off the man's muscular build and good looks.

A moment of surprise widened his dark eyes as he saw Aisling.

Chapter 16

Then he entered the elevator with a casual step and the barest hint of a smile.

Catharine stepped forward, expecting Aisling to follow, but the young woman was seemingly frozen to the spot, her posture one of determined nonchalance.

Feeling totally foolish, Catharine barely had time to dive back in the elevator before Mr. Misogynist pressed the button for B-2, and the doors closed once more.

"Hello," Aisling said, offering a casual smile.

"Hello," came the equally casual reply.

"How are you doing?" she asked politely.

The man's eyes met hers with weary frankness. "Pretty tired, actually."

"I know what you mean," Aisling mumbled, nodding agreement.

Catharine groaned inwardly. If this generic seesaw was a typical example of their conversation, it was little wonder Aisling said she'd never really talked to the man. Whatever the two lacked in verbal skills, they more than made up for in sparks of unspoken awareness. As potent looks and equally potent silence filled the elevator's small space, Catharine felt her own presence shrinking to the size of a fly on the wall.

Seconds later, the elevator came to a metallic halt, the doors opened and Mr. M. was on his way with a soft-spoken, "See you," offered in parting.

"See you," Aisling answered in return, and drifted out with Catharine following after. Aisling took one more step then paused, her expression a trifle blank.

"Did you change your mind about going for a walk?" Catharine asked innocently.

The blankness lifted and Aisling let out a small moan. "I don't believe this," she said under her breath. "I told you I don't function when he's around."

Only a few yards away, Mr. M. was exchanging greetings with a staff member at the Information Desk. He laughed at something that was said, and Aisling turned pleading eyes to Catharine.

"Now that we're here, we've got to do something legitimate. Otherwise, it will look as if—well, you know."

Catharine smiled indulgently. "I'll give you five minutes to enlighten me with some nineteenth century map of Ireland."

"Thank you."

After the prescribed five minutes, they returned to the elevators without incident and left the library. Catharine managed to keep her amusement under control until they were outside and walking briskly down the sidewalk. She glanced at her daughter, unable to contain the laughter bubbling up inside.

"I think I may have to revise my earlier statement," she said.

"What statement is that?"

"The one about finding romance in the Family History Library."

"This is hardly what you'd call romance!" Aisling protested with flaming cheeks. "This is just—well, it's just weird, that's all."

Catharine laughed. "On the contrary. I think it's fascinating."

AFTER A BRISK half-hour walk and no further mention of Mr. Misogynist, they returned to the second floor and began their search of Kings County death records. The procedure was simple, but time consuming, with Catharine taking microfilms covering the first half of the decade, and Aisling the latter. It was more than a little disturbing to see the large percentage of infants and young children on the mortality lists, with very few entries for persons over the age of sixty. Thankfully, the years 1871 and '72 contained only a handful of Clifford's, with no Henry's among them.

Then in 1873, Catharine was scrolling through the C's and discovered death dates for two Henry Clifford's—one in May, the other in July, barely two months apart. Seeing the names she felt a sudden ache inside, as if father and son had died in that very moment, and not over a century before.

"I think I've found them," she said, moving her chair to the side so Aisling could view the screen.

Aisling checked the names and nodded, touched by the note of sadness in Catharine's voice. "I'll write down the dates and numbers, then we can get the film with the actual certificates."

Minutes later, they found themselves looking at the Death Certificate for Esther's brother, Henry Forbes Clifford.

"Age forty-two years, five months and six days," Catharine said softly. "And he never married. Oh, how his father must have grieved."

Aisling frowned, noting the cause of death. "Peritonitis, due to 'exposure.' Every time I see something like this, I feel new appreciation for penicillin and modern medicine."

The next certificate revealed that Henry Sr. had died at the goodly age of seventy-nine with the cause listed simply as 'old age.'

"What a shame young Henry died first," Aisling commented. "I'm sure that must have been a contributing factor in the father's death." She stood up and carefully removed the microfilm from the machine. "I'll make copies of the certificates, if you wouldn't mind putting the rest of the films away."

When Catharine didn't respond, Aisling put a tentative hand on her arm. "Are you all right?"

"What? Oh ... yes. I was just thinking that Esther and I have this in common as well. It's a sad sort of parallel. We both lost brothers that we loved, and they both died painful deaths far away from home … mine in the jungles of Viet Nam."

"I didn't know you had a brother."

Catharine nodded slowly. "Robert was only twenty-two when he died. Strange, how finding this, and thinking about Esther's loss, brings it all back. The day we heard…."

Aisling placed a gentle hand on her shoulder, and left to make the copies. Catharine was scarcely aware she had gone.

# 17

Henry & Rose Marie

Thoughts of the Clifford family hovered on the edge of Catharine's sleep all that night, and met her as soon as dreams drifted into wakefulness the next morning. Brothers, sisters, spouses and children—unknown until the day before, now moved through her thoughts with the affection of the long familiar. And with the affection, came the corresponding sorrow for the family's grief and loss. Father and son, dying within two months of one another, an entire continent away from Esther Clark.

Catharine turned over and saw Aisling watching her from a chair near the window. Notebooks and census pages were spread out on the table nearby.

"Good morning," she said. "I hope you slept well."

Catharine sighed, then stretched. "I did. What time is it?"

"Quarter to eleven."

"What?" Catharine sat up with a start. "You shouldn't have let me sleep so long. I'll hurry and get dressed."

"No need to hurry. It's Sunday, and the library's closed. I was thinking it might be nice to attend the Choir broadcast at the Tabernacle, but I didn't have the heart to wake you."

"Is it too late to go?"

Aisling smiled and nodded. "The broadcast ended over an hour ago."

"I'm sorry." Catharine lay back down and succumbed to the softness of her pillow. "I never sleep this late."

"You were seven seas under," Aisling said, "and I don't blame you. We've put in some long hours the past few days."

"Well, you look disgustingly awake," Catharine told her daughter. "Don't you ever get tired? Or is my age starting to show?"

Aisling laughed at this. "I have to admit, last night I was feeling pretty worn out, but early this morning I woke up with visions of Clifford's dancing in my head." She picked up a copy of one of the death certificates. "Thanks to these, I think we're one step closer to finding the family in Ireland."

"Why is that? What have you found?"

"It's not really a question of finding anything new—just realizing the importance of what's already here. These death certificates are a literal gold mine of information."

Catharine needed no more encouragement than this to be out of bed and at Aisling's side. "Tell me more about the gold mine."

"Well, to start with, there's Esther's brother and his middle name. I'm sure Forbes must be a significant surname for the family."

"The maiden name of Esther's mother, perhaps?" Catharine suggested, her thoughts jumping ahead.

Aisling smiled. "Possibly. Or it might be a surname on the paternal side. Either way, I think Forbes is an important clue. Then we have brother Henry's precise age at the time of his death. As specific as it is, right down to the month and the day, I've been able to estimate his birth date as January 1, 1831."

"Which would have made Esther around eight years old when Henry was born."

Aisling nodded. "And something else. Henry had been living in the U.S. for twenty years when he died, which gives us the year he immigrated from Ireland."

"1853," Catharine filled in, excitement running through her voice.

"Exactly. And since father Henry had only lived in Brooklyn for eleven years, we can assume he didn't come over until the early 1860's —a full decade later. The library has some new CD's with expanded passenger lists for Irish immigrants. I'm going to check into those first thing tomorrow. If either or both Henry's are listed, we can look up the film for the actual ship's manifest."

"But I thought you said ship manifests rarely give more information than the country of origin."

"That's true in many cases, but there's always the chance there might be more. And I don't want to eliminate any source that could identify the county where the Clifford's lived."

"What about doing some research into the Forbes name?" Catharine suggested. "Wouldn't there be some books in the Irish section with pedigrees and other information on the landed gentry of the time?"

"There are tons of them," Aisling said, not visibly affected by the mention of the infamous B2 level of the library. "And now that we know Esther's father was still living in Ireland as late as 1860, there's another source I want to check—Griffith's Primary Valuation Lists."

"I've heard you mention that one before," Catharine said. "What is it exactly?"

"Basically, it's a list of all the people, heads of household that is, who paid taxes to the Irish government between 1840 and 1864. Since most of the census records were destroyed in the Four Courts' fire back in 1922, Griffith's survey has become an important substitute."

"But if we don't know the county, how will this help?"

"Ordinarily, you would need to know a specific county," Aisling said. "But using the new CD-ROM Index, all I have to do is enter Esther's father's name and it will give us a list of all the Henry Clifford's recorded in Griffith's. If we were looking for a name like John Clark, I wouldn't even attempt it, but with a surname like Clifford, there shouldn't be that many."

"So what are we going to do today, besides count the hours until the library opens in the morning."

Aisling grinned. "Well, for starters, I think we should call Grace and let her know what we've found so far."

"Good heavens, I meant to call Mother last night!" Catharine said, putting a hand to her head. "I don't know where my mind was."

"I think I do. It was in Brooklyn ... about a hundred and thirty years ago, grieving with an immigrant family who lived on the corner of Commerce and Imlay streets." Aisling's eyes met Catharine's with tender understanding. "The way you care about these people, I know it's going to be a wonderful book."

"I hope so."

Aisling's smile held confidence as well as warmth. "It will."

THE HOURS PASSED in contented ways, with a leisurely lunch and a long phone conversation with Grace, followed by a tour of Temple Square. In late afternoon, the phone rang and Catharine answered, thinking it might be her mother calling back. She was totally taken back to hear a pleasant male voice asking for Aisling.

"It's for you," Catharine said, putting a hand over the receiver. She couldn't resist adding, "Maybe it's Mr. Misogynist."

"Right." Aisling raised her eyes heavenward and left the desk to take the phone from Catharine. "Hello? Oh, hi, Darren. I didn't think you'd be in town until tomorrow. No ... no, I'm not busy."

Catharine picked up a magazine and stretched out on the bed, not wanting to eavesdrop on her daughter's conversation.

Moments later, Aisling put a hand over the receiver and turned to Catharine. "Darren wants me to have dinner with him tonight. Do you mind?"

"Of course not. Go right ahead," Catharine urged, touched that Aisling would consider her feelings enough to ask.

The entire conversation lasted less than three minutes, and after hanging up, Aisling returned to the desk where she'd been organizing her notes and research materials. Her movements were confident and methodical, with the same brisk energy that Catharine had come to enjoy. Whoever this Darren might be, he didn't seem to inspire the kind of reaction she'd witnessed whenever Mr. Misogynist appeared on the scene.

"Are you sure you don't mind me taking off for the evening?" Aisling said. "I hate to just abandon you."

"Don't be silly, you're not abandoning me. I hope you don't feel like you have to be at my 'beck and call' around the clock."

"I don't, but—"

"No buts. Just go out and have a good time. There's only one thing I want to know. Who's Darren?"

"His name is Darren Taylor," Aisling filled in. "We've been seeing each other off and on for the past few months. I knew he was going to fly in for a business conference at the Salt Palace this week, but I wasn't expecting him until tomorrow."

"Is he nice?"

The question prompted a smile that was part teasing, part provocative. "That all depends on how you define 'nice.' If you mean good looking—yes, very. But I'll let you judge that for yourself. Darren's picking me up at six-thirty, and he's always punctual."

"Are you and Darren—you know, an item?"

Aisling laughed at this. "An item?"

"Well, if you've been seeing each other 'off and on' for several months, I'm curious as to how you'd describe your relationship. Is it more off than on, or the other way round?"

"Good question," Aisling said with a little shrug. "I haven't quite decided the answer."

By six twenty-five Aisling was dressed and ready, but with none of the nervous flurry that occurred when she'd 'freshened up' for Mr. Misogynist. This evening she'd chosen a pair of dressy gray slacks with a gray blazer over a silky black top. With her vivid hair and fair coloring, the overall effect was very striking, Catharine thought. Even if it did look more business-like than romantic.

At six thirty-two, the phone rang and Aisling took the call.

"No. No, that's not a problem. I'll meet you there in say, ten minutes? All right, fifteen." She hung up and explained, "Darren's boss kept him on the phone longer than he thought, so I'm going to meet him at the restaurant. See you in a few hours."

"Have a good time," Catharine said, biting off the urge to give some maternal instructions. The temperature had dropped markedly during the day, and now the sky looked threatening. How far away was this restaurant? And what was so earth shaking in its importance that the punctual Mr. Taylor couldn't take the time to pick Aisling up at her hotel room? Good grief, she thought, giving herself the stern reminder that Aisling was thirty years old, and not some teenager on her first date.

The room seemed strangely silent after she had gone, uncomfortably so. Catharine tried to fill it with the sound of the television, but flippant, sexual sitcoms and violent police dramas were not the solution she wanted or needed. During the daylight hours, she felt comfortably safe in her surroundings; her mind occupied every minute. But there were moments after darkness fell, that she found herself struggling with nervous fears and the incessant playback of a shot that had very nearly found its mark.

So what to do? The evening hours suddenly loomed long ahead of her. Catharine moved restlessly to the corner table where Aisling had left a scattering of family history notes and papers. Trying to find a positive focus for her thoughts, she picked up a handwritten note with a list of various Clifford family members and the estimated year of their birth. The absence of Esther's mother from the list prompted some reflection as well as curiosity.

When did you lose your mother, Esther? she wondered. *Was it during the famine, when fever and dysentery claimed as many lives as the terrible hunger? Or perhaps even earlier.*

A span of some eight years existed between the time of Esther's birth in 1822 and that of her beloved brother Henry. Had there been other children born during this period, infants who lived only days or a few precious months? Questions wandered through her mind like the twisting path of a river whose source lay hidden just around the next bend.

If Rose Marie had died when Esther was fairly young, then Esther could have been raised by a stepmother—not unlike Aisling, who had known no other mother than Helen Montgomery. As she sat staring at the names, Catharine had a strong feeling this was so, that Henry Clifford had indeed married a second time. There were no facts to support this assumption on her part; nothing to give any substance to the feeling, yet it was there, all the same.

Rose Marie. The woman and the name continued to haunt her thoughts as Catharine ate a simple dinner ordered from room service. It might be that she would never learn all the facts, but already, her heart and mind were shaping the face of the woman whose death had been lost somewhere in the blurred pages of the past.

It could have happened in any of a dozen ways, from childbirth to an accident, but perhaps the actual cause didn't matter after all. What really mattered was that Rose Marie should be remembered.

Taking a fresh legal pad and her favorite black pen, Catharine sat down and began to write.

IT WAS WELL after midnight before Aisling returned to their hotel room. The apology on her lips was stilled the moment she felt the room's silence and took in the fact that the only light burning was a small one on the table. Moving quietly past Catharine's sleeping form, Aisling got out her pajamas and began to undress. The heavy ache of disappointment inside told her just how much she'd counted on Catharine being awake, how badly she needed to talk with her about the evening just past. The hours spent with Darren had left her feeling unsettled and confused, but somehow, if she could just talk with Catharine, she knew she'd see things more clearly.

Strange, how quickly she'd come to enjoy and even rely on their talks together at each day's end. She'd been on her own for over ten years now, taking pride in her independence and self-reliant ways, yet knowing Catharine for even a short span of weeks had taught her so much. There were times she was frankly in awe of Catharine's gentle wisdom, her total lack of arrogance, and her rich sense of humor—

even when the joke was on her. She remembered their first day at the Family History Library, when Catharine had been all thumbs trying to figure out how to operate a microfilm reader.

But Catharine was quick, too. Amazingly so when it came to spotting names that were barely legible or misspelled. As a rule, Aisling avoided doing research with her clients, a policy with which most people were only too happy to comply. They had little interest in going through the tedious and often frustrating research process. What they wanted were results, preferably, the 'immediate if not sooner' kind of results. But the past week of working with Catharine had been thoroughly enjoyable, as well as fulfilling.

Aisling's professional determination to find the Clifford family was sparked by a personal fervor that she didn't fully understand. She only knew it was there, rich and strong, turning seemingly dead ends into detours, and making their discoveries all the more satisfying.

Somewhere along the way, genealogy aside, her respect and fondness for Catharine Cavanagh had grown into a rich, delightful friendship, one entirely different from those shared with her peers. Catharine's opinions and feelings had come to mean a great deal and her advice, always given in the gentlest of ways, was something Aisling knew she could rely on.

After the evening with Darren, Aisling knew she was in need of some solid motherly advice. She stared into the room's dimness, as a fuzzy sort of realization came clear in her mind. In many ways, Catharine seemed more like a mother than a friend. But how could that be?

Moving wearily to the desk to turn out the light, she saw a small note propped against the lamp.

Hope you had an enjoyable evening. Feel free to wake me if you want to talk. Or, if you're too tired, sweet dreams and I'll see you in the morning.

Catharine

P.S. Don't let me sleep in!!

Aisling glanced toward Catharine's sleeping form with a smile, hearing the peaceful, even sound of her breathing. Their talk would just have to wait. There was no way she would disturb her now.

Then, turning her gaze back to the desk, Aisling noticed the handwritten pages of Catharine's notebook. Without making a conscious decision to do so, her eyes traveled over half a page of flowing black script, before her conscience put a sudden halt to the reading. Would Catharine object if she read a few pages? Somehow, she didn't think so. It wasn't as if she were prying into her private journal. The two of them had discussed scenes and plot possibilities for the story about Esther Clifford several times during recent weeks.

Sitting down, Aisling picked up the notebook and sent Catharine a silent message. *If I'm assuming too much and you don't approve, you'll just have to scold me in the morning.*

Then she settled back in the chair to read.

December — 1830

The Irish have long considered Christmas to be the most joyous time of the year, yet along with the joy, there is an old saying that, "A green Christmas makes a fat churchyard." This proverb reveals much about the Irish character, for 'tis a simple fact that it does not often snow in Ireland. Green Christmases are far more common than not, and sadly enough,

Irish history has shown ample cause for churchyards to grow fat with new graves.

Naturally, being Irish, there is yet another proverb that says, "When it snows on Christmas Eve, the angels in heaven are plucking geese for the feast on the morrow." Christmas, then, like life itself, may be bitter or sweet. Sometimes it is green and melancholy, other times, white and joyous. Most often, it can and will be both.

Like the last Christmas I had with my mother. Thinking back, that Christmas signaled the last of many things, my childhood being one of them. I was but eight years of age at the time, yet it remains ever clear in my memory.

Mother had a special way of bringing even more joy to a holiday already known for its good cheer. Like other Irish homes, ours had candles in every window on Christmas Eve, fragrant holly boughs and ivy on the mantle, and the tantalizing smell of spicy puddings and cakes filled with currents and raisins. Preparations began many weeks before, with the house undergoing a thorough cleaning, sweeping and scouring. All the best dishes were brought out and Mother's silver was polished until it shone.

On Christmas Eve, tradition called for either the youngest child or a daughter named Mary to be given the honor of lighting the first candle. To my chagrin, my sister Mary was always the one who earned this privilege, but on this Christmas, Mother suggested to Father that I should be given my fair turn.

Mary sulked for two days after learning the news, whilst I could scarcely contain my joy. The candle itself was fat and red, and sat in a lovely glass holder on the sill of the sitting room window. From this, all the other candles in the house were to be lit.

John Richard and his family placed candles in their windows as well, but with only two windows in their small cottage, the sight was not nearly so grand. And lacking holders, the candles had to be stuffed into two large turnips. Yet, they were merry with the season, for all that.

At Christmas time, Father was always more generous to the poor. I knew for a fact, that a goose and a fine plum pudding had been delivered to John Richard's mother in time for the Clark's Christmas dinner. And Mother had insisted that gifts of warm woolen stockings be given to all the children in the family.

Mother had been lying abed much more in recent months due to her 'condition,' of which I understood little at the time. Bouts of nausea are not significant symptoms to a child of eight. Nor was Mother's increasing girth anything that gave me serious pause to wonder.

On this Christmas Day, she insisted on joining us at the table. I will never forget the sight of her, eyes shining in the glow of candlelight and her smile, so sweet and merry. Wearing a dress of deepest emerald, with a red garnet brooch on her breast, Mother was the very vision of Christmas itself. I'm sure Father thought so as well, for I never remember him smiling quite so much or so tenderly.

In my excitement and happiness, I chattered even more than usual, which was always overmuch, as far as Father was concerned. Yet, at this Christmas dinner, I received not one scolding, and once, he even laughed at something I had said. Just hearing the sound of his laughter, coming so hearty and unexpected, fair struck me dumb for at least five minutes.

I'm sure Mary and I received a small gift or two in our stockings, but I have no recollection now what it was. My greatest gift that Christmas was the memory of my mother's love. I hear her voice yet, telling a bedtime story to Mary and me, her arms holding us close on either side.

It was a green Christmas that year, but I drifted off to sleep that night, never once thinking of bad omens or fat churchyards.

St. Stephen's Day with its frolicking mummers and 'Wren Boys' passed in a happy sort of blur, and I awoke one crisp, cold morning with a pale sun shining feebly through my window. It was the first day of the New Year, but for some reason, no one in our household seemed mindful of the fact.

Mrs. Murphy had served breakfast in a dither of clattering dishes and apologies. "I'm sorry, Miss Esther, but the porridge is a wee bit on the thick side. I've given you more cream though, to make up for it. And the sausage, sweet Mother of God, is nigh burnt to a crisp."

Mother didn't come downstairs for breakfast, and Father was busy with something in the library that seemed to require a great deal of slamming of books and drawers. I saw Mother's maid slip into the kitchen for a quick cup of tea, whisper something to the cook, then scurry back upstairs, her face flushed and eyes unusually bright.

After breakfast, Mary and I were scooted upstairs to our room by Mrs. Whelan, the housekeeper, who instructed us firmly to "busy ourselves with embroidery like good girls." My wishes to say a brief good morning to Mother were quickly denied.

"Your mother's not feeling well, right now," she explained. "A little later, perhaps." Although the words were spoken softly, something in her tone told me it was best not to argue.

The morning dragged slowly by, with Mary dutifully stitching a pillowslip and me, alternately playing with my doll or watching the rooks in the branches of the oaks outside my window. I hated embroidery. My stitches were clumsy and uneven, while Mary's were always neat as you please. And despite the use of thimbles, I managed to prick my fingers more often than not.

I was sitting at the window when I saw the horse and carriage of old Dr. Campbell come racing up the drive. As they clattered into the yard, John Richard's father ran around the corner of the house and grabbed the reins, while Dr. Campbell jumped down from the carriage. I can see him yet, hurrying toward the house, his straggly gray hair and long coattails blowing in the rising wind. At that moment, something inside me shivered and went cold.

Not long after, a muffled cry coming from somewhere down the hall confirmed my fears.

"That was Mother!" I said, jumping to my feet.

Mary frowned at me with the superior knowledge of a ten-year old. "I'm sure you're mistaken, Ettie. 'Twas probably one of the servants."

"It was not a servant!" I flung back. "That was Mother."

I would have been out the door and down the hall to investigate, but for the fact Annie Murphy, cook's daughter, knocked and entered our room only seconds later.

"Excuse me, Miss Mary, Miss Esther," she said with flushed cheeks and wide, frightened eyes. "I'm to fetch you both and take you downstairs."

"What's happened to Mother?" I asked, the fear inside me growing bigger and colder when I saw the look in Annie's eyes.

"Now don't you be worryin' your heads about your mother. Dr. Campbell's with her and he'll soon put things to right," she said stoutly. "Before day's end, God willin', you and Mary will have a wee brother or sister. Come along now, both of you. There's tea and biscuits waiting in the kitchen."

A brother or sister? The words filled me with a sense of pure wonder, for there's no way Annie Murphy could have known that I had long been praying for just such a miracle. Yet even in this, my gladness was dampened by the worrisome feeling that all was not right.

Much later, it may have been hours or minutes, my sister and I were fetched once more, this time by Mrs. Whelan, who took us by the hand to Mother's room. The stillness spoke to me, long before father's stilted, painful words. His voice seemed more lifeless even than the sight of my mother, lying in the bed with eyes closed and her white hands folded neatly on her breast.

"Your mother has left us," he said. "God has taken her from us. Come give her a kiss, then you may go."

Mary approached the bed first, pressing a quivering, but obedient kiss on Mother's pale cheek, while a few tears trickled slowly down her face. I moved woodenly forward to do the same, staring at the lifeless features with a mixture of confusion and shock. This lovely, waxen form couldn't be Mother.

Where had God taken the living, vibrant part of her, if this was all that was left behind? My lips felt the strangeness that death had given her skin, and a sob tore from my throat. Mother was gone. I knew it now. And only this white shell remained.

In those first days after my mother's death, I wasn't allowed to see the baby for more than a minute or two. I didn't understand why this should be so, except that adults seemed to feel children should be kept separate and apart from all that had happened.

But how could I remain apart from the death of my mother? Especially, when everywhere I went, someone was weeping. The servants had all adored her, and Mother's maid was inconsolable. A sturdy young Irish girl, Bridget Reynolds fairly worshipped my mother. In truth, I can understand her admiration, for Bridget was big-boned and often clumsy, with a freckled face and arms, while Mother was like a delicate English flower.

I once chanced to overhear a conversation between my parents where Father had been trying to convince Mother that she should have an English maid to see to her needs. Mother had remained firm, in her quiet, positive way.

"Bridget's a good girl, Henry. She tries hard, and she's very quick to learn."

"I only want you to be well cared for, my darling," Father had said in a voice reserved only for Mother.

"I know that, dearest. And I am cared for. I have you, do I not?"

I'd slipped away unnoticed and totally embarrassed because I'd seen my parents kissing. Not in the cool, polite way I'd seen before. Father often kissed Mother's cheek or her hand. But that was nothing like the kiss I'd witnessed on this occasion.

My mind whirled with such memories in those days immediately before and after the burial. Sometimes I heard Mother's lovely voice telling me stories or reciting poetry. Other times I saw her slim, white fingers playing the harp on rainy afternoons, the silvery notes as graceful as musical raindrops. I remembered her looking like a queen in her green silk dress on evenings when she and father had attended a special dinner or a ball. Things I would never see or experience again.

The memories and images ebbed and flowed between life and death. One moment, my mind saw her sparkling and alive, as she had been on Christmas Day; and the next, it was tortured with the sight of her body lying waxen and cold. What a fascinating, terrible difference death made in the body once the soul has departed. So empty. No more than a shell.

I wanted to cry like all the others, but I felt too dead to cry. One has to be alive for tears to flow.

Father was dead like me, moving through the grim necessities like a pale, sad-eyed ghost of his former self. He was rarely home, and when he was, he took meals in his study alone.

It was as if a gray film covered everything and everyone within our home.

Then one morning, a sweet living sound penetrated the grayness of my world. Singing. A woman's voice, low and rich, crooning a simple lullaby.

I was alone in my room, my sister Mary having gone to visit some cousins a few miles distant. Lying on my bed, I had been staring at a feathery crack in the ceiling, and listening to the steady drip of rain that had been falling since breakfast.

Then I heard the singing. It came from the nursery down the hall. I got off my bed to follow the sound, drawn to it as surely as if it had been issued from some mysterious siren of the sea.

In the adjoining nursery was no siren, but John Richard's mother, Anna Clark, who had been retained as wet nurse for my infant brother. The latest addition to the Clark family was but sixteen months old, which brought the number of children to seven. What was it Father had once remarked about the Clarks? "A vulgar assortment of ragamuffins who haven't the sense to know how wretched they are."

The words, flung out with such careless and cruel superiority, had filled me with anger and a confused sense of shame. It was true that the Clark children were more often dirty as not, and their clothes always needed mending. They lived in a small two-room cottage near the stables, which seemed far too small for nine people, let alone the stray chickens that often came to roost there. Yet for all this, they seemed happy enough. James and Anna Clark always had time for a story or two and were openly affectionate with one another as well as their offspring.

John Richard's father had a canny knack with horses and was a hard worker. Even Father couldn't find fault with him, other than the fact he was

Catholic, of course. The way Father said the word made it sound as if people of that faith had two heads or some grotesque malady.

I never could understand what made Catholics so loathsome and the Established Church so superior, or vice-versa. Shouldn't a loving God love all His children, rich and poor alike, whether Catholic, Protestant, or Jew?

The adult world of prejudice and privilege made no sense to me. All I knew was that the Clarks were a likeable family who seemed ever so much happier than my father, despite their poverty and so-called vulgarity.

Just now, peeping into the nursery in search of that wonderful singing, I don't think I had ever seen such a lovely sight as Anna Clark, rocking gently near the window, with my infant brother in her arms. Her plain cotton dress was unbuttoned to the waist, with one breast exposed. I watched, fascinated, as my brother suckled eagerly, one hand balled in a tiny fist against the woman's white flesh.

Her plain face, with its unruly tendrils of brown hair escaping from a crude bun, seemed radiantly beautiful seen in the soft gray light. Her voice, soft and low, crooning love and warmth to this motherless infant, touched me to the core.

She glanced up then, becoming aware of my presence, and instead of ordering me to leave, or covering her nakedness, included me in the radiance of that smile.

"Miss Esther . . . come closer, child, and see this fine little man."

I swallowed and felt a nervous tingle of curiosity. Did I dare? But my feet were already moving in the direction of the wondrous sight.

Anna Clark didn't seem at all embarrassed that I should be present, so I tried my best to respond in kind, although I know my cheeks were hot. I stood next to her side and stared down at my brother's contented nuzzling. "Does it hurt?" I asked.

She let go a delighted chuckle. "Good gracious, no, although I know some who've had a hard time of it. My James always said I had enough milk for a dozen babes, and pure cream at that. 'Tis glad I am for it now."

Inserting a finger near the corner of the baby's mouth, she released his fierce hold and after buttoning the front of her dress, plopped him handily to her shoulder. "Have you ever seen such a perfect little head?" she crooned, patting his back and holding him close. "And look at those dear little ears. So nice and flat against his head. He has his father's chin and mouth, that he does, but those eyes . . . ah, I see your dear mother's eyes lookin' up at me every time I take him in my arms."

The tears came then, dripping down my cheeks in a quiet stream, then filling my throat with thick sobs.

"Oh darlin,' it's all right," Anna said, pulling me close with her free hand. "Let it out now, Miss Esther."

I dropped to my knees with my head in her lap, where all the grief and aching loss spilled out. Anna stroked my head and crooned soft words, while the baby slept quietly on her shoulder.

When my sobs quieted, she asked in her lovely lilting voice, "Would you be wantin' to hold him, Miss? Take the chair next to mine and just sit yourself down."

I wiped my cheeks and eyes with my apron, then did as she said.

"Mind you support his wee head, now. That's the way. Ah, what a fine little brother ye have."

Wrapped snugly in a blanket, the infant felt warm and right in my arms. My ragged breathing calmed as I held him and the tortuous ache in my throat subsided.

He was beautiful. And so perfect. Love filled the emptiness inside me and tears clouded my vision once more as I gazed down at little Henry.

"Why did God take Mother?" I asked in a mumbled whisper. "Is it my fault, Anna?"

"God love you, child, of course, it's not your fault. Why on earth would you be thinkin' such a thing?"

"Because I prayed so hard that God would send me a brother . . . and then I heard the Vicar say, 'the Lord giveth and the Lord taketh away.' I thought God didn't want me to have the baby and Mother."

"Ah, you poor sweet child. 'Tis not for any of us to be tellin' the Lord what He wants and doesn't want. I do know that life sends us sunshine and rain, and we must learn to accept them both." She cupped my face gently in one of her work-worn hands. "Little Henry is that lucky to have you," she said.

"And who's to say Heaven is all that far away? Your blessed mother will be looking down on the two of you, I'm sure."

18

Darren

"I have a confession to make. Two confessions, actually," Aisling said the next morning, as she and Catharine ate a quick breakfast of juice and bagels in the hotel coffee shop.

Catharine glanced up from spreading cream cheese on her bagel. "This sounds serious."

"The seriousness depends partly on you." Aisling said, her smile tentative. "Last night, I read the scene you wrote about Esther and the death of her mother."

"That's your confession?" Catharine regarded her daughter's discomfort with gentle humor. "I purposely left the notebook out hoping we'd have time to discuss it after you got back—but then I totally faded."

"I was a lot later than I thought," Aisling said. "Darren and I had a lot to talk about."

Catharine wondered what that might be, but decided now was not the time to ask. Instead, she gave Aisling a hesitant look. "Well, what did you think?"

"That's the other confession. It made me cry, and books rarely do that, let alone an excerpt from one."

"I'm so glad you liked it. I was hoping you would."

Aisling shook her head at this. "After all the books you've written, I can't imagine why my opinion should mean much of anything."

"Trust me. It means a great deal," Catharine told her. "And as long as we're making confessions … when I was writing that scene, I shed a few tears myself."

"I can imagine. Reading it made me love Esther all the more—and Anna Clark, too. They're so real."

"It's amazing how it happens, sometimes. While I was writing, the whole experience seemed very real.…"

"I wonder if you realize what you've done in writing that scene," Aisling said, her expression thoughtful.

"What do you mean?"

"Well, aside from the emotional impact, it got me thinking about other angles of the story. You may have given us the real reason Esther's father objected to her feelings for John Clark, something much stronger than the obvious difference in their social class."

Catharine met her daughter's eyes with dawning understanding. "Religion."

"Exactly. If Esther's family belonged to the Church of Ireland, it's little wonder she was disinherited. In the Ireland of her day, there couldn't be a bigger barrier to a relationship. Those same walls exist even now."

"Yes ... walls," Catharine said faintly, remembering a long ago conversation with Eamonn, walls that her own father, much like Esther's, had been determined to keep firmly in place. She glanced down, afraid Aisling would see something in her eyes.

"We know from the parish records in Grass Valley that Esther and her children were Roman Catholic," Aisling went on, "but you and Grace weren't sure about the Cliffords. I'm curious—when you wrote that scene, did you make a conscious decision to have Henry Clifford belong to the Established Church, or did you just write it?"

Catharine shrugged. "I just wrote it, and it felt right."

"I think it is right," Aisling told her. "Both Henry Sr.'s and Jr.'s death certificates list their burial place as Greenwood Cemetery and back then, Greenwood was largely a Protestant cemetery. Most Irish Catholics were buried in the Cemetery of the Evergreens."

Catharine smiled at her daughter. "You keep this up, and I'm going to have to hire you as my permanent research assistant."

"As if you need one," Aisling said with a laugh, then added with touching sincerity, "But thanks. I'm—well—more than glad I could help." Suddenly embarrassed, she quickly finished her juice. Then her tone became casual once more. "Oh, before I forget, Darren's invited us to have dinner with him tonight, but I don't want you to feel obligated to come."

"I'd love to come, if you're sure you don't mind me tagging along."

"How can you even say that? Of course you wouldn't be tagging along. Darren's very excited to meet you."

"I'm looking forward to meeting him as well," Catharine said and couldn't resist adding, "He must be something special if you're willing to give up an entire evening's research."

Aisling smiled at this. "We won't be. The library closes at five on Monday evenings, remember?"

"Well then, if we're going to have a shorter day, we'd better get going. What's the plan?"

"I have a couple more things I want to check in a New York State census, then I'll join you in the Irish section."

CATHARINE HAD TO smile as she got off the elevator on the B-2 level of the library. Her first impulse was to glance around for a baseball cap and the bearded good looks of Aisling's Mr. M. This morning, the man was nowhere in sight. In fact, unlike most other days, the area was fairly sparse in patrons. Catharine settled comfortably at a quiet table near the back of the room, surrounded by half a dozen books on Anglo-Irish Nobility and Peerage.

Minutes disappeared into hours, as she entered the privileged world of Ireland's eighteenth and nineteenth-century gentry and estate owners. There had been Cliffords living in Ireland since the time of Queen Elizabeth I, with some receiving grants of land for their loyal service to the crown, and others acquiring property through an advantageous marriage. There was a Lord Baron de Clifford who had married Elizabeth Bourke in Dublin's St. Anne's Church in the late 1700's, and succeeding Baron de Clifford who owned extensive tracts of land in several counties. In County Wexford, she found reference to several Clifford families, among them a Henry Clifford of Great Gurtins.

As a surname, Forbes was nearly as scarce as Clifford, with the earliest settlers coming to Ireland from Scotland during the 'plantation' period of Queen Elizabeth I. Among their descendants was one George John Forbes, the Earl of Granard, who, unlike many 'absentee' landlords, spent a good portion of his time at Castle Forbes in County Longford.

The names soon blurred and blended into a pretentious, frothy mixture of titles—the third and fourth Earl of this and the fifth Marquis of that. There were dukes and dutchesses, counts and viscounts, a goodly amount never having set foot on their estates in Ireland, while others built lavish country houses that often left them hopelessly in debt. All in all, the social ladder set up by the Crown placed a mere 12% of the population in possession of over 90% of the land, while the Irish were left to scrape out a meager existence in one or two room hovels. Sandwiched between the two extremes was a small middle class, comprised of merchants, farmers and gentlemen who leased comfortable land holdings from titled peers.

Had her Clifford's been part of that extravagant world, she wondered? True, the pedigrees of the privileged had the advantage of being well documented, but after reading about the excesses of their lavish lifestyle, Catharine rather hoped her ancestors weren't among them. Nobility might make genealogy easier to trace, but had very little to do with a man's character, much less the worth of his soul.

By the time Aisling joined her, it was going on noon. One look at her sparkling eyes and smile told Catharine she must have found what she was looking for.

"Another clue?" Catharine said, putting aside her own books as Aisling sat down in the chair next to hers.

"Better than a clue! I have proof," she announced with a flourish. "And I want you to know, I also have a very healthy respect for those 'feelings' of yours. You were absolutely right."

Catharine smiled at the young woman's enthusiasm, and said dryly, "I'm right about so many things—which one is it this time?"

"About Esther's father being married more than once." Aisling placed a xeroxed copy of a census page in front of Catharine. "It took a little digging, but I found it. In the 1865 State Census for Kings

County, here's Henry Clifford, newly arrived in this country along with his daughters, Mary and Eliza!"

"Oh, good heavens, not another sister?"

Aisling grinned and nodded. "And there's more. Check out the columns following Henry's name. *Number of times married*—two! And the next one—*widowed twice*. I knew there was a state census that had detailed information on a person's marital status, but I wasn't sure of the year. This is incredible!"

"And so are you," Catharine said warmly.

Aisling shrugged aside the praise and placed another xeroxed copy on top of the first. "Find #2. I tried to tell myself I shouldn't take the time to do this one, but for some reason, I have an unexplainable fondness for Esther's brother George. Anyway, I got to thinking, if I could find his marriage certificate, it might give us a little more information on the parents. Take a look."

Reading over the certificate, Catharine found herself suddenly speechless. When she looked up at Aisling, her shining eyes said it all.

"Not only were you right about the Clifford's being Protestant, we now have the name of Henry's second wife," Aisling said, hardly able to contain herself.

"Mary McCormack—Aisling, this is too wonderful! You really are incredible!"

"I just followed a hunch and one of your feelings," she said with a pleased smile. "And right now, I'm also incredibly hungry! Let's go eat!"

Forty-five minutes later, they were back at it, this time, working on the main floor at one of the computers designed for CD-ROMs. Aisling had reserved the CD containing a Surname Index to Griffith's Primary Valuation and moments later, they had a printout of all the

Henry Clifford's living in Ireland during the years the survey was taken.

The puzzle pieces that had seemed so vast and widely scattered when they first began their research were suddenly narrowed to six. Six names from five counties.

"Grace told me that family information gave Esther's birthplace as Dublin," Aisling said. "And there's a Henry Clifford listed in County Dublin. Shall we start with that one?"

Catharine gave an excited nod, but moments later, found her soaring hopes taking a nosedive. The Henry Clifford in County Dublin lived a few miles north of the city in the parish of Balrothery. The man owned no land, and was leasing a small house whose worth was estimated at nine shillings.

"This can't be our Henry," Catharine said adamantly.

"How do you know?" Aisling countered. "The survey for Dublin was taken several years after the famine. He could have lost everything by then."

"I realize that, but—"

"Don't tell me. It doesn't *feel* right."

Catharine gave her daughter a wry look. "What happened to all this new found respect for my feelings?"

Aisling grinned at this. "All right. What county do you *feel* we should try next? I think we can safely eliminate the Henry C. in County Kerry, because those were Irish/Catholic Cliffords. That leaves us two in Sligo and one in Leitrim."

"Let's try Leitrim," Catharine said, feeling more than a bit breathless at the possibility and wanting to eliminate Eamonn's home county as soon as possible.

"Hmm. Ireland's *Cinderella* county," was Aisling's comment.

"Cinderella county? Why is that?"

"Partly because Leitrim's so small, and often overlooked by all the big travel guides. Partly because the land itself is incredibly poor—even for Connaught. Leitrim was especially hard-hit during the famine," she added.

"Well, Leitrim might be the Cinderella county," Catharine put in, her tone slightly defensive, "but let's not forget who got the Prince and lived happily ever after."

Aisling shook her head. "Catharine, you are such a romantic."

"I know, and it's far too late to do anything about it."

"Even if it weren't, I'd be the last one to ask you to change. County Leitrim it is."

Moments later, Aisling had the necessary volume with a list of land owners and occupants living in Mohill Parish, County Leitrim. With each turn of the page, Catharine felt a breathless expectancy that hovered on dread.

"Here he is," Aisling said, "living in the townland of Moher. This one's much better off than the last Henry. He's leasing 23 acres and 22 perches. With the house and office, that makes it worth about...." Her voice trailed off as she glanced up and saw the expression on Catharine's face. "What is it? Is something wrong?"

"Nothing's wrong," Catharine answered, her voice slightly breathless. "Look at the name of the land owner that Henry's leasing from."

Aisling glanced down. "What about him? This Earl of Granard owns a ton of property all through Leitrim."

"The surname of the Earl of Granard was Forbes," Catharine told her. "George John Forbes to be exact. I was reading about the family shortly before you came."

Aisling gave her an incredulous look, then threw her arms around

Catharine in an impetuous hug. "I think we've found them," she said. "And if this is right, not only the county, but the parish and the actual townland where Esther and her family lived. Leitrim—who would have thought."

"Yes ... who would have thought," Catharine repeated faintly, stunned by the irony of their discovery as much as the discovery itself. How the fates must be laughing. To think that out of Ireland's twenty-six counties, her ancestors and Eamonn's shared the same birthplace.

"I don't think we need to check the Henry Clifford's living in Sligo. At least, not yet," Aisling was saying. "The name Forbes has to be more than just coincidence. There is one more source I'd like to check though. Catharine—are you all right?"

"What? Oh, yes ... just a little dazed, that's all. What were you saying?"

"That I'd like to check the film with the Tithe Applotment records to see if Henry was living in Moher back in 1834."

And he was. Aisling was jubilant.

"Grace is going to be thrilled when we tell her. What do you want to bet, she'll be booking the trip to Ireland before we get back?" Aisling glanced at her watch. "We still have almost thirty minutes before the library closes. If we hurry, there might be time to take a look at the CD with Irish passenger lists."

"That's fine. Whatever you think...."

Aisling gave Catharine a close look, suddenly aware of the pallor in her face and the almost haunted look in her eyes. "On second thought, I think we should leave the passenger lists until tomorrow. Sometimes, I don't know when to stop. Would you like to go back to the hotel? That way, we can take it easy and have plenty of time to get ready for dinner."

Catharine managed a smile for Aisling's benefit. "Maybe that's not such a bad idea. I promise, I'll revive in time for dinner."

A HOT SHOWER and short rest helped restore Catharine's perspective as far as the day's discoveries were concerned, but the idea of tagging along on Aisling's dinner date was still less than appealing. She took two *Advil* for her pounding head and told herself the most she could expect from the evening was a passable meal and that Darren Taylor wouldn't treat her like a maidenly aunt.

Forty-five minutes later, as the three of them sat at a corner table in the Carriage House restaurant, Catharine knew she wouldn't have missed this experience for the world. Not only did the food exceed her expectations, the *Advil* had done its work, and the writer in her was totally intrigued by the young man at their table.

Darren Taylor was as good looking as Aisling had said, on the early side of thirty, with a pleasant smile, intelligent gray eyes and thick brown hair neatly combed into submission. He dressed well, with Ralph Lauren's signature logo very much in evidence, from the tailored beige shirt, to his dark brown slacks and highly polished shoes. Catharine wouldn't have been at all surprised to see his socks and underwear bearing the same *Polo* logo. But somehow, on Darren, it was strictly a borrowed image.

Catharine had been trying to figure out exactly what it was that bothered her about the man ever since he arrived at their hotel room, all smiles and politeness, with a small bouquet of flowers for her and a single red rose for Aisling. Was she being overly protective where her daughter was concerned? Or were her feminine instincts sending another message?

Aisling was looking particularly lovely, in a silk blouse of periwinkle blue that brought out the deeper blue of her eyes, and black slacks that showed her slender figure to good advantage.

Darren was clearly not unaware of the young woman's beauty. Catharine could see that much in his eyes. Still, there was something in his manner that she found vaguely irritating, but as yet, it was something she was unable to identify.

They chatted fairly easily through the *h'ors oeuvres* and salads, with Darren plying Catharine with a few polite questions.

"Is this your first trip to Salt Lake?"

"No, it isn't."

A nod and no further comment.

"Aisling tells me your research is going well."

"Yes."

Another nod. "That's good."

Catharine tried to give his non-interested eyes and voice the benefit of the doubt. It could be he was feeling a little awkward or even shy because of her presence. Darren livened up considerably when Aisling asked about his seminars for the business conference at the Salt Palace. Listening to him, Catharine had to admit the man was intelligent and hard working.

Yet, as she observed the interplay between the two, it was almost as if Darren and Aisling were reading lines from two different plays, each making the proper entrance and delivering the proper lines, but with no continuity or cohesiveness, and certainly no enjoyment.

As they talked, Catharine found herself studying Aisling's voice and demeanor. There was no glow on her lovely face, not even the hint of one. There was no sparkle when her eyes met his.

She doesn't love him, Catharine decided. And he doesn't love her. Not the real Aisling. He's enchanted with the outer wrappings, but he hasn't a clue about the worth and fineness of the package contents.

Then the main course arrived and Catharine sat in silent fascination, trying not to stare at the phenomenon occurring at their table.

Darren had ordered prime rib with mashed potatoes and gravy, and petite peas on the side. While she could find nothing overt to criticize in his manners, Catharine had never witnessed anything quite like the way Darren approached his food.

The white mound of potatoes vaguely resembled one of the ring forts she had seen in Ireland, with the sides neatly fortified and the brown well of gravy carefully contained by the constant maneuverings of his fork. After each bite, the walls of the ring fort were quickly mended and shaped by that ever-moving fork, a little pushing here. Some quick arranging there.

It was all Catharine could do to tear her eyes away from the ring-fort of potatoes long enough to eat her own meal. At the moment, Aisling was intent on telling Darren about their latest discoveries at the Family History Library and didn't seem to notice the construction project going on at the dinner place next to hers.

The man's obsession with neatness was as revealing as it was bizarre. The regiment of peas was kept properly in line and even his meat didn't escape unscathed. In no time at all, Darren had the thick slice of juicy prime rib cut into neat little squares and rectangles, so closely identical in size that Catharine began to wonder if he had a built-in ruler for a brain, neatly calibrating and measuring the size of each piece.

As the meal progressed, the ring-fort slowly diminished in size, but never lost its shape. Always, there was that deftly moving fork, shaping, patting, pushing and scooping, never losing control until the last bite was taken.

Catharine felt as if she had just witnessed the building of the Pyramids in reverse.

Dessert was no less amazing. A chocolate brownie was set in front of him, looking for all the world like a chubby Italianate villa with a dome of vanilla ice cream on top and a drizzle of hot fudge oozing down the sides. The deconstruction project began immediately. This time it was hallmarked by the rhythmic scraping of Darren's fork against the china plate, rather than the pushing and shoving reserved for the potatoes.

Scra-a-a-pe, scra-a-pe, scra-a-pe, scrape, scrape. The villa neatly disappeared along with its swirls of chocolate syrup. The rhythm between bites was as jarring to the ear as the drilling of a metallic woodpecker. *Scra-a-a-pe, scra-a-pe, scra-a-pe, scrape, scrape.*

When Darren asked a question about her new novel, Catharine found it difficult not to answer in the same rhythm as the fork. More than once, she had to douse her smiles and rising laughter in her glass of ice water.

As they were leaving the restaurant, Darren made and withdrew an invitation in the same moment. "I'd love to take you to a movie, that is, if there were anything worth seeing; but I'm supposed to give a seminar at seven-thirty in the morning, and I really ought to spend some time going over my notes."

Aisling didn't seem to be the least bit disappointed by this, and it was all Catharine could do to contain her relief. Thinking what he might do with a bag of popcorn was enough to boggle the mind, and more than she was up to.

After thanking him for the dinner, Catharine wished Darren well with his seminar. She even managed a little good-bye kiss on the cheek.

A half-hour later, she and Aisling were relaxing in their pajamas, but unlike other evenings, Aisling showed no interest in going over their genealogy research or watching the news.

Turning off the TV, she said, "Darren really liked you."

"He did? I wasn't sure."

"Oh, yes. He's never very demonstrative with his feelings, but I could tell." She paused, and then with an anxious look, "What did you think of him?"

Catharine hesitated, searching for a balance between honesty and tact. "He's—very nice, and very good-looking, just as you said."

"You don't like him."

"No, no it's not that." Catharine searched wildly for a word to describe him, then said, "He's—uh, certainly very focused."

"Focused?" Aisling's mouth curved upwards in a wry grin.

Catharine took in the appealing youthfulness of her daughter's expression and her slender figure in silky Nile-green pajamas. In many ways, Aisling not only looked, but seemed much younger than her years. "What do *you* think of Darren?" she countered. "I think that's much more important."

Aisling frowned at this and gave a little shrug. "I'm not sure." She blew out a sigh and said without an ounce of joy or enthusiasm. "Last night, he asked me to marry him. Well, not asked exactly. It wasn't anything that formal or definite. We just sort of discussed where our relationship was going, and Darren thought that marriage was the next logical step."

"Logical?" Catharine said. "That doesn't sound very romantic."

"I know, but romance is such a fleeting thing, and we really do get along very well," Aisling put in quickly. "We have a lot of things in common."

"I hope love is one of those things."

Aisling shrugged once more, this time in a gesture of fatalistic resignation. "I have to admit, Darren doesn't inspire any great passion in me, but maybe that's a good thing. It helps you stay more clear headed and more—"

"Focused?" Catharine supplied, and they both laughed.

"I don't know that passion is always necessary to be happy," Aisling observed with the easy nonchalance of youth. "Most of the time, it does nothing but get people into trouble."

Catharine smiled. "True, but passion and love aren't the same thing, any more than lust and love are."

Aisling had no reply to this, just sat, thoughtfully twirling a strand of red-gold hair.

"And there are all kinds of passion," Catharine went on. "You approach your work with real passion, as well as intelligence. I've seen that sparkle in your eyes, and heard the excitement in your voice. The passion inside you brings more meaning and enjoyment to everything you do."

"So what are you trying to tell me?"

Catharine took a deep breath, as her reluctance to give advice wrestled with more protective, maternal emotions.

"It's okay," Aisling said with a little smile. "I know you don't want to interfere, so just tell me how you feel."

"All right. In spite of Darren's good qualities—and I'm sure he has a lot of them—I just don't think you could be happy with a man—a man who has such an unnatural relationship with his potatoes."

Aisling's open-mouthed astonishment widened into a grin. "With his potatoes?"

"It's true. Richard Dreyfuss in 'Close Encounters' could take lessons from Darren. Didn't you notice? All through dinner he was arranging, and patting and straightening the edges with his fork. And it wasn't only the potatoes. The way he maneuvered his peas was just as bad. He practically had them lined up in regiments, and if a straggler so much as dared get out of line, he'd scoot that little green deserter right back with the others."

Aisling was nearly doubled over by this time, with tears running down her cheeks. "Catharine, stop! My sides are killing me."

"Well, you wanted to know what I thought," Catharine said, joining in the laughter. "The truth is, I'd much rather see you end up with someone like Mr. Misogynist than Mr. Potato Head."

Aisling fell back across the bed and it took some time before either one of them could stop laughing long enough to talk.

"I'll never be able to look Darren in the eyes again without thinking of Mr. Potato Head," Aisling gasped, wiping her eyes.

Looking at her daughter, Catharine felt a wave of overwhelming love. "Aisling, you have this incredibly tender, yet passionate spirit—and watching Darren tonight, I couldn't stand the thought of him mashing you down and constantly trying to keep you in line. Sooner or later, he'd realize he couldn't control you, and you'd both end up miserable." She paused, then added quietly, "I know, because I married my husband for all the wrong reasons."

Aisling's smile faded as she glimpsed the shadow of pain in Catharine's eyes.

"I was your age when I met Justin," she went on, "and at the time, all I could see was how handsome and charming he was. No, that's not true. There were other things," she amended with some honest introspection, "but I didn't want to see them. I was very lonely, and very aware that the clock of my youth was ticking away. It was fairly easy to convince myself that whether I loved Justin or not, didn't really matter ... that my feelings for him would grow with time. He was widowed with a little boy, and all I wanted was to be married and part of a family."

"Those don't sound like the wrong reasons," Aisling said. "Not really. I've felt the same way this past year, ever since I turned thirty. No matter how fulfilling my work is—it can't take the place of being married and having a family."

"I know, but a marriage without love? Believe me, that can be even emptier and more lonely than being single."

Aisling's shoulders slumped and she released a groan of pure frustration. "Why does it have to be so complicated? Sometimes I think life would be much simpler if we left love out of the equation altogether, and just lined up and took a number."

"Simpler, maybe," Catharine agreed with a little smile, "but—oh my, what we'd miss...."

Aisling straightened at something in Catharine's tone. "There was someone else, wasn't there? Someone you really loved."

"Yes, but that ended years before I met Justin."

"What happened?"

Catharine was silent for a moment, not sure how much to say. "Something that should have been simple, got very complicated," she said. "There were others who interfered and—well—I mistakenly thought he no longer cared. It all happened a long time ago...."

"But you still love him, don't you." The softly spoken words were a statement, rather than a question.

"Yes...."

"I'm so sorry."

"No, don't be sorry. I'm not."

"But the pain, and the loneliness—"

Catharine smiled and told her, "It doesn't always hurt. I know it sounds trite, but time really is a great healer."

"It may heal, but it hasn't changed the love," Aisling said with quiet wonder.

Catharine sat very still, staring at nothing. "It's amazing how it happens. Sometimes, when I least expect it, a feeling or a memory will come back ... like the wind on a breathless day. He's like that for me. Just when I think I've grown accustomed to a stifling lack of air, his memory breezes by, and I know all over again that I'll always love him.... "

Aisling's eyes glistened with unshed tears as she got up and put her arms around Catharine. "Thank you for telling me," she said.

19

"Star of the West"

Rain fell during the night, leaving its freshness and a newly washed clarity to the morning. Sidewalks and roads were still damp, as Catharine and Aisling made the familiar walk from the Marriott to the Family History Library.

"Mmm. The air smells like spring," Aisling drew a deep lung full of its sweetness, then smiled at Catharine. "I feel like spring," she said with touching exuberance. "And I can hardly wait to get hold of those passenger lists. No matter how good I feel about the Henry Clifford we found in Griffith's, I'll feel a lot better if we have one more source to link him to County Leitrim."

Catharine nodded, only half-listening. *I should have told her*, she thought. *Last night, I had the perfect opportunity and I let it go by*.

"You're awfully quiet this morning," Aisling commented. "Didn't you sleep well?"

As a matter of fact, she had tossed and turned half the night, alternately tortured by memories of Eamonn and the increasingly heavy weight of telling her daughter the truth. Mother was right,

Catharine thought, about not waiting too long. Last night would have been the perfect time, but once again, fear had kept her silent. The fear that, if Aisling knew the truth, it would bring an end to everything.

"I was just thinking how fast the week's gone by," Catharine said. "And how much I've enjoyed it. Do you think we'll still be taking the flight back in the morning, or do you want to stay a little longer?"

Aisling smiled. "Let's see what the day brings."

Minutes later, they were sitting side by side in a cubicle with a computer and CD-ROM containing information on nearly a million and a half names of Irish immigrants who had arrived in the ports of New York City and Boston.

Aisling typed in the name of Henry Clifford, and they began examining the various passengers by that name, checking the person's age and date of arrival for a match with that of Esther's father and brother. Ordinarily, Catharine's enthusiasm for the work would have kept pace with her daughter's, but not today, not when she felt this desperate urgency growing inside.

"All right!" Aisling said in an excited whisper. "Here's a Henry C., age 58, who arrived in New York, on March 24, 1863. The age is way off, but the year of arrival is right for him to be Esther's father."

Catharine wrote down the information that Aisling gave her, including the ship's name. Moments later, another Henry Clifford caught their attention. This one, age 23, who sailed to New York from Liverpool on the 'Star of the West.'

"Esther's brother. It has to be," Aisling said. "Let's go upstairs and get the films for the ship manifests."

Catharine gathered up her things and followed after, feeling like a weary tug boat, trailing along in the wake of a winged clipper ship.

Aisling didn't seem to notice Catharine's pensive silence, as all her excitement and energy focused on following this particular 'clue.' "I think there's a good chance we'll find more information on Henry Sr.'s ship," she said once they were settled with films in hand. "Coming over at a later date and on a steamship, the steward often made more detailed entries."

But this was not the case. After searching through the list of two hundred plus steerage passengers, they finally spotted Esther's father, brothers and sister Mary—but in the column designated for country of origin, there was only the abbreviation, *Ire.*, with a trail of ditto marks going down the page.

"Well, we tried," Aisling said, disappointment evident in her face as well as her voice. "At least now, you'll have the name of the ship and the exact date of their arrival for your book. That's something, I suppose."

"It certainly is. It's a good deal more than I hoped to find," Catharine told her, trying to lift her crestfallen expression. "What about the manifest for young Henry's ship? We still haven't checked that one, and I like the name of his ship a lot more than the 'City of Manchester.'"

This comment produced a smile. "Don't tell me," Aisling said dryly. "The 'Star of the West' is more—"

"Romantic," Catharine filled in. "And it is. The name fairly reeks of romance."

"Considering the times, the ship probably reeked of a lot of things."

"True, but think how much better 'Star of the West' will look on a page than some of the others we've seen, like 'Webster' or 'Yorkshire.' Who wants to read about a ship that sounds like a dictionary or a pudding?"

Aisling's gloom gave way to laughter as she deftly threaded the film into the machine. Moments later, she turned to Catharine with a frown. "The name may be more poetic, but the steward's penmanship is atrocious. Reading the passenger list for the 'Manchester' was a breeze compared to this one."

Catharine had to agree. Between the tight black cursive and the blurred darkness of the film itself, their progress slowed to a crawl. With so much concentration needed to decipher the names, Catharine gave heed to little else, until Aisling's gasp brought her up short.

"What? Have you found him?"

"Not yet—but I just realized something. Look at the column under country of origin."

Catharine did so, and felt her pulse quicken. In addition to each passenger's name, age, sex and occupation, their home county had been painstakingly recorded. *Limerick. Galway. Dublin and Wicklow.* The musical names flowed down the page like a litany.

"God bless the man who took the time to do this," she whispered.

Heightened expectancy mingled with the fear of disappointment as they began searching the massive list of steerage passengers. Name after name went slowly by. Catharine could almost see them in her mind, answering the captain's roll call: work-weary young men, with nothing more than the clothes on their backs and a few shillings in their pockets; nervous young spinsters, hoping to find work as a domestic. And small, ragged children, kept anxiously in tow by haggard parents—a deck crowded with exiles, leaving heart and homeland behind.

Aisling stopped the film. Her breath came out in a long sigh.

That same moment, Catharine's eyes found the name Henry Clifford and she was almost afraid to look at anything else.

Then Aisling was gripping her hand, her voice breathless with excitement. "Oh, Catharine...."

There, beside the occupation of common laborer was written clearly and unmistakably, *Leitrim*. The name blurred as tears filled Catharine's eyes and spilled down her cheeks.

"Thank you ... oh, thank you," was all she could say.

Aisling's grip tightened on her hand. "We've found them! We've found your family in Ireland!"

Catharine met her daughter's eyes. "They're your family, too, Aisling."

"What are you saying?" Aisling's look was uncomprehending, then searching. "How can they be my family?"

Catharine hesitated, then glanced at the other patrons working in the dimly lit area. "Could we go someplace more private? I need to talk to you ... about something very important."

CATHARINE'S WORDS AND voice played like an echo to the nervous beating of Aisling's heart as she picked up her purse and jacket and followed Catharine out of the library, into the chilly clarity of the afternoon. The sunlight had a harshness to it, and the cold breeze cut through her thin jacket.

Aisling tried to think what could be so important to merit that look in Catharine's eyes, and the almost determined grimness in her tone. *They're your family, too...* How could the Clifford's be her family, unless...? Aisling refused to carry the thought further, but her heart was pounding hard and fast. She saw Catharine glancing around the area between the genealogy library and the Church Art Museum. Then, with that same look of determination, she headed across the street to Temple Square.

"Is there anywhere private where we could talk?" Catharine asked when they were inside the grounds.

Aisling glanced toward the gothic-styled structure of the Assembly Hall where a tour was just exiting. "The Assembly Hall is open," she said. "I'm sure it would be all right if we went in for a few minutes."

The guide confirmed this, assuring Catharine and Aisling they were welcome to sit and visit, as there wouldn't be another tour along for at least half an hour.

Inside, the building was reminiscent of an old English church, with its high arched ceiling, stained-glass windows, and wooden pews. Their footsteps echoed hollowly on the hardwood floors as Catharine, after taking a brief look around, chose a bench in a secluded corner alcove.

Aisling sat down without a word, feeling her heart beat faster as her thoughts pounded out questions with no answers.

"I've been trying to find the right way and the right time to tell you this for weeks," Catharine said, "but I haven't known how. Maybe there isn't a right way or time, but you need to know...."

"Know what?" Aisling asked in a dry voice.

Catharine's blue eyes met hers. "That thirty-one years ago in May, I had a baby out of wedlock ... a beautiful baby girl ... and I gave her up for adoption. Not because I didn't love her—" She paused, then corrected herself. "Not because I didn't love *you*, Aisling—but because I wanted you to grow up in a home with two parents who loved you. And at the time, I had no hope of seeing your father again."

Aisling could only stare as her mind struggled with the enormity of what she was hearing.

Catharine was silent, probably waiting for her to respond or say something. But there were no words … no feelings … only a hard knot that hurt deep inside.

After a moment, Catharine drew a ragged breath and went on in halting tones. "I hope … in time, that you'll forgive me … and please … I don't want you to think I'd ever try to replace your adoptive mother. I'm sure she was a wonderful woman … I wish I could thank her for all she did. But I hope there'll be some place for me in your life. And for your grandmother."

Aisling felt dizzy with the realization. Grace, her grandmother? And Catharine Cavanagh, her birth mother?

Silence stretched out like an aching thread between them. "I don't know what to say," she said finally. "I don't know what to do with this … where to put it." It was strange, to be handed a missing piece of one's life—a huge piece—and not know where to put it, but it was true. Aisling found herself looking at Catharine as if she were seeing a stranger, as if someone had taken away her friend, her confidante and companion, and put a stranger in her place—a stranger she was supposed to call Mother.

"I think we should be heading back to the hotel," she said.

DINNER WAS AWKWARD and silent, with neither Aisling nor Catharine having much appetite. Where Aisling usually had to curb her tendency to talk all through dinner, she now had difficulty saying anything at all. The contrast between this painful new silence and their usual uninhibited chatter was keenly felt.

By the time they returned to their room, the numbness was fading, and shock waves of resentment had taken its place. Catharine and Grace must have known all this when they first hired her to work on the Clifford line. How could they have used her in such a way? She felt like a pawn being moved about at the whim of two chess players.

A quiet voice inside argued that neither one would intentionally want to hurt her, but she refused to listen. Anger helped her to function, at least, and anything was better than the cold numbness she had experienced when Catharine told her the truth. One moment, she felt like accusing and tossing out blame, and the next, she would see the silent suffering in Catharine's eyes and feel a pang of guilt for her reaction to the situation. Hadn't she longed to find her birth parents? Yearned to discover and know her parentage? Then, why wasn't she feeling overjoyed or at least grateful to know that Catharine Cavanagh was her mother?

"Would you like to call Grace this evening, and tell her about the ship manifests?" Catharine asked. "Or did you want to go back to the library?"

The library. The words brought Aisling back to the surface from the deeps of her own thoughts where she had been floundering.

"The library ..." she said aloud. "I left my portfolio ... and I forgot to make copies of the manifests. I think the microfilm's still on the machine." She hesitated an awkward moment before asking, "Do you want to come?"

Catharine shook her head, and there was a sad sort of patience in her voice. "No, you go ahead. Do what you need to do."

Aisling walked swiftly up West Temple Street toward the library, feeling a mixture of guilt and relief. Relief to be outside and alone with her feelings, and guilt that she should so badly want and need to get away.

Evening was coming on with gentle grayness, the colors and confusing elements of the day fading into softness that soothed the sharp edges of her hurt and anger. She wasn't angry—not really. But so much new knowledge left her feeling helpless and vulnerable. When she acknowledged that, the tears were never far away. Crying was something she refused to allow. Not now.

Entering the library, Aisling gave her watch a quick glance. Seven fifty. She took the stairs to the second floor at a near run and headed for the area of reader machines, as two conflicting voices argued inside her. One was resentful and full of self-pity, whispering that two strangers were trying to encroach on her safe existence, telling her she belonged to them. The other acknowledged with quiet wonder that Catharine and Grace had never felt like strangers, that her heart seemed to recognize a kinship and comfortable companionship with them both from the beginning.

Weaving her way along a narrow aisle between desks, chairs and patrons, Aisling felt hot tears pricking her eyelids and angrily blinked them back. The next moment she nearly collided with a familiar, dark-bearded man in a baseball cap.

Surprise and recognition flickered in his dark eyes as the two of them stopped short of a head-on collision.

"Sorry," Aisling said, and after a helpless shrug, hurried past, not seeing the concerned glance that followed her down the aisle.

Where was it she and Catharine been sitting? What if one of the staff members had come along and taken their things to the lost and found? Then, turning down the next row, she caught sight of her portfolio, still lying on the desk top, along with her notebook and pens. The microfilm they had been checking was still in the machine.

Aisling blew out a shaky breath, silently blessing the consideration of patrons and staff alike for leaving their things undisturbed. She hurriedly gathered them up, putting notebooks and pens in her portfolio, then removed the film. Glancing over the top of the machine, she caught sight of a baseball cap on the next aisle over, only a few feet away.

Why, of all evenings did *he* have to be here? Didn't she have enough to deal with already?

Self-pity yielded to guilt as she remembered the look in Catharine's eyes when she left the hotel. Aisling knew she ought to do nothing more than make the necessary copies, then return to the Marriott. She also knew she wasn't ready to go back. Not yet. And since Mr. M. was occupied on the second floor, where was the harm in spending a few minutes on the B-2 level?

Still wrestling with the should's versus the want to do's, Aisling made copies of the revelatory ship's manifest for Henry Clifford. Somehow, just seeing his name and beside it, the long sought after county in Ireland, brought a measure of peace into her mixed-up soul. *This really is my family,* she thought. *I've been doing genealogy for my own people.*

So why wasn't I told before? the other voice demanded. *Why string me along, letting me believe I was just doing another job?*

Aisling snatched up the copies and the rest of her things and headed for the elevator. She couldn't go back to the hotel, not with tears and anger still so close to the surface. Stepping inside the elevator, she punched the button for B-2 with a vengeance that widened the eyes of the diminutive, gray-haired little soul standing next to her.

"Some days can be awfully frustrating," the woman ventured timidly. "But don't give up, dear. I'm sure you'll find what you're looking for."

Aisling forced a smile and semi-pleasant nod. That's just it, she thought. I have found what I was looking for. So why aren't I thrilled and grateful? What's wrong with me?

Getting off on the B-2 level, Aisling noticed that only a small handful of patrons were on the computers, and even fewer occupied the study area. In spite of this, she found herself unable to concentrate or enjoy the luxury of some quiet research.

Feeling as if she had to justify her stay, Aisling looked up the surname Clifford in the Index for the Dublin Register of Deeds. She would allow herself thirty minutes, no longer, then return to the hotel. Catharine would understand. Dropping her portfolio on one of the tables, she hurried to the filing cabinets where the films were stored, determined to shut out confusing thoughts of the present with a doorway to the past.

The 1700's, long known as the 'silent century' for Irish research, had several entries for the name Clifford, but most were concerned with the land and property of those Clifford families living in County Wexford or Dublin. Then, in the late 1700's and early 1800's she discovered a few deeds for one Henry Clifford and his brother Samuel, living in County Leitrim.

Frustration soon yielded to fascination as she read the wordy legalese of some two centuries before. One deed in particular, describing the business dealings between Henry Clifford, gentleman, of Mount Campbell in County Leitrim, and Samuel Crawford of Newtown Forbes, in neighboring County Longford caught her attention. Forbes. There was that name again. Checking the town's location on a map, she discovered it was very near Castle Forbes, less than a mile from the demesne itself.

The surname Crawford struck a significant note as well. But why? Then she remembered the marriage certificate she'd recently found for Esther's brother. Along with other pertinent information, his full name had been given: *George Crawford Clifford*.

There had to be some sort of connection between the families. Cliffords. Forbes. And now, Crawfords. All living within a five to ten-mile radius of each other. Possibilities raced through her mind as she read and took notes. And through it all, was a growing sense of pride. These people were her ancestors, not someone else's, but her own.

On her way back from making a copy of the deed, Aisling gave the wall clock near the information desk a quick glance. Nine-fifteen! Guilt shifted into panic mode as she hurriedly returned the films to their proper file drawers, then went back for her jacket and portfolio. The jacket was there, draped across the back of the chair, but what had she done with her portfolio? Glancing around, her heart skipped a beat as she caught sight of Mr. M. heading in her direction. *Not again.* She'd had enough encounters for one day.

The next moment, her searching eyes found the stray portfolio lying on a chair beside one of the tables. Attention focused straight ahead, she marched over to the chair and snatched up the portfolio.

Aisling was halfway to the information desk, when she heard a familiar masculine voice call out something from behind. Ignoring the voice, she kept on walking, dropped off the Index to the Registry of Deeds without missing a step, and headed for the elevators like a racehorse for the finish line.

The voice came again, closer now, and more insistent. "Excuse me … could you wait a second?"

Aisling punched the Up elevator button and mentally willed the blasted doors to open.

Then the running footsteps halted and a voice close beside her said, "Hi, I think there's been a slight mix-up."

Aisling turned and gave Mr. M. an innocently inquiring look, as if she hadn't known exactly whose voice and footsteps had been behind her. "A mix-up?"

The bearded lips parted in a smile, and his dark eyes met hers with more than a glint of amusement. "I think you may have taken my portfolio by mistake."

The elevator doors opened, seeming to wait a breathless moment while Aisling glanced at the leather valise in her hands, before shutting firmly once more.

"I don't think so," she said. "Mine has my initials on the front. *A. M.*"

"So does mine," he said, his smile broadening to a devastating grin. "Same initials. *A. M.*"

"They can't be...." Aisling stared at the black leather portfolio in his hands, then back to the one she was clutching. "They are the same."

"The similarity ends there," he said, "unless your name happens to be Alex Moran."

She smiled and shook her head, feeling more foolish by the moment.

"Well, if your name isn't Alex, the initials must stand for something—other than the time of day, that is."

"Aisling Montgomery," she said and meekly offered him the portfolio. "I'm sorry about the mix-up. I was in kind of a hurry."

"So I noticed," he said as they made the exchange. "You would have been even more sorry if you'd got home and discovered the estate papers of Loftus Tottenham. The man kept meticulous accounts of everything he owned, down to the last turnip and cabbage, but completely ignored any mention of his wife and seven children."

She couldn't help laughing a little. "Then it's a good thing you caught up to me. After all the work I went to to find this family, I'd hate to lose them now...." The words were lightly spoken, but she knew in one jolting moment, that they were true. She didn't want to lose them. Or Catharine.

"Are you all right?" Alex asked, knowing full well she wasn't. He'd known it ever since their near collision upstairs, when he'd glimpsed the hurt and confusion staring out of those incredible blue eyes. He had to fight the impulse to follow after her right then. All the teasing and the lightness vanished as he watched her now. "I had the feeling something was wrong when I saw you upstairs a while ago."

A dozen denials passed through her mind—easy verbal dodges and ways to avoid admitting the truth. But somehow, she couldn't give voice to one. "I–I've had something of a shock today," she confessed. "And my mind can't seem to focus on much of anything ... which is probably why I took your portfolio instead of mine."

"I have an excellent remedy for shock," he said with a gentle smile.

"You do?"

He nodded. "A steaming mug of hot chocolate, with a fat dab of whipping cream on top. And if the symptoms are really serious, you can always add a sticky cinnamon bun. Works wonders."

She smiled back. "Thanks. I'll have to try it sometime."

"What about now? We could go somewhere and talk. J.B.'s is just down the street."

Her lips parted as she stared at his darkly handsome face, with common sense making a feeble attempt to win out over much stronger desires. "But ... we don't really know each other."

Alex pushed the Up button on the elevator. "Yes, we do," he said. "We've known each other for a long time. We just haven't talked much, that's all."

Aisling was still trying to take in the full import of this remarkable statement when the elevator doors parted. Smiling, Alex Moran took her arm, and they stepped inside.

20

Alex

Aisling slowly stirred the dollop of cream into her steaming mug of chocolate, watching it mix, then melt into the drink. "Alex Moran," she said, still intent on stirring the cream. "That's very Irish."

"It is at that," he answered, with a bit of the brogue. "My father's grandfather came over during the famine years. My mother's people are mostly English, with a little Danish on the side. What about you? With a name like Aisling and that hair, you must have more than just a touch of the Irish."

She could feel the warmth of his gaze on her face as surely as she felt the warmth of the chocolate sliding down her throat. And something in the way he said *'that hair'* quickened her pulse in a way that was not at all unpleasant.

"Yes, I do."

"And what about Montgomery? Are your father's people Scottish or English?"

She hesitated, and Alex sensed rather than saw a shadow cross her features. "English, for the most part," she answered, adding quietly, "but that isn't my actual bloodline. I was adopted by the Montgomery's."

"And … is that a sensitive issue with you?" he asked, not unkindly. "I didn't mean to pry."

"No, I know you didn't. I've known I was adopted since I was a child, but … it's only been since this afternoon that I've known anything about my birth parents."

Alex was silent, watching the play of emotion on her lovely face. Hurt and confusion, even a little anger, were evident on the expressive features. "Is that the shock you were referring to?" he asked quietly.

She nodded.

He waited a moment, watching as she sipped the hot chocolate. "Didn't you want to know about them?"

"Oh no, it's not that. I've wondered about them for years," she admitted. "I think most people who are adopted have some curiosity about their birth parents. But I've never really pursued anything, or even thought seriously about the issue until after my mother—my adoptive mother died."

"And when was that?"

"Five years ago. She and my father were both quite a bit older when they got me—in their late forties."

"And is your adoptive father still living?"

Again, she nodded. "He remarried a couple of years ago, to a mutual friend whose husband passed away not long after my mother did. I'm very glad they have each other," she said with a little smile. "I hated seeing Dad so lonely."

Alex was silent for a moment, not wanting to push her. She

glanced up then and their glances met in a way that suddenly had him wondering, *What the hell was I thinking to deny myself this for so long? I could have spoken to her months ago.* More than that. It had been well over a year since he'd first noticed her working alone on B-2. Aloud, he asked casually, "So how did you find your birth parents?"

"I didn't. They—she found me."

He watched her draw a steadying breath, and saw that mixture of hurt and confusion cloud her eyes once more.

"Do you remember the woman I was with when I saw you in the elevator the other day?" she began.

He tried to think, then shook his head. "I don't remember any other woman."

Warm color flooded her cheeks, and the sudden soft shine in her eyes was far from displeased. "You honestly didn't notice?"

He shrugged. "There may have been someone else there. I didn't pay much attention," he said, thinking back to the afternoon in question. He'd been more than a little weary, after an eleven-hour stint in his photography shop the day before, and a miserable migraine that kept him up half the night. To add to the frustration, his genealogy research for an English family by the name of Rix was leading him in a merry chase with nothing but frustrating circles and dead-ends. Then he'd seen her, standing in the blasted elevator, looking as fresh as the first day of spring. He remembered the tentative sound of her hello. And the scent of her perfume, something light and flowery, not overpowering or sickly sweet. Why had he made that stupid remark about being tired? But she had asked, and he'd answered without thinking. She seemed slightly uncomfortable in his presence, and he wondered why.

"The woman I was with is Catharine Cavanagh—the author," Aisling was saying. "I've been helping her with family history research for a new book she's writing...."

"The name sounds familiar," Alex answered with a noncommittal shrug. "What sort of books does she write?"

Aisling's look was incredulous. "Historical romances, and I can't believe you haven't heard of her. Why, practically every book she writes hits the *New York Times*' bestseller list."

"Then I'm sure she must be a very good writer," Alex said easily, "but historical romances have never been my preferred genre."

"She's not just good—she's incredible! I've read all her novels at least a dozen times each."

"Okay. So you're here with Catharine Cavanagh, and her books are incredible." The teasing glint was back in his dark eyes. "What exactly does all this have to do with finding your birth parents?"

"It has everything to do with it," Aisling said in a dazed sort of voice. "Catharine Cavanagh is...." She cleared her throat and glanced down at the mug of chocolate. "Catharine is my birth mother. She told me this afternoon...."

Alex leaned against the cushions of the booth and stared at her. "And you had no idea?"

"No ... how could I?"

He blew out a stunned breath. "How do you feel about all this?"

"Like the song says, 'dazed and confused.'" Aisling shook her head. "It's something I've longed to know and now that I do ... I don't know what to do with it."

"What's she like? A lot of authors, like any other kind of celebrity, I suppose, have insufferable egos."

"Catharine's not like that at all. Just the opposite. She's very kind, and funny and sympathetic...."

"Then, you like her?" he asked carefully.

"Of course I do."

"And you're not disappointed, or ashamed to know that she's your birth mother?"

"Ashamed? Good heavens, why would I be ashamed? Catharine's a wonderful person and ... and ... oh, I don't know what's wrong with me, except that it was so much simpler the other way—before I knew." She glanced at him with a helpless shrug. "That probably makes no sense at all...."

"Actually, it makes a lot of sense. I think what you're really saying is that it's a lot easier to be in awe of Catharine Cavanagh the author, than to know she's the mother who gave you up."

Aisling bit her lip, feeling the sudden sting of tears as his words rang true deep inside. She nodded, struggling to control her emotions. "Yes, I guess it is. That makes me sound very small, doesn't it?"

"No, not small ... just human." Alex's dark eyes were warm on her face. "Besides, I'm not telling you anything that you don't already know."

"If I did, I didn't want to admit it," she said, somehow not minding that he should know this about her. "And I do care about Catharine. But it's so odd—no, not odd—somewhere between incredible and uncomfortable to think of her as my mother."

"Maybe that's because you've given her just one role to play in your life."

She stared. "One role?"

"Well, maybe a limited role says it better," he said, rubbing his bearded chin in an unconscious gesture that she was coming to know and enjoy. "People do it all the time. Parents, children. Especially, husbands and wives. Some women go into marriage expecting their husbands to play the dual role of 'white knight hero' and romantic lover. When real life requires something else—like a friend—they're disappointed and disillusioned. Men can be just as bad. Some want nothing more from a wife than a glamorous mistress who doubles as a maid. Others want a beautifully wrapped package who doesn't think or threaten their fragile egos with opinions of her own. And then—" Alex broke off mid word to give her a crooked grin. "Sorry. I'll bet you didn't know that one of my many roles is part-time philosopher."

Aisling smiled and rested her chin on her hand. "I always liked philosophy."

A warm moment followed, when feelings instead of words hung suspended in the air between them, building intimacy's slender bridge.

Aisling was the first to glance away, shaken by the intensity of her response to him. Not thinking, she said, "You know, you don't sound at all like a misogynist."

"Misogynist?" Alex coughed and half-choked on the word. "Where did you get that idea?"

"From you, actually." She answered his blank look with, "One evening at the library, I couldn't help overhearing part of a conversation you were having with some of the staff."

Alex's smile was still faintly puzzled as he tried to find a place for this in his memory. "And when exactly did this illuminating conversation take place?"

"The last time I was in Salt Lake. Around the first week in October."

"Well...." The dark brows lifted slightly. "Either I must have made an indelible impression, or you have an amazing memory."

"I have an excellent memory," she answered lightly, but her cheeks bloomed with sudden color. "And even though it sounds incriminating, I really wasn't trying to eavesdrop. I just happened to be working nearby and—well, one doesn't meet a self-confessed misogynist every day. You told them you came from a long line of misogynists."

Alex started to chuckle, then threw back his head and laughed. "I remember now. I shocked Dave right out of his complacency, but poor old Helen—she's one of the volunteers—thought I meant massage therapist, and was all set to send me some of her elderly friends with back problems."

Aisling laughed, too, then asked, "Well, are you?"

He was thoughtful for a moment, then fixed her with an enigmatic smile. "Let's just say there've been times when I convinced myself that I had reason to be." The smile deepened. "But we'll talk about me another time."

Aisling felt a secret thrill of pleasure at the promise in his voice, as well as the words. Then she straightened up with a start. "Time!" she blurted out, glancing down at her watch. "Good heavens, how did it get to be so late? Catharine's going to be worried sick. I'd better get back to the hotel."

"Where are you staying? I'll walk you there."

"Just down the street at the Marriott, but you don't need to bother."

"It's no bother," Alex answered and, getting up, put some bills on the table beside his plate.

They left the restaurant and Aisling felt the gentle pressure of Alex's hand on her arm, as they crossed the street. They walked in silence for a few moments, and along with increased awareness, Aisling felt some of her former shyness return.

"Thanks for the shock treatment," she said, needing to say something, and trying to keep her voice light.

"I'm glad it helped. Will I see you tomorrow?"

"Tomorrow?"

"Will you be at the library?"

"No. Catharine and I will be flying home first thing in the morning."

"Where's home?"

"Sacramento, for me. Catharine and her mother live in Alameda."

"She lives with her mother?"

"It's a temporary thing. She's going through a divorce. Her husband is a real putz, let me tell you. I met him the night before we flew to Salt Lake."

"When will I see you again?" Alex asked, determined not to be sidetracked. "Do you have any more trips planned for Salt Lake in the near future?"

"Not right away. We'll be flying to Ireland in the next few weeks to do research there."

"Who's we? You and Catharine?"

"Actually, there'll be three of us. Grace is coming, too."

"Your grandmother?"

He said the words so easily, but their significance suddenly struck Aisling as nothing less than earth shattering. She would be traveling to Ireland with her mother and grandmother.

"That's right," she said, feeling a little dazed with the realization.

"Then I assume you'll be attending the conference," he went on.

"What conference?"

"The genealogy conference at Trinity College."

"Oh, I–we haven't got that far with our plans."

Alex put a detaining hand on her arm. "Didn't you say you were staying at the Marriott?"

Aisling gave the huge hotel to their left a surprised look as if it had suddenly dropped out of the sky. "Are we here already?"

"I'm afraid so," he said, and meant it.

They stood a few feet away from the gleaming glass entrance doors, both hesitating over good-byes that neither wanted to say.

"Do you have the right portfolio?" Alex asked with a teasing grin, "Or have we switched A.M.'s again?"

Aisling laughed and unzipped hers to check. "This is definitely mine. I'll leave the Tottenham's to you." She smiled into his eyes, aware that she had no idea when she would see him, and realizing that she very much wanted to. "Thank you again," she said softly. "For everything."

He nodded, but there was no answering smile on his face. Instead, he gave her a long, steady look, as if his eyes were drawing a picture for his mind to remember. He didn't want to miss a single detail. She glanced down in confusion, feeling warm and breathless inside. When she looked up once more, his dark eyes were still intent on her face. Then he leaned forward and for a brief moment, she felt his bearded lips against her cheek. There was promise, rather than passion in the kiss.

"Goodnight, Aisling," he said in a husky tone. "And sweet dreams." Then he turned and walked back up the street.

Aisling drifted into the hotel and floated toward the elevators. Not until she reached the door of their room, did reality's weight pull her back down to earth. She stood, key card in hand, knowing that her first impulse had been to rush in and share the evening's amazing events with Catharine. Then a secondary wave smothered the first, as she remembered the painful awkwardness that had marked her leaving. Gathering her tangled emotions together, she shoved the card into the slot. Whether she felt awkward or comfortable at this point didn't really matter. What mattered was Catharine.

She entered to see Catharine sitting in bed with a book in her lap.

"I'm sorry to be so late. I–I found our things and stayed to do a little more research."

"That's fine," Catharine told her, but the anguish in her red-rimmed eyes betrayed the calmness of her voice. "Darren called. Twice. He'd like you to call him."

"This late?"

"He said it was important, and to call as soon as you came in—no matter what time it was."

Aisling tossed her portfolio and purse on the bed with a frustrated sigh. Calling Darren was not the way she wanted to end the evening, but she might as well get it over with.

"Would you like some privacy?" Catharine asked. "I could always take another shower—or a long soak in the tub."

"No need," Aisling assured her, touched that Catharine would offer, and feeling more than a little guilty at her own insensitivity. Sitting down on the bed, Aisling kicked off her shoes, then picked up the phone and punched in the numbers.

"Hi, Darren. Catharine gave me your message."

"Well … I was beginning to wonder if you'd been kidnapped or something." His voice had a wounded sound with a hint of anger.

"Actually, I was kidnapped by Blackbeard the pirate," Aisling said wickedly. Glancing across at Catharine, she saw a spark of curiosity replace the bruised look in her eyes.

"You'll have to excuse me if I don't appreciate the sarcasm," Darren answered.

"Sorry," Aisling said with a sigh, unconsciously putting a hand to the cheek Alex had kissed. "I wasn't trying to be sarcastic."

"I certainly hope not."

The self-righteous reproof in his voice caused her spine to stiffen.

"What was it you wanted, Darren?"

"I wanted to let you know that there's been a change—a very important change in my job. That is, if you're interested in knowing."

Aisling raised her eyes heavenward and leaned back against the pillows. She hated his wounded martyr voice. "Do you want me to know?" she countered.

"Well, of course I do. I should think that much would be obvious since I've stayed up so late waiting for your call."

"Well then, I hope it's good news," was all she trusted herself to say.

"It is. I've been offered a promotion and a management position at the Seattle branch."

"That's wonderful, Darren. Congratulations."

"You don't sound very excited."

"Of course I'm excited," she said, trying to summon some warmth in her voice. "I'm thrilled for you."

"For *us*," he said meaningfully. "There's no reason now to wait. I think we should get married right away. Well, not right away—but soon, in a couple of months, as soon as I've had a chance to shape up the Seattle office and get things in order."

Listening to him, her mind produced the image of a white mound of potatoes on a plate, with Darren neatly shaping and pushing and getting it in order. Catharine was right. All in the same moment she knew that she did not love this man—that she could never marry him. Nor did she want to become one of the many things that needed 'shaping up.'

"Aisling ... are you there?"

His voice sounded worlds away. She smiled, hearing another voice telling her in words like a husky caress, " ... sweet dreams."

"I'm here," she sighed.

"Well … I'm waiting." The petulance and long-suffering was back.

Still smiling she said, "I'm sorry, Darren. I can't marry you."

In the bed next to hers, Catharine dropped the book, totally abandoning any pretense of reading.

"What do you mean, you can't?"

"What do you mean, what do I mean—I mean, I can't marry you. It wouldn't work for either of us."

Silence, followed by a stunned, "I can't believe you're saying this. What's happened? What changed your mind?"

"I haven't changed my mind. It's more like clarifying, rather than changing."

"What in hell's name are you talking about? Aisling, you're not making any sense."

"Really? I think I'm making perfect sense."

"And I think I should come over to your hotel right now. We need to talk."

"We are talking," Aisling said. "I'm sorry, Darren. I don't want to hurt you, but I–I just can't marry you."

"Give me one good reason!" he demanded.

"You mean, other than the fact that I'm not in love with you?" she answered quietly.

There was a potent moment of silence, followed by a long sigh. "We've discussed all this before," he said, his voice a mixture of weary patience and annoyance. "And you know I'm willing to wait … to be patient with your feelings. It's not like you to be so—unfair."

"Darren, please," Aisling began, then caught her breath as words suddenly came to her mind. "You said it yourself," she went on. "I'm not being fair." Glancing over at Catharine, she said, "If we got married, neither one of us would be happy, and we'd be breaking all the rules."

"What rules?"

"Share, care and be fair," Aisling said, her voice breaking a little. Still looking at Catharine, she felt tears coming to her eyes. "My mother shared those rules with me and I ... I think she's right. Goodbye, Darren."

She hung up as tears and a torrent of pent-up emotion broke the surface. All she could do was sit there, shaking and crying, the sobs hurting her chest. Then Catharine was beside her, holding her, and it felt right. Wonderfully right.

"Oh, Aisling ... Aisling, dear...."

Still half-blinded by tears, Aisling lifted her head and saw the tears in Catharine's eyes, and so much love that she couldn't speak. There was so much she wanted to tell her, if only she could find the words, but no words would come, only the tears.

Catharine held her close, murmuring, "It's all right. Everything will be all right now.... Oh, Aisling, I thought I'd lost you a second time."

Aisling met her mother's eyes. "You haven't lost me ... we both found a lot today."

21

I am sick of the showy seeming
Of a life that is half a lie;
Of the faces lined with scheming
In the throng that hurries by.

John Boyle O'Reilly

They talked late into the night, and as they talked the painful burden of years was gently lifted off Catharine's shoulders, never to return. Neither one felt any constraint, either in what should be asked, or how to answer. Like a spring rain that prepares the ground for planting, tears had softened and prepared the earth of their understanding. Hearts were open. This was their time to know and to share.

"Tell me about my father … how you met…."

"His name is Eamonn. Eamonn Gallagher from County Leitrim, and we…."

"Leitrim!" Aisling burst out before Catharine could say another word. "My father and the Cliffords are from the same county?"

Catharine smiled and nodded. "Believe me, the irony of that discovery wasn't entirely lost on me."

"No wonder you reacted the way you did…." Aisling straightened suddenly, her blue eyes wide. "I really am Irish—not just my ancestors—me!"

"Yes, you certainly are." Catharine smiled at the pride shining in her daughter's eyes.

"Tell me about him," Aisling said again. "How you met. Everything."

Catharine had barely begun, when Aisling interrupted once again, this time with a quiet, "He was the one. My father is the one you were talking about last night. The man you were in love with…."

"Yes," Catharine said. "Your father and I were very much in love."

After that, Aisling was content to listen to how it all happened so long ago….

"BEFORE I LEFT Ireland, your father gave me the Claddagh ring you're wearing. We were going to be married as soon as he finished school at Trinity." She watched as Aisling's glance went to the gold ring on her finger, then shook her head. "The first time you came to the house and I saw that ring … I was in such a state of shock I nearly fainted."

Aisling stared. You mean, you didn't know about me until then? Grace didn't—my grandmother didn't tell you?"

"No. Afterwards, Mother felt terrible about it. She wanted to prepare me, but didn't know how. I'm not sure it would have helped that much, even if she had. One doesn't have a script for things like this," she added, remembering her mother's words.

Aisling was silent, thinking of Catharine's emotional reaction at their first meeting, and Grace's hurried explanation about difficulties with a divorce. New respect for the way Catharine had handled the situation touched her understanding. Along with the respect, came added appreciation for the gold ring she wore. That Catharine would give it to her was no small sacrifice.

"You resemble your father much more than me," Catharine was saying.

"Don't tell me he has red hair."

Catharine laughed at this. "No. Eamonn's hair was dark brown, but very thick like yours, and curly. And you have his eyes...." She smiled tenderly at the young woman sitting beside her. "You get your hair from your great-great grandmother, Esther's daughter, Annie."

The wonder of it all was like sunlight filling a room that had long been dark. John and Esther ... Annie and Hugh.... The names danced in Aisling's mind like beams of light. These were her people. Her family. Then the light fell on another room, this one peopled by her father and his family. What were the Gallaghers like, she wondered?

"When we go to Ireland, will you—are you going to see my father?" she asked.

"I hope so. He needs to know about you, and you deserve to know him. No matter what the circumstances might be. I know there's a good chance Eamonn will be married with a family of his own. That's something I've had to face."

"Oh Catharine, I don't know how you can be so brave and unselfish...." Aisling broke off and a tinge of self-consciousness suddenly colored her voice. "Do you mind if I still call you Catharine?"

Catharine hesitated only slightly, privately acknowledging that having Aisling call her 'Mother' was something she longed to hear, but had no right to expect. "Of course not," she said aloud. "Whatever you feel comfortable with."

Aisling gave her a close look. "Are you sure? It's not that I—well, I don't want you to think—"

"It's all right," Catharine told her with a gentle smile. "It isn't as if I'm going to stop calling you Aisling and start referring to you as 'daughter' all the time."

"Thank you." Aisling reached out and covered Catharine's hand with her own.

Seeing their hands together, with the gold ring on Aisling's finger, Catharine felt as if a torn place inside her heart had been seamlessly mended. She swallowed hard, trying to keep emotions in check. "Before he gave it to me, your father explained the symbolism of the Claddagh, and how it should be worn. You have it on the correct hand, but after tonight—don't you think you should turn the ring around, so the heart faces outward? The way it is now means you have friendship and love is being considered."

"That's right. I'd forgotten which way meant what." Aisling was about to slip the ring off her finger, when the image of Alex Moran's bearded face moved into her thoughts. "Mmm, I think maybe I'll keep the ring the way it is."

Catharine's glance was puzzled. "But—you told Darren you wouldn't marry him."

"I certainly did. You were so right about him." A mischievous sparkle lit her blue eyes. "I was thinking of someone else…."

"Someone else?"

"Alex," came the soft answer.

"Who's Alex?"

"Until tonight, you knew him by another name," Aisling said with laughter in her voice. "Mr. Misogynist." She laughed again, at the stunned look on Catharine's face. "I ran into him at the library tonight. We nearly had a head-on this time. It was wonderful. And later, I was such a wreck I took his portfolio by mistake. And you'll never guess—"

Catharine shook her head, feeling more than a little dizzy with this account. "I'm sure I won't."

"We have the same initials," Aisling announced, as if that fact were of cataclysmic importance. "Which is partly why I picked up his portfolio, instead of mine, but still—isn't it amazing?"

"Amazing," Catharine agreed. "And what do the initials stand for? Surely not Alex Misogynist?"

Aisling laughed again, then sighed. "His name is Alex Moran. Don't you love that name? It just sort of rolls off the tongue, don't you think?"

Catharine managed a vague nod, as a moment of *déjà vu* sweetened her memory. *Catharine Gallagher ... Isn't that a wonderful name? It just sort of rolls off the tongue, don't you think?*

"It is a wonderful name," she said aloud. "And very Irish."

"I know, and of course, he's not really a misogynist. Although he did tell me there were times in his life when he felt he had reason to be...."

"Obviously, tonight wasn't one of those times," Catharine said dryly.

"No ... it wasn't."

Catharine smiled at the dreamy look in her daughter's eyes. "Well ... do I get to hear more about this amazing man or not?"

"The answer is a definite 'yes'," Aisling said and launched into a detailed account of her evening.

"Talking with Alex helped put everything into perspective," she said at length. "He was so understanding. I hope you'll forgive me for the way I acted earlier, but I was feeling so overwhelmed by everything."

"I know that. There's really nothing to forgive," Catharine said.

"You're going to make me start crying again," Aisling said, and took a deep breath. "Anyway, there's something about him ... the questions he asked, and the way he listened.... He just opened the doors and windows to all those stuffed up feelings, and let in the fresh air."

"And this from the woman who didn't believe it was possible to have an intelligent conversation with a man."

Aisling's face flushed with color. "I did say that, didn't I?"

"You did indeed."

"Talking with Alex was nothing like my conversations with Darren," she said. "With him, I always had the feeling that he wasn't listening so much as waiting for me to finish, so he could get on with whatever he was going to say. Either that or it was like talking to a wall."

"I noticed."

"You did?"

Catharine nodded. "What's more important, you know it now." She smiled and her voice took on a provocative note. "You realize, of course, that having an intelligent conversation with the right man can lead to other activities, none of which would be described as intellectual."

Aisling's face went from pink to scarlet. "I can't believe you're telling me this."

Catharine's laughter was as young as her daughter's. "Sorry. I couldn't resist teasing you a little. That day we met Alex in the elevator, there was enough chemistry in the air between you two to create nuclear fission, but your conversation was anything but intelligent. I'm glad to know you've progressed beyond the generic level."

"It was pretty awful," Aisling admitted. "But do you want to know something really incredible about that experience?"

"What's that?"

"He didn't know you were there."

"Well, that is incredible," Catharine said with a laugh. "And it does wonders for my ego." Her smile softened, as she took in her daughter's happiness. "Will you be seeing him again?"

"I don't know. I hope so, but ...since we're flying back in the morning—later today, I should say, I have no idea when that will be."

"Is there more that you'd like to accomplish at the library?" Catharine asked. "We could always change our flight for a later date."

"No, I don't think we should. Especially on my account. There's a lot I want to do with Irish records, of course, but most of that can be done in Dublin and Leitrim when we get there." Aisling sighed, trying to resign herself to the fact that it might be weeks or even months before she saw Alex Moran again. At least she had the promise of his words ... *We'll talk about me another time* ... and the unspoken promise in his kiss.

"I wouldn't worry too much about seeing him again," Catharine said. "Not when you two have such a fondness for head-on collisions. Serendipity is bound to provide you with another chance—"

A yawn surprised her in mid-word, and she glanced at the clock on the night table. "Good heavens, we've talked more than half the night. I suppose we'd better get some sleep." Catharine leaned over to give Aisling an affectionate hug, and felt her heart swell when the hug was returned without reserve or hesitation.

They smiled into each other's eyes for a quiet moment, needing no more than that to acknowledge their newfound closeness.

Sometime later, Aisling whispered into the darkness. "Catharine … are you asleep?"

"No."

"Can I ask you something?"

"Of course."

Instead of a question, there was silence followed by a restless sigh.

Catharine sent a little smile in her daughter's direction. "Don't worry. You'll see him again."

"Do you have one of your feelings about it?"

"A very good feeling."

"I'm glad." Another sigh. "Good night."

SOUND AND SMOKE colored the large room of a casino where two men sat huddled over their drinks in a corner booth. The air was thick with the choking haze of half-smoked cigarettes and a circus-like cacophony of bells, whistles, and electronic music jangling from slot machines and other games of chance.

"Are you sure he's coming?" Justin asked in a low tone, although no one was sitting nearby, and the electronic noise level made it difficult to hear the sound of his own voice, let alone anyone else's.

"He'll be here," the man sitting across the table assured him. "Have you got the money?"

Justin gave a short nod, looking at the man with barely concealed disgust. Two day's growth covered his fatty jowls with a briar patch of wiry stubble and tattoos made a wasteland of graffiti on his upper arms. Mitch was such a slob, a slob and a coward. If he'd had the guts to finish the job the first time, instead of high-tailing it out of that parking lot, this meeting tonight wouldn't be necessary.

Chapter 21

Justin's attention was momentarily diverted by the long legs and promising smile of their server who arrived with another round of drinks. Long legs were only one of her many assets, Justin decided, as the young woman leaned seductively over the table, offering him a generous view of her silicon-enhanced measurements.

"Is there anything else I can get for you?" she asked, leaning closer still to wipe up the misty film left by his glass. "I'm off at eleven...."

Justin smiled and answered the sultry invitation in her eyes by tucking a twenty-dollar bill into the tempting valley of her cleavage. "This'll do for now. I'll see you later, honey."

Moments later, a man approached their booth and slid onto the seat beside him.

"Mr. Waller. Nicholas Foscari."

They shook hands and Justin found himself having to revise his earlier assessment of what his contact would look like. He'd been expecting a cross between Marlon Brando and Al Pacino, and Foscari definitely didn't fit the "Godfather" image. The man was slender, fit, in his late thirties or early forties, with a benign expression in his gray-green eyes, brown hair cut short, and impeccable taste in clothes. They were understated to the point of seeming ordinary, but classy, very classy.

"Mitch tells me you've been having some health problems with a family member," Foscari said. "I'm sorry to hear that. You understand of course, that treatment for this particular illness can be very expensive."

Justin gave a jerky nod, hating the fact that his palms were suddenly sweating. "Whatever it costs, I want the job done—and this time, done right," he added for the benefit of the man sitting opposite him.

Mitch ignored the comment, more interested in nursing his drink.

"I don't know that it's wise to attempt another treatment so soon after the last one," Foscari went on mildly. "Why the rush?"

"Because she's leaving the country—going to Ireland."

"How soon?"

Justin shook his head. "I don't know. Sometime in the next few weeks."

Foscari was silent as he considered this, his expression focused somewhere beyond the haze of smoke above their table. "Lovely country, Ireland," he said at length, still looking past Justin to that undefined place in the haze. "The people are quite friendly, I'm told, and very helpful."

"So what are you saying? Can you help me or not?" Justin found himself growing impatient with the man's vague innuendos and hints. Why not just come out and say what needed to be said?

Nicholas Foscari smiled and fixed Justin with a look from those gray-green eyes that had him sweating even more. "I hope your wife is properly insured for such a trip. As I said, Ireland is a lovely place, but it can also be quite dangerous at times. One never knows what might happen ... do you remember that car bomb in the town of Omagh a couple of years ago? Tragic."

"Then you'll do it?" Justin found his throat was suddenly dry.

"I have some friends there who are very experienced in the kind of treatment we've been discussing. But as I said before, the cost is considerable, more than double what you paid the last time, and right now, my 'insurance company' has some valid concerns about your ability to pay."

Justin's voice was casual, even careless, although his grip on the drink in his hands turned shaky. "I brought a down payment with me. You can tell your *company* that cost won't be an issue—not after the

Chapter 21

job's done. Charge me triple the amount, if you like. It won't be a problem." Reaching into an inside pocket of his jacket, Justin brought out a thick envelope. Then, needing to show Foscari his disdain for the money issue, tossed it carelessly on the table.

Foscari pocketed the envelope with a slight frown. "I'm sure we can work out an equitable amount for everyone concerned," he said. "Mitch will keep you informed of the progress."

"But how will you know when she's leaving, or where she's staying?"

"There are ways, Mr. Waller. There are ways. My advice to you would be to keep your distance and let the professionals take care of the job. In other words, don't do anything that might draw undue attention to yourself."

"That advice is hardly necessary," Justin said, annoyed with the man's infuriating attitude of superiority.

"Purely a case of semantics," Foscari said, the mildness of his voice a marked contrast to the hardness in those gray-green eyes. "If I might offer a word of *caution*, then, rather than advice. Until your wife's treatment has been completed and paid for, you'd be wise to curb your tendency toward melodrama."

"Melodrama? What the hell are you talking about?" Justin demanded in a defensive bluster.

"I'm talking about those notes on the windshield of your wife's car. The last one in particular."

"That wasn't melodrama. I was just stacking the cards in my favor. The police already know about Barrett Saunder's obsession with my wife."

"And if someone had seen you?"

Justin had no ready comeback for the question other than to finish his drink in a careless swig. The burn down his throat felt good.

"As I said before, I'm only offering a word of caution," Foscari went on. "If that offends you, I'm sorry. You're the one who has the most to lose."

Justin answered this with a conciliatory shrug. "When will I hear from you again?"

"You have e-mail, I believe?"

"Yeah."

"Either Mitch or 'Uncle Oscar' will keep you up to date." Nicholas Foscari rose and offered Justin his hand. "Good luck, Mr. Waller. And give my best to your lovely wife."

IT TOOK SEVERAL days for Justin's bruised ego to recover from the meeting with Nicholas Foscari. Anger seethed and simmered inside him every time he recalled the man's patronizing attitude. Who the hell did he think he was to be offering words of caution, when it was his man who screwed up the first attempt? Now he had to pay double for someone else's mistake. That phony Foscari had the gall to tell him what to do. Melodrama, he said. Even the word rankled. Those notes were brilliant, and there was no way they could be traced. Foscari had no right telling him what he could or couldn't do. If he felt like putting a dozen notes on Catharine's car, then he'd damn well do it.

Thinking of Catharine brought the seething even closer to the surface. The way she'd looked and acted when he dropped by her mother's house, so distant, so cool, and so damned beautiful. Still, he'd managed to ruffle her feathers a bit when he asked about the trip to Ireland. It was obvious she hadn't wanted him to know she was leaving the country.

He had every right to know. They weren't divorced yet, dammit,

Chapter 21

even though that cool, detached look in her eyes told him they might as well be.

Caution and ego continued to play out their dangerous dance during the weeks that followed, as Justin's thinning patience competed with his curiosity. Several times, he found himself drawn to Alameda, casually cruising the streets near the Cavanagh home. More and more, he found himself searching for Catharine's car in nearby malls or stores. Once, he'd seen her leaving the local library. Her steps had been light and carefree in a way that suddenly brought all his anger to the surface.

How dare she be happy when he was hurting and alone? How dare she look so free, while he felt dragged down by the weighty chains of his own making? No. Not his making. Just bad luck. And Catharine was the cause. Once she was gone, his luck would change. But knowing that didn't stop Justin from wanting her to suffer a little now. He didn't care what Foscari said. One more note wouldn't hurt....

THE AFTERGLOW OF a lavender sunset was fast fading into a twilight of muted blue and gray. The calm waters of the San Francisco Bay picked up the remaining lavender tints and held them in liquid reflection of the sky's passing glory. Far across the bay, lights glimmered like pale stars.

An asphalt path running parallel with Alameda's Shoreline Drive and the narrow strip of sandy beach bordering the bay was a place frequented by joggers as well as those desiring a leisurely walk. With apartments, businesses and shopping malls confined across the street to the east, the beachside path offered an unobstructed view of the bay, as well as of San Francisco's distinctive skyline to the west.

Catharine found it an ideal place for a quick morning run or quiet evening stroll. It was convenient and comparatively safe to park her car streetside and then enjoy a solitary half hour, or however long she might have, to breathe in the sea-scented freshness of the air and clear her mind.

With the trip to Ireland only days away, and the prospect of finding and facing Eamonn ever constant in her thoughts, she badly needed the solace and beauty offered by tonight's sunset. Looking at the lavender sky, with its delicate tints and shadings, her heart and mind had enjoyed a moment's respite from worry and strain. Worry would accomplish nothing. Trust and faith would serve her far better. She knew that. But it was so easy to forget, when life's hectic pace often pushed calmer thoughts aside.

Less than a mile away from the strip of beach where Catharine stood watching the sky, a tall man was slumped low in the driver's seat of a tan Ford *Escort*. Barrett Saunders saw neither sea nor sky. His attention was focused solely on the Toyota he'd been following for the past hour. Keeping a safe distance behind the car, Saunders watched with interest as the Toyota pulled up curbside, behind Catharine's dark-green Subaru.

Moments later, Justin Waller got out of the car, for all intents and purposes, to do nothing more than enjoy the soft, sea-scented air. Hands in his jacket pockets, his dark hair ruffled slightly by the evening breeze, Justin stood facing the bay. Then, after a casual glance around, he approached the Subaru, his pace deliberate, but unhurried.

Barrett saw him pause and bend down, as if he were tying the laces of his jogging shoes. There was no one else close by. Only an elderly couple walking in the opposite direction, and they were a good twenty yards away. Justin straightened, then after another quick glance around, slipped something narrow and white under the Subaru's wiper blade. The next moment, he was walking back to his own car. The sound of his tuneless whistle carried clearly on the evening air.

Chapter 21

Barrett waited until the Toyota's taillights had melted into the furry gray dusk, before getting out of his own car and swiftly crossing to the Subaru. Removing the envelope, he pocketed it in his jeans with a satisfied smile.

BARRETT'S THOUGHTS TRAVELED a twisted road between clarity and confusion as he made the drive back to his apartment in Oakland. There was that initial moment of euphoria when he'd pictured himself walking into Lyle Adams' office and handing over the envelope with Justin's damning message inside. "I told you it wasn't me! I told you I'd never want to harm her! Now do you believe me?" This was followed by the sinking realization that, even with the note, chances were slim to nonexistent that Adams would believe him. Why should he? More likely, the detective would probably accuse him of writing the note himself.

Ever since the police had hauled him in for questioning, Saunders had had a feeling in his gut that the real threat to Catharine was someone close to her—someone who would stop at nothing to keep her from him. Who had a better motive for this than her husband? Who else would cleverly try to poison Catharine's mind against him, when all Barrett had ever wanted was to love and take care of her?

Let the police fumble about in their half-hearted efforts. Barrett was convinced it was up to him to save her. So he had waited and watched, knowing that sooner or later, Justin Waller would reveal his true self. For weeks now, he'd been following the man—to his real estate office in San Anselmo, to bars, even to Reno and those fancy casinos where he'd seen Justin throwing his money away with such careless abandon.

Now he knew, but simply knowing wasn't enough. He had to find a way to stop him from harming Catharine. Simply following Justin from a distance wouldn't reveal what the man was thinking and planning. He needed information and proof.

Like the complex paths and mazes created for his computer fantasy games, Saunder's mind pursued its convoluted course, searching for the right path that would lead him to his goal. Late into the night, smoking cigarette after cigarette, he pondered the problem with dogged determination. Fear for Catharine's safety grew stronger every time he read the note he'd intercepted.

Then it came to him. The note had been printed on a computer. By now, Justin would have deleted the information, but there had to be other, equally damning evidence on the machine. Saunders smiled as the circuitous path of his thoughts suddenly turned a corner to reveal a straight road ahead. It would take some doing, of course, but the task was far from impossible. Barrett stubbed his cigarette into the overflowing ashtray, and still smiling, turned out the light.

22

Serendipity

The morning before their flight to Ireland, Aisling awoke with a clear sense of purpose, knowing exactly what she must do. Two weeks had passed since her return from Salt Lake. Two weeks filled with the flurry of preparations for the future and poignant visits to the past—a past newly discovered, with people and places unknown to her before now. She'd had several visits with Grace and Catharine, simple times of sharing and caring, as she'd come to call them. One evening had been especially touching. In answer to her questions about her birth father, Catharine had brought out the photo album with pictures of that long ago trip to Ireland. Seeing her then nineteen-year old mother and putting a face to the name of her birth father was an unusually stirring moment. In the photo, Catharine and Eamonn were standing in front of an old white-washed farmhouse, arms about each other's waists. Catharine looked so beautiful and so young, the expression on her face a shining mirror of her hopes and dreams as she smiled up at the young man with a rakish grin and tousled dark hair. And her father. Even in a small photo, his roguish charm was clearly evident. It was little wonder Catharine hadn't forgotten him. Seeing the two of them together, so young and carefree, and so much in love made Aisling ache inside. At the same time, studying her father's features, she felt a thrill of pride, recognizing the strong resemblance that she bore to him. I do have his eyes, she thought, and my mother's smile.

Then there was the morning she had accompanied Grace to the cemetery where her grandfather and uncle were buried. Observing the tender way Grace arranged a vase of spring flowers beside her husband's headstone, told Aisling more clearly than any words, that her grandmother had deeply loved this man. Her own feelings toward Gordon Cavanagh were still a mixture of resentment and pity, rather than any real fondness. Knowing even a few details of what he had done in an effort to keep her parents apart, was enough to light the spark of anger inside her. It was all in the past. She knew and accepted that, but the far-reaching repercussions of her grandfather's actions were not lost on her. Yet, if he hadn't interfered, she never would have been adopted by the Montgomerys, or known the warm security of their love and home. Would she want to change all that, even if she could? Looking at Gordon Cavanagh's headstone, she found herself silently acknowledging that perhaps it was better after all, to simply forgive and go on, the way Catharine had.

Young Robert Cavanagh had been buried beside his father. Seeing the dates of his birth and untimely death in Viet Nam etched in granite, Aisling was reminded of that moment when Catharine discovered the death date of Esther's brother Henry. She glanced over at Grace who stood, lost in thoughts of her own. Even now, thirty-one years later, Aisling could see the pain of loss in her grandmother's eyes as she gazed at the resting place of her only son.

Not speaking, she'd put an arm about Grace's shoulders, and they shared a moment of silent reflection.

Afterwards, Grace had taken her for a short walking tour around the cemetery, introducing her, as it were, to various members of the

Cavanagh clan, and giving brief vignettes that brought the names of long ago relatives to life. The genealogist in her was fascinated with the stories and scope of history, and now there was the added dimension of knowing these people had played a vital part in her own life history.

All in all, it had been a memorable morning, but now, on the day before her departure to Ireland, Aisling knew there was yet another visit to make. There was one more grave that needed spring flowers and loving remembrance—that of Helen Montgomery.

Early afternoon found her sitting on the sun-drenched patio of her father's home in Santa Clara, enjoying a tall glass of lemonade with Joseph Montgomery. Although Aisling was genuinely fond of her new stepmother, she was grateful that Fran was away for the day, visiting a married daughter. Besides wanting to see her father before leaving for Ireland, there were other matters that needed the intimacy of a one-on-one talk.

As she sat looking into the eyes of the only father she had ever known, Aisling realized with sudden sadness that Joe Montgomery was looking all of his seventy-nine years. In a few months' time, he would be eighty. Those hazel eyes were still as sharp and bright as ever, but how long had he had that tremble in his hand? Or had it been there and she had just not noticed?

They spent a few minutes talking about the garden and his beloved roses. Then Joe's conversation shifted to a tender little experience recently shared with his new wife. Seeing the love shining in his eyes for a woman who was not the wife of his youth, Aisling suddenly found herself asking, "Do you ever have trouble sorting things out?"

"What kind of things are we trying to sort?" he asked in return.

Aisling hesitated only slightly. "Love ... the way we love people. I know you loved Mom, and you know how glad I am that you're not alone any more—but does it ever bother you, that you can love Fran, too?"

Joe Montgomery regarded his daughter's earnest expression with tenderness. "I wonder if what we're really talking about here is loyalty, rather than love. It didn't take long after meeting Fran, to know that I loved her. What I really had to deal with after that were feelings of guilt—that my loving Fran was somehow being disloyal to Helen. Is that what you mean?"

"Yes ... yes, it is," Aisling said, grateful that he could put plain words to the muddy mixture of emotions she'd been trying to sort out.

"We humans are a strange lot," he said. "We make up all kinds of rules for ourselves that the good Lord never intended. Then we wonder why our lives get so complicated."

Aisling smiled at this, enjoying the easy-going sound of his voice. It was so comfortable and unpretentious, like a favorite chair that invites you to sit and rest awhile.

"I don't know why we try to put limits or boundaries on love," he went on, "but there was a time when I felt terribly guilty for loving Fran. Then I made myself ask why. Did loving her take anything away from the love and all the years I had with your mother? And I knew that it didn't, any more than a parent who has three children is only capable of loving his first born and not the rest. I finally decided that if I was feeling guilty or disloyal, it was really a lack of understanding on my part, rather than a lack of love." He smiled at Aisling, then said, "But this really isn't about Fran and me, or your Mother and me ... is it?"

Aisling met his steady look and shook her head. "The past month or so I've gotten to know my birth mother, and my grandmother...." She paused, searching for the words, as well as trying to contain emotions very near the surface. "They're both so wonderful, but I–I find myself wondering how Mom would feel about everything. I don't want to hurt her … or you."

Joe Montgomery reached over to give her hand a little pat, content to wait a moment while she blew her nose. "And why do you think that loving them would hurt us?"

Aisling couldn't answer this, with tears so near the surface. The most she could manage was a confused little shrug.

"Do you remember the time—I think you were in the second or third grade—that you came home from school crying and all upset because one of your friends told you that she wouldn't be your friend any more if you played with another little girl in the class?"

Aisling gave him a brief nod, then reached for another tissue from the box on the patio table.

"You were torturing yourself, thinking you had to choose between one or the other. Your feelings now are kind of a grown-up version of the same problem. The answer I gave you then, is still the same. Love them both."

When Aisling glanced up to give him a smile, Joe saw the tears sliding down her cheeks.

"Almost thirty-one years ago, your birthmother—Catharine—gave Helen and me a priceless gift. We were the first ones to see you smile and make you laugh. We were the ones to see your first steps, the ones you ran to when you were hurt. We experienced all he milestones, large and small, and all of the joys. None of that will change or be taken away. Before you came into our lives, your mother's arms were empty and aching. It was Catharine who filled them by giving you to us. Now how could your mother and I be anything but grateful to someone who gave us all that?"

Aisling went into his arms with a strangled little sob. "I love you, Dad."

"I know you do. And it's all right to love her, honey. I'd feel terrible if you didn't. There's more than enough love to go around for all of us."

Aisling kissed his cheek and smiled through her tears. When she'd gathered enough control to speak, she said, "My birth father is Irish. He doesn't know about me yet, but there's a good chance I'll be meeting him when we go to Ireland."

Joe just smiled and nodded. "Well, you can tell him from me, that I'm real proud of my girl!"

A TRIO OF fervent hopes and silent prayers walked with them as Aisling, Catharine and Grace made their way to the Aer Lingus check-in counter in Los Angeles' mammoth airport. *Please help Catharine not to be hurt ... Please help Eamonn to love and accept her ... Dear Lord, please help us all and be with us on our journey ...* The silent thoughts of each were communicated from heart to heaven as clearly as the constant stream of intercom announcements given in a host of languages, from English and Spanish to Mandarin Chinese.

That morning, they had flown from Oakland to Los Angeles where Aer Lingus based its flights to Ireland. Now, step by step, they moved through the necessary hurdles of policy and procedure, checking luggage, passports and I.D.'s, until at last, the announcement came for their flight's boarding in a voice that was liltingly Irish.

Through a window beyond the Aer Lingus counter, Catharine could see the large jet with its distinctive green shamrock emblazoned on the side. She was going back ... back to Erin. The dogged necessities and day to day requirements that had kept her functioning for the past few weeks were behind her now, and the journey itself—with all its attendant possibilities, whether painful or promising—was at hand.

Catharine felt a gentle squeeze of encouragement at her elbow, and glanced away from the aircraft to find her daughter's blue eyes on her face.

"No matter how it turns out … I know we're doing the right thing," Aisling said with calm assurance.

Catharine drew a steadying breath. "Yes, we are…."

Seeing the smile exchanged by her daughter and granddaughter, Grace felt her own nervousness disappear, and eagerness take its place. "Then let's do it!" she said with a gingery gusto that had Catharine and Aisling laughing.

The three headed down the jetway and onto the plane where flight attendants wearing deep green blazers and slim green skirts, offered a warm greeting. One of the attendants smiled at Aisling and, assuming she was Irish said, "You look very happy to be going home."

Aisling gave her a glowing smile, not bothering to explain that this was her first visit to the country. In many ways, it truly felt as if she were going home.

Seating on the large aircraft was divided into three sections, with rows of two seats on either side and a broad center section, six seats across. Catharine and Grace found their assigned row and seats on the plane's right side, with Aisling taking the window seat on the row in front of theirs.

"I still think you should have let me be the one to sit by myself, rather than Aisling," Grace grumbled as Catharine reached up to put their carry-ons in the overhead bin.

"Now Mother, we've been through all that."

"But you know you two will want to discuss research and genealogy on the way over. And who knows? If I sit by myself, some distinguished widower with an Irish accent might be my companion."

"Mother, the seating is fine the way it is," Catharine said with a laugh.

Ignoring her, Grace went on, "Why don't I talk to one of those delightful flight attendants. I'm sure they wouldn't mind if we made the change—"

"You'll do no such thing," Catharine said, putting a hand on her mother's arm.

"But I—"

"Mother, trust me on this one," Catharine said in an undertone, "and let's give serendipity a chance."

"Serendipity? What on earth are you talking about?"

Aisling turned around, partly kneeling on her seat to give them an amused glance. "All right, what's going on? Are you two plotting something behind my back?"

"Not a thing," Catharine said, smiling in a way that only served to whet Aisling's curiosity. "Your grandmother's just being a little difficult."

"Difficult?" Grace said with a snort. "You're the one who's—"

"Actually, we were having a little discussion about serendipity." Catharine was smiling broadly now and her eyes had an unmistakable sparkle.

"We were not," Grace contradicted with a huff, then turned to Aisling. "I simply offered to trade seats, so you and Catharine could work together. I don't see what's so difficult about that."

Aisling pushed back a lock of red-gold hair, and looked at the two with puzzled amusement. "If you want to trade seats, that's fine. It doesn't really matter to me where I sit—"

"It matters to me," said a masculine voice very close by.

Aisling turned slightly, then did a neck-jerking double-take. "Alex!"

Smiling, he slid onto the aisle seat beside hers. "Hello."

She stared, open-mouthed. "How—?"

His dark eyes held a smile even warmer than the one parting his bearded mouth, and Aisling had to fight the sudden impulse to fling herself into his arms. Wearing a light tan blazer over a black tee shirt and jeans, he looked every inch the gentleman pirate. A shiver of amazement tinged with disbelief shook her and she said again, "How—?"

"It's like your mother said ... serendipity," he answered.

Aisling's stunned gaze left Alex long enough to glance over her shoulder at Catharine, who was looking extremely pleased with herself.

"How—?"

"Aisling, dear, could you please stop stuttering and introduce me to this young man," Grace inserted mildly.

At this, Alex got to his feet and offered Grace his hand. "You must be Mrs. Cavanagh," he said, then turned his smile on Catharine. "Your daughter and I met briefly in Salt Lake at the genealogy library—in the elevator, I believe, although I was somewhat distracted at the time."

It was Grace's turn to stare. "Good heavens! Are you the Mr. Misogynist I've been hearing so much about?"

Aisling shrank down in her seat with a moan, but Alex was chuckling with obvious enjoyment.

"That's *former* misogynist," he said, white teeth flashing. "Since I've reformed, the title no longer applies."

"I'm glad to hear it," Grace told him. "You're far too good looking to be a misogynist. It would be a total waste."

Alex chucked, then sat down beside Aisling, whose head was in her hands by this time.

Grace turned to Catharine with a knowing look. "Something tells me you gave serendipity a hand in all this."

"No more than a nudge, really," Catharine said, leaning back with a happy sigh. "Alex already had things well in hand. He called a few days after I got back from Salt Lake, and we made the necessary adjustments."

"And you never said a word to me!"

"Alex and I decided that a surprise attack might be the best approach."

"Assuming of course, that Aisling recovers enough to say more than 'how'."

Catharine laughed. "Don't worry. She'll do just fine."

"How long did you say this flight was?"

"A little over eleven hours."

Grace glanced toward the row in front of them, her eyes twinkling. "Well, that's about ten hours too long for me, but I have a feeling it'll be the shortest transatlantic flight on record for those two."

A FEW MINUTES AFTER takeoff, Aisling found that her insides were still all a-tremble, a condition that had nothing to do with the plane's rapid ascent. That Alex Moran had talked with Catharine, not once but several times in recent weeks, was something she could hardly take in.

"I hope that answers the 'how's' to your satisfaction," he teased, dark eyes on her face.

"Yes, it does, but—"

"But what?"

Please don't look at me that way, she thought, *or I will melt into a warm puddle of butter right here and now. On the other hand, please don't stop looking at me that way.*

"I still can't help wondering why," she said.

"Why what?"

"Why go to so much trouble, just to—well—"

"Just to see you again?" he filled in, enjoying the color that stained her cheeks. "I believe in serendipity as much as anyone, but some things shouldn't be left to chance. Quite frankly, I didn't like the odds of trying to find you at the genealogy conference in Dublin. Especially since you're so good at running away from me."

"I do not run away from you," she retorted.

"Yes, you do."

Aisling lowered her voice. "I do not."

'What about all those times you ducked down behind your microfilm reader when I walked by—or purposely chose one as far away from mine as you could get."

"What? I don't know what you're talking about."

His smile widened into a wickedly devastating grin. "Then there were the times you suddenly changed course and headed for the elevator whenever you saw me taking the stairs.... Shall I go on?"

Aisling glanced away and her chin lifted defensively. "I don't know why you're asking all this, but—if you're trying to embarrass and humiliate me, you're doing a very good job."

"I'm sorry."

She shot him an unbelieving look, and he went on in a husky tone, "Maybe I'm just curious … wondering why you'd want to run away from me."

Denials died as she met his eyes and heard the serious note in his voice. "I don't know that it's really you, so much as the way you make me feel…."

"I don't understand."

"That's the whole point—I don't understand it either," she said with frustration. "All I know is, whenever you're around—even if it's halfway across the room—something happens. One minute, I'm reading a deed or a will, and the next, everything around me turns into meaningless static. All I hear is your voice telling someone what your plans are for the weekend, or why you won't be working on a certain day because you're going to have your boys with you and—"

Aisling's explanation was effectively silenced as Alex leaned closer and pressed a warm kiss on her mouth. Her surprised gasp only served to make the kiss deeper and more intimate. One of his hands cupped her face, while the other raised the arm that divided their seats. That barrier eliminated, his arm moved around her waist and back.

Her own hands that should have pushed him away, suddenly turned traitor—one finding the darkness of his bearded cheek, and the other resting weakly against his chest. The kiss went on, tormenting her with its tenderness and tantalizing in its promise that this was only a beginning, a prelude of passion waiting in the wings.

Alex drew back and smiled into her eyes, one hand still cupping the soft curve of her cheek.

"Is that why I was running?" she asked in a happy daze.

"It could be."

"I think we'd better make sure ... would you mind explaining it to me again?"

"My pleasure ..." His mouth found hers once more, and she melted against him, like wax to a flame.

"By the way, they're not my boys," he said at length, his voice unsteady and slightly breathless. "They're my nephews ... my brother's sons."

Aisling stared and straightened. "They are?"

He nodded. "I've never been married, let alone divorced."

"Really? Then you couldn't possibly be a misogynist."

At this, Alex threw back his head and laughed.

In the row behind them, Grace turned to Catharine with a wry glance. "I was beginning to think they'd never come up for air."

Catharine just smiled and reached for the headphones in the seat pocket in front of her. "Here, Mother. Put these on and watch the movie."

"That's what I was trying to do," Grace said, her lips twitching, "but the seat was in the way."

EVENING MOVED INTO night. Dinner had long since been served and trays removed. Cabin lights were dimmed and after the intermittent wandering in the aisles, passengers were settling in for the long nighttime hours and transatlantic portion of the flight.

Catharine gave her mother a fond glance. Only a half hour earlier, Grace had announced she might shut her eyes for a few minutes, but stoutly insisted she couldn't sleep on a plane. Now, her deep, even breathing attested otherwise. Catharine tucked the green and blue lap robe more snugly about her mother's slender frame, then turned her gaze out the plane's small window. Somewhere in the blackness far below lay the Atlantic, the same ocean John and Esther had crossed as exiles a century and a half before, the same watery gulf that she had crossed over thirty years ago, believing with all the fervent desperation of youth that her parting from Eamonn would only be temporary. She didn't often allow her heart and mind to dwell on that scene. The tears ... the aching promises ... trying to hold on to the last glimpse of his tall figure at the airport ... with neither of them knowing what lay ahead, or that she was already carrying the seed born of their love. Now she was returning. Her own hopes and dreams felt much like the ocean below—unseen, dark, and unfathomable. But she was not returning alone. The seed had blossomed into a lovely flower.

Even if you can't forgive me ... please love her, she thought, staring out into the night.

23

O Ireland, isn't it grand you look –
Like a bride in her rich adornin'
And with all the pent-up love of my heart
I bid you the top o' the mornin'!"

John Locke—The Exile's Return

Aisling took the copy of the ship's manifest Alex handed her and slipped it back inside the portfolio. For the past several hours while other passengers read or slept, they had examined and discussed her research on the Clifford line, with Alex asking questions as well as making comments on her work.

"I haven't had time yet to go through all the entries in the Registry of Deeds," she told him, "but I have a feeling there's a connection between Esther's father and the Henry Clifford living at Mount Campbell. He might even be Esther's grandfather. Then I want to look for a possible link between the Cliffords in Leitrim and the Forbes and Crawfords in County Longford. I can't prove anything yet," she admitted freely. "In fact, my thinking may be way off ..."

"I like the way you think," he said. "You've done some good work here."

Aisling glanced down in happy confusion. Compliments were not unknown to her. Darren and others before him had praised her eyes, her hair and her smile. That was all well and good, of course, yet something in Alex's voice and words struck a much deeper chord. There had been times during recent months when she sensed that her thinking was a source of real irritation to Darren, that he would have been much happier if she'd just given him simple 'yes' and 'no' answers, and left it at that, especially during those moments when her thinking conflicted in any way with his. Yet, for the past two hours or more, she and Alex had enjoyed a spirited discussion, arguing some points, defending others, and suggesting possibilities. And now, he was telling her that he liked the way she thought. Incredible. Also, she had to admit, it was very stimulating. What was it Catharine had told her on their last night in Salt Lake, that having an intelligent conversation with the right man could lead to other things?

Aisling smiled and permitted herself a subtle sideways glance at Alex's mouth and bearded jaw. The sensual effect on her insides was immediate, and just as Catharine had said ... *far from intellectual.*

"What was that look about?" he asked.

"Oh, nothing. Just thinking."

His smile was no more than a sensual curve of his mouth, but his eyes said he knew exactly what was on her mind. His kiss said it even better. She melted against him, mindless of the papers and portfolio in her lap until they went sliding onto the floor.

Alex chuckled softly at the jumbled assortment of research now scattered at their feet. "I think we'd better put away the past, before we concentrate on the present."

Unbuckling their seat beats, they began picking up the notebooks and papers, trying not to disturb the sleeping passengers in front and around them.

Chapter 23

Alex reached under the seat in front of him to retrieve some census copies, and handed them to Aisling with a smile turned thoughtful. "How does it feel, now that you know these are your people?"

"It feels good," she said softly, putting the sheets back in her portfolio. "Sometimes I'm totally amazed by it all, and other times, it's as if part of me knew all along that this family belonged to me. The first time Catharine told me about her great-great grandmother, I felt something inside—a kinship maybe—I don't really have the right words. I just knew there was some kind of connection between Esther Clifford and me. I still feel it. Am I making any sense?"

Alex nodded, handing her the last of the fallen goods. "For one thing, you're both dreamers. I think you and Esther share a lot more than the same name. Whatever it is that links people together, probably has very little to do with the way we try to define things." He sat back down and softly fingered a strand of her hair. "You tell me you get your hair from Esther's daughter ... and when you smile, I can see a lot of Catharine. Yet there's a part of you that's totally unique ... unlike anyone else I've ever known."

Aisling glanced up from sorting the loose papers in her lap, her lips parted and her blue eyes alight. "Alex, please don't say things like that...."

"Why not?" He frowned slightly and a shade of worry crossed his face.

"Well, for one thing ... we just barely finished picking everything up, and right now, I'm more than tempted to send it all flying again...."

His dark eyes regarded her with a steady look that made her tremble from the inside out.

Aisling stuffed the remaining papers inside her portfolio, not caring that they were totally out of order, then zipped it up and tossed it aside. "There. The past's out of the way," she said and went into his arms. "Let's concentrate on the present."

"YOU PROMISED TO tell me about yourself," Aisling said with drowsy contentment, her head resting against Alex's shoulder. "You already know so much about me...."

"Not nearly as much as I'd like to," he said, neatly side-stepping her request. Sharing pieces of his life meant trusting, and Alex wasn't entirely sure he was ready for that. She hadn't been the only one running away. He had done his share of avoiding her this past year. Refusing to look up when he knew she was working just a few feet away—forcing himself to concentrate, and denying himself the pleasure of talking with her, or even enjoying the sight of her sitting across the room, afraid what might happen if he yielded.

And this is why, he thought. Part of him must have known it would be this way, that if he ever allowed himself to talk with her or touch her, there would be no turning back. So if it was already too late, why was he holding back now? Wasn't having her worth the risk of losing himself?

"What's wrong?" she was asking, her blue eyes searching for the answer to his troubled silence.

He gave a careless shrug. "I'm—uh, not sure where to begin," he admitted with a crooked grin.

The look in her eyes was even warmer than her smile. "Catharine told me that a good way to begin a story is the way you hold a puppy—somewhere around the middle."

He grinned back, wondering if and when Aisling would make the transition from 'Catharine' to 'mother' in her heart and mind. Aloud, he said, "You really do care about her, don't you?"

"Yes, but I thought we were going to talk about you—not me."

Chapter 23

"Are you sure you're up to this?" he said, only half-joking.

Aisling was silent for a moment, then she put a hand to his face and kissed him softly. "Yes," she answered, "I am. But if you're not, it can wait until another time."

The trust in her eyes melted the last bastion of his resistance. Putting an arm about her shoulders, he drew her close once more, needing to feel the softness of her against him, and amazed there could be so much strength in softness rather than the hard walls he'd built around his heart.

Alex Moran watched the gradual approach of morning and marveled at the dawning clarity in his own life.

Aisling lay sleeping in his arms, her head resting in the curve between his neck and shoulder, one of her hands on his chest. He turned his head slightly to see the night's blackness retreating to a soft blue-gray, and caught the light fragrance of her hair, felt its silky softness against his cheek. The wonder of the night just passed, and the miracle of the approaching day suddenly swept through him, filling him with a profound sense of gratitude.

Six years ago, if anyone had tried to tell him that he could be this happy ... that anything good could ever come from that bitter season of his life ... he would have told them to take a flying leap.

Alex had taken all his savings and borrowed a good deal more to set up a photography studio in Denver with his best friend and business partner. The venture had been on shaky ground for the first couple of years, as he and Dave struggled to build a clientele and compete with older, more established portrait studios. They had toughed it out though, doing spreads on everything from county fairs and rodeos to classes of graduating seniors.

It was during that time of financial struggle that Alex met Robyn Whittaker, a college beauty queen, doing the pageant circuit and garnering a variety of titles and conquests along the way, everything from Miss Rodeo Days to Dream Girl of Phi Kappa Phi. A leggy blonde with a long, golden mane and a staggering set of vital statistics, Robyn had first come to the studio wanting a series of glamour shots to impress a modeling agency. She'd posed in everything from glittering evening gowns to an eye-popping bikini that hid very little and flaunted even more.

He and Dave had jokingly made bets on who would be the first to get a date with the tantalizing Miss Whittaker, but it soon became obvious that Robyn had already made up her own mind in that regard. She asked for extra sittings and specifically requested that Alex do the shoots instead of Dave.

His ego had been flattered and his photographer's eye was intoxicated by her beauty. Before he knew what was happening, they were seeing each other on a regular basis, and Dave was offering good-natured congratulations to the victor. Two months later Alex gave her an engagement ring and told himself he was the luckiest guy in the world.

Business began picking up soon after, and so did Robyn's modeling career. The marriage date was postponed once, then twice, as she traveled to New York and San Francisco for photo shoots with big agencies. Then, two weeks before the wedding, she flew to New York for an interview with *Vogue,* and never came back. Robyn's mother offered Alex an embarrassed apology for the inconvenience, saying, surely he knew what an incredible opportunity this was, one much too important for her daughter to refuse. Marriage right now was out of the question. She hoped he understood.

Of course he understood. Mainly that he was a fool for getting involved with Robyn in the first place. Ten months later, his heart and ego had recovered and the photography business was doing well enough that he and Dave agreed they needed to hire a receptionist/secretary. They eventually settled on a young single mom that Alex had met at the gym where he worked out a few times a week. Holly's typing skills were negligible, but she was great with customers and Alex knew how much she needed the job; especially one with flexible hours that would allow her to spend more time with her children, a boy and a girl, just two and four years old.

Looking back, Alex knew he'd fallen in love with those kids long before he came to care for their mother. They were a little on the hyper side, but that was understandable given the circumstances of their mother's divorce and having a real deadbeat for a dad. Six months later, Alex began seeing them as a family—he and Holly, with Travis and Tiffany. When he proposed, Holly said she needed a little more time—just to make sure she wasn't doing anything on the rebound, especially with the children to consider.

That was only fair, Alex thought, and assured her she could have whatever time she needed. A few weeks later, he'd come into work earlier than usual to take care of some pressing business, and found Holly and Dave actively engaged on the floor of the back room.

It had taken well over a year before he could rid his mind of the disgusting scene and the couple's hurried attempts to get dressed.

Alex left Denver not long after that, bought out his share of the partnership and accepted his brother Brian's invitation to move to Salt Lake and stay with him and his family for awhile. It would be just until he got back on his feet.

In spite of the circumstances that prompted it, the move had been a good one. It was then that Alex discovered the art of photo restoration. He might not be able to repair the flaws and ragged edges of his own life, but it was satisfying to take something old and torn and turn it into a valuable keepsake for someone else. His interest in genealogy was a natural offshoot of the photography business, as his clients brought in fragile pieces of their family history to share with him.

Work filled the daytime hours, and during those long evenings, Alex often found himself visiting the Family History Library. Delving into the past, searching for long ago pieces of the Moran family puzzle kept painful memories at bay and gradually helped to rid his mind of that sordid backroom scene. He had a good life, he told himself. His photo restoration business was doing well—so well, he could take or leave a job, and pretty much set his own hours. He kept his body fit with running and regular workouts at the gym, and even managed to take some classes, becoming an accredited genealogist, with the British Isles his specialty.

Alex filled the empty well of his own emotional needs by pouring out love and attention on his nephews. As far as his dreams of having a family of his own … well, they'd simply have to lie fallow. Dreams couldn't be trusted. They were far too fragile, and their destruction too painful. Reality would just have to do.

Telling Aisling about it all, Alex suddenly saw that period of his life in a much clearer light. He hadn't been the victim of fate or circumstance at all. Marrying either of those women would have been the real tragedy. Instead, he'd been fortunate enough to come away from both experiences, a little wiser and with a great deal more understanding.

There'd been moments after his evening with Aisling in Salt Lake, when Alex found his fears warring with his desires, and he wondered if he were only asking for more heartbreak to allow this 'dreamer' into his life. But now, holding her, thinking of their conversation throughout the night, and the trust offered in those incredible eyes of hers, Alex knew this was a dream worth fighting for. More than that. Whatever the cost, he wanted to make Aisling a permanent part of his reality.

Chapter 23

Moving out of his thoughts, his gaze focused on the brightening sky. Not only had morning come, but a sight as lovely as any dream.

"Aisling..." He spoke her name in a whisper, lips against her hair, but she roused quickly, raising her head to smile at him.

"Look there," was all he said, and the next moment she was pressing her face against the plane's small oval window.

Far below them, shining through the gauzy mists of cloud was a verdant landscape of patchwork fields and darker hedgerows. Seen in the fragile light of dawn, the shades and tints seemed almost surreal, ranging from light apple green, to moss and jade and deepest emerald.

"Ireland," she breathed. "Oh, Alex, it's Ireland."

24

Ballinamore, County Leitrim

Dublin met them like an old friend whose smile has been missed for many a year, but is ever the same. It had all the bigness and busyness of any large city, yet still retained its unique Irishness when it came to offering visitors 'a hundred thousand welcomes.' Riding in the taxi to their hotel, Catharine was amazed by the addition of wide new motorways fanning out from the city's perimeters. Yet as they drew closer to the heart of the capital, she began to recognize traditional landmarks and sites. No matter how big the city had grown, Dublin was still Dublin, and there was always time for a chat, whether you were merely buying a few stamps at the nearest post, catching a bus on the street corner, or, as in their case, arriving at a hotel.

Catharine had made reservations at the Jurys Skylon Hotel on Drumcondra Road, and after the weary blur of necessary regulations at the airport, it was a welcome relief to settle in and indulge in a short rest. Grace had initially attributed Aisling's exuberance and energy after the eleven-hour flight to the resilience of youth, but soon discovered it had far more to do with Alex Moran. The two were inseparable, and since the genealogy conference was still a day away, Alex had booked a room at the Skylon for the night. That evening, all four had dinner together in the hotel's attractive dining room.

Listening to Aisling and Alex's animated conversation, Catharine found it nearly impossible to do little more than insert a word now and then. Her condition was more than the natural result of jet lag and a sleepless night on the plane. Mounting tension that was soul-deep had had a relentless grip on her emotions ever since their arrival.

Tomorrow. Tomorrow morning they would drive to Leitrim and that lime-washed farmhouse in Ballinamore. Tomorrow she would face the ghosts of her past and confront her future. She found herself trying to rehearse what she would say to Eamonn, how she would introduce the daughter he had no idea existed ... but her mind was a weary blank.

It was a relief to finally go back to the privacy of their room. There was no need to plead the excuse of a headache. Her head was pounding.

For weeks, she'd tried to prepare herself, knowing it was best to have no expectations one way or the other. Yet, now that they were here in Ireland, and the moment of facing Eamonn was nearly at hand, Catharine found there was no sensible way to approach this pivotal event in her life. It was like the legendary tale of the knight whose fate lay behind one of two doors—a beautiful lady waited on one side and a ferocious tiger, on the other. Which would it be? How does one prepare for such exquisite pain or delight, especially when the largest part of her believed far more in the reality of the tiger being behind both doors?

The battle to keep her emotional struggle strictly on the inside and not spoil things for Aisling and Grace was well fought, but far from successful.

"I'm so worried about her," Aisling confided to Alex as they took an evening walk through a quiet neighborhood near the hotel. "The strain is greater than I think she expected it to be. Even when she smiles, her eyes are so haunted. I want to help, but I don't know what to do...."

"Just you being here will help more than you know," Alex said. "I wouldn't worry too much. She'll feel your love and support. Besides, everything seems worse when you're tired. It'll be better in the morning." Silently, he wished he were coming with them, but knew he'd only be in the way. "Promise me you'll call tomorrow night."

"I will."

"Who's going to do the driving—you or Catharine?"

"Probably me. I'm not sure what she'll feel up to."

"Have you ever driven on the left before?"

Aisling smiled and shook her head. "No, but I'll manage. Will being left-handed give me any advantage, do you think?" she asked, trying to lighten the worry in his eyes, touched that the worry was for her. *What would I do if he weren't here?* she thought suddenly. *Could I face any of this if I had to do it alone? Like Catharine....*

From somewhere nearby, the mellow peal of bells chimed the hour, and Aisling stopped to listen. A few yards farther down the street, she glimpsed a gray stone church with its adjacent cemetery, and quickly turned her steps in that direction. Smiling, Alex followed indulgently after.

The wrought iron gate hung crooked on its hinges and groaned a rusty complaint as Aisling pushed it open. Inside, the grass was long and thick, and clumps of yellow daffodils sang a song of spring's renewal and life triumphant amidst the silent, lichen-encrusted gravestones.

"Oh, how beautiful … look at the daffodils," Aisling exclaimed, taking it all in. "Alex, I'm really here … we're here … in Ireland. Can you believe it?"

For answer, his arms reached out for her and his kiss held none of the gentle reassurance he told himself he should be offering. All his worry and concern combined with his need for her, resulting in a rough, bruising hunger. He'd half expected her to pull away. Instead, she yielded her mouth with a little moan and her body went soft and boneless against him.

"Sorry," he said, when reason and speech returned. "The last thing I want to do is give you a reason to run away from me again."

Aisling smiled and wrapped her arms around his neck. "Do I look like I'm running?" she murmured, lifting her lips to his.

MORNING CAME WITH a mottled sky of blue and gray, and more than a hint of rain in the offing. Much to her own surprise, as well as the relief of the others, Catharine found herself facing the day with quiet resolve rather than determined grimness. It was as if some previously untapped well of strength had been discovered deep inside and was now flowing free.

Grace immediately sensed the change and knew her prayers had been answered. Aisling saw it as well and felt a new layer of admiration for the remarkable woman who was her mother.

After breakfast, Alex insisted on accompanying them back to the airport where they had reserved a car for the journey west. He and Aisling had spent some time going over maps and choosing the most direct route out of Dublin, then to their surprise, Catharine announced that she would be driving for at least the first half of the journey.

Alex had his doubts about the wisdom of this, but Aisling readily agreed with the plan.

"She needs to do this," Aisling told him, as he loaded their luggage in the trunk of the car. "It's part of facing things, I think."

He nodded, then said softly, "Call me."

"I will."

He gave her a quick hard kiss, and her radiant smile made him long to tell her all the things that he'd convinced himself it was far too soon to say—even if they were true. Instead, he kissed her again.

The last thing he saw as they drove out of the rental agency's lot was Aisling's red-gold hair blowing in the breeze as she leaned out the car window to wave good-bye.

"ARE YOU SURE you want to sit in the back?" Aisling asked Grace for the third time as they headed west out of Dublin. "I hate to have you miss seeing anything."

"In this case, I think it will be much better for my nerves to miss seeing as much as possible," Grace said.

"Thanks for the vote of confidence," Catharine said with a chuckle.

"That's no reflection on your driving, dear," Grace added hastily. "You're doing just fine, but until I can get myself used to this backward approach to driving down a road, I'll feel a lot better staying right where I am. Besides which, Aisling is a much better navigator. Those roundabouts turn me inside out."

"They're not so bad, once you get the hang of it," Aisling said. "It's simply a matter of knowing which position on the clock we need for our exit ... three o'clock, six o'clock, or whatever."

Catharine gave her daughter a sidelong glance. "Then I'd hate to hear what happens to your breathing when you're really nervous. Every time we get within fifty yards of one, you start huffing and puffing like a woman practicing her Lamaze."

Aisling's rippling laugh acknowledged the truth of this. "Oh, all right. It does take a little getting used to."

For the first two hours or so out of Dublin, both the drive and the weather were fairly trouble-free. Concentrating on the road and her driving was a mixed blessing, forcing Catharine's thoughts and attention on something immediate and concrete, rather than the nebulous uncertainty of what lay ahead at their journey's end.

They had passed through the grassy midlands of County Meath, with its lush farmland and legendary towns that in centuries long past had been great seats of learning and home to Ireland's high kings. Soon they would be 'beyond the Pale' of what was once considered the civilized influence of the British Crown.

Even though the centuries of conflict and conquest were long since over in Ireland, one always had the feeling that the past happened only yesterday, especially with evidence of the conqueror such a visible reminder: ancient abbeys and monasteries torn down by the Normans ... the gray ruin of Norman, castles, grim remains of Cromwell's brutal march through the country, stones and walls, built up and torn down again and again.... The destructive cycle of man's greed and intolerance toward his fellow man is everywhere.

Stones and walls ... Is that what she would find when she saw Eamonn again, a wall of hurt and misunderstanding, built by her father's stony determination to keep the two of them apart? Or would she see the blank wall of indifference staring back at her from Eamonn's dark blue eyes?

His voice came back to her, so faint, it seemed even less than a whisper, promising that ... *all the years and all the walls in the world can never keep us apart.* ... Catharine drove on, finding little consolation in the words spoken so long ago.

R AIN WAS FALLING steadily by the time they crossed the Shannon at Roosky Bridge in County Leitrim.

Aisling looked out on the gray-green landscape with a mixture of wonder and growing apprehension, thinking that somewhere nearby, Henry Clifford and his family had made their home. Most likely, they had traveled this same road in another century. Somewhere, in that long ago time, Esther Clifford and her coachman had made the life-altering decision to marry and flee Ireland. Her life was the direct result of that decision, not only John and Esther's, but the unique parallel path followed by her own parents over a century later.

Leaving the Shannon behind, they turned north on a road that would take them to the market town of Mohill. Rain was falling heavily now, a cold, soaking rain, and skies were bleakly gray.

Catharine scarcely heard Aisling's voice indicating highway numbers or a direction they should follow. Her heart and memory knew the way. After Mohill, she continued north, past hilly farms with black-faced sheep huddled beneath the scant shelter offered by still leafless elms and oaks, past whiskey-colored streams and boggy meadows, past small lochs looking like rippled sheets of iron and gray stone ruins on green hillsides.

Then they were in Ballinamore, with its narrow streets and even narrower cluster of houses.

"Our bed and breakfast isn't much farther, only a couple of miles outside of town," Catharine said, feeling a strange calm now that they were here.

"I wish the rain would let up a little," Aisling said, thinking the town didn't seem nearly as appealing as Catharine's descriptions had led her to believe.

"Are you going to call the Gallaghers?" Grace asked, hoping her voice sounded no more than matter-of-fact.

"No. I can't do this over the phone. You and Aisling can rest and freshen up at the B & B while I'm gone."

After that, there was nothing more to say. The road, which was narrow enough to have Grace cringing at the lack of shoulder space, grew more narrow still. The terrain was hilly and wooded, with rivulets and streams threading their way through small pieces of pasture and solemn stands of trees.

Glenview House was a large two-story home, set well back from the road, with white-washed walls and a slate gray roof. Off to one side of the main house was a parking area for guests and a smaller thatched cottage with a bright red door.

They made a quick dash through the rain from car to house and felt some of the day's oppressive grayness immediately dispelled by the cheerful entry hall. Painted a bright salmon red with white lace curtains at the windows and a multitude of potted plants spilling over table tops and window sills, the room would have been bright and welcoming on the grayest of days.

The owner, Mrs. Kennedy, was a small woman with a big voice and a hearty, bustling manner. "Ah, you're here then. Welcome, ladies. It's a dreadful day we've got, isn't it? Just dreadful," she said, answering her own question. "Come all the way from Dublin, have you? You'll be wanting a rest then, I'm sure. Let me show you to your rooms and we'll have someone help you with the luggage. I hope the smell of paint isn't too strong for you. We've just finished with a little remodeling."

"The house is lovely," Grace managed to get in, as Mrs. Kennedy led the way up a narrow flight of stairs.

"Thank you very much, and I hope you'll be comfortable. Dinner is served between six and seven, did I tell you? You've only to let me know if there's anything you need before then. Anything at all. I'll be letting you settle in now."

After Mrs. Kennedy had gone and their luggage was brought up, Catharine went into the bathroom to comb her rain damp hair and apply fresh lipstick. Staring at her reflection, she could see only the flaws … the shadow of weariness under her eyes, the pallor of her skin.

I look so old, she thought. *I feel so old. Will he even know me?*

She added a little powdered blush to her cheeks, then left the bathroom with a nervous sigh.

Grace got up from the bed and put her arms around her daughter. "I love you, dear. My prayers are with you."

"Thanks, Mother." Catharine gave her a grateful hug and bit down on her lower lip to stop its trembling. Grabbing her jacket and purse, she turned to Aisling, who stood beside the door with a smile that was held in place by sheer determination and eyes that were suspiciously bright.

They exchanged a quick hug, and Catharine said, "Thanks for understanding why I need to do this alone."

Aisling just nodded, finding it impossible to get any words past the sudden lump in her throat.

"Hold a good thought for me," Catharine said softly. Then she shut the door quietly behind her.

MEMORIES MET HER at every bend and curve of the road as Catharine made the short drive to the Gallagher's farmhouse. Her heart was pounding louder than the rain pelting the windshield as she pulled into the muddy yard and parked in the gravel drive beside the house. Peering through the rain, she could see no one about, but there was a light in the window nearest the kitchen door. On legs that were none too steady, Catharine approached the peacock-blue door and gave the knocker some loud taps. She tried to calm her racing heart with the thought that chances were, more than likely, Eamonn wouldn't be here at all.

Seconds later, a young woman with dark hair and cautious eyes answered her knock. "Yes? Can I help you?"

Catharine stared at the stranger in surprise. "I–I was looking for the Gallaghers. Are they at home?"

"The Gallaghers don't live here."

"Oh … I'm sorry. Perhaps I have the wrong house." Catharine glanced about in momentary confusion.

"You've not the wrong house. It's like I said. The Gallagher's don't live here any more. Are you a friend of theirs, then?"

"Yes." Catharine brushed a damp strand of hair away from her face, feeling her nervous heartbeat slow to a dull thud. "I knew their son—a long time ago."

"Which son would that be?"

Catharine swallowed and answered bleakly, "Eamonn."

The young woman opened the door a little wider. "You're welcome to come in out of the rain."

"Thank you. I don't want to bother you."

"It's no bother." The woman stood aside, ushering her inside the kitchen where a warm fire crackled in the hearth and smells of supper issued from the stove.

Catharine glanced around the familiar room, finding it painfully the same, yet sadly different than the place her memory had kept so lovingly. The old blue cupboard was still against one wall, but the long wooden table with its benches had been replaced by a tidy little round one with a lace cloth and a vase of daffodils.

"Would you care to sit and warm yourself for a moment or two? It's been a dreadful day, with the rain and all."

"Thank you, but I really can't stay. Would you … do you know where I can find the Gallaghers? Or how I could get in touch with them?"

"John died some nine years back now," the woman answered. "And it bein' too much for her to take care of alone, Mary sold the farm to my husband Tom and myself. Last I heard, she was living with one of her daughters, near Ballymote in County Sligo."

The facts, offered in such a matter-of-fact way, struck Catharine like a physical blow.

"Come sit yourself down," the young woman urged, seeing her guest suddenly sag. "You're lookin' more than a bit done in. Are you sure you don't have time for a cup of tea?"

"Thank you … I–I didn't know John had died." Catharine glanced toward the hearth and the empty spot where the hedgerow chair once had its place of honor.

"I'm guessin' you're from America, so how could you know?" she said, taking Catharine's arm and directing her to a chair beside the table. "Murphy's my name. Jeannie Murphy. As I said, my Tom and I've been farming the place for the past few years. Himself'll be out in the barn finishing up with the chores."

"Thank you, Jeannie." Catharine met the young woman's concerned eyes and managed a smile. "It's been a long time since I've been in touch with any of the family. I'm Catharine … Catharine Cavanagh."

"And you're friends with Eamonn, you said?"

"Yes. Do you know where I could find him?"

A slight frown crossed the woman's pleasant features. "I never knew Eamonn all that well. My mother, she was very good friends with one of his sisters, though. Maggie, I believe it was. The last I heard, I think Eamonn and his wife were livin' somewhere north of Dublin. Here now, the kettle's near to boilin' and I'll get you that tea."

"Thank you, but I can't stay. I'm sorry for all the trouble, but I really have to go...."

"It's no trouble," Jeannie assured her, but Catharine had already turned away and was hurrying out into the rain.

25

Trinity College

Rain followed them all the way back to Dublin, adding its own element of tension to a drive that was anything but relaxed. Catharine was composed and quiet, the only indicator of her physical and emotional state being her request that Aisling please drive.

Grace sat in the rear seat, watching curling ribbons of rain slide down the car window, and wishing there were something she could do to lessen the blow of the previous evening. Both she and Aisling had been surprised by Catharine's quick return and thought at first, the Gallagher family might not have been home. When Catharine told them what she had learned, Grace felt waves of sinking disappointment. To come so far ... for this? She could still hear the deadness in her daughter's voice as she told them, "It's better this way. I've known all along there was far more chance of Eamonn being married than not. I just need a little time to adjust to the fact, that's all. And it really doesn't change anything. He still needs to know about Aisling."

Grace knew better than to weaken Catharine's ragged grip on control with too much pity. "So what do we do now?" she'd asked.

"First of all, we need to go downstairs and enjoy the meal Mrs. Kennedy has prepared, and then get a good night's sleep." Catharine had turned to Aisling then with an apologetic look. "I know you wanted to visit the Heritage Center and check the records, but I think, under the circumstances, we ought to drive back to Dublin first thing in the morning."

"That's fine. Please don't worry about me," Aisling said. "The records aren't going anywhere. But how are you going to find him?"

Catharine answered this with a philosophical sigh. "As soon as we get to the hotel, I'll start looking up Gallaghers in the phone directory. There can't be that many Eamonn Gallagher's living north of the city."

THERE WERE, IN fact, eleven E. Gallaghers listed in the Dublin Directory, which included several Eamonn's. With a look of grim determination, Catharine picked up the phone and started dialing the first number on the list.

Grace sat nearby, making an outward attempt to watch television, and aching with the agony of listening to Catharine's voice politely asking if this particular Gallagher were from County Leitrim. By evening's end, all but four names had been eliminated. Of these, three were not at home, and one line was consistently busy.

Two stressful days and long hours of driving, along with Grace's emotional empathy, were more than enough to produce all the necessary ingredients for a raging headache, and Catharine had gone to bed.

Aisling escaped to the hotel lobby to call Alex with the disappointing results of their trip to Leitrim.

"Would you like me to come over?" he wanted to know. "I can get a bus or taxi and be at your hotel in half an hour."

"No ... not tonight. I'm sorry, Alex, but I need to be with Catharine right now."

"When will I see you?"

"I don't know ... tomorrow. Sometime tomorrow."

"Are you all right?"

"Yes ... no. Oh, Alex, I don't know anything right now. Why did he have to be married?" she burst out.

"Aren't you forgetting something? Catharine's married, too."

"I know, but her husband is an egotistical creep and she's getting a divorce. My father probably married some—some selfless, long-suffering woman who adores him. It's all just horrible."

There was a soft chuckle on the other end of the line, then a quiet, "Aisling...."

"I know what you're going to say. That I'm not being reasonable and I'm just tired, and things won't seem so horrible in the morning."

"That isn't what I was going to say."

"Well, if you did you'd be right. What were you going to say?"

"That I love you."

Aisling stood very still, feeling as if everything inside—her thoughts, her feelings, even her breathing had suddenly been captured into one impossible moment of pure joy.

"Aisling? Are you there?"

"I'm here."

She heard a muttered expletive, then a pause. "Look, I'm sorry. I know my timing's rotten. After what's happened, I have no right to—oh, hell. Can I see you tomorrow? We can talk then."

Aisling smiled, listening to his frustrated rambling, feeling light and life spilling into all the weary sad places inside her. "Does that mean I should wait until tomorrow to say that I love you, too?" She cradled the receiver and said softly, "Because, I do."

There was a stunned silence. Then, "Do you have any idea how much I want to hold you right now," he said with some husky-voiced additions that left her weak with longing.

"Darling Alex ... I don't think you should be saying things like that—at least not while I'm here in the lobby."

"Why? No one can hear me. Unless of course, you're on a speaker phone," he added with a chuckle.

She gave a shaky laugh. "No ... but right now my legs are so weak, I'll be lucky if I can crawl over to the elevator. Oh, Alex, it just doesn't seem fair that we should be so happy when Catharine's hurting and miserable."

"I know, but somehow, I don't think she'd mind. Your mother is an amazing woman, and she's stronger than you think. I don't know her well, but enough to know that your happiness means a lot more to her than her own."

"Thank you," she whispered.

"For what?"

"For understanding me. And loving me...."

"I'd much rather express my feelings in person. Since I can't see you tonight, is there any way you could meet me at Trinity College in the morning?"

"Yes. I know Catharine will need the car, but there's a bus stop right across the street from the hotel. Where shall I meet you, and what time?"

"I have a seminar on Irish Estate Records at 8:50, but I'll be free by ten or a little after. Why don't we say 10:30 by the campanile?"

"Where's that?"

"Straight past the main entrance in the center of the grounds. You can't miss it."

"Ten-thirty. I'll be there."

"I love you. Sleep well ... "

"I love you, too," she said, glancing around to make sure she wouldn't be overheard. "And here's a little something to dream about...."

Alex groaned, listening to her. "Not fair. Now I won't be able to sleep at all."

AISLING'S EMOTIONS WERE as mixed as the weather the following morning: one moment sunny and singing, her heart filled with love and eagerness to see Alex, and the next, clouded over with concern for Catharine and the sobering thought that this might very well be the day she met her birth father for the first time.

She showered and dressed with special care, then went in to check on Grace who was sitting up in bed with the *Irish Times* in her lap, and a cup of hot tea on the bedside table.

"How's the headache? Any better?"

"That depends. Do you want the stock answer or the honest answer?" Grace replied, giving her a warm smile nonetheless.

Aisling bent over to give her grandmother a kiss on the cheek. "I'm sorry you're not feeling well."

"Thank you, dear." Grace took in Aisling's radiant appearance with a knowing smile. "There's no point in even asking how you're feeling this morning. Love agrees with you."

Aisling sat down on the edge of the bed with a blissful smile. "Is it that obvious?"

Grace nodded. "Alex is a lucky person. You both are. Not that my opinion will change anything, of course."

"It wouldn't change the love, but I'm very glad you approve." Aisling gave one of Grace's hands an affectionate squeeze. "I just wish the timing were a little different, for Catharine's sake."

"Love's timing is never convenient, dear, but don't worry. In the long run, I think it will be a blessing. Your happiness means everything to her."

"That's what Alex said. He is the most incredible man...."

"So I gather." Grace smiled, seeing the soft shine in Aisling's eyes, and suddenly feeling every one of her seventy-five years. "Tell me something. Doesn't that beard sort of ... get in the way at times?"

Aisling's smile was impish. "Not really. You might say it just adds another texture to the experience."

"Texture," Grace repeated dryly. "I gather you'll be seeing him this morning?"

She nodded happily. "Yes. I'd better go. See you later."

Entering the main room of their suite, Aisling saw that Catharine was already on the phone and talking with someone in a voice that was curiously flat and totally unlike her.

Her heart gave a curious little leap as she watched Catharine write something on a note pad.

"Yes. Yes, I think I've got it all. Thank you. I should be arriving sometime between nine-thirty and ten ... yes, that's right. Good-bye."

"Have you found him?" Aisling asked as Catharine hung up the phone.

Catharine nodded and released a nervous sigh. "That was Eamonn's wife, Ellen Gallagher. She's invited me to come out to their home this morning."

"Will my—will Eamonn be there?"

"I think so ... I was in such a state just talking to her, I didn't think to ask."

"You didn't sound nervous," Aisling said.

"Maybe not on the outside, but on the inside ..." Catharine gave a little shiver and stood up.

"Are you sure you want to go alone?" Aisling asked. "Alex wanted to meet me at the college this morning, but I can try to get hold of him and—"

"No, no, I wouldn't want you to change your plans. Until I've had a chance to talk with Eamonn and explain, I think it's better if—well, anyway—I'm glad you're going to see Alex. I should be back around lunch time and we can make our plans then." Catharine put the note with the directions in her purse, then smoothed her hair with nervous hands. "Are you through in the bathroom? I suppose I'd better do something with this hair." Glancing at Aisling, she asked with a little catch in her voice. "Tell me something. Do I look too ancient?"

Aisling looked at her mother, touched by the question as well as the underlying motive that prompted it. It doesn't change, she marveled silently—a woman's need to be beautiful in the eyes of the man she loves, even when, as in Catharine's case, the circumstances were far from ideal.

With the exception of a blue scarf the same shade as her eyes, she was dressed entirely in soft ivory, from her silk top to the linen slacks and jacket. Other than the strain around her eyes, Aisling didn't know when she had seen Catharine look lovelier.

"Not ancient ... incredible, and very beautiful. Ellen Gallagher will probably hate you," she added.

This last comment produced a real smile. The first Aisling had seen in two days.

"Thanks," Catharine whispered, giving her a hug and quick kiss on the cheek. "I needed that." Then, crossing to the doorway of Grace's room, she announced briskly, "I'm going to be leaving in a few minutes to see the Gallaghers. Do I need to worry about you this morning, or will you behave yourself?"

"Since when is a headache worth worrying about?" Grace answered. "I'm going to order a poached egg on toast, then see if I can find something totally mindless to watch on Irish television."

Listening to them, Aisling shook her head and thought, *Alex was right. Catharine is an amazing woman. They both are....*

Promptly at nine-fifteen, Aisling boarded a large two-tiered bus with a brilliant smile and cheerful, "Isn't it a beautiful morning?"

The driver, who'd left home grumbling over burnt toast and the state of the world in general, blinked at her and said, "God love you, Miss, it is at that."

After finding a seat, Aisling glanced at the various Irish faces on the bus, knowing that most probably took this same route to work every morning. For them, driving past Dublin's city streets had long since been assimilated and absorbed into the commonplace, while to her, even the bus ride itself was an adventure—a ride through history, as it were, into the very heart of the city. Her eyes eagerly drank in the sight of quaint old pubs that had been serving up pints, along with Irish wit and conversation, for centuries. Then, from the backways and byways, the bus turned down historic O'Connell Street near the River Liffey, where the impressive dome of the eighteenth-century Customs House shared the skyline with the ultra-modern Financial Center.

Dublin had witnessed everything from marauding Vikings to the grandeur of English aristocracy and bloody insurrection of Ireland's Civil War. Now it was a modern thoroughfare, choked with cars and buses, the sidewalks filled with people on the move. If the ghost of poor 'Molly Malone' still walked its busy streets, she would find little space for her cart of 'cockles and mussels.'

Aisling got off the bus near Trinity College's impressive granite façade. Entering the front gates, her thoughts were not on the distant past, nor even on the pleasure of her upcoming meeting with Alex. This is where they met, she thought. This is where my parents first saw one another and fell in love. There was no point in dwelling on what might have been. She knew that. Yet knowing couldn't prevent the poignant tug of emotion as she walked across the cobbled square toward the campanile.

Was Catharine with him even now, meeting her father, his wife and family? How would she break the news that there was yet another member of the family—someone he had no idea even existed?

Aisling's leisurely steps turned suddenly restless, and she paused to glance at her watch. Only nine forty-seven. In her eagerness to see Alex and allow enough time to find the place, she had arrived nearly forty-five minutes early. So what to do? The next moment she was smiling. It shouldn't be too difficult to find the lecture hall where his seminar was being held. No matter that she didn't have the foggiest notion where to look or which way to turn. This was Ireland. All she had to do was ask.

Some fifteen minutes and three delightful encounters later brought Aisling to the Arts Block of the campus quadrangle and a large lecture hall. One glance at the name badges worn by people exiting the hall told her she was in the right place. She moved through the crowd, enjoying the mixed babble of conversation all around her. Some voices were immediately identifiable as American, and some had the soft lilt of the Irish, while others the articulate precision of the British.

Aisling entered the back of the lecture hall and glanced around. Sloping rows of some fifty to sixty chairs descended in fan-like fashion to a narrower front where there was a blackboard and desk-type podium. Only a handful of people still remained. Aisling's heart gave a happy leap as she spotted Alex near the podium, talking with a tall gentleman in a dark suit. No baseball cap and tee shirt for Alex today, she thought with a smile, noting his tweed jacket and dark shirt, a scholarly pirate with just a touch of the rogue. That was Alex. And he loved her. This incredible, wonderful man that she had been trying to elude for the past year, loved her. From now on, it's definitely going to be a case of running to and not from, she thought, seeing only him as she made her way down the narrow aisle between desks.

Alex must have sensed her presence, much the same way she always seemed to be aware of his, for Aisling was little more than half way down the aisle when he glanced up and saw her. The smile that parted his mouth and kindled dark fire in his eyes was for her alone.

"Aisling!" He reached for her hands, and caught them in a firm grip.

"I know I'm early, but—"

"I'm glad you are," he said, his voice offering a warm kiss of welcome. Drawing her close, he went on, "I'd like you to meet one of Ireland's foremost experts on estate records."

"Now don't be attaching any fancy titles to my name, young Alex," the man beside him interrupted with a modest grin and chuckle. "If I'm foremost at anything, it's in knowing how much I've yet to learn." Turning to Aisling, he offered his hand. "Aisling, did you say? It's a rare treat for a man to meet such a lovely dream first thing in the morning."

Aisling smiled, then felt her heart begin to pound with blinding recognition even before Alex finished the introductions.

The dark hair was liberally salted with gray now, but still thick and curly, framing his rugged, square-jawed face. The smiling mouth was exactly the same as the one that had been captured on film over thirty years before.

Aisling felt a sudden weakness that nearly caused her knees to buckle. She hadn't expected it to be this way, that she should feel such breath-stopping emotion just looking into his face.

Somewhere outside the pounding of her heart, she heard her voice asking faintly, "Are you ... were you born in County Leitrim?"

"I was, yes."

"And ... and was your father's name John?"

"It was," he said slowly. The dark blue eyes stared down at her in sudden confusion, seeing something familiar, yet not able to identify what it was or why this should be. "How would you be knowing this?"

"Catharine told me," she answered in a small tight voice.

Eamonn's face blanched, and the firm straight mouth suddenly trembled. "Catharine...?"

Tears spilled down Aisling's cheeks, as she tried to swallow a choking sob. "My mother."

He stared at her with dawning realization. "Oh, dear God," he whispered. Then he opened his arms and wrapped her inside.

Alex stood in stunned silence, feeling the sting of tears in his own eyes as Eamonn Gallagher held his daughter for the first time. Aisling's arms clung to her father's neck. She was weeping freely now, her face buried against his broad shoulder. Then Alex saw the big man's shoulders begin to shake and heard the sob that escaped his throat. Alex bowed his head and swiped at the tears that slipped down his bearded face.

It was a long moment before either father or daughter gained enough control to speak.

"There now … there now," Eamonn got out at last, stroking her red-gold hair. "Let's have a look at you." With his hands on her shoulders, Eamonn's eyes met those of his daughter. He took a ragged breath, then asked, "Where's your mother?"

Aisling smiled through her tears. "She went to find you."

26

Ellen

Catharine parked the rental car alongside the curb and glanced at the gray two-story house a few yards away. This had to be the one. For the past half hour, she'd been driving through a confusing maze of neighborhoods, hunting for the address Ellen Gallagher had given her. What seemed like straight forward directions, had ended up resembling the intricate twistings and turnings of a Celtic knot. She had forgotten how challenging finding an address in Ireland could be, and even more so, Irish directions to find a given address.

"We live in Huntstown," Ellen Gallagher had said. "Not far at all from N–3, the Navan Road, just past Blanchardstown and Mulhuddart, but not as far as Cloonee."

Finding Huntstown had been a major victory, but not the end of the war, as Catharine slowly cruised the narrow streets searching for Huntstown Court, where the Gallaghers lived. First there was a Huntstown Road, which intersected with Huntstown Way. Then a few streets over, she'd found Huntstown Close and Huntstown Avenue.

Street signs and house numbers seemed to be purely optional commodities, which one had to suppose, only added more interest to the search and an excuse to stop and chat along the way. *Someone else must be having as much difficulty with directions as I am,* Catharine thought. More than once she'd noticed the same dark blue Fiat traveling slowly behind her car, only to pull off into a side street, then reappear a few blocks later.

At long last Catharine discovered the elusive Huntstown Court, sandwiched between Huntstown Green and Huntstown Glen. Now, seeing the gray stucco house with its dark slate roof and Georgian-style door, she had to admit searching for the house was far easier than finding it. How does one confront a moment like this after thirty years and a thousand lifetimes apart? She had no idea, except to do it and hope for the best.

Walking up to the door, Catharine thought she detected movement in the white lace curtains at the window. Her back straightened automatically, and her chin lifted a little. In spite of her rapidly beating heart, she made sure her knock was definite and unapologetic.

Would Eamonn answer? The mere thought sent a nervous tingle shooting through her veins.

Moments later, the door was opened by a diminutive woman with a softly-rounded face and short, grayish-blonde hair.

Catharine offered a smile. "Hello. I'm Catharine and—"

"Yes, I gathered that. I'm Ellen Gallagher. Please come in, Mrs. Waller." The names alone neatly divided them, without the crisp coolness of her tone.

Catharine followed her past the entry hall into the adjoining living room. Instead of the bright reds, blues, and yellows commonly found in Irish decorating, the room was a subdued study in grays and mauve, echoing the same pale hues worn by the woman herself.

Ellen Gallagher was not a stunning woman, nor was she unattractive. An honest smile would do wonders for those chilly blue eyes, Catharine decided, as Eamonn's wife gestured to a chair and said with the same cold politeness, "Please, sit down."

Catharine sank rather than sat in the softness of the faded chintz, while Ellen Gallagher faced her on a gray sofa directly opposite.

The woman's silent appraisal probably lasted no more than a second or two, but felt uncomfortably longer. Wanting to avoid those eyes, Catharine's gaze wandered briefly around the room, finding a framed photo of two teenage boys atop the television set. One had unruly dark curls, the other, a shock of sandy hair and healthy dusting of freckles. The likeness they bore their father sent a bittersweet shaft of pain straight to her heart.

"Are these your sons?" Catharine asked, feeling an uncomfortable stiffness in her smile.

"John and Martin, yes."

"They're very handsome."

"Thank you."

Another silence followed. Then Ellen asked, "Are you still writing books? I was once quite a fan of yours."

Catharine could think of no appropriate response to this double-edged remark. Rather than try, she said, "Thank you for agreeing to see me. I–I'm sure this is probably awkward for us both. Will Eamonn be here soon?"

"No, I'm afraid not."

Catharine's lips parted. "You mean, he's refused to see me?"

"Eamonn doesn't know you're here."

Catharine searched the woman's closed expression for an answer to this. "I don't understand."

"Then perhaps you're not aware that Eamonn and I are divorced. We have been for some seven years now."

The coldly stated announcement sent Catharine's mind and senses reeling. "You're—then why?"

"Why did I invite you to come?" Ellen Gallagher's thin lips parted in an even thinner smile. "Quite frankly, I was curious. I wanted to meet the legend."

Catharine got to her feet, her heart thudding hard and fast. "I should go now. Do you know where I can reach Eamonn? It's very important, or I wouldn't ask."

"He should be listed in the directory," Ellen said, rising also. "He has a flat in Glesnevin."

"Thank you. I'm sorry to take your time."

"Not at all."

Ellen Gallagher saw her to the door and Catharine felt the woman's burning resentment follow her every step of the way.

She walked away from the muted grayness of the house into a morning that seemed shockingly bright and sunlit by comparison, even though clouds were moving in from the west. A fresh breeze blew through her hair, and she lifted her face to its coolness.

"Eamonn...."

At last she could allow herself the luxury of saying his name aloud. As she did, the hard shell of control that had encased her emotions began to shatter and break. Eamonn ... not married, but divorced. She didn't dare think beyond that.

As she approached her car, a tall man ran toward her from a parked car a few yards away. She glanced in his direction, then froze, her heart constricting in a tight knot of fear. It couldn't be.

"Catharine, wait!"

Chapter 26

She stared, unbelieving, at Barrett Saunder's lanky form and stringy hair. His eyes were wild and feverishly alight.

"Get away from the car!"

Instinctively, she made a dive for it, yanking frantically at the door handle, but he was too fast for her. She screamed as he grabbed her roughly by the shoulders and shoved her away.

"Run!" he yelled, and something in his voice freed her from fear's paralysis. Stumbling, she turned and ran. Then the air around her was shattered with sound and blinding heat, and a force that knocked her off her feet.

SOMEONE WAS TELLING her not to move and be still, which was odd because there was no way she could have moved. Not when everything inside felt so weak and broken. All she could do was lie there, clutching handfuls of grass and earth, her face pressed against the cool, moist green and her mouth tasting strangely of earth and blood.

Then there were other voices, frightened screams and cries, and waves of burning heat somewhere behind her. Someone took hold of her arms, dragging her across the grass, while another voice asked, "Are you all right?"

She heard her voice answering quite calmly, "No...." and that was all she could say. She was alive. And breathing. That much she knew because her chest hurt every time she drew breath. She lay still, not understanding the screams or the strange fan of heat and burning smells.

Sirens replaced the screams and her dazed mind knew the jarring sing-song meant help was on the way.

Catharine was conscious during the ambulance ride to the hospital. Her ears heard the soft Irish voices of the paramedics giving efficient instructions, and her eyes saw the swaying bottle of IV fluid and plastic tubing above her. Yet her shocked mind couldn't grasp the situation fully enough to ask questions or speak.

Barrett Saunders, running toward her, his eyes and voice desperately alight. The explosion. Had she been dreaming? But if she were, why did she feel this pain?

Then they were at the hospital, with a flurry of doctors and nurses in green scrubs and gowns. One of them bent over her, as they wheeled the gurney down the hall and into a treatment room. "Rest easy now, Miss," he said calmly. "You're going to be fine."

Kind hands and arms moved her from one gurney to another and someone else tucked a warm blanket around her. She would have loved to melt into that heavenly warmth, but somewhere close by, she could hear a man's painful moans mingling with the terse instructions of doctors. Rapid orders were given for vitals and blood and, all the while, there was the man's soft moans.

Turning her head, Catharine realized that only a canvas drape divided her from the injured man and the doctors treating him. Then the moan became the sound of her name and everything suddenly came clear. It was Barrett. Barrett Saunders lay only a few feet away, bleeding internally while doctors struggled to save his life—as he had saved hers. The moments before the explosion ... the crazed look she'd seen in his eyes. He'd been trying to warn her, not harm her.

"Catharine...."

Her loins twisted at the raw pain in his voice, and grabbing the metal sides of the gurney, she pulled herself to a sitting position. Maneuvering the IV tubing out of the way, she made it to her feet, and reached for the curtain that divided them.

"I'm here …" She yanked the drape back and recoiled at the sight of Barrett's mangled body and the blood.

"No, Miss. You mustn't!" One of the nurses rushed to her side, taking her by the arm. "Lie back down, please."

"I can't … I'm the one he's calling for."

One of the doctors ordered sharply, "Get her out of the way," and another answered in quiet tones, "If it helps, where's the harm?" Catharine saw the brief, telling look they exchanged, and knew what it meant.

That same moment, Barrett's pain-glazed eyes caught sight of her. "Catharine! You're all right…."

"Yes … I'm here. I'm fine." She moved closer, trying to block out the sight of the blood and his torn flesh.

"I wasn't trying to hurt you," he got out.

"I know … I know that now."

"The bomb … someone put a package in the car. Your husband made a deal … paid someone to do it…."

Catharine felt the nurse's grip on her arm tighten, and saw the sudden stiffening of the doctors who were working frantically to stabilize Barrett's condition.

"How do you know?"

"I followed him … and I hacked into his computer…." Barrett struggled for breath, the sound rasping and thick, as blood trickled from the corner of his mouth. "It's all there.… I made copies. Justin wrote those notes … planned everything.… It's all there. Please, believe me…."

She leaned over and touched his cheek. "I believe you. Please rest now…."

His eyes drank in the sight of her, as she cradled his bloody cheek with her hand. "I told you … I told you I was meant to be in your life…."

"Yes, you were," she said softly.

CATHARINE HUNG UP the phone at the nurse's station, not knowing what to do or where to go. For the past ten minutes, she'd been trying to reach Aisling and her mother at their hotel, without success. Where could they be? Did they know about the bomb?

One of the nurses gave her a sympathetic look. "Don't you think you ought to be resting, Ms. Cavanagh? You've had a nasty shock."

A nasty shock. Yes. Discovering that her husband had tried to kill her, not once but twice, was not exactly pleasant. But somehow, the full reality of it all hadn't hit her. It was as if some painkiller had dulled her mind as well as the places where shrapnel and bits of glass had been removed. Everything felt numb and slightly unreal.

Doctors said her wounds had been mostly superficial and x-rays showed that she'd suffered no broken bones or internal injuries, only some bruised ribs from the fall. It was a miracle, they said, that she was alive. If she'd been any closer to her car, or inside the vehicle when the bomb went off, the story would have been much different. It was a miracle … one afforded by another man's sacrifice.

Her mind was still haunted by the subdued voice of the surgical nurse who had come into the treatment room while Dr. Kelly finished removing the last piece of shrapnel, lodged in the fleshy part of her hip. "Ms. Cavanagh? I'm so sorry … but I thought you'd want to know. Your friend died on the way to surgery. We couldn't stop the hemorrhaging. I'm very sorry…."

In the truest sense of the word, he was my friend, she thought, feeling the hot sting of tears.

Chapter 26

Soon after Dr. Kelly had finished, two officers of the *Garda* arrived, wanting to know if she were up to answering a few questions and making a statement. The men had been respectful and considerate, assuring her that minimal information was being given to the press at this time, in an effort to apprehend those responsible. Those responsible. Was Justin waiting near a phone, she wondered, fully expecting to hear the news of her tragic demise and ready to assume the role of the properly grieving husband? The thought sickened her.

What would happen when he learned that this latest attempt had failed? Her mind couldn't go there. Not now. What she needed most was to know Aisling and Grace were all right.

Catharine left the nurses station and wandered aimlessly down a long hall with patient rooms on either side. Something in her refused to rest, needed to move, if nothing more than to walk down this hallway.

An elderly man left his room on the arm of a nurse, staring at Catharine with open-mouthed curiosity. It occurred to her suddenly, that she must be quite a sight. Her white linen slacks torn and stained with blood, bandages on both arms, her face wan and shock-weary.

But I'm alive. And needing to affirm the fact, she gave the poor old fellow the best smile she could muster.

Catharine reached the end of the hallway and turned back, thinking she would try calling the hotel once more. Then, glancing ahead, she saw a young woman with red-gold hair approach the nurses' station, with a bearded man at her side.

"Aisling...."

The name was little more than a heartfelt whisper—nothing like the joyful shout that followed, echoing down the long hallway as clearly as a church bell on the sabbath.

"Mother!"

Aisling left Alex's side and broke into a frantic run, rushing headlong into Catharine's arms.

"Thank God you're alive," she cried, holding her in a fierce grip of joy and relief. "The bomb ... when we heard ... we thought you were dead," she got out, before tears caught her voice in a trembling sob.

"I'm so sorry. I tried to call you...."

Aisling scarcely heard. "I thought it was too late ... too late to say how much I love you."

Catharine met her daughter's eyes as words tumbled out between tears and smiles. "I love you, too...."

Then, over Aisling's shoulder, she saw Grace hurrying toward them. At her side, holding her mother's arm in a firm grip of support was a tall man with worried eyes and a tight mouth.

"Eamonn...."

If Aisling's arms hadn't held her, Catharine knew she would have fallen. The stark reality of their thirty years apart was evident in his face and in his eyes, yet even as her heart reached out to him, uncertainty and fear held her back. What right did she have to hope that he might still care, that love could somehow bridge the gap of hurt and pain that stood like an aching chasm between them.

Blinded by fear and doubt, Catharine didn't see the soft shine in Grace's eyes, or the smile on Aisling's face as she gazed up at her father. All she could see was that firm, straight mouth, and the stark look in Eamonn's dark blue eyes.

Then the mouth softened. His voice, still the same, reached out to her, not merely bridging the gap, but closing it as if it had never been.

"Come into my arms, darling girl ... you've been far too long from home."

27

"... the heart & the hands of the golden ring...."

The winter inside her was over at last. That part which had lain sleeping for so long was alive and blooming once more. Held close within his arms, it was as if all the lost springs and denied hopes had suddenly emerged to the joyful call of the sun. His love was her sun, and she basked in its warmth and sureness. Even as her eyes saw the passage that time had written in his features, her heart recognized the face of love that would never change. The touch and taste of his tear-wet cheek against hers ... the feel of those dark, unruly curls, now sprinkled liberally with gray ... the sound of his voice speaking her name in the same soft way.

A work-weary nurse just ending her shift approached the scene in the hall and stopped to stare. During some sixteen years at the hospital, Peggy O'Shea had seen her share of life and death and most everything in between. Now, after working a double shift, giving smiles and injections to crotchety old complainers, filling vials and emptying bedpans, all she wanted was to go home where a hot cup of tea was waiting, along with a cushion for her aching feet.

At first glance, Peggy thought sure someone must have died because they were all weeping, every blessed one of them—from the sweet-faced older lady to the good-looking, black-bearded bloke with his arms around a pretty red-haired woman. Then she saw past the tears to the smile on the face of the dark-haired woman with the bloodstained clothes and the near worshipful fervor in the eyes of the tall man with curly gray hair who was holding her the way one clings to life itself. *Holy Mother,* she thought, *to love someone like that,* and she discovered her own eyes were suddenly smarting.

Then the tall gentleman turned and offered an arm to the young red-haired woman. All three of them blended into a happy embrace of laughter and tears.

Feeling their joy, a few tears slipped down Peggy's cheeks, and instead of walking discreetly past, she found herself stopping to pat the shoulder of the dark-haired woman. "God bless you, dearie," she sniffed. "God bless you all."

Then she went on her way, feeling the weariness and cares of her long hours suddenly lifted.

REALITY SEEMED AS fleeting as the cloud shadows on the far off hills, as Eamonn drove away from the hospital with Catharine beside him. Was this really happening, or only some fantastic dream that the two of them were driving down the Navan Road toward Dublin like any other ordinary couple? After the events of today, could anything ever be ordinary again?

Chapter 27   "... the heart & the hands...."

Eamonn's day had begun like any other. He got up this morning, performed the same old rituals, thinking he knew exactly what the day held in store. Shortly before nine he was scheduled to give a lecture at the college for a group of English, Irish and American genealogists. His mind wasn't worried about the subject matter. Irish estate records and their genealogical value had been a passion of his for years now, a passion that he was fortunate enough to share with some wealthy American colleagues of Irish descent, who'd helped turn his dreams into reality—one of identifying and filming existing estate records. There was no use lamenting the tragic loss of records at the Four Courts fire some eighty years back. It was time now for individuals as well as governments to work together to preserve and make available the information that still existed.

At noon he had a luncheon with a group of individuals from the National Archives and the Family History Library in Salt Lake City, to discuss a joint venture in filming some eighteenth century records. Then it was back to Trinity for another seminar.

His life was full of purpose, and he was reasonably content. What other choice did he have? You tell yourself you have a good life and you believe it because you need to. For the most part, it was true. He loved his work. His boys were young men now, twenty-six and twenty-four. John and Martin were good lads, eager, intelligent, and he'd remained close to both in spite of the divorce.

Ellen was well cared for. He couldn't fault himself there, even though the failure of his marriage still brought occasional feelings of guilt. He didn't blame her for wanting the divorce. No woman deserves to feel second best, as if she's merely a stand-in or replacement for someone else.

He and Ellen had been faculty members at the same school when they'd met. Their relationship amounted to little more than casual friendship, at least on his part. When she asked if he would like to come over for dinner some time, he told himself, where's the harm?

He was fond of Ellen. She was a lovely woman and pleasant to be with. Eamonn made it clear from the first there had been someone else. That his heart still lived at another address. She insisted it didn't matter, that in time, he would forget and they could be happy together. In his loneliness, he needed to believe that she was right.

But it was a surface kind of happiness, never reaching the depths of meaning and emotion his soul had known before. Instead of helping him forget, somehow being with Ellen only made him love Catharine more. A part of him always wondered where she was—what had happened—and if she still wore his ring.

In those early years after their parting, Catharine's memory moved from place to place. For a while, she'd haunted his dreams and every waking moment. Love songs and poetry were constant reminders. He thought he'd never be rid of the pain.

Then, she'd moved to a shelf—a treasured place where the past was still visible and not far from reach. After he married Ellen, he'd tucked Catharine's memory into a drawer, somewhere safe and dark where those blue eyes and the love they'd shared would be out of sight.

He loved Ellen as best he could, but it felt more like a duty without the joy, and it was never enough to satisfy her. One night, he'd come home late and found Ellen in bed reading a novel. She was wearing a new nightgown, some filmy peach concoction that was as transparent as the look in her eyes.

Eamonn had approached the bed, trying to summon some emotion inside. Suddenly found himself staring at the photograph on the book's back cover. All in an instant, the drawer was flung open and there she was—those blue eyes and smiling lips, the soft, dark hair—still the same, yet even more beautiful than he remembered.

There was no way he could disguise his reaction.

"What is it? What's wrong?" Ellen had asked.

He didn't answer. Instead he picked up the book, hating the fact that his hands were shaking and his heart pounding hard and fast. The brief bio beneath her picture tore open the wound. *Catharine Cavanagh, best-selling author of historical romance novels ... wife of Justin Waller ...*

Wife ... What did he expect? It was fifteen years since she'd left. Seeing her picture, knowing she was married, shouldn't mean anything to him by now. Eamonn tossed the book angrily aside, then made love to his wife with a desperation that shocked and pleased her, but afterwards left him feeling empty and ashamed.

She wasn't Catharine. She never could be. He had no right to expect her to be anything more than she was. He wasn't aware that he'd spoken Catharine's name aloud until Ellen drew away from him, her eyes hurt and confused.

Catharine ... At last the shadow of the past had a name. Ellen demanded to know the rest, and in a strange way, it was a relief just to talk about her, to give his longing and loneliness a few moments of verbal release.

The next morning, Eamonn found the book in the trash and a bitterness in Ellen's eyes that never went away. Their divorce didn't come until a few years later, but in many ways it was only a formality. Their hearts had been divorced long before any papers were signed.

And Catharine? His love for her refused to be shut away in a drawer, or put on a shelf. Instead, her memory was pressed upon his heart, like a flower kept within the pages of a book. Life went on and he functioned very well. And even though the book was rarely opened, he knew the flower was still there.

Now, in the midst of what he thought would be just another day—all that he'd lost was restored to him. And more. His mind still reeled with the fact that he and Catharine had a daughter. Aisling ... their little dreamer, a beautiful young woman.

Eamonn had driven only a few miles from the hospital when he felt the magnitude and emotion of all that had happened welling up inside him. Without a word, he turned off the main road, onto a roundabout that brought them into the wooded acres of Phoenix Park. Catharine didn't question his actions as he pulled onto a secluded side road and parked the car. One look at her eyes said she understood.

The moment was too deep for words. Holding her, feeling the softness of her in his arms, while the quiet paths of their tears met and merged, he breathed in the reality of her return. She was here. And he was whole again.

"There's so much I need to tell you," she said at length. "So many things to explain. I don't know where to begin ... except to say, I love you ... I always have."

"That's all I need to know. There'll be plenty of time for talking later." He kissed her gently, then smiled. "As for explaining, our daughter has already delivered a heavy dose."

"Aisling has?"

Eamonn nodded, his smile widening. "And what she didn't give, your mother was more than willing to supply. Those two women, both so earnest and intent, trying to cover thirty years in thirty seconds from the sound of it." He touched her face where a few tears still lingered, and said gently, "Don't be reproaching yourself over the past, darling girl. You're here now and that's all that matters."

With a little cry, she pulled him close. Then, in the midst of a kiss, he felt her wince and stiffen.

"What is it?"

Gingerly shifting position on the seat, Catharine gave him a sheepish look. "Nothing serious. The numbness is starting to fade in certain areas, that's all."

"Have the doctors prescribed something for pain? Do we need to stop at the chemists?"

"Being with you is the best pain medication," she said, then admitted with a rueful smile, "although sitting on a pillow sounds very appealing right now."

Eamonn chuckled. "Whatever you need, you've only to ask. Say the word and I'll have you carried in on a litter by Nubian slaves."

Catharine smiled and reached for his hand. "It really is you," she whispered. "I may need to be convinced of that for awhile…"

"And so will I, darlin'. Every day for the rest of our lives…."

EAMONN TURNED ON the TV news at ten, anxious to know if there'd been any updates or new information on the bombing. Grace and Catharine were both sleeping, and he'd sent Alex and Aisling over to his flat to get some clothes and a few of his things. Until he knew there was no further threat to Catharine, he wasn't leaving her alone for even a minute.

The news report was little more than a repeat of earlier broadcasts, but just seeing the burned and twisted metal of her rental car, was enough to turn him inside out.

"Citizens in a quiet suburb north of Dublin are still shocked and puzzled over the explosion of a car bomb that killed one man and injured American author Catharine Cavanagh…. It is believed there was no political motivation for the incident…. no arrests have been made at this time…."

Eamonn reached for the remote control and switched off the TV, shocked and puzzled. They'd be even more shocked if they knew the details withheld from the press and general public—namely, that Catharine's husband, cowardly piece of scum that he was, had hired someone with mob connections to kill his wife. Every time he remembered the tremble in Catharine's voice, and the way her eyes had looked when she told them about Barrett Saunders' revealing information, Eamonn felt another surge of helpless anger. He'd come so close … so close to losing her, and now he couldn't even thank the poor bastard that had saved her life.

Two detectives from the *Garda* had stopped by the hotel room that afternoon to let them know a warrant had been issued for Justin Waller's arrest. But as yet, the man who put the packaged bomb in Catharine's car had not been apprehended.

Did Waller know this latest attempt had failed? Eamonn wondered. Would there be another? The mere possibility gnawed at his insides. He hadn't wanted to frighten her, but whatever precautions hotel security and the Garda had made weren't enough to calm the gut-wrenching fear that whoever was responsible might try again. He'd insisted on staying the night. If someone tried to get through that door, he'd have to get past him first.

Thinking over the events of the day, Eamonn's anger shifted from Catharine's husband to his ex-wife. Damn her bitterness and jealousy. If Ellen had just told Catharine that they were divorced or how to reach him, she never would have driven out there in the first place. At least Ellen had had the decency to call the hotel after the explosion, though it would be a long while before he forgot the horror of that call.

The four of them, he, Grace, Alex and Aisling, were sitting together and talking, expecting Catharine to come walking in at any moment. The anticipation of seeing her again was turning him into a blithering fool. His palms were sweating and he couldn't stop himself from checking the time every few seconds. Then the call came. Aisling had jumped up to answer the phone, thinking it might be her mother. All in an instant her smiling eagerness had turned to white-faced horror.

"No ... oh, no ..." was all she could say.

Eamonn was on his feet in a moment, knowing that whatever had happened must concern Catharine. Aisling handed him the phone in shocked silence. Then he'd listened to Ellen's voice, crying and near hysterical telling him about the car bomb.

"It was horrible ... deafening.... All the windows in the house shook. I ran outside and there they were ... lying on the front lawn, the two of them ... with bits of metal and glass everywhere ... and the car on fire...."

"Is Catharine all right? Was she hurt?" he demanded, but Ellen didn't answer. Instead, she kept rattling on about the windows and the burning car and the neighbors all frightened and screaming.

"Ellen, get hold of yourself. I don't care about the damned windows or the car," he'd yelled into the phone. "What happened to Catharine?"

There had been silence then; taut, stretched-out seconds of anguish before her cold voice told him, "She was alive when the ambulance came. That's all I know. I found her purse on the lawn, and there was a card with the hotel's number...."

The worst moment had come on the drive to the hospital. Alex had driven Aisling and he'd taken Grace in his car. Traffic was heavy and sluggish. He'd kept the radio on a news station, hoping to hear something, anything that would let him know Catharine was all right. Instead, the announcement came that one person was confirmed dead, with another in serious condition. Eamonn felt as if the entire world had suddenly gone black. *Please God, don't take her from me now....* Then he felt a gentle hand on his arm.

"It's not Catharine," Grace told him quietly. "She's alive. I know it."

And so he'd hung onto that, praying and pleading the whole way. They'd arrived at the hospital to find the news media and officers of the Garda everywhere. Their mere presence seemed to confirm his worse fears. Finally, they made their way through the gauntlet and there she was ... the reality more beautiful than any dream. After all these years, to hold her again.... How could something be exactly the same and yet, even better?

Eamonn got up from the couch and moved restlessly to the window, staring out into the darkness. He wanted to hold her now. Ached with his need for her. Alex and Aisling would be properly shocked if they could read his thoughts at the moment. Give them thirty or forty years, he thought, and they might have a proper glimpse of what love was all about.

He wondered how long they'd have to wait for her divorce to be final. The fact that Catharine still had to go through those legal hurdles to divorce a man who'd tried to kill her not once, but twice, was galling to him and sheer mockery. But however long it took, she was more than worth it.

A movement behind him, slight though it was, had him instantly alert. Turning, Eamonn saw Catharine standing in the shadows of the doorway between the sitting room and bedroom. Her dark hair was loose about her shoulders, and her slender form was softly outlined by a silky robe of pale lavender.

"I thought you were sleeping," he said, just the sight of her nearly taking his breath away.

She shook her head and pushed her hair away from her face in a little gesture he remembered well. "I can't sleep."

"Is it the pain that's keeping you awake?"

"No ... it's you."

He swallowed hard, trying to keep his emotions in check.

"For thirty years there's been an ocean and an entire continent between us," she said. "Now having you in the next room seems much too far away."

The next moment they were in each other's arms.

"Are you sure you haven't come back to me from T'ir N-a-Nog, the land of the ever young?" he asked, kissing the smooth hollow of her throat. "You're more beautiful now than ever, while the years have made me a grizzled old badger."

Her laughter was young and free, as she ran her fingers through the thick curls of his hair "You, old? Never...."

A sharp rapping on the door interrupted the gentle rhythm of their kiss and Catharine stiffened in his arms. "Would that be Aisling?"

Eamonn shook his head. "No. She and Alex have a key. Stay here, darlin'. I'll see to it."

"Who is it?" he asked before unlocking and opening the door.

"Detective O'Donnell, of the Garda."

Opening the door a crack, Eamonn gave the sandy-haired man standing outside a close look.

O'Donnell held out his I.D. "I'm sorry to disturb you at such a late hour, but I need to have a word with Mrs. Waller."

"Mrs. Waller is resting," he said, resenting having to use the name. "Can it wait 'til morning?"

"I'm afraid not, sir. It's very important or I wouldn't trouble you."

"It's all right, Eamonn," Catharine said, coming to the door. "Please come in, Mr. O'Donnell."

Rory O'Donnell was a big-shouldered, square-jawed man who looked as if he'd be more comfortable on the soccer field than wearing a suit. Before stating his business, he politely inquired how Catharine was feeling, and offered an apology for what had happened as sincerely as if he himself had somehow been at fault.

"As you might expect, we've been in close communication with authorities in the States, trying to verify the information given to you by Mr. Saunders. Our office received word a short time ago from a Detective Adams. He and some other officers went to your husband's home to question him."

"What did he say?" Catharine asked, her mind leaping ahead to imagine the confrontation between Justin and the police.

Detective O'Donnell paused slightly and gave her a close look. "It seems Detective Adams and the others weren't able to question your husband. Mr. Waller was dead when they arrived."

Catharine's lips parted. She stared at O'Donnell's serious face, feeling as if a sudden gust of wind had just passed by, but left her standing. Eamonn's hand moved to cover hers, and she clung to its warmth.

"How did it happen?" she asked. "Did he ... was it suicide?"

"No, ma'am. I'm sorry to distress you with the details, but apparently, he was shot twice, at fairly close range. There were no signs of struggle. Detective Adams felt that your husband must have known whoever did it. Nothing in the house was disturbed, except for the fact that his computer was missing."

"The evidence," Catharine said slowly. "They would take that."

"I'm afraid so." O'Donnell nodded. Then a pleased glint came into his eyes. "But it seems, whoever shot your husband didn't know about Barrett Saunders' involvement. When authorities went to his apartment, they found copies of several incriminating e-mails, some sent and others received by your husband. Detective Adams wanted me to assure you that they have some good leads."

"Thank you."

Catharine saw him to the door, giving wooden responses to his polite expressions of concern and repeated apologies for disturbing her.

"Katie, darlin', are you all right?" Eamonn asked when O'Donnell had gone.

"Yes, I–I think so…." Then her knees buckled and the room swam.

CATHARINE FELT SOMETHING moist and cool against her forehead, and a man's voice echoed in her head along with the sick dizziness. She opened her eyes to see Eamonn's face bending over her, worry darkening his eyes. The dizziness gradually receded, and she realized she was lying on the couch.

"Did I faint?"

"You did, love. It's no wonder." He put the cool washcloth against her forehead and asked, "Can you take a sip of something? I've a glass of water here."

She nodded and he put an arm around her shoulders to help lift her head.

The water was cold and tasted wonderful, but just the effort of drinking seemed to tap all her strength. She lay back down with a sigh and looked at Eamonn.

"Justin," was all she said, then shuddered. "Such a wasted life…."

Eamonn gave her a close look. "Surely, you're not grievin' the man, after what he's done."

Catharine lay still, looking bewildered and a little lost. "I don't know what to feel.... It's so strange. I was dreading having to see him again, but I–I never wanted him to die."

Eamonn's firm mouth tightened with the effort to control his anger. "His death was a lot quicker and less painful than the one he planned for you," he said. "Forgive me, if I can't spare much pity for the man."

"Such a wasted life," she said again, then lifted her arms to him as shock and reaction quaked through her. "Hold me, Eamonn.... the only thing that seems real right now is you. Just hold me...."

"I have you, love. It's all right."

Catharine clung to him, her head pressed against his chest, feeling the steady, strong beat of his heart. "It's over ... but it's not over," she whispered.

"What do you mean? You're safe now, Katie. He can't touch you ever again."

"I know that, but—" Her arms tightened around his back and she looked into his eyes with a desperate plea for understanding. "Oh, Eamonn ..., all I want is to be with you, and now I have to go back."

He stiffened slightly. "What are you saying?"

"Only that, no matter what Justin did, there's his son to consider. I don't want to go, but I can't let David face all this alone."

Eamonn took one of her hands in his. "And what makes you think you have to face this all by yourself?"

"Well, I–I can't expect you to just leave your work and—"

Eamonn bent his head and kissed her the way he'd been wanting to kiss her all day long. "There now. Whatever needs to be done, we'll face together," he said with a confident smile. "We've had thirty years denied to us, darlin.' You'll not be leavin' me again."

28

*True love's the gift which God has given
To man alone beneath the Heaven;
It is the secret sympathy,
The silver link, the silken tie,
Which heart to heart, and mind to mind
In body and in soul can bind.*

Sir Walter Scott

October 30, 1902

I am eighty years old today. I never thought to live this long or see so much. Annie and Jim's wife Susie gave me a lovely party, with a cake and all, and the grandchildren sang to me. How I love their dear sweet voices.

It is late and the family have all gone to bed. Yet even though my body is weary, my mind is not yet ready to rest. It is pleasant to sit here by the fire, with a quilt tucked around me. The embers are still warm and glowing gold. Outside, the night is cold and there is fresh snow on the hills. I wonder if these old bones will survive another winter.

So many that I love are gone now. My husband and son, buried side by side in Silver Reef. Annie's Hugh passed on six years ago, and it's been such a struggle for her to make ends meet. Yet she never complains and works harder than most men, keeping up the boarding house over in Mammoth. Her children are nearly all grown. Whenever I look at young Alex, I see the Irish blue eyes of my husband John. Alex is such a handsome lad and full of mischief, just like his grandfather. I can't help loving the dear boy. And in Henrietta, I see much of myself at her age. Though, to look at me now, one would never guess that I was once widely sought after by many young men. Or that my days and years have seen many an adventure. No. All anyone would see is an old woman sitting by the fire. Memories are fading like my eyesight and soon all will be forgotten. I wonder sometimes, if my life has made any difference, or what it will mean to those who come after. I do so want to be remembered. . . .

Chapter 28

May—2002

Catharine Gallagher sat with pen in hand in the upstairs study of the old Cavanagh home. The last chapter of Esther Clifford Clark's story lay on the desk in front of her, but her mind couldn't seem to find the right words or the feeling to finish it.

"Katie, darlin', I hate to interrupt you, but there's a young gentleman downstairs who's waiting to see you."

Catharine put down her pen and turned to her husband with a smile. "That's all right. I wasn't making much progress. The right ending just hasn't come to me yet. Or maybe the story doesn't want to end, I'm not sure which."

Eamonn leaned over and kissed her. "If it doesn't want to end, maybe you should try a pregnant pause instead."

Catharine smiled at him. "A pregnant pause? Now that's an interesting concept. What young gentleman is it, by the way? I didn't know we were expecting company."

"He didn't give me his name, but I gather he's come a long way to be with his grandmother on her birthday."

Catharine gasped with pleasure. "Are Alex and Aisling here with the baby? Why didn't you tell me? I didn't think they could come until the end of next week."

"I thought I was telling you," he chuckled, but she was already out of the chair and rushing toward the stairs.

Catharine entered the living room to find year-old Eamonn Alexander on his great grandmother's lap playing pat-a-cake, much to the delight of his parents, who sat nearby, totally enthralled with this timeless form of entertainment.

Between hugs and kisses, Aisling explained, "Alex finished his photo shoot nearly a week early, so we decided to surprise you."

Catharine gave her daughter another hug, then held out her arms to her grandson. "Oh, Aisling, he's grown so much, I hardly know him. And look at that hair!"

"He looks more like his grandpa every day," Eamonn said proudly, as Catharine cuddled and kissed the curly-haired boy.

"He certainly does. But he has his daddy's eyes," Aisling added, smiling at Alex. "How's the book coming along, Mother? Is Chapter 27 still giving you fits?"

"Your mother's not sure about the ending," Eamonn filled in, as Catharine was too involved in baby worship to respond. "She's considering a pregnant pause instead."

Alex and Aisling exchanged a significant look at this. Then Alex put an arm around his wife. "That pretty much describes our own situation right now," he said with a pleased smile. "Very pregnant, but without the pause."

Catharine stared at the two of them and Eamonn started to chuckle. "Is this an announcement?"

"It is." Aisling's smile was radiant. "Little Eamonn's going to have a brother or sister in about six months. Will you be here, do you think, or in Ireland?"

Since their marriage, Catharine and Eamonn divided their time between the Cavanagh home in Alameda, and a comfortable townhouse outside of Dublin, with frequent trips to Salt Lake City to visit Alex and Aisling.

"We'll be right here with you," Eamonn told her. "Can you imagine your mother anywhere else?"

"Or you," Catharine put in, giving her husband a fond smile. "I wasn't the one who wore a groove in the waiting room floor when little Eamonn was born."

"How are you feeling, dear?" Grace wanted to know.

Chapter 28　　　　　　　　　　　　　　　　413

"Disgustingly healthy," Aisling answered. "And hungry all the time."

"That's good because I have some gingerbread and hot lemon sauce out in the kitchen, just waiting for someone to eat it."

The words sparked a sudden memory of the day Aisling had first come to the Cavanagh home, smiling and eager to do genealogy research on the Clifford line. Catharine gave Grace a fond glance as they went out to the kitchen, knowing the same memory tugged at her mother's heart. So much had happened in the two years that followed. So many milestones of love renewed and restored. And in a large way, nearly all of it was a result of her great great grandmother's life and story.

LATE THAT NIGHT, Catharine found her thoughts drifting back to Esther Clifford Clark and the unfinished chapter she had left earlier in the day. Sitting in bed with book in hand, her eyes were not focused on the page of Irish poetry, but someplace far distant.

"You're looking very thoughtful, Katie," Eamonn said, climbing into bed beside her.

Catharine readily abandoned the book to snuggle close within his arms. "I was thinking of Esther.... Wondering if she'd be pleased with what I've done."

"And why wouldn't she be?"

"I don't know ... sometimes I can't help wondering if I've done justice to who she was and all her life means. There's still so much we don't know about her, in spite of the research you and Aisling did. To fill in the blanks, I've had to take quite a bit of literary license."

"That's true, but think of the gift you've given her."

"Gift?"

"To be remembered is a great gift," he said. "Years from now, little Eamonn and his children, and all the children who come after that, will be telling the story of the lovely Irish lady who ran away with her coachman and came to Amerikay." Eamonn's arms pulled her closer, and his mouth found hers in a lingering kiss. "Only books have last chapters, darling girl. Our family and Esther's legacy will go on and on...."

Afterword

On the old Mail Coach road from Drumsna to Dublin, a quarter mile east of Roosky Bridge where it spans the river Shannon, there lies a small townland by the name of Moher. In Gaelic the name literally means a ruin, either of a house or cluster of trees. On this townland one can find both. Thick stands of alders and oak grow near the riverbank and across the grassy fields there stands an old white farmhouse near a shady copse of elms. Not far from the road, there is a small ring fort, a remnant of the Iron Age when early Celts inhabited the area. Overgrown and all but camouflaged by woodsy brush and grass, only the keen and discerning eye would recognize the ancient mound.

Today, a smooth asphalt highway covers the ruts of the old road, and in most modern maps of the region, one rarely finds any mention of the townland. The eastern boundaries of Moher are largely bog, with a few acres of arable pasture. The farmhouse is much like any other Irish farmhouse, and the land itself, though lovely, is unremarkable. Most travelers would scarce remember the place or the road, only as a blur of pleasant scenery between one destination and another.

Yet it was here in 1822, that a baby girl was born to Henry and Rose Marie Clifford. They named her Esther ... Aisling, the dreamer. It was here, that the child grew into a young woman who had the misfortune, according to some, to fall in love with the wrong man—a poor coachman not of her faith or social standing.

On this same road the lovers made their escape, away from censure and famine, to a new world and a new life.

The Clifford name is all but gone from the area now, along with most of the big houses and memories of that long ago time. But the dreamer and her coachman have not been forgotten, and their grateful posterity lives on.